Reclaiming
Mni Sota

An Alternate History of
the U.S. – Dakota War of 1862

By Colin Mustful

ISBNs: 978-1-7364990-8-5 (pb);
978-1-7364990-9-2 (hc);
979-8-9873191-0-9 (eBook)

Book Cover Design: The Book Cover Whisperer, OpenBookDesign.biz
Interior Book Design: Inanna Arthen, inannaarthen.com
Title page image attribution: FreeVectorFlags.com
Library of Congress Control Number: 2022951445
First Printing: 2023
Printed in the United States of America

Names: Mustful, Colin, author. | Loso, Michael AmikoGaabaw, writer of supplementary textual content.

Title: Reclaiming Mni Sota : an alternate history of the U.S.-Dakota War of 1862 / by Colin Mustful ; with sensitivity reading from Michael AmikoGaabaw Loso.

Other titles: Reclaiming Minnesota

Description: [Roseville, Minnesota] : [History Through Fiction], [2023] | Includes bibliographical references.

Identifiers: ISBN: 978-1-7364990-8-5 (paperback) | 978-1-7364990-9-2 (hardcover) | 979-8-9873191-0-9 (ebook) | LCCN: 2022951445

Subjects: LCSH: Dakota War, Minnesota, 1862--Fiction. | Dakota Indians--Wars, 1862-1865--Fiction. | Indians peoples of North America--Minnesota River Valley (S.D. and Minn.)--History-- 19th century--Fiction. | Settler colonialism--Minnesota--History--19th century--Fiction. | Executions and executioners--Minnesota--History--19th century--Fiction. | LCGFT: Historical fiction. | Alternative histories (Fiction) | BISAC: FICTION / Historical / General. | FICTION / Alternative History. | FICTION / Indigenous.

Classification: LCC: PS3613.U847 R43 2023 | DDC: 813/.6--dc23

Dedication

To writers everywhere.
Don't give up on yourselves. Don't give up on the process.

Your pioneers are encircling the last home of the red man, as with a wall of fire. Their encroachments are perceptible, in the restlessness and belligerent demonstrations of the powerful bands who inhabit your remote western plains. You must approach these with terms of conciliation and of real friendship, or you must very soon suffer the consequences of a bloody and remorseless Indian war. Sir, what is to become of the fifty or sixty thousand savage warriors and their families, who line your frontier, when the buffalo and other game upon which they now depend for subsistence are exhausted? Think you they will lie down and die without a struggle? No, sir, no. The time is not far distant, when pent in on all sides, and suffering from want, a Philip or a Tecumseh will arise to band them together for a last and desperate onset upon their white foes. What then will avail the handful of soldiers stationed to guard the frontier? Sir, they, and your extreme western settlements, will be swept away as with the besom of destruction.

Henry Hastings Sibley, 1850

Author's Note

In August of 1862 war erupted in the state of Minnesota. Commonly known as The U.S. - Dakota War of 1862, the war was brief but its results were tragic and long-lasting—perhaps everlasting. During the war, which started August 18 and ended September 23, an estimated 400 to 800 white Euro-American settlers lost their lives, while more than seventy United States soldiers were killed. For the Dakota—the Indigenous population Native to Minnesota— an estimated seventy-five to one-hundred fifty soldiers were killed during the war while thirty-eight men were executed by hanging in Mankato, Minnesota, on December 26, 1862. Another two were later hanged at Fort Snelling on November 11, 1865. Additionally, several hundred Dakota were imprisoned while about 1700 were interned at Fort Snelling and later exiled to Crow Creek, South Dakota. In each case, conditions for the Dakota were poor and several hundred died from disease and starvation.

But this book is not an attempt to quantify the U.S. - Dakota War and its aftermath. Neither is it an assessment of the actions of those involved or an attempt to clarify or interpret those actions. This is not a direct attempt at reconciliation. Rather, as someone who has spent years researching and writing about Minnesota's complicated and often heinous past, I want to take a new look at the past—not as history, but as it exists today. History is intertwined with the present in such an inextricable way that the two cannot be separated. What happened in the past has a direct and meaningful impact on everything we do, see, and think as time moves forward. This, of course, is obvious but can be easily overlooked. We study history in the past tense, viewing people and events as a segment of time rather than an unbroken string that links our present moment with the people and events that have gone before us.

I was born in Minneapolis and have spent most of my life in the state of Minnesota. I enjoy all of the benefits of a wealthy, modern, abundant, and privileged society while also enjoying access to the peace and recreation of a vast and beautiful landscape of lakes, forests, rivers, hills, and prairies. On any given day I can use the land to hike, climb, fish, swim, run, bike, camp, canoe, kayak, hunt, ski, or make use of it in any other way. I also benefit from the abundance of its resources and everything the land produces such as food, water, timber, iron, coal, energy, limestone, and so on. It is a place of remarkable beauty and abundance.

Acknowledgment of the past and the impacts it has on the world today is a good place to start. But to truly understand history we must move beyond acknowledgement and toward empathy. That's why I've written this book. It is my attempt, through the creativity and power of fiction, to create a direct link to the past—one that engenders empathy rather than just acknowledgment. There are no shortages of facts surrounding the history of the U.S. - Dakota War of 1862 or the Sandy Lake Tragedy, both of which are covered in previous novels of mine. I've learned the facts as they are presented, and I cannot change what happened. But I can change the way I perceive it.

What if my family was forced to move from the land we lived upon for generations? What if my family was stripped of its language, history, and culture? What if my family was executed for trying to survive? What if my family was imprisoned, maltreated, and exiled—placed aboard steamships and sent away to a small, inhospitable reservation on arid, rocky ground?

As a white American, I will never fully comprehend the loss, grief, and historical trauma of Native populations in this country. I can try to understand and acknowledge the realities of the past and what it means for Native peoples today, but I cannot bring myself to a place of parallelism with the Native experience. What I've learned through research and writing is right and good and leads to understanding, but it does not bring us all the way to empathy. That requires more effort.

This story is an alternate history of the U.S. - Dakota War of 1862. It relies on real people, events, and settings, but it does not represent the facts. It is not meant as an indictment on any one person or group of people. It is a way to connect the past with the present by showing readers what the world might look like if the events of the past happened a little differently. It is meant to bring out the humanity in all of us—to enlighten us on all we've gained, all we've lost, and why we must make things right.

A note on language, sources, and appropriation – I identify as a white male who grew up in a suburban setting in the 1980s and 1990s. What I create through fiction is, inevitably, an expression of my own experience and viewpoint. I've relied on my professional and educational backgrounds to create, to the best of my ability, a meaningful and important story. While I've worked hard to represent history and culture in an accurate and respectful manner, I acknowledge that there may be shortcomings or errors in my representation. Furthermore, I do not claim ownership or authority over the people, places, history, or culture shared in this fictional representation of the world. I encourage readers to seek out more sources and perspectives, especially those from Native peoples, about this history.

Regarding Native history and culture, I've relied heavily on a book titled *Chippewa Customs* by Frances Densmore. I've also relied on a variety of other sources such as *Ojibwe Waasa Inaabidaa* by Thomas Peacock and Marlene Wisuri, *History of the Ojibway People* by William W. Warren, and various other print, digital, and online sources. Regarding language, I have relied upon a variety of online resources such as The Ojibwe People's Dictionary, Ojibwe. net, and the Great Lakes Indian, Fish, and Wildlife Commission's Language Poster. I do not speak Ojibwemowin or Dakota and there remains much I do not understand about the tradition and complexities of these languages. However, I decided to include both the Ojibwemowin and Dakota languages in this novel to create a sense of veracity and to show support for the current growth and revitalization of these languages.

Finally, I am indebted to Michael A. (AmikoGaabaw) Loso for his help to correct and verify elements of Native representation in this novel. Any mistakes that remain are my own.

Prologue

WasabishkiMakwa
Gayaashko-zaaga'igan
Manominike-giizis
(August 1862, Gull Lake, Minnesota)

Ignoring his tired legs, WasabishkiMakwa hopped from one foot to another, raising his voice and banging his chest as if he were at a summer pow-wow. Like the rest of the young Ojibwe men, he was filled with excitement as they followed the old messenger, Niskigwun, to Gayaashko-zaaga'igan where their leader, Bagone-giizhig, awaited his new soldiers.

Though he was absorbed in the thrill of the moment, deep down Waabi, as he was known by his friends and community, carried a sense of fear and doubt. He had never counted coupe or claimed a scalp. He did not consider himself a soldier. By the time he came of age, his people lived in relative peace with the Bwaan—their eternal enemy. He knew only stories of revenge raids and territorial battles. When he raised his weapon it was only to kill little vermin—rodents, and rabbits—never a man.

As a young boy, he remembered his grandfather telling him about raids led by his people against the Naadowens. At the time, the Naadowens had no firearms or gunpowder. But the Ojibwe, who had been trading with the French, did. His grandfather told him that the Ojibwe used to fall upon sleeping villages of Bwaan, crawl silently upon the tops of their lodges, and drop bags of gunpowder through the opening in the top, which would land in the fire causing it to explode and kill or injure those living inside. Using methods like these, his grandfather told him that they were able to force the Naadowens out of the upper river region. They even forced them from their great villages on Misi-zaaga'iganing, a place called Mille Lacs by the whites.

As the men continued their march to Gayaashko-zaaga'igan, Waabi recalled one of his earliest memories. In a field, not far from his family's lodge, human hair hung from hoops swaying in the wind. There were more than Waabi could count with his fingers. They whipped and twirled with each gust, some gathering dried leaves that had been caught like flies in a web.

"What are those?" he asked his mother.

"Those are reminders, my son. They remind us that no life is lost without another being taken. This way we do not harm another without first judging the consequences."

"They look like hair," Waabi said. "Like father's hair and uncle's hair."

"Yes," his mother answered. "They are the scalps of our enemies hung at the graves of our kin."

"Our enemies?"

Waabi's mother gently stroked the back of his head. "Nothing is gained without loss. For everything that is given, something is taken. For every friend, there is a foe."

The scalps remained there for many seasons, blowing in the wind, suffering through the elements, wasting away. Eventually, they drifted off into the wind rejoining the circle of all things. The image he had of them, haunting and ominous, was seared deep in Waabi's memory.

Samuel

The Road to Fort Ridgely, Minnesota
August 1862

Cannon fire echoed down the river valley as Private Samuel Copeland walked warily along the road to Fort Ridgely. A few hours earlier the eighteen year-old army private experienced his first skirmish—something, after months of drilling, he thought he longed for. Now, as he walked past another lifeless body that lay face down and scalped, and having lost most of his company to a surprise attack, he realized he was wrong. Who would wish for this?

He felt a sudden, stinging pain in his left forearm causing him to bend over while grimacing in discomfort. The pain was a constant reminder that he had been grazed by a shotgun pellet in a futile effort to repel an Indian ambush, all the while secretly begging the spirit of his father to help him survive. Samuel closed his eyes as he gripped his injured forearm and clenched his jaw. Once the surge of pain passed, he took a deep breath, straightened himself, and reopened his eyes. There, floating in the shallows of the Minnesota River, he saw the body of a Union army soldier face down in the water.

Samuel retched in his mouth, bending over involuntarily and coughing out rancid water. "Dammit," he cursed as he wiped his mouth. He took a few sips of water from his canteen before moving to the side of the road to investigate the dead soldier. Feeling the heaviness of his feet and legs, he edged his way down the river bank toward the bloated body. Putting one foot in the water, he reached for the exposed back of the blue army coat which had dried in the sun. Using his right arm he managed to pull the over-turned body on shore. With a trembling curiosity, Samuel grabbed the dead soldier's body by the side of the torso and tried to flip it over. He grunted, struggling with the weight of it. With one final push he flipped the body over and then toppled forward landing hard against the dirt and sand. Samuel rose to his knees, spit sand from his mouth, and turned to look at the face of the dead soldier.

Immediately he recognized the cold, discolored face to be that of his Company Commander, Lt. John Marsh. Kneeling there, tired and grief-stricken, Samuel slumped his shoulders and hung his head. The last time he had seen Marsh, less than twenty-four hours earlier, he was negotiating peacefully with an Upper Sioux standing on the opposite side of the river. That's when all hell broke loose.

With the sun beating down on him, and the distant sounds of cannon fire still echoing through the valley, he realized there was no time to dwell. The body had to be buried, or at least hidden until a burial party could be sent later. Samuel stood up. Ignoring his aches and pains he took hold of Lt. Marsh's body and dragged it to a thicket of hazel brush. Breathing heavily and sweating under the August sun, Samuel laid the body carefully among the shrubs. He straightened the lieutenant's collar, wiped the sand from his jacket, and placed his arms over his chest. With one last look, Samuel said a silent prayer and then rose up from the thicket, returned to the road, and continued walking toward the fort.

Cannon fire exploded once again sounding like a thunderstorm in the distance. But there were no clouds. The fort, he was certain, was under attack. His life, the lives of his fellow soldiers, the lives of his family, were in peril. He pushed the thoughts of fear from his mind and continue walking toward the fort. He knew it was purposeless, but he didn't know where else to go. He only knew that he longed to be home, years past, chopping wood with his father, putting up with his brother's idleness, and taking care of his younger siblings. Now he was alone with his fear and his pain, walking slowly toward certain danger, hoping he might find anyone that could give him food, water, shelter, and rest. His feet were heavy and blistered, his arm throbbed, and his head ached from the heat.

Samuel paused for a moment. He looked to his right and left and saw only that the world around him was peaceful and quiet. The wind brushed gently against the leaves of the nearby oak trees. The birds called back-and-forth, exchanging harmonious trills. The river offered a soothing and constant burble. He could see, in the absence of chaos—of war—why people gave up their old lives and came to this place called Minnesota.

Chapter 1

WasabishkiMakwa
Winter Lodge
Onnaabaw-giizia
(Near Bad River, March 1850)

Waabi dug through layers of hard, frozen snow attempting to find the ground. Below, somewhere, he knew lay thousands of maple seeds that months earlier had spun and fluttered to the ground like wounded birds.

"I can't find any," his younger cousin, White Cloud, said as he stood, straightened his back, and looked at his sister, Star.

"I can't either," Star agreed, squeezing her face in displeasure.

"Just keep digging," Waabi said, hiding the desperation from his voice. "They're here somewhere."

Waabi had never dug through the snow for maple seeds before. But this, his tenth winter, held on much longer than usual, and he and his relatives had used up most of their stored provisions. Hunger had become a daily companion.

"Ayah!" Waabi exclaimed, pushing aside layers of crunchy ice with his beaver skin gloves. "Over here!"

White Cloud and Star raced over to Waabi's side and began shoveling through the crunchy snow. Underneath it they found layers of maple seeds.

Star wiggled her way between the two older boys and reached down to scoop up a handful.

"Wait!" Waabi said, ignoring his own eagerness. "We must make an offering of tobacco." The air stilled as Waabi removed his glove, reached inside the pocket of his leather coat, and pulled out a pinch of dried tobacco leaves. Holding his hand straight out, he released the leaves from between his thumb and forefinger watching as they fluttered to the ground. "A gift for what we receive," he said in a hushed tone.

Moments later, Waabi and his cousins filled their parfleche bags with handfuls of decayed, frozen maple seeds and returned to the winter wigwam bounding through the snow like little rabbits. Inside the fire-lit lodge Waabi's father, grandmother, aunt, and uncle were smearing their faces with wet ash. As they paused to look up, Waabi thought they looked like a war party of gloomy ghosts.

"It's for the goodwill of the spirit," his father, Giizhigoon said, his fingers blackened to the knuckle and his face half-covered in ash.

Waabi laid his parfleche beside the fire revealing the pile of seeds he had collected. "Are you going hunting?" he asked.

"We are going hunting," his father said. "We must all blacken our faces and fast until the hunt is complete. If we are steadfast, together, the Great Spirit will end our famine."

Waabi turned to his young cousins who nodded innocently. Because he had no brothers or sisters, Waabi felt protective of them. From the back of the wigwam, seated on a bright yellow and red beaded pillow, Waabi's grandmother held forward the wooden bowl of dark wet ash. Waabi walked around the fire and knelt next to the bowl. He placed his fingers in the warm paste and dabbed streaks of it across his forehead and cheeks. Like a balm to his stomach, his hunger pangs drifted away. He didn't feel like eating cooked maple seeds anyway.

"We will depart at first light," Giizhigoon said, speaking with confidence.

It had been sixteen days since their winter camp, comprised of five families, had eaten any meat, surviving only on rice, dried blueberries, and various seeds. Until then, Waabi had not known hunger, he knew only abundance. He was surprised when his father told him he'd be joining him on a winter hunt. He had never hunted game that he could not trap or beat over the head with a heavy stick. When he was hungry he caught and ate pigeons or rabbits. But little rodents and fowl would not satiate them for long.

Morning came early with the sun bursting through the narrow slits of weaved bulrush at the corners of the wigwam. Waabi was offered only hot water as a morning meal, then was told to ready himself for the day at hand. Before departing, his cousins smiled at him, their faces bright and encouraging, though their ash covered skin was dark.

Outside the air was fresh, but bitterly cold, working its way up Waabi's nostrils and causing his lips to go numb. He followed his father north alongside the frozen creek, walking lightly over the glistening snow. On his back he carried a sled made of hardwood and strung together with basswood cord. On his feet he wore snowshoes made of elm and netted by a crisscrossing pattern of rawhide. Snowshoes were one of his most important tools. Waabi's grandmother and aunt, and other women from their lodge, dedicated much time during the winter months toward the repair and maintenance of snowshoes. Without them, trekking through the snow would cause overwhelming exhaustion.

As they followed the creek to the east, Waabi's father paused and held his breath. Using great care, he lowered himself to one knee and looked steadily in the direction of the trees ahead. Waabi stopped and crouched in his father's long morning shadow. From over his father's shoulder he could see a deer picking at the bark of a young sapling. It was a beautiful creature with dark, glassy eyes and a smooth, tannish sheen. The animal was completely unaware of their presence.

As Waabi admired the graceful creature, an arrow struck it between the lower ribs, causing it to yelp and lift itself off its forelegs. Then, it spurted away, meandering frantically through the birch trees.

Without a word Waabi's father rose and strode in the direction of the fleeing deer. Waabi stumbled, the weight of the sled heavy on his back, but he managed to right himself and follow quickly along his father's path. Reaching the spot where the deer was hit, his father pulled out another arrow, notched it on his bowstring, and drew back. Waabi planted his feet firmly as he bent forward to watch as his father lowered the bow but never released the arrow.

"Let's chase it," Waabi said over his quickened heartbeat.

Waabi's father shook his head and looked back at him. "We do not kill the deer," he said. "We allow the deer to give itself to us. We will track him until he is ready to die."

Waabi thought of the members of his lodge—waiting, hoping—without food, fasting until their return. Then he thought of himself.

"I am hungry, father."

"You must be patient. The deer will make a great circle trying to escape us, but he will tire out. We need only stay close. Come," his father said. "Let us follow its trail."

Waabi's father located the trail of the deer but did not walk directly in its path, staying parallel to it instead. Just as his father had predicted, the deer, who started north, turned west and then gradually turned south in a large circle. After several hours Waabi grew tired, his face was numb, and his fingers stung with coldness. He longed to be back at camp, inside the wigwam by the warmth of the fire. He wanted so much to return that he had forgotten his hunger and thought only of rest and comfort.

His father stopped. "The animal is weary, but it still walks."

"Why have we stopped? Should we follow?"

Waabi's father took out his bandolier bag and pipe from inside his robe of woven blankets. "Sit," he said. "We will smoke kinnikinnick. It will fill the air with a sweet smell, and the deer will come to us."

Heavy with fatigue, Waabi plopped down into the cold but comfortable snow. As the pain in his back and legs eased, he looked with admiration at the colorfully beaded bandolier bag. Its red, blue, and green floral design shone like a rainbow against the whiteness of the landscape. The bag was more than just beautiful, it was the last thing his mother ever made before she passed away from illness when Waabi was barely more than a papoose.

Waabi's father struck a wooden match and lit the pipe. Instantly, Waabi smelled a rich aroma that reminded him of milk-weed in the summer. His father took three long inhales of the pipe, then leaned his head back and exhaled puffs of white smoke that wafted toward the blue sky. Satisfied, his father handed him the pipe. Waabi took it in his hand, adoring the carved red stone of the bowl, then, placing the stem between his lips, he inhaled, feeling the warm air enter his lungs. He released it in one long exhale and then smiled at his father.

"A Bwaan gave me that pipe," his father said. "It is made of sacred stone."

Waabi tilted his head, giving his father a sideways glance. "But the Bwaan are our enemy."

"They are not our enemy, son. Counterpart. They are our counterparts. At times we fight. At times we live in peace. This creates balance so that one group does not have more than another... so that all things remain in harmony."

Waabi nodded and took another puff on the pipe. Harmony, he thought, sounded nice. But he was old enough to know that a new threat lurked. One that showed compassion and contempt all in the same breath. The white man.

They sat in silence, passing the pipe between one another. As they did, the sun began to fall in the west.

"Shouldn't we continue tracking the deer?" Waabi asked.

In that moment, Waabi heard the soft crunch of snow in the distance behind him. His father pointed over Waabi's shoulder. Waabi turned and saw the wounded deer. It sniffed the air and took a step forward, shaking as if it might fall. It sniffed again, but then collapsed, groaning in pain.

"Our hunt is successful," his father said as he stood and pulled tobacco from his pouch. "But first a gift, our spiritual currency."

By the light of the moon, Waabi and his father trudged heavily through the deep snow. Waabi grunted and sweated, struggling against the weight of the deer on the sled as he pulled it forward by two leather straps around his shoulders. Tired as he was, Waabi did not dare ask for rest because he knew the winter camp was fasting while waiting for their return.

Peering through the darkness of the dense forest, Waabi saw a glimmer of light in the distance signifying that camp was near. When he and his father finally arrived, the ashen faces of his lodge members shone bright with smiles. Hearing shouts of exaltation, each of the five lodges was emptied as men, women, and children hurried out in front of the central fire pit to congratulate the successful hunters. As men slapped Waabi on the back, he tried his best to hide his staggering exhaustion. He wanted to fall over—to land face first in the snow, close his eyes, and sleep. Instead, he straightened his back, let go of the straps on his shoulders, and walked into camp like it was a leisurely stroll.

"Congratulations, Waabi," his aunt Memengwaa said. "You have killed your first deer and now we can celebrate... and eat!" Her round cheeks became flush with color as she grinned.

"Father killed the deer," Waabi said. "I only carried it on the sled."

"We shall break our fast by having a feast of the first fruits. You have ended our hunger with your steady aim," his aunt said.

Waabi raised an eyebrow. "But I told you, I did not..."

Meme, as he called his aunt, brought a raised finger to her lips. "Let us celebrate this accomplishment."

Waabi smiled as Meme stepped aside inviting him to enter the inner circle of the camp. As he did, he was rushed upon by his cousins White Cloud and Star, along with the other children of the camp. They patted his back and poked at his belly causing Waabi to laugh and giggle to the point where he fell helplessly into the snow.

Waabi's father looked back at him; first with a glare as if he might scold his son, but then he raised a fist, smiled and said, "Let us have a feast!"

The families gathered as the deer was dressed, and then the meat was prepared over the central fire. The fire danced and sparkled, warming and lighting the faces of their close-knit winter community. Meanwhile, Waabi's grandmother, Nokomis, prepared a stew thickened by pumpkin flowers and wild rice—ingredients she had secretly been saving.

When all was ready, the Mide, a man called Noodin, who was a member of the Grand Medicine Society, stood to offer words to Manidoog, the spirits. With his face shaded by deep wrinkles Noodin began by offering a portion of the meal back to the creator, throwing a hunk of meat into the fire. "We are grateful for the deer of the forest," he said. "We offer a piece back to you, Manidoo, as a first fruit. We petition you for our health and safety during this time of need. We ask for happiness and long life, here, where our ancestors are buried, where the food grows on water, where our fathers and grandfathers, mothers and grandmothers, lived before us, free from the dangers of the war, protected from the growing presence of the white man and his hunger for our land. We suffer with gratitude and we feast with gratitude. We take nothing for granted."

Noodin stepped back from the fire, brought his hood over his head, and sat down upon a bulrush mat. A great *Hi-ya!* was raised echoing through the surrounding darkness of the forest. Others began shouting and the celebration began. The women sang while the children danced and laughed. The men gathered together and told jokes while laughing uproariously and holding their satisfied bellies. Waabi forgot all about the long, tedious hunt and the hunger that preceded it. He forgot the struggle he endured to haul the deer back to camp.

Having wiped his bowl clean and tired of singing, Waabi entered the wigwam ready for rest after a long day. The lodge was warm and satisfying, as it always seemed to be, even on the coldest biboon nights. The walls, layered in bulrush and covered in birch bark, held the heat in. As Waabi slid underneath his covers, he never felt so comfortable as he did lying atop his feather bed, and below his furry, bear-skin blanket with his naked feet hanging out and angled toward the fire. It was sheer bliss to feel the heat of the crackling fire against the soles of his tired feet as he laid himself down, tucked himself in, and rested his head against his soft duck feather pillow. He would sleep with ease knowing his father rested near the entrance of the lodge while his grandmother kept watch over the fire. Not wild animal, nor hostile intruder, nor winter chill could disturb or destroy his solace and comfort. As he drifted off to sleep, even hunger, which had tormented him so recently, seemed far away.

Chapter 2

Samuel
Londonderry, Vermont
July 1859

Like a tree with roots, Samuel stood steady and balanced, heels
planted on the ground, knees slightly bent, shoulders square.
With a soft but firm grip he held the ax in front of him, resting the
sharp metal edge against the three-foot log of elm that stood round
and upright. He focused. If the ax came down in the center of the
log it would stick to it like an arrow to a bullseye. If he struck it too
wide, it would only chip the log. If he was going to split the log, he
had to hit it in just the right spot, not too close to the edge, not too
near the center.

Samuel raised the ax high above his head, keeping his eyes
locked on the target—a spot where the wood was smooth and white,
without knots or gnarls. He took a deep breath, held it, tightened
his stomach, and brought the head of the ax down with force and
speed.

Smack. The sharp metal edge of the ax hit its spot, cracking
the log like a peanut shell and sending the halves in opposite directions. The sound, the sight, the feel of it was satisfying.

With the log successfully split, he grabbed the next one,
placed it upright in front of him, and repeated the chore. Sometimes
the log split, sometimes it didn't. Sometimes the blade stuck into
the top of the log and he had to wiggle and pull and fight to get it
out. Sometimes it split as easily as an egg.

Samuel leaned back, tilted his head up, and took a deep
breath, inhaling the warm Vermont summer air. He could feel the
sweat dripping slowly down his forehead as he removed his cap and
wiped it away with the back of his forearm. The sky, he couldn't
help but notice, was an endless deep blue that seemed impossible.

"Samuel!" he heard the voice of his father from behind him.

He turned to see his father walking toward him. His sandy brown hair flopped against his forehead with each long stride. His pants were muddied and his overstretched shirt was drenched in sweat.

"Samuel," he said again, now close enough for Samuel to see the beads of sweat that gathered in his father's gray-speckled patchy beard.

Samuel marveled at the contrast between them. His father was short, well-built, with a square jaw and gleaming blue eyes. Samuel was thin, with a narrow face, plain brown eyes, and, at the age of fifteen, was already taller than his father.

"Yes, Pa?"

His father stopped a few feet in front of him. His face brightened, revealing deep smile lines that stretched from the corners of his eyes down the curve of his cheeks.

"Later today," his father explained, "we need to cut down a few trees—make sure we keep building up our stock of firewood."

Samuel nodded.

"Except this time we have to bring your brother along. It's time he learns to fell a tree."

Samuel felt a sudden heaviness. He slumped.

"Hey," Samuel's father said, recognizing his son's dismay. "It'll be fun! You can teach him." He smiled and winked.

Samuel was not encouraged by his father's enthusiasm. At thirteen years old, his little brother Thomas was just two years younger than he, but not half as mature. Worse, Thomas was his father's closest companion. The two of them were like best friends, always joking and laughing with each other, never including Samuel in any of their fun. Plus, it seemed like they teamed up against him, forcing him to complete the harder chores while they acted like school children at recess.

Samuel knew why, of course. Ever since he was a baby, Thomas had shortness of breath; a wheezing caused by any task or challenge that was too onerous. The doctor called it asthma and said there was no cure. Samuel was protective of his little brother, and so was his father. But Samuel was also envious of the relationship they had, one that he and his father would never have.

Samuel nodded. "All right, Pa."

"Good! Good!" he said, smiling. "You finish up splitting these logs and then we'll head out."

With a nod of his head he turned and left just as quickly as he came. Samuel took a deep breath, leaned his head back, and took another long look at the eternal blue sky.

It was a hot afternoon and the sun was directly overhead by the time Samuel, his brother Thomas, and his father Randolph, headed into the woods behind their third-generation Vermont homestead. Samuel carried a thick, heavy rope over his shoulder that scratched the side of his neck as he walked. Worse, the weight of it gave him a pinching pain that felt like a hook in his skin. His father led the way while carrying a wooden-handled felling hatchet and a two-man crosscut saw which he struggled to balance in his gloved hand. Thomas, whom Samuel had lost track of somewhere behind them, was given nothing to carry.

They reached an opening in the woods when Samuel's father paused to look around. Relieved, Samuel dropped the rope like an anchor. He looked behind them, but didn't see Thomas.

"Thomas! Thomas!" he yelled.

Thomas' shaggy head of brown hair appeared from behind a knoll bouncing up and down. He whipped by Samuel dropping bright red raspberries along the way.

"Thomas!" he said. "You ain't supposed to be pickin' raspberries, you're supposed to be learnin' how to cut down a tree."

Thomas continued toward their father without looking back. "Pa," he said as he stopped next to him. "Look what I got." Thomas held out his right hand which was filled with berries.

Their father looked down at Thomas' open hand and tipped his cap. "Those look perfect for eatin'," he said, then he pinched a few berries between his thumb and forefinger and tossed them into his open mouth.

Samuel shook his head in displeasure. "Pa," he said, breaking up their little berry eating session, "I got the rope ready. Just tell me which tree to tie it to."

"Just hold up a second Samuel," he said, brushing away his willingness like it was a pesky horse fly. "I got to teach your brother how to select a tree."

Samuel clenched his fists in frustration but tried not to let his father see that he was upset. While he waited for them to eat their berries, he saw that there was a white ash tree about twenty yards in front of them that was scarred from years of a quiet and lonely existence. Its branches were dead and drooping, its leaves were brown and dried up, and it leaned to one side like it had given up living. Above it, to the west, clouds were gathering.

"There's an old tree we can cut down," Thomas said pointing at the white ash.

Their father stood and rubbed his hand through Thomas' shaggy hair, congratulating him like he might a dog who had just obeyed a command. "Yes! Well done!"

Thomas squinted and smiled, soaking up his father's praise. Samuel rolled his eyes.

"Yeah," Samuel said, "and we'd better get a move on because I see some storm clouds gathering."

Their father leaned back, peering up at the sky. "Yeah, we've got time," he said, then turned to Samuel. "You can tie the rope to that white ash tree. Make sure you tie it above the cut."

Without a word Samuel grabbed the rope and headed for the tree. As he unrolled the heavy rope and began to wrap it around the thick trunk of the tree, his father and brother just stood there talking and laughing. They didn't seem to care to help him one bit.

As Samuel was finishing the knot, Thomas asked, "What's the rope for anyway?"

"Ain't that common sense?" Samuel said with a snide tilt of his head.

His father whipped his head around and looked at Samuel hard, like he could see right through him. "It ain't common sense, Samuel! You had to learn this, too."

Samuel's body turned to stone, shocked by the sudden remark.

His father turned back to Thomas and spoke gently. "We use it to keep the tree from falling in the wrong direction," he explained.

"We tie one end of the rope to the tree we're cuttin' down, and the other end of the rope to a strong, sturdy tree. The sturdy tree will keep tension on the rope pulling the weak tree toward it until it falls to the ground. That way we know which way it'll fall. We wouldn't want anybody gettin' hurt."

Thomas blushed in response to their father's wide grin.

"Samuel," their father said, pointing. "Take the other end of the rope to that tree there and show your brother how to tie it up. That's our sturdy tree," he said, looking back toward Thomas.

The tree was a maple, about two and a half feet thick with leaves so green they were startling. Samuel grabbed the end of the rope and walked toward the maple tree without looking to see if Thomas followed. When he reached the tree, he immediately began tying the rope. He started by walking around to the back side of the trunk and then continued another quarter of the way around. With his right foot against the trunk of the tree and his hands wrapped tightly around the rope, he pulled as hard as he could using the trunk of the tree as a pivot. By this time Thomas had arrived.

"You gotta pull the rope tight," Samuel explained, "using all your weight and strength."

Thomas tilted his head and watched, squeezing his eyes into narrow slits.

"Give the rope a tug," Samuel said. "Is it stiff?"

With his middle and forefinger Thomas plucked the rope, sending a singing vibration through the entire length of it. "Sure is," he said.

"Good. Now, keeping the rope tight, I'm going to walk around the tree three times."

With the rope wrapped around his knuckles, Samuel walked around the tree, ducking underneath the rope each time he reached the front. Thomas stood there quietly with his hands at his side—it was the most obedient Samuel had seen him all day and it filled Samuel with a sense of pride.

"Hurry up, Samuel!" their father called, erasing the pride from his heart. "I'm not trying to be rude, but you may have been right about those clouds. They're moving faster than I thought."

Samuel paused and looked at his father who was leaning against the white ash tree and pointing toward the sky. It had turned dark and was filled with heavy rain clouds coming their way. But, in his own form of personal protest, Samuel gave him no sign that he meant to hurry and kept wrapping the rope around the maple tree.

"All right, Thomas," Samuel said once he'd finished. "We're going to use a taut line hitch."

Samuel handed the end of the rope to Thomas who slowly lifted his open palms looking like he thought the rope might be dangerous. "What do I do?"

"It's simple," Samuel said. "Take the very end of the rope—"

"This?"

"Yes. Take the end of the rope and wrap it over the line twice."

Thomas moved slowly, but did exactly as Samuel told him.

"Good. Now take the end and wrap it over, under, and through the loop you just made."

Samuel guided Thomas with his fingers, but he didn't seem to need the help.

"Good. Good!" Samuel said. "Now pull the knot tight."

With his left hand on the knot, which was waist high, and his right hand on the taut rope, Thomas edged the knot toward the tree.

"Like this?"

"Exactly."

For a moment Samuel's pride returned, but then Thomas let go of the knot, dropped his hands, and turned and ran toward their father.

"Hey!" Samuel yelled. "You didn't finish."

Thomas continued running until he reached their father who stood waiting at the white ash tree. Samuel pulled the knot himself, making sure it was snug against the trunk of the maple tree.

"Good job, Thomas!" their father said.

Samuel walked across the open space separating him from his father and brother, dragging his feet as he went.

"Now we cut it down?" Thomas said.

"Not quite," their father said, shaking his head as if he wasn't the least bit bothered by Thomas' constant questions. He took hold of the ax, raised it up, and rested it against his broad shoulder. "Now we cut a wedge into the side of the tree, underneath the rope. This will help the tree fall the way we want it to fall."

Thomas looked on silently.

"Step back while I take a few whacks at it," their father said with a wink.

Samuel took Thomas by the shoulder and they both stepped back.

Taking a wide, bent stance, their father held the ax, his right hand above his left. He looked carefully for his spot, then drew the ax back and swung it forward with as much speed and power as he could gather. The sharp, metal end of the ax struck the bark with a heavy, dull thud that echoed through the forest. He drew back and swung again, aiming for the same spot. Over and over he swung, striking the tree hard each time and sending chunks of bark and wood flying speedily through the air. It was mesmerizing to watch.

Their father stopped, set the head of the ax on the ground and leaned against it like a crutch. He breathed heavily as he wiped the sweat from his eyes. He managed to cut a wedge in the tree that was about six inches deep.

"All right, Samuel," he said. "You ready to saw?"

Samuel turned his eyes to the saw lying in the grass as lifeless as a stick. He walked over and grabbed the handle while his father did the same. It was a six-foot, two-man saw that wobbled like a sheet of paper in the middle, but had long and sharp jagged teeth that looked threatening. As a boy, Samuel was scared of it when he saw it hanging in the shed, but now he knew better. It was a tool that helped them build things up and cut things down. It helped them survive. As a sawyer, like his father, the saw was instrumental. Plus, it required the work of two men, which meant it was work he could do with his father.

"Step back, Thomas," their father said with yet another broad and carefree grin. "This tree will crush you like an ant if you don't get out of the way."

Thomas smiled back. "Like an ant? More like a boot to a spider!"

They both laughed, sounding like two clattering windchimes. Samuel ignored them.

"Come on, Samuel," his father said. "Have a sense of humor."

Samuel repressed the urge to smile but couldn't fight it for long.

"There it is!" their father said and all three of them shared a laugh.

After a few moments, Thomas stepped back as Samuel and their father raised the saw into position, underneath the rope and opposite the wedge.

"Ready?"

Samuel nodded.

They began slowly, with little pushes and pulls, letting the jagged edge of the blade cut into the thick gray bark. Once the saw found its place, they began to push and pull harder and faster moving the blade back and forth, rhythmically. The blade pushed through the bark and into the hard, yellow wood. Samuel closed his eyes and listened to the constant grating sound of the saw while focusing on the flex and release of his straining shoulders. The smell of sawdust, the whooshing of the saw, the labor of his muscles—it felt good.

As they continued to cut, pushing the saw hard, Samuel's skin grew hot and beads of sweat rolled down his forehead, across his eyebrows, and down the curve of his cheeks until they reached his jawline where they fell like drops of melting ice. A cold breeze cooled his hot skin, and the entire forest dimmed as if a shadow had been cast upon it. Samuel looked up and saw that the dark clouds he'd seen earlier were now directly overhead.

"I think rain's comin'," Thomas said.

Their father paused to wipe his brow and look up. "Let's get this tree down before the rain starts."

Randolph looked at Samuel. Acknowledging each other, they continued sawing, this time faster and stronger than before. With each push Samuel's father began to grunt and with each pull Samuel became more and more worried that he couldn't keep up with his father's determined pace. His shoulders ached like he had been holding a canoe over his head, and his hands became sore and red.

"Just another minute or so," his father grunted. "Make sure you stand back, Thomas."

The once proud white ash tree, which had probably survived centuries, began to creak and bend telling the world that its life was coming to an end. The wind grew heavier—thicker—filled with dust and moisture.

Samuel concentrated hard, eager to finish the cut. The blade was nearing the wedge on the other side, and it was only a matter of moments before the tree would finally give in to gravity.

"Get ready!" their father said.

But just before either of them had a chance to step back and observe the results of their labor, a heavy gust of cold wind moved through, catching the tree by its branches and twisting it a quarter way around. For a moment the rope held tight against the weight of the tree, but then, like the snapping of a whip, the knot on the opposite tree unraveled and the rope slung from its hold. Another heavy gust moved through, this one stronger than the one before, twisting and pushing the tree in their father's direction. Samuel gasped as the tree fell quickly, forcing his father to leap from its path. The tree crashed with a roar against the ground, shaking the whole earth and trapping his father's right leg beneath it.

Their father screamed like a bleating goat, crying loudly over and over. He lay face down with his head turned and his arms bent, holding his chest just off the ground. His left leg was curled into his body and his right leg was trapped under the trunk of the tree from the knee down. His face was red and scrunched tight as he gritted his teeth and breathed heavily.

Samuel's heart beat through his chest. He felt scared and dizzy.

Thomas ran to their father's side and bent down next to him. "Pa! Pa!"

Their father clenched his jaw enduring the pain.

Thomas brought his hand to his chest and began wheezing. He opened his mouth wide and tried to take big breaths, but each time he was forced to exhale and try again, as if someone had their hands around his throat. Thomas looked up in a panic. His eyes and face reddened and he bobbed back-and-forth trying desperately to breathe.

For a moment, Samuel stood there, unable to move.

"Dammit!" Randolph groaned. "Help your little brother."

Samuel nodded before finally springing into action. He ran to his brother's side, kneeled down and put his hand around his back. "Breathe," Samuel said. "It's all right. Pa's gonna be all right."

Thomas was beyond gasping and started to choke. His face was red as an apple, his eyes filled with desperation.

"Relax," Samuel said, though he was enveloped with fear. "Like this," he said as he kneeled closer to Thomas and made eye contact. Samuel took small, patterned breaths, using his hand to show Thomas the rhythm.

It worked. Thomas' wheeze returned as the airways slowly opened up. Then his breaths grew longer, bigger. The wheeze went away and the color returned to his face. Thomas turned away from Samuel and back to their father.

Randolph, too, began to take deep, regular breaths and the tightness in his face softened.

Samuel said, "What do we do, Pa? We can't move that tree ourselves."

"You'll have to fetch help," he groaned.

"And leave us here?" Thomas said, a look of helplessness on his face.

"It'll be all right, but hurry, Samuel," their father said through pained breaths.

Samuel put his hand on Thomas' shoulder and nodded with assurance. He stood and said, "I'll be quick, Pa."

His father, still grimacing in pain, turned his face toward the ground and sighed, exhaling against the dry dirt. "Just..." he breathed in, struggling. "Just go get help. And hurry."

Chapter 3

WasabishkiMakwa
Winter Lodge / Mooniingwanekaaning-minis
Onnaabaw-giizia
(Winter Lodge / Madeline Island, March 1850)

The warming temperatures of ziigwan could not be held off forever. Waabi sensed it when the snow began to soften during the day and harden at night, often causing the netting of his snowshoes to break. It was called Onnaabaw-giizia for a reason, the hard crust on the snow moon. He knew they would soon pack up their winter camp and head for the sugarbush. This excited Waabi. After several moons wintering he grew restless and welcomed the change of scenery and the chance to be more active. He was told by his father that he was born in the sugarbush and he could still remember his mother calling him "Little Sugar." Being back there, once a year, Waabi felt connected to her, as if they were still together.

"Waabi," Grandmother Nokomis said as Waabi swept the hard ground around the fire pit.

Light poured in from the open entrance and songbirds could be heard in the trees, along with the intermittent but joyful shrieks of his cousins who were playing a game of hide-and-seek.

"Tomorrow we will pack up the winter camp. I need you to help take down the wigwam and show your cousins how it should be folded and stored."

"Yes, Nokomis," Waabi answered. "I am glad to be going to the sugar camp. I look forward to it all year long." Waabi flashed his grandmother an innocent smile.

"I know you do, grandson," she said looking at him with dark and heavy eyes. "But you will not go to the sugarbush tomorrow. You are going to the island with your father. The sugarbush will come later. Soon, but later."

"But summer is still far off. Why would we go to the island already?"

"Do not whine like a dog who begs," his grandmother said. "The sugarbush will not go anywhere, and there will always be plenty of work for you to do."

Waabi was curious. They had never traveled to the island so early in the season and he wanted to know why, but he knew better than to prod his grandmother further.

"Grandmother," he said. "When I am done sweeping, may I go outside to play with White Cloud and Star?"

His grandmother, seated in the back of the wigwam, lifted her face to the light. Her dark eyes filled with a sudden glint of sun as she said yes and then lowered her face back down.

The next day, early in the afternoon after Waabi helped break down the winter camp, he departed with his father, uncle, and three of the men from camp.

"Why haven't any of the other boys joined us?" Waabi asked his father.

"Because they have brothers and sisters to watch after while we are gone," his father said.

"But I have my cousins. Don't I have to watch after them?"

"You do," his father said. "But you are an only child. You must grow up sooner than the other boys. You must learn about the world so that you can care for yourself, then you can care for others."

Waabi's eyes locked onto the heels of his father's snowshoes as numerous thoughts and questions swirled in his head.

"Think of the animals who travel alone," his father said. "Such as the bear or the wolverine. You too may have to travel alone and you must be prepared."

"Or the skunk!" his uncle Ogimaa said walking up from behind him.

Waabi turned to see uncle smiling from ear to ear. "We can call you little skunk boy."

Waabi leaned down and reached for a handful of wet snow, but before taking aim at his uncle he was bombarded with snowballs from the men of the group.

"Hey!" Waabi said with a giggle, then he started throwing snow in every direction in playful retaliation.

30

"It's two against three, son," Waabi's father said as he took aim at his sister's husband.

"Skunk-boy, skunk-boy," the men chanted as they flung snowballs in Waabi's direction.

Waabi leaped from side to side but he became overwhelmed and fell to the ground.

Waabi's father fought valiantly. Spry and quick, he avoided each snowball while striking his opponents with every throw. But, as he leaned down to gather more snow he was struck in the top of the head. He tried to retaliate with a quick, sidearm throw but he missed and was hit again. Then again. Then again. "All right, all right," Waabi's father said. "We surrender."

"Had enough, Giizighoon!" Ogimaa said. Then, raising his snow filled hand, he turned to his comrades and said, "Claim your scalps, men!"

A new barrage of snowballs came hurling through the air, striking Waabi's father across the chest and arms. He turned his face and closed his eyes and fell to the ground beside Waabi, rolling in the snow and laughing. "You got me, you win."

The victors buckled over with laughter. Waabi sat up and smiled, admiring the carefree and joyful attitude of his father and uncle. Ogimaa, barely able to catch his breath, walked over and helped Waabi to his feet.

"Do we have a truce?" Ogimaa said.

Waabi's cheeks hurt because he was unable to repress his smile. Catching his breath he said, "I think we've had our fun."

Waabi's father finally stopped rolling through the snow. He stood and wiped the mushy slush from his hair and fur-lined coat. "You should be careful, Ogimaa," he said with a smirk. "Every good attack is followed by a revenge raid."

Waabi took a deep, grateful breath. Surrounded by his family—his community—he felt happy.

The group continued north along the Mashkii-ziibi and past Oodenaang, a small village started by the white missionary Leonard Wheeler where the people farmed and practiced Christianity. When they reached Zaagawaamikong-wiikwed, called Chequamegon Bay by the missionaries and traders, they continued on the frozen bay until they reached the island—Mooniingwanekaaning-minis.

This was home to Waabi, his family, and his clan members. It had become known as Madeline Island by the foreign visitors even though it was the traditional homeland of the Ojibwe people where their ancestors had settled centuries earlier after a long migration. The island was long and narrow, with endless shores and deep, abundant woodlands. The waters surrounding the island provided food, protection, and seclusion. It was close enough to the mainland to provide convenient travel to and from the island, but far enough away to offer a real sense of community pride and safety.

Stepping off the ice and onto the island, Waabi felt an intimate connection that softened and soothed his body as if sliding into a warm spring. He didn't understand the feeling. Certainly he had fond memories of long summer months on the island spending time with his friends and family, gathering berries, and learning how to hunt and fish, but the connection he felt came from deep inside him. It was a collective memory built through generations. Looking on, Waabi could see that they had arrived at an important gathering. Hundreds of people assembled outside the traders' stores and in the forefront of the protestant church, the place where Waabi attended school in the summer months.

The town and agency was called La Pointe and it was established years before Waabi's birth when the French fur traders built trading posts where they could exchange tools and cloth for furs and pelts. His grandfather used to speak of the fur trade as an even exchange between nations, sharing important valuables and establishing crucial alliances. But that exchange changed over time to something done only between store clerks and individuals. Waabi watched his father many times enter the trader's store with nothing and depart with ammunition or blankets, only to be settled months later when his father returned with thick winter pelts. It was an exchange based on credit that Waabi didn't fully understand.

The traders were all present for the gathering along with a multitude of various other La Pointe residents. Among them Waabi saw voyageurs with names like Le Fevre, Robidoux, Charette, and St. Jean. There were store clerks, missionaries, teachers, laborers, and fishermen. Of course, there were the Ojibwe of La Pointe, but there were also the Ojibwe from other parts of the region such as Nagaajiwanaang, Odaawaa-Zaaga'iganiing, Waaswaagan, and Gakiiwe'onaning, all of them just as eager as Waabi to know why they had been called by the government agent.

"Many hundreds have gathered," Ogimaa said as the group edged closer to the agency center crushing the wet snow beneath them as they walked.

"This council will determine much for our people," Waabi's father said, sending a shock of surprise through Waabi's spine.

Hesitant, Waabi spoke up. "What do you mean father, much for our people?"

Waabi's father paused and looked down at him. His steady eyes did not blink or wander. "Eight years ago, when you were still confined to a cradleboard, the government agents came asking for our land. We said no, we would not give up our homeland. But then they said they did not want our land; they wanted the rocks inside the land and a thing called copper. In return, they told us that they would provide for us food, clothing, ammunition, and all the things we needed for survival. And so we agreed."

"That is why we collect food and blankets on the island in the time after ricing?" Waabi said, trying hard to contemplate what his father was explaining.

"Yes, that is why," his father said. "They told us that for many years afterward they would supply us with goods, if they could only have a way to get the minerals in the land along the shores of Gichigami. And they told us we would never be asked to move from our lands."

"But they lied," Waabi's uncle said.

"They lied?" Waabi said.

Waabi's father took a long, drawn out breath. "There are rumors that the American government changed their minds. We believe they want us to move west into the land of the Dakota and the land of the Misi-ziibi where other clans and other tribes of Ojibwe already live."

"How can they tell us to go where others already live?" Waabi asked.

33

"They do not make rules like our rules. They are not passed down from father to son or from grandmother to granddaughter. Their rules change with the seasons depending on what suits them. Their words do not mean the same as our words. Our words are written on scrolls of birch bark and have been carried through generations from the time we lived near the Great Salt Water Sea. Their words are written on paper with ink that can be scratched out or destroyed. They shake our hands rather than exchange gifts. They say one thing and do another."

Listening to his father, Waabi was confused and hurt. He remembered his mother, every night before he slept, saying to him, "Be brave young one. Honest and true. Love your family and your people. Never hurt someone lesser than you, always respect those older than you. Never turn away from those in need. Learn from the world around you and be grateful for everything it provides." Waabi couldn't understand what his father was telling him. Until now, the world he knew made sense.

"I can see you are confused," his father said. "But do not worry. Our people have been a part of this land for much longer than the Americans. We are a part of the land and cannot be removed from it. We are resilient and strong. We will fight back against their lies."

Ogimaa placed his hand gently upon Waabi's back. "Come along, nephew. You have much to learn but that will come with time. For now, let us move forward; the council is about to start."

The speaker was a white man who stood atop a wooden crate.

"I am your agent, Jon Livermore," he said. "I am responsible for all transactions between yourselves and the United States government officials in Washington. I communicate to you all the policies handed down from Washington and in return I communicate your condition and needs back to Washington."

The agent wore a long, black, fur-lined overcoat that hung open exposing a gold-buttoned vest and dark trousers. His shoes were polished, and on his head he wore a tall black top-hat. A red and white scarf was tucked neatly into his vest and fluffed high around his neck and chest. He was unlike any white trader Waabi had ever seen, nor was he like any of the farmer Ojibwe who had cut their hair and spoke of a thing called the gospel.

Around him the Ojibwe, traders, merchants, and people of all kinds packed tightly together with their chins lifted and shoulders leaning forward. The agent's voice did not carry well in the empty late winter air, but was amplified somewhat by the surrounding buildings. The interpreter's voice was no clearer. Waabi craned his neck left and right to get a view of the man who was instructing them.

"Last fall," the agent continued, "the Legislative Assembly of the newly created Minnesota Territory determined that the Lake Superior Ojibwe living upon the ceded territory should be removed to the unceded territory."

Shouts of disapproval rose up from the crowd. Waabi was confused. "What does that mean? What is the ceded territory?" Waabi's questions went unanswered.

The agent spoke over the disapproval. "For which, a proposal for your permanent removal was signed and passed in October of last year. The measure was forwarded to Congress who approved it and placed it on the President's desk. President Taylor signed the order which officially cancels the usufructuary rights—that is, the right to live upon and use the land—of the Lake Superior Ojibwe and requires their removal from the ceded to the unceded lands."

The shouts of disapproval swelled like a powerful gust of wind rising up from the crowd and into the clear blue sky.

"What does that mean?" Waabi said, but he could not be heard among his father, uncle, and lodge members. Seeing their fists in the air, their mouths agape, and their eyes filled with anger, Waabi felt apprehensive and scared.

"You told us we would never be removed from our homes!" one elder Ojibwe man shouted toward the agent.

The agent held out his arms, palms pointed to the ground, but the accusations and questioning continued.

Turning away from the excitement, Waabi suddenly caught the eye of Agnes, a girl his own age and the daughter of the protestant missionary, who was also his school teacher. She raised her hand and waved. Her blue eyes sparkled and her plump, rosy cheeks were lifted by her smile. The chaos surrounding Waabi faded and he responded similarly, with a wave and a smile. He had never waved before, but it was common among the whites. She began walking toward him.

"Hey!" she said, putting her mitten covered hand on Waabi's forearm and steering him away from the derisive crowd. Worried of straying, Waabi turned toward his father and uncle for approval, but neither were paying attention. Waabi followed Agnes. A lightness filled his belly.

Clear of the crowd Waabi and Agnes stood face to face. He wanted to speak, but he was still learning English and he felt embarrassed. "What this means?" he said, unable to endure the silence between them. "We leave? Live somewhere else?"

"I hope not," Agnes said, her voice uncertain and innocent. "If the Ojibwe have to leave, my father would have to close down the school and mission." She looked nervously toward the ground, then back up at Waabi. "You are attending school this summer, right?"

Waabi could barely think. He was confused by the directions of the government agent and now he was startled by Agnes, a girl who caused his heart to beat fast and his palms to sweat. They had spoken before, but mostly Waabi just observed her from across the Mission schoolhouse. She had wide set eyes and smooth, wavy hair the color of basswood twine that swept across her forehead. Waabi noticed that she often adjusted her hair and turned her head away from him, presumably to cover a bean-shaped birthmark on her right temple. Waabi felt drawn to this imperfection and the bashful way Agnes covered it up. Realizing he hadn't yet answered, Waabi just nodded, afraid to speak English again.

"You will!" she said, raising herself up off her toes gleefully.

"I..." Waabi stuttered. "I think. If my grandmother need no help. If she say it okay."

"My mother is working hard to prepare the lessons," Agnes said. "She is so tired of winter and is looking forward to teaching and gardening this summer. Maybe you can help us in the garden?"

Waabi was surprised but not displeased by the attention Agnes gave him. It seemed forbidden to take a liking to a girl who was not Ojibwe, but that did not change the way he felt. Standing there, looking into her bright, wide eyes, it felt good. The world around him didn't matter at that moment.

"Enya'. Yes. I hope," Waabi said, unable to repress his smile.

"WasabishkiMakwa!" A man's voice called for him.

Agnes raised her chin and looked behind Waabi. "I think it's your father," she said.

Waabi's father came striding toward him, his face severe and hard as if he were ready to chasten his son. "Come along Waabi," he said. "I shouldn't have brought you here."

"What's happening?"

"Your uncle is going to take you to the sugarbush. I am going to stay here along with the other men from our lodge. We have important things to discuss."

Before Waabi could ask more questions, his father grabbed him by the arm and pulled him away. Having no choice, Waabi went with his father. He looked back at Agnes and waved. Lifting her hand waist-high, she waved goodbye, a quiet look of concern on her graceful face.

Chapter 4

Samuel
Londonderry, Vermont
July 1859

"The lower leg and ankle are broken," the doctor explained, "not to mention the damage to the foot. He'll be laid up for probably six months."

"Six months!" Samuel's mother, Alexandra, said. She took a deep, labored breath and placed a hand on her husband's shoulder as he lay in bed. Next to him were his children: Samuel, Thomas, Isabel, and Edward. In a crib at the foot of the bed, Eva Marie slept peacefully.

"Are you certain, doctor?" Alexandra asked in a strained voice.

Samuel gazed up at his mother. Her face was lined with anguish, and she was visibly shaking. Samuel knew, as well as she did, that the family would suffer without his father's income from his work at the sawmill. They would also suffer without the work he provided around the homestead. Six months seemed a lifetime.

"I understand you're upset, ma'am," the doctor said, "but your husband is lucky not to lose the leg—he's lucky just to be alive. That tree could easily have killed him. Or, your two sons. You should be very grateful."

Samuel's mother brought her hand to her forehead and sighed. Her normally pale skin had turned red.

Lying in bed and looking up at his distressed wife, Randolph offered an assuring smile. "I'll get better in no time. It'll be all right."

"Of course we're grateful no one was hurt worse," Alexandra said to the doctor, moving her hands to her hips. "I just don't know what we'll do with Randolph laid up like this."

"I'm sorry, I really am. But with a break like that he'll need a lot of rest. Months of rest." The doctor leaned over to pick up his leather pouch, reached in and pulled out a brown glass bottle. "Give him this for the pain, just a teaspoon each morning and each night," he said, handing Alexandra the bottle. "I'll be back to check on him and rewrap his stint once a week. With any luck, he'll be up walking around in no time. But six months is my professional opinion."

Alexandra grabbed the bottle and dropped it in her apron pocket. Expressionless, she showed the doctor to the door.

Before leaving, the doctor pulled a small envelope from his pouch and handed it to Alexandra.

"Here's my bill," he said in a hushed tone as if trying to keep it a secret. "Stop by the office sometime and my assistant will arrange a manageable payment plan."

Alexandra stared at the envelope for a moment before taking it in her hand. Then she held the door open for the doctor who gave a tender look at the children and left. The rusty hinges creaked loudly as the door came to a close. Turning around, Alexandra looked weary, as if she'd suddenly fallen ill.

"Can you believe this, Alexandra?" Randolph said in a playful manner. "Now you'll have to wait on me hand and foot!" It was a poor attempt at humor, but Thomas chuckled.

"Thomas!" Alexandra snapped. Looking at her husband she said, "This is no time to joke, Randolph. We're already behind on payments for the barn, and we've got a whole list of chores to do before winter comes."

Samuel looked at his father, awaiting his response. His blue eyes sparkled despite the condition he was in with his head cushioned against several pillows, and his leg in a splint held up by hanging bed sheets. "It's going to be fine, honey," he said. "Everything is going to be all right."

Alexandra bristled, stamping her foot to the ground like an angry child.

"We can talk about this later," Randolph said, "when the children aren't around."

Samuel turned his head toward his younger brothers and sisters. Edward, who was just four years old, had a look of sheer distress like he may burst into tears. Isabel, who was nine, looked worried, almost pained. And Thomas... he seemed to finally understand that he should just keep his mouth shut.

Glancing at her children, Alexandra hesitated, but did not relent. "No, Randolph. We can talk about this now. You always do this."

"Do what?"

"Pretend... pretend everything's all right!" Alexandra blurted, her hands still held firmly to her hips, her posture determined. "Just look at yourself. You'll be laid up in that bed for months. Not only will we be without your wages but we'll be without your labor around the homestead: hauling water, chopping wood, feeding the livestock. And I'll be pulled away from my chores just trying to make you comfortable. How can you just smile and say everything will be all right?"

"We can help—Thomas and I," Samuel said to his mother. "I am capable of doing all of Pa's chores and I can teach Thomas how to do some of mine."

Alexandra shook her head in frustration. "It's more than that, honey," she said plainly, sweeping her light red hair away from her tired eyes. "I know you and Thomas and Isabel will help out, but we've been struggling as it is. I just don't know how we're going to get by."

Silence settled over the small, one-room cabin. Candles burned bright as dusk brought with it the fading light of the setting sun. Eva Marie whimpered from her crib tussling back and forth.

"Thomas will have to go down to the mill with you," Randolph said, looking at Samuel and speaking with a tone of sincerity. "I will pen a letter to the foreman, Mr. Blake, telling him what happened and asking him if he can give Thomas a job in place of me."

Thomas stood straight and nodded, though he looked like a frightened puppy. Samuel bit his lip, worried by the idea of putting Thomas in a taxing situation.

Samuel leaned in close to his father's ear. "Will Thomas be all right working at the mill? His breathing, I'm not sure it'll be good for him."

Thomas wacked Samuel on the back. "I'll be fine you nincompoop!"

Samuel's father laughed heartily at the insult. Catching his breath he said, "He'll be fine, Samuel. He can do the work just fine."

Samuel straightened up. "All right, Pa. Long as you're certain."

Samuel's father nodded and scanned the family with his eyes. "Thomas can earn some money for the family, and if everybody pitches in this six months will slip by in a breeze. Then I'll be back on my feet and more vigorous than ever." He grinned sheepishly, looking at his wife for approval.

"It's already past supper time," Alexandra said, changing the subject entirely. "Thomas, fetch a pail of water from the pond for boiling. Samuel, take the slop bucket out to the goats and take in the oxen. Isabel, help me with supper and keep an eye on your little brother and sister. Randolph..." she paused, looking at her now incapacitated husband. "We'll think of something for you," she said with a hint of a smile.

"I've got an idea," he said, raising his index finger. "I will ponder."

Alexandra blushed as she whirled toward the kitchen counter behind her. "All right, dear. You ponder. You'll be having plenty of time to do that. Everyone else, let's get to work."

The next day Samuel and Thomas rose with the sun, ate a quick breakfast of oats and honey, and headed down the road to the sawmill.

"Be on your best behavior," their mother said as she pushed them toward the door, each with an apple, bread, and apple butter. "Oh, don't forget your book, Samuel."

Samuel spun around and grabbed the small, well-worn book from his mother's hand.

"What's that?" Thomas said. "You can't read a book at the sawmill. It's not even thick enough to be a book."

"Settle down," Samuel said as he headed out the door and into the cool morning air. Thomas followed like a dog on a leash.

41

"Just tell me what it is," Thomas said.

"It's poetry. I like to read it on my way to the sawmill, all right? So just be quiet and let me read."

"Poetry? Why do you like that?"

"I just do, Thomas. Now quiet."

Thomas remained silent the rest of the walk. Rather than talk, he occupied himself by looking at the plants and birds along the road. After fifteen minutes, the slanted roof of the old sawmill came into sight, framed brilliantly by the rising sun behind it. The waterwheel, which normally purred with activity, stood still as the waters of the West River flowed quietly by.

Samuel led Thomas around the end of the building to an open door on the back side. Within a small room Mr. Blake sat at his desk leaning over some papers. A pair of spectacles rested on the tip of his nose.

"'Scuse me," Samuel said knocking on the open door.

Mr. Blake turned his bearded face and removed his spectacles. "Ah, morning Samuel," he said. "Is that your brother you got with you?"

Mr. Blake stood from his desk and walked over to greet Thomas.

"Yes, sir. This is my brother, Thomas."

Thomas held out his hand which was quickly enveloped by Mr. Blake's larger, coarse fingers. "Nice to meet you, son, but where's your Pa? Where's Randolph?"

"There was an accident," Thomas said, before Samuel had a chance to.

"Accident? What kind of accident? Is your Pa all right?"

"Yes, yes, he's all right," Samuel assured the sawmill operator while handing him the letter Randolph had written, "but he'll be laid up for quite a while."

As Mr. Blake opened and read the letter Samuel explained what happened—the storm that rolled through, the burst of wind that took the tree down, the roar of the tree as it hit the ground.

"That's why I brought Thomas down, sir. I was hoping he could pitch in, earn some wages while Pa is laid up."

Mr. Blake, standing a whole head and shoulders above

Thomas, eyed him carefully. "I suppose that'd be all right. Let's put him in the boiler room."

Samuel snapped back at the suggestion. "The boiler room? Are you sure? Isn't there something...easier we can give him?"

Mr. Blake grinned widely, leaning his head back. "This is a sawmill, Samuel. Ain't no easy jobs, you know that. Besides, we start everybody in the boiler. Just like you did, too."

"But Thomas has got asth—"

Thomas struck Samuel on the arm. "I can handle it just find Mr. Blake. Just show me what do to."

Samuel looked at Thomas with concern, but Thomas peered up at Mr. Blake and smiled.

"That's the right attitude," Mr. Blake said reaching to shake Thomas' hand once again. "Samuel, take him down to the boiler room and show him what to do."

As Mr. Blake disappeared back into his office, Samuel turned to Thomas.

"I'll be fine," Thomas said. "Don't worry about my breathing. Besides, I know how important it is to fill in for Pa and help out the family, no matter what you think about what I am and ain't capable of."

Samuel opened his mouth to respond harshly, but looking at the determination his brother's eyes, he thought better of it. "Just follow me," he said.

Samuel led Thomas through the building and past the now quiet cutting room floor, eventually reaching stairs that led down into the foundation of the building. With Thomas right behind him, Samuel proceeded down the stairs and into the darkness of the boiler room.

"Sure is cold down here," Thomas said, entering the room.

"That'll change real quick," Samuel said.

In the middle of the room was a large, rounded, steel furnace. Held up by four short legs, it was wide in the middle and narrow at the top, like a giant metal pear. In the center it had a square opening with a metal door and at the top was a steel pipe that led into the steam room.

"So?" Thomas said. "What am I supposed to do down here?"

Samuel rolled his eyes at his brother's impatience. "See that?" he said, pointing at a box of scrap wood. "That's the fuel. During the workday sawdust and scrap wood will fall down that chute and you got to use the shovel to dump it into the boiler."

"All day?"

"All day," Samuel said. "It's the most important job because the fire creates the steam that powers the saws."

Unimpressed, Thomas shrugged. "What do I do first?"

"You got to load the boiler."

Thomas shuffled to the box of scrap wood, picked up the shovel, and forced the blade into the pile of sawdust. "Like this?"

"Yeah. Now, bring the shovel to the door of the boiler and rest it on the lip of the opening," Samuel said.

"No problem," Thomas said, leaning back to bear the weight of the wood and sawdust before resting the shovel with a thud against the lip of the boiler.

"Now we light it with a match," Samuel said, holding a long wooden match in front of his face. He struck the match against the side of the boiler and held the flame against the sawdust. Slowly, the sawdust turned to embers and then became a growing flame.

"Just let it burn like that for a minute," Samuel said. "Once it's burning good, dump it into the opening and stir it around to get the leftover ash burning."

Thomas did exactly as Samuel told him and before long the boiler was producing heat.

"You just keep shoveling until that fire gets nice and big," Samuel said. "Every now and then, you throw some scrap wood on there to really get it going."

"How do I know when to stop?" Thomas asked.

"The whistle. This is the most important part, all right? When you hear one whistle, it means you can start shoveling and you just keep feeding the fire at a steady pace. When you hear a double whistle, you stop. And, when you hear a triple whistle, you get that boiler as hot as you can as fast as you can, but be ready to stop when the whistle blows."

Thomas stared at Samuel, nodding like a cattail in the wind.

"You got that?" Samuel said.

"Yeah, yeah, I got it," Thomas said as if he were annoyed by the question.

"Repeat it back to me," Samuel said.

Thomas sighed. "One whistle means start. Two whistles means stop. Three means shovel fast."

"All right, good. I'll be back to check on you and let you know when you can take a break. I have to go to sharpen the saws. You sure you can do this?"

"Don't worry about me, Samuel. I'll be fine. This is easy," Thomas said with a wink.

Samuel paused and looked at his little brother. Feeling hesitant, he gave him a subtle nod and then bounded up the steps and on to his next task.

After greasing the machinery and sharpening the saws, Samuel stepped onto the cutting floor to meet with Mr. Blake and the crew members to be assigned a position for the day. Seeing Samuel, the men all lowered their heads solemnly letting Samuel know that Mr. Blake had told them about the accident.

"I spoke to the men and we're all real sorry about what happened to your Pa," Mr. Blake said while the rest of the men kept their heads low and removed their caps like it were a funeral. "I know that'll be hard on your family, but I'm glad Thomas can fill in down in the boiler."

"Thank you," Samuel said while tapping his foot impatiently. "You got the daily assignments?"

There was a pause as each of the men looked at Samuel as if he should be grieving.

"No sense wasting time or feeling sorry for ourselves," Samuel said. "My Pa will be all right, he just needs time to get better."

"Good, that's real good," Mr. Blake said, looking at Samuel. "If that's the case, your assignment is in the mill pond today, sorting and cleaning the logs."

"Yes, sir, Mr. Blake. I'll get going right away."

Samuel left the cutting room floor and headed to the mill pond, a man-made drainage along the river used to collect logs that were sent floating downstream.

Samuel went to work finding pleasure in his task. He was alone, sorting logs and inspecting them for rocks and dirt. When he found the logs satisfactory, he pushed them through the water and next to the rope and pulleys to be lifted onto the cutting floor. Pushing the heavy logs while wading through waist deep water was exhausting, but Samuel enjoyed the strain in his muscles and the quickening in his breath. He felt useful and alive and he enjoyed being outside. It wasn't nearly as noisy or hot as the mill. He also loved watching the ducks move gently through the pond and listening to the constant rush of the river. At times Samuel closed his eyes and let the breeze cool his face while feeling the heaviness of the water lap against his thighs. He felt lucky to be outside. He was certainly luckier than Thomas who was stuck in the darkness and confinement of the boiler.

After pushing enough logs to be well ahead of the cutters, Samuel went to check on his brother and give him a break. As he descended the stairs to the boiler room, he heard the whistle sounding, but he did not hear Thomas shoveling. When he entered the room he saw that the fire was dying and Thomas was nowhere to be found.

Thomas! Samuel said to himself. *Where are you?*

Samuel rushed to the shovel, picked it up, and started shoveling sawdust into the boiler as fast as he could. After seven or eight loads, Samuel grabbed some larger pieces of scrap wood and hurled them into the boiler. The fire surged and was burning strong once again. That's when Thomas walked casually down the steps.

"Where were you!" Samuel hissed. "You can't leave whenever you feel like it."

Thomas stopped, wide-eyed, at the bottom steps. "I just needed a break, that's all."

"I told you I'd come down and give you a break. You can't leave unless someone is here to relieve you."

Thomas turned his head aside unwilling to make eye contact.

"Wait. Was it your asthma?"

Thomas shook his head, but still wouldn't look up.

"If it's too hard you gotta tell me. Your health is more important, otherwise both you and Pa will be laid up. Or worse..."

46

"It ain't such a big deal!" Thomas shouted, as he brought his head back up and glared at Samuel. "I just left for a couple minutes. I'm fine! Now let it be."

Samuel stood there in silence, uncertain what to say. He wanted to protect his brother, his family. He wanted to them to be happy and safe. After a few moments, Samuel sighed and brought the shovel to Thomas, thrusting it forward. "I'll be back to give you a break, all right?"

His eyes softened as Thomas took hold of the shovel. "Yeah."

Samuel rushed back up the steps, meeting Mr. Blake at the top. "Everything all right down there?" Mr. Blake asked, appearing annoyed.

"Yes, sir. It'll be fine. Thomas is still just getting the hang of it."

"I hope so," Mr. Blake said. "You know we can't afford a slowdown in production."

"I know. Don't worry."

Samuel returned to his duties, sorting and cleaning logs, wading through the water and pushing heavy timber from one side of the pond to the other. The sun had come out and was bearing down on Samuel's neck and cheeks, causing his skin to redden and his forehead to sweat. In a way it felt good. It felt rewarding.

After what must have been an hour, but felt like ten minutes, Samuel went again to check on Thomas. Walking by the noise and clatter of the cutting room, some of the men lightheartedly chided Samuel, but he ignored them. With slow, wary steps, Samuel descended to the boiler room once again.

Light glowed from beneath the square metal door of the burning furnace. The rest of the room was dark and quiet. "Thomas?"

"I'm here," Thomas said from a darkened corner.

Squinting, Samuel saw his brother sitting on a stump, hunched over but head up, the shovel in his right hand. "What's wrong Thomas, you gettin' tired?"

His face was sallow and dirty. "No, no. I can do this. Besides, I know we ain't got many other options." He paused. "And I want to make Pa proud."

Samuel was not expecting Thomas to say that. "What? But you and Pa are always so friendly. It's me who's got to work to make him proud."

"What? No," Thomas said, standing up from the stump. "Can't you see he's always explaining stuff to me, telling me what to do and how to do it. Never giving me any hard work. But with you he doesn't need to say anything. He knows you'll do the work and do it right. He's not proud of me, he's proud of you."

Samuel had never thought of it that way. He felt ashamed if it were true. "Maybe you're right. I don't know. I've always just been so jealous that you two get along so well."

"Believe me," Thomas said as he turned to pick up another shovelful of sawdust. "You got it much better. You got Pa's respect. I just got his friendship."

Samuel breathed deep preparing a reply, but couldn't think of what to say. Instead he just watched his little brother toss more sawdust into the boiler and then turned and walked slowly up the stairs, thinking about what Thomas said.

Chapter 5

WasabishkiMakwa
Mooniingwanekaaning-minis
Abitaa-niibino-giizis
(Madeline Island, July 1850)

While crouched behind a purple spotted lilac, Waabi leaned forward and focused his right eye down the shaft of his wooden arrow. At the end of his sight was a cottontail rabbit—its ears perked and nose quivering. Waabi drew back with his right index and middle fingers until his bow was taut. He breathed deeply and released.

"Hay'!" Waabi exclaimed in disappointment as he watched his arrow strike the dirt, causing the rabbit to flee faster than lightning. Waabi stood from his kneeling position and turned to look toward the sun at his back. Realizing it was nearly mid-morning, he knew he couldn't wait for another rabbit because it was time for school.

When Waabi asked his grandmother if he could leave early, he told her it was to practice his bow and arrow. Though he was practicing, that was a lie. He wanted to catch a rabbit for Agnes. He wasn't sure why exactly, he just knew he liked her, and he wanted to come to school with a gift for her.

"I don't know why your father insists on sending you to school," his grandmother said before agreeing he could leave early. "You can learn nothing of use from those pale-face foreigners. Everything you need to learn is here, on this island, among your people."

"Father says the times are changing, grandmother," Waabi said. "He thinks we need to change with them or our people will not survive."

"Survive?" his grandmother said with a downcast turn of her mouth. "Your people have survived for generations with the knowledge of the seasons and the natural gifts of the land and its animals. School cannot teach you what is already in your bloodline. It cannot teach you what is written on our scrolls or passed down through our Aadizookaan."

Waabi hesitated, unsure how to reply. "I am eager to learn, grandmother," he finally said. "But the whites have shown us that there is a world outside our own. One filled with wonder and knowledge. Many have become my friends."

"You have very few years, noozhis," she said, "and you cannot see all that has come before you." She paused. "No good can from them. You should never trust a white man."

Waabi stared back, again unsure what to say. He understood what his grandmother was telling him, but she did not know the wisdom of the white man or his kindliness toward them.

"Be gone to shoot your bow and arrow, and then to school," his grandmother said, throwing the back of her hand forward through the empty air. "When you return you will help me collect the gum of the evergreen for the making of a pitch."

"Yes, grandmother," Waabi said, then he rushed away from his grandmother's attentive eye.

After missing his gift of prey, Waabi walked to the school-house feeling disappointed but not unpleasant. He weaved effort-lessly through the tall forests of yellow and white birch enjoying the comfortable summer air that blew in off the bay. Birds chirped happily and rodents scurried out from under his path. Along the way he passed lodges and groups of lodges where people were busy pruning their gardens, weaving bulrush mats, drying berries, playing games, or just sleeping out in the open air. Men played music on drums while women created delicate floral patterns on their bead-work. Waabi saw nets of carefully woven nettle fibers hung to dry and piles of basswood twine alongside birch bark to be used later to create makak baskets and other useful tools.

"Boozhoo!" some exclaimed as Waabi walked by while others maintained their independent focus.

But Waabi also noticed something different than usual. Something he'd noticed throughout the summer moons. The gardens were not as lush as they had been in years past. And the community was quieter and less active. Canoes were not being built and the lodges were not decorated with the color and life that he was used to seeing. Boys did not gather for games of hide-and-seek and girls did not collect dry grass for the making of dolls. Even the men rarely played baaga'adowewin, a favorite pastime that used to be played on a near daily basis in the summer. Even the sky had a heaviness about it, casting a constant shadow on Mooningwanekaaning.

Carrying his deer skin pouch across his shoulder, Waabi stepped out from the woods and into the village called La Pointe by the traders. It was the only white settlement with wood frame buildings that Waabi had ever seen, but it had been built well before his birth. There were several one-room, wood-frame houses all neatly painted red and standing in a row. Opposite the houses was the trader's post, a large, long building with a slanted roof and numerous windows. It was operated by Julius Austrian, a rotund man with red cheeks and a strange way of talking. Mr. Austrian was a Bavarian, Waabi was told, from a place on the other side of the sea.

At the far side of the trader's post were various storehouses for goods and fish. These buildings were locked at nearly all times except when the men returned from a hunt, eager to exchange their furs, or at the time of the annuity payment, when the Indian agent arrived with wagons of blankets, flour, pork, and other goods.

Finally there was the Catholic church, an old building with chipped blue paint and broken shingles that soared above the rest of the buildings with its tall pointed steeple. Waabi admired the steeple with its cross that glittered in the sun and cast a long shadow on the center of the village.

But Waabi did not attend school at the Catholic church. The schoolhouse was behind the church about a stone's throw, somewhat secluded from the rest of the village. It was a relatively new building made of large round logs held together with a mixture of clay, mud, and sand called chinking. The schoolhouse was just one room, which was more than enough for Waabi who often felt uncomfortable being inside where he felt confined.

"Hurry up, Waabi," Agnes shouted from the open doorway. "Class is nearly starting."

Feeling a pleasant jolt that traveled from his heart down to his feet, Waabi pushed himself forward quick as the rabbit he let get away.

Entering the schoolhouse, Waabi was surprised to see several rows of empty desks. In the front, near the chalkboard, were several of the white children—sons and daughters of the traders, miners, and fishermen, who lived permanently on the island. In the back were only three Ojibwe children. In the middle rows were two Metis girls—daughters of French fur trading men and Ojibwe women.

"Where is everyone?" Waabi whispered to Agnes.

As Waabi said this, Pastor Hall, who was writing the daily schedule on the chalkboard, turned to face Waabi and Agnes. "It's nearly time for class to start, please take your seats," he said, not impolitely. The pastor paused looking at Waabi through tired, heavy eyes and a steely face. "Waabi," he said. "Why are you wearing leggings and buckskin? You have been told that when you come to school you are to wear trousers and calico."

Somewhat frightened by the pastor's rebuke, Waabi didn't answer.

"Do you understand me?" Pastor Hall asked. "Do you need me to interpret?"

"Sorry," Waabi said, shaking his head. "My grand-grand-mother," he stuttered, "does not want me to dress that way."

Pastor Hall pursed his lips. "You are not to dress like an Indian while in class," he said. "Every time that you do, you will receive ten demerits to be paid back with chores."

"Father!" Agnes pleaded. "That's not fair. Can't you just give him a warning?"

"No!" Pastor Hall said with uncommon zeal, but then stopped himself before saying anything further. He raised his hand to his forehead and took a deep breath.

There was a long pause. Agnes looked at Waabi with concern and whispered, "I've never seen my father yell in class before."

Waabi tried to appear sympathetic, but he was still smarting from the sudden outburst.

"What's wrong, Father?" Agnes asked.

"I'm sorry," he said, dropping his hand from his forehead.

He looked distraught and tired, like he'd been carrying a weight. "You'll notice we have very few students today, and it's a cause of great concern to me."

Waabi and Agnes took their seats while the other students stared silently at their normally composed teacher.

"Attendance is even lower than usual," Pastor Hall said, motioning his arm sideways in front of him.

"It's not your fault," Eliza, the daughter of a local laborer, said. "My Pa says it's all this talk of moving the Ojibwe out of Wisconsin. He says the government has no right to move them."

"Your father is right," Pastor Hall said. "The Ojibwe have been here for centuries and there is no need that they be moved. It keeps me up at night wondering about the future, wondering what might happen to this place if the removal goes through. But," he said, looking at Waabi and the other Ojibwe students, "the Indians do not help themselves by living in ignorance and failing to become industrious and educated."

Chibines, a tall, teenage boy with high cheeks and a square jaw who had cut his hair short and frequently carried a Bible, furrowed his brow and looked hard at the pastor. "For whatsoever a man soweth, that shall he also reap," Chibines said, quoting Galatians 6:7.

"Yes?" Pastor Hall said, expecting Chibines to say more.

"Our people do not live in ignorance," Chibines said, speaking perfect English. "The Midewiwin share your beliefs that doing good things makes for a long life; doing evil brings consequences. We learn from what we see all around us, not only in your books and language, but in the flight of the birds and the sound of the lake against the shore. Good will come from good and bad will come from bad. The future, whether it is here or some other place, will be just and fair for those who do good and those who do evil."

Waabi was amazed to see Chibines speak back to a white man the way he did. He slunk down in his chair, worried about how Pastor Hall might react.

The teacher raised his arm and opened his mouth like he might rebuke his student. But then he lowered his arm and let his eyes wander for a moment. "You're right, Chibines. There is much to learn from the world around us. In fact," he said with a sudden change in mood, "You've reminded me of one of my favorite poems."

"Poems?" Chibines said. "Like Psalms?"

"Yes, exactly. They are elegant words that flow together in a beautiful pattern."

As Pastor Hall turned toward the blackboard and grabbed a piece of chalk, Waabi leaned forward in his chair.

"Continuous as the stars that shine," Pastor Hall said as he wrote the words on the blackboard.

> *And twinkle on the milky way,*
> *they stretched in never-ending line*
> *Along the margin of the bay.*
> *The waves beside them danced; but they*
> *Out-did the sparkling waves in glee*
> *I gazed—and gazed—but little thought*
> *What wealth to me the show had brought.*

"What wealth to me the show had brought," Pastor Hall said repeating the last line as he turned back to the class. "Those are the words of an Englishman—William Wordsworth—but you see, he has expressed many of the views that you have, Chibines."

Waabi continued to lean forward in his chair but he no longer heard the words of his teacher. His mind wandered as he imagined glittering stars forming a path against the night sky, and he heard the swirling murmur of continuous white-capped waves as they landed harmlessly against the shore wetting his naked feet. He was lost in the words of the poem. English words that had somehow captivated him—words he understood with clarity.

"Waabi," Agnes whispered. "Waabi," she said again, this time poking him in the shoulder.

Waabi suddenly awoke from his mental wandering. When he did, he saw that the whole class was eyeing him.

Pastor Hall, who stared at Waabi like an eagle from a perch, cleared his throat. "As I was saying, I'm sorry for my earlier outburst. I spoke too candidly and was thinking only of myself by expressing my concern about classroom attendance. I only hope the removal does not go through."

The mention of removal brought Waabi all the way back to the present as he was struck with worry.

"I have taken up too much time already speaking of myself and of poetry," Pastor Hall continued. "It's time for the arithmetic lesson."

As the Pastor Hall turned back to the chalkboard, Agnes glanced sideways at Waabi. "Waabi?" she said, barely audible. "Everything all right?"

Waabi nodded reassuringly and then turned his head forward to avoid showing his concern. He was moved by the poetry but even more, he felt flushed with worry. Would his people be forced to leave the island, he wondered? Would the white leaders go against the wishes of the people—good people like Agnes and Pastor Hall?

Chapter 6

Samuel
Londonderry, Vermont
September 1859

Samuel took a deep breath, enjoying the crisp late summer air as he stepped out of the mill pond. After a few heavy, wet steps he untied and removed his boots. Bending over he felt a tinge of pain in his lower back from a hard day of labor. When he straightened back up, Mr. Blake was standing directly in front of him.

"I can't keep him on," Mr. Blake said bluntly. "He's a liability."

"A liability?"

"It means—"

"I know what liability means," Samuel said. "I just can't believe you won't give him more time to learn. More time to get used to the work. It's only been five weeks. And with my Pa laid up like he is, we need the money."

"I'm sorry, Samuel. He's takin' too many breaks," Mr. Blake said, with a sharpness to his voice. "This is a business and I got to think of what's best for the business. I need someone more dependable."

"But..." Samuel stopped himself. He was about to blame it on Thomas' asthma, but he knew that was a bad idea—he knew that might prevent Thomas from ever getting a job again.

"What about switchin' jobs...with me," Samuel pleaded. "I can work down in the boiler and he can work out here in the fresh air. In the mill pond, I mean."

A closed-lip smile stretched across Mr. Blake's face, holding back a chuckle. "Ha! Thomas is too little. He might drown just tryin' to keep up."

Samuel opened his mouth to continue his plea, but Mr. Blake spoke too quickly.

"Listen, I know this is hard on your family but I'm not changin' my mind. Besides, look at the bright side. I've still got plenty of hours for you. Plenty of work. You deserve it."

Samuel nodded, half-pleased by the compliment, but totally dejected by the situation. He thought of arguing further, but he knew it wouldn't do any good. "All right. I understand. You gonna tell Thomas, or do I have to?"

Mr. Blake clenched his teeth forming an awkward grin. "I think it would be better if you did. He didn't work here long, and I'm no good at that kind of thing."

"Yeah," Samuel said in a long, drawn out sigh. "I'll do it."

Mr. Blake held out his large right hand. "I'll see you tomorrow, Samuel."

"Bright and early," Samuel said, then quickly turned to find Thomas without giving Mr. Blake the pleasure of shaking his hand.

"Thomas!" Samuel called, finding his little brother waiting for him on a wooden bench near the road entrance to the mill.

"What was that all about?" Thomas asked, getting up and following after his fast-walking brother. "Slow down," he said. "Are you mad or what?"

"I'll tell you later."

"Tell me later? Tell me now."

Samuel stopped and turned toward Thomas. Narrowing his eyes, he said, "I'll tell you later!"

Thomas shrunk back, noticeably startled by Samuel's tone. Samuel continued walking and Thomas followed after, not saying another word.

A few minutes later, Samuel turned left at the fork in the road and headed toward town, rather than heading home. Sensing Thomas' curiosity Samuel said, "I gotta go to the general store. Ma asked me to pick up some wire and nails."

Thomas hesitated before asking, "What for?"

"I don't know what for. To fix things."

The two walked side by side now. The sound of their leather work boots against the dirt road filled the silence between them.

As the road crested and became a gentle downward slope they passed the town's wooden sign that declared *Londonderry - Elev.*

1,916. A mixture of oak, maple, and birch trees lined the road. In the distance, the hills looked like an unbroken sea of green and yellow.

"Listen," Samuel finally said as the town came into view. "Mr. Blake told me that you can't come back to the mill."

"What do you mean I can't come back?"

"It means—it means you're no longer employed by the mill. Mr. Blake said he wants someone more dependable."

"What? I did good work down there, didn't I?"

"You took too many breaks," Samuel said as he stopped to face his brother.

"You know I had to, Samuel. I couldn't breathe in that tiny room filled with dirt, sawdust, and smoke. I coulda died!"

Samuel brought a hand to forehead and closed his eyes tight. Opening them he said, "I know. I know that, Thomas. And it's better that you lose this job than you getting hurt. I just don't know what we're gonna do now."

They both just stood for a moment, the sound of cicadas filling the air.

"We're going to get wire and nails," Thomas said.

"What?"

"That's what we're going to do next. We're gonna get wire and nails." A smile slowly formed across Thomas' face, breaking the momentary tension.

Samuel rolled his eyes and then smiled in return. "Yeah," he chuckled. "I suppose we are."

Together they turned and continued down the hill, stride for stride.

Londonderry was little more than a street, a quarter-mile long, with two-story wood frame buildings on each side. Across the bridge on the opposite side of the river was the church with its red steeple peeking out above the evergreens and ash. But, other than the schoolhouse, there was little else within the confines of the humble downtown.

Samuel and Thomas stepped up to the boardwalk to avoid the muddy street and walked past the post office, the feed store, and the saloon. There were a few men doing business and some women holding the hands of young children walking in and out of the shops, but the town was mostly quiet.

"Let's be quick," Thomas said as he turned to step inside the general store. "It's been a long day."

As Samuel turned to follow, he paused for a moment, seeing a man he didn't recognize on the bench outside the store. "I'll be just a minute," he said to Thomas.

The man, though seated, looked tall and refined. He wore a three-piece suit, black leather dress shoes, and a top-hat unlike any Samuel had ever seen. In his right hand he clutched a sweaty bottle of sarsaparilla. He was no Vermonter.

The man turned, tilted his head up, and looked at Samuel under the brim of his hat. He smiled in a manner that Samuel thought mischievous, then took a long swig of his sarsaparilla.

"Excuse me?" Samuel said. "You ain't from around here are you?"

The man stood, showing himself to be more than six feet tall, moved his beverage to his left hand and then reached out his right. Samuel grabbed hold and shook, feeling the wetness from the bottle now on his own hand.

"The name's James McPherson," he said, holding Samuel's hand for longer than was necessary.

"So you aren't?" Samuel said.

"James McPherson?"

"No, I mean, from around here?"

"Oh, no," he said, arching backward and chuckling. "I'm from Washington D.C. I work for the office of land management."

He took another sip of his soda.

"Wow," Samuel said. "I never met nobody from Washington D.C."

"You'll have to pardon me," he said. "I was just taking a little break."

"A break from what?"

"I'm handing out flyers about all the frontier land that's open in the middle west. You ever been out west?"

"Ha," Samuel gasped. "I never been out of Londonderry."

"I can't say I'm surprised," McPherson said, "but that

really is a shame. It's a beautiful country out there. And vast, too. Stretches as far as the imagination. Bet you know some families, too, that already made the move."

"S'pose I do," Samuel said, thinking for a moment. "The Murrays, Donnellys, Bakers...said they were off to find a better life."

"That's right! A better life." McPherson reached inside his breast pocket like he'd forgotten something. "Here," he said, pulling out a folded piece of paper. "I'm handing out flyers, letting folks know about all the free land in the prairies. Open prairie as far as the eye can see. All you have to do is claim it. Show this flyer to your Pa."

Samuel took the paper and unfolded it. It was an advertisement. The wording stretched across the top of the flyer said, *Millions of Acres Open for Settlement.* Below the words was a sketch of uninhabited grassland dotted with trees and a stream. To one side was an Indian on a horse who appeared to be galloping toward the sunset. Below the sketch were the words *Land! Opportunity! Adventure!* At the very bottom it read: *The New State of Minnesota.*

"What's this all about? What's Minn-es-sota?" Samuel said, raising his eyes to his new acquaintance.

"The frontier, my friend," McPherson said. "The dream of every adventurous American. Land for the taking. To start over. To run away. Wealth. Opportunity. Whatever you can imagine."

"I thought that was California. Where all those gold miners went."

"You're geography's off, kid. You're missing the middle of the country. The endless plains. The fresh air. A place where people tame the land and build the future." McPherson spoke in a lively and energetic tone, moving his arms and being expressive with his bearded face.

Samuel hesitated, thinking to himself before asking, "Isn't that Indian country?"

McPherson's lip curled and his eyes shined. "Not anymore. The Indians sold the land and have been moved onto reservations. That's why the government's practically giving away the land. The Indians are gone and we need good, decent, hardworking folk to populate the land and put it to good use. Folk like you and your family I suppose."

Before Samuel could form a response he heard Thomas from behind him. "Hey!" he said rather loudly. "What are you doin' out here? Are you gonna buy some wire or not?"

Samuel turned his head and looked sharply at his brother. "Just a minute." Then he turned back to McPherson.

"You keep that flyer," McPherson said, "and show it to your Pa. Think real hard about it, too. It could be the opportunity of a lifetime for you and your family. It could change your lives for the better."

McPherson smiled, a big, almost exaggerated grin. Samuel felt his heart jump—a feeling of nervousness but also of wonder, of hopefulness.

"Sure will, thanks sir," he said.

"Who was that?" Thomas asked as Samuel walked by him to enter the store.

"Never mind, Thomas," Samuel said. "Just never mind about it."

On the way home Thomas was exceptionally quiet. Samuel thought it was odd, but he didn't mind either. Just before they came in sight of the homestead, Thomas broke his silence pulling what looked like a small pamphlet or book from his inside pocket.

"I bought this for you," he said, holding the thing out in front of Samuel. "I know how you like poetry."

Leaves of Grass it read in gold lettering and plant-like font. "How did you pay for this?" Samuel said.

"Mr. Blake. He gave me some money before I left today. My final payment I suppose, but he didn't tell me he'd ended my employment."

"You shouldn't be spending it on books!"

"Don't act so bothered," Thomas said. "I was just trying to do something nice."

Samuel quickly realized that Thomas was right. With the book held gently in his right hand, Samuel examined the textured green cover and opened the pages.

"Do you like it?" Thomas said.

Samuel huffed, then sighed. "Yeah," he said. "I do like it. Thank you, Thomas. I'll read it every night."

Thomas blushed revealing the dimples of his child-like face. "Race you home!" he said and then took off running.

"Hey!" Samuel protested and took off after him.

Chapter 7

WasabishkiMakwa
Mooniingwanekaaning-minis
Binaakwe-giizis
(Madeline Island, October 1850)

Thick, rolling clouds gathered overhead reflecting off the waters of Zaagawaamikong-wiikwed. In the distance, Waabi heard the low rumble of thunder. A gust of wind blew in off the choppy waters of the bay picking up leaves of red and yellow and sending them up from the ground in a whirlwind of color. Standing alongside his aunt and cousins, Waabi watched nervously as his father and uncle loaded their canoe for the journey to Gaa-mitaawangaagamaag.

"I am nearly old enough to care for myself," Waabi said as his uncle loaded the last bag of provisions. He looked toward his father who stood facing the lake, his long hair blowing across his shoulder. He watched as his father dropped an offering of tobacco into the water. "I should come along... to help paddle, and hunt, and carry back the annuity goods," Waabi said.

As he waited for his father's response, Meme put her arm around Waabi pulling him close, her fingers curled tenderly around his arm.

Waabi wiggled free, denying his aunt's embrace. "You heard the instructions of the government agent. He said you are to bring your families to the payment. Why are you and uncle the only ones who are going?"

His father did not turn around. Waabi felt as if he were talking to the wind.

"Father!" Waabi pleaded. "I will not be a bother to you. Soon I will be old enough to collect annuities on my own. I must learn the travel routes. I must become familiar with the agent. It's different now that they will not pay us at Mooningwanekaaning. How else will I learn?"

Lightning pierced the sky to the west above the horizon of golden, brown, and red hued leaves. A few seconds later, as thunder clapped over the landscape, Waabi's father finally turned and walked toward his son. His face appeared pensive but calm, without fear or worry. From his shoulder he removed his bandolier bag and held it out toward his son.

"I'd like you to have this bag while I'm gone," he said.

Waabi squeezed his face with concern. "But that's the bag mother made for you. It is yours to remember her by."

"Your mother lives in my heart. She will be with me on the journey to and from Sandy Lake. But the bag may become lost. I'd like you to watch over it for me."

Waabi grasped the bag softly in his hands, feeling its smooth beads against his fingertips. He felt a sudden warmth from the vague memories of his mother and his nervous anger suddenly fell away. He looked up at his father. Meeting his eyes, he nodded.

"We will return in a few weeks," his father said, now speaking to the group, "loaded with provisions for the long winter ahead."

Waabi wiped the corners of his eyes to stop himself from visibly crying. His father patted White Cloud and Star on the head giving them each a hard piece of maple sugar candy, then he said goodbye to his sister, Memengwaa, with a long embrace.

Coming back to Waabi he said, "Be good nigozis. Care for your family and community. Never let hate enter your heart."

Waabi nodded as a tear rolled down his cheek. He wrapped his arms around his father and whispered into his ear, "Gigawaabamin."

Waabi's father and uncle said their last goodbyes to everyone and pushed their canoe into the splashing waters. Ahead of them were numerous canoes converging in a line around the point, all headed west toward the storm—toward the 1850 annuity payment at Sandy Lake, Minnesota Territory.

The season of Dagwaagin passed slowly into Biboon. For Waabi, the days were long and the nights were endless. Several moons passed and not a single man or messenger had returned from Sandy Lake. One night, with the Month of the Big Spirit

Moon nearly upon them, Waabi lay awake listening to the snow that fell continuously, rolling down the curved roof of the wigwam and piling up along the sides as tall as a man stood. It was the third night in a row of snow in what was already a long, hopeless winter.

"The snow still falls," White Cloud said as he sat up, the light of the fire illuminating half his face. "I can hear it piling up around us."

"Are you restless?" Waabi said. "It is the middle of the night and you should be sleeping."

"I could say the same to you," Waabi's cousin answered.

"I am worried. Father and Uncle must be out there somewhere. It has been two and half-moons since they left for the annuity payment. The water is frozen and the only way back is on foot."

"I am worried, too," White Cloud said, wiping his eyes and yawning. "They have never been gone this long."

From a dark corner of the wigwam, Nokomis spoke. "Worrying will not help you, nor will it help them." The old woman scooted into the dying light, her deep wrinkles casting long shadows on her face.

"Nokomis," Waabi said, "we did not mean to wake you."

"I sleep like a Bwaan, fearful of a revenge raid—always alert." She paused. "Would you like the snow to stop, young one?" she said to White Cloud.

White Cloud nodded. "Yes, but I do not control the sky."

"There is a way," Nokomis said, revealing a sly grin. With her right hand she picked up a small piece of birch bark and held it up to the light. "You must shoot a flaming arrow into the eye of the storm. If you do that, before you wake up in the morning, the snow will stop falling."

White Cloud swallowed nervously and looked at Waabi who shrugged, playing along.

"I will," White Cloud said, turning back to his grandmother. "I will shoot a flaming arrow into the eye of the storm."

"That is good, noozhis," Nokomis said. "You must fit this birch bark to your arrow and then drop it in the fire, setting it ablaze. You must be careful, though, not to disturb our little wigwam."

White Cloud lifted his chin slowly and deliberately, up and

down, acknowledging the weight of his new responsibility.

"Here," Waabi said, "you may use my bow and arrow." From under his yellow yarn bag he used as a pillow, Waabi pulled out his bow and one arrow, then handed it to his little cousin.

White Cloud took it like it was a fragile jewel. Being very careful, he stuck the birch bark to the tip of the arrow, placed the shaft on the bowstring, and then leaned the point of the arrow into the glowing fire. After a few moments, the birch bark caught fire. White Cloud raised the arrow and began moving toward the entrance, shuffling carefully around his still sleeping mother and sister.

From the back of the wigwam, Nokomis gestured toward Waabi. "Go with him," she said.

Waabi was old enough to know the futility of shooting an arrow into the vast and empty sky; nevertheless he felt an innocent glimpse of hope. His concern for his father was so great that he believed it was better to do something than to do nothing. And his grandmother, wise and mysterious as she appeared to him, gave him this sense of hope.

Stepping outside, the snow was deep, but not impassable. It came down in large, light flakes that appeared to float more than fall.

White Cloud, with the snow above his knees, leaned back and pointed the arrow skyward. He pulled back as far as he could, straining the bow with all the strength of his chest and arms. He released and the arrow sprung forward cutting through the snow leaving behind it a trail of spotted light and a curious sound like a knife through water. Waabi and White Cloud watched as the path of the arrow curved, eventually falling back toward the earth before the light finally gave out and the arrow disappeared.

"Do you think I hit the eye of the snowstorm?" White Cloud said.

"Yes, cousin. I think you did."

Waabi and White Cloud returned inside the wigwam, wiping large flakes of snow from their hair. Nokomis had slunk back from the light to the far end of the wigwam where she could be heard snoring. Waabi and White Cloud looked at each other and smiled, trying hard to withhold their laughter. Then they slid back down under their covers and closed their eyes for what they hoped would be a peaceful slumber.

The cold winter days continued their slow procession with the pace of a turtle. For Waabi and his family, most of the time was spent in the wigwam hiding from the bite of the frigid air. The sun remained bright while it was up and the landscape, frozen as it was, looked barren and tranquil, almost naked. Not a single hoof print or feathered bird broke the endless blue and white horizon. "Don't worry," his aunt assured Waabi, "your father and uncle must be wintering at Gaa-mitaawangaagamaag. They will return in Ziigwan loaded with supplies."

One afternoon, while Waabi helped his grandmother weave a blanket of rabbit fur, the shallow but distinct sound of sleds cutting through the hard packed snow could be heard through the bearskin mat that covered the entrance of the wigwam. Waabi, along with his cousins, aunt, and the rest of their small community, scurried out of their lodges expecting to find the return of their fathers and brothers, uncles and sons. Though they had departed by canoe, they had to return by foot because the rivers and streams had been frozen for several moons.

With his hand against his forehead, Waabi shielded his eyes from the brightness of the sun reflecting off the snow and looked into the distance. Like dark shadows a handful of figures appeared over the crest of the windswept landscape. Waabi felt a surge of conflicting emotions. He was excited to see the return of the men and women who had made the trip to Sandy Lake, but knew that their long delay meant that something had gone terribly wrong.

Without his snowshoes, Waabi trudged forward, barely able to pass through the thigh-high snow. But he pressed on, breathing heavy and forcing his tired muscles forward. As Waabi approached the oncoming group, he could barely see their faces from inside the hoods of their frost covered blankets. They moved slowly and heavily, backs slumped and steps short. Several pulled sleds but the packs they carried looked to be nearly empty.

"Father?" Waabi called as he came within twenty paces of

the group. No one returned his call. "Father?" he said again. He was among them now, but still they ignored him. Men walked by slowly, looking at Waabi through strained eyes as they continued moving toward the lodges. Waabi looked left and right but could not identify his father. As he craned his neck a hand settled on his shoulder.

"Father?" he said again, turning to the person who caught his attention. At first it appeared to be a stranger—an older man Waabi had not seen before. Looking more closely he recognized the amber specked eyes of his uncle. He looked gaunt, almost dead.

"Where is my father?" Waabi asked.

Waabi's uncle, Ogimaa, dropped his eyes and shook his head.

Waabi's heart beat heavy and fast. "Is he in the rear? Has he fallen behind?"

Without looking up, Ogimaa shook his head again.

Pleading now, Waabi said, "When will he return?"

In a soft, broken tone, Waabi's uncle replied, "Your father will never return. He has joined your ancestors on the spirit path." He raised his hand to Waabi's eye level. In it was an eagle-bone whistle that had belonged to his father. "For your spirit bundle," he said.

Taking the eagle-bone whistle in his hand, Waabi began gasping for breath, then he dropped to his knees and sunk into the snow, crying like the day he was born. Behind him, from the community of lodges, he could hear his aunt wailing.

Hundreds died at Sandy Lake, Waabi later learned. Hundreds more died trying to return to their homes in the cold, harsh winter. The government agent, who had promised payment in late October, did not arrive until late November. While they waited, men became sick from government supplied rations. They experienced stomach cramping and fevers, followed by vomiting, diarrhea, and dehydration. Then they started dying. It was only a few at first, but then five or six every evening. When the government agent finally did arrive, he had no money or goods to provide the Ojibwe. Instead, they had to rely on the credit of traders just to be given enough supplies to last the long, difficult trek home. With the waterways frozen over, they had to throw away their canoes and travel on foot. The snow was already deep and the land was nearly bare of game. Many suffered and died trying desperately to return to their loved ones.

Waabi painted his face black, mourning the loss of his father and the other men from his community. His father, Waabi's uncle told him, died of dysentery a few weeks after arriving at the lake. Because so many had died in such a short period of time, his father could not be wrapped in birch bark nor given a wooden structure to mark his burial.

"I laid him in a shallow grave along with several others," Ogimaa lamented one evening in the wigwam. "I placed his face toward the west so that he might find his way to the spirit road. I buried him with his knife and tobacco pouch, and for four days after his death I returned each day to offer advice and to ask him to be careful on the spirit journey."

"Did you mark the grave?" Memengwaa asked.

"He was buried with so many others," Ogimaa said, "there was no way to distinguish his place from that of another."

Outside the cold winter wind whipped and howled against the sides of the wigwam. Inside the light of the fire flickered causing the shadows of Waabi's cousins, aunt, uncle, and grandmother to dance on the bulrush walls behind them. Waabi clung tightly to his father's bandolier bag, a sad reminder of not only his mother's death, but his father's now too. A tear slipped down Waabi's cheek, cutting a streak of gray down his painted face.

"We will not let your father die without purpose," Ogimaa said, looking at Waabi with solace in his eyes. "We will not let the white officials remove us from our land. Though we may not be able to visit the graves of our brethren or find them on the spirit path, we must ensure that they can find us."

Looking back at his uncle, Waabi was expressionless. He closed his eyes, then he closed his heart. The pain of loss had lodged deep inside him. He knew then, he was no longer a child.

Chapter 8

Samuel
Londonderry, Vermont
December 1859

Months passed as the rolling Vermont hills changed from an ocean of green, to waves of red, yellow, and brown, before finally being covered with layers of white snow. Once the mill pond froze over, Samuel's work at the sawmill ended and wouldn't begin again until the spring when logs could be sent down river. His work was replaced with an endless monotony of chores at home. Each night he went to bed with sore hands and an aching back. But, as he lay in his woolen blankets, sleeping on the floor alongside his younger siblings, he would wait until the stillness of the night and pull out Mr. McPherson's flyer from under his pillow. By the dim light of the wood-burning stove he would stare at the scene of the open, abundant prairie and wonder if life was better there. Others had packed up and gone. Some to northern Vermont, others to places like Ohio, Indiana, and Illinois. It could be done, he only needed the courage to ask his family to go with him. He would ask soon, he told himself, before folding the flyer, slipping it back under his pillow, and finally succumbing to his exhaustion.

As for Thomas, their father had scolded him for losing his job at the mill, but he had done it gently.

"Is that it?" Alexandra said, confronting Randolph in front of the entire family. "Thomas is dismissed from the mill and you just give him a pat on the back? Your son is putting the whole family in a tough situation. He needs to learn from it."

Randolph, lying in bed with his foot up, showed no signs of anger. He looked at his children, then back at his wife. "What would you have me say, Alexandra? The boy needs to work outside, in the fresh air. It wasn't his fault and scolding him ain't gonna make him..." He paused. "Better."

Alexandra sighed and turned away. Isabel rushed to console her.

Samuel looked on, conflicted. He wanted to be upset at the favor his father had shown Thomas, but he knew his father was right.

"The sun is down early," Samuel said one evening as he entered the one-room homestead after clearing a path of snow between the outhouse and the barn. "The orange light over the western hills looks very pretty."

No one seemed to notice Samuel in the dying light of dusk, oil lamps having yet to be lit. His mother and sister Isabel were busy peeling, cutting, and boiling potatoes for supper. His father lay in bed, asleep, with his splint covered leg visible through a break in his bedroom curtain. His little brother Edward and little sister Eva Marie were on the wood planked floor playing with two cotton-stuffed ragdolls.

Looking around the pinewood cabin that he called home, Samuel couldn't help but notice the plainness of it. One long rectangular room with a table in the middle. To one side, where his mother prepared supper, was a large pit for cooking and a shelf filled with kitchen utensils. On the other side, in the corner, was the wood burning stove. Beside it was a metal tub for bathing and a bucket with clean water. On the far wall was his parents' bedroom where his father now rested. There was a curtain hung for privacy, but one could hardly call it private. Two scratched and murky windows let light in—one on each end of the cabin.

As Samuel removed his coat and mittens, the door flung open behind him as Thomas entered and announced his presence.

"What's for supper?" he said in a tone so loud he could not be ignored.

"Boiled potatoes," Isabel said looking over her shoulder.

Thomas stuck his tongue out in disgust. "Boiled potatoes? That's all we're eatin' is boiled potatoes?"

"And bread," Isabel added.

"That's all we can eat right now," Alexandra said as she glanced over at her snoring husband. "It's going to be a long winter so you better get used to eating potatoes."

Thomas huffed but didn't argue further.

After hanging up their coats, Samuel's mother said, not unkindly, "Boys, will you wash up and then set the table? Once the table's set, Samuel, will you get your father out of bed?"

"Yes, Ma," Thomas and Samuel said, one after another.

Stepping around their little brother and sister, Samuel and Thomas went over to the pail of clean water and soap next to the stove. Before washing up, Samuel quietly walked over to his bed of folded blankets.

"Where are you going?" Thomas said. "Ma told us to wash up."

In a hushed voice Samuel snapped back, "I will in a second, I just have to get something."

With his father still asleep and his sister and mother occupied, Samuel slid his hand underneath his pillow, grabbed the folded flyer, and placed it quickly and quietly in his breast pocket.

"What did you grab?" Thomas insisted as Samuel sidled up beside him to wash his hands.

"Never mind!" Samuel said.

Thomas eyed Samuel, but didn't prod him further.

After setting the table with wooden bowls and stained silverware, Samuel walked over beside his father's bed. Behind the drawn curtain his father looked blissfully unaware of anyone or anything. "Come on, Pa," Samuel said leaning toward his father's unshaven face. "You can't just lie there forever."

With a yawn and a few blinks of his eyelids, Samuel's father finally woke up. "Samuel," he said, pleasantly. "Smells like potatoes."

"That's cause it *is* potatoes, Pa," Samuel said with a smile, unable to resist his father's natural charm.

"Seems like I remember having potatoes yesterday," Samuel's father said, sitting up. "And the day before that come to think of it."

Samuel's mother released an audible groan. "Of all people," she said, "you are the last one allowed to complain."

"I'm sorry, I'm sorry," Samuel's father said. "I've gotten too used to the comfort of this bed."

"Come on, Pa," Samuel said, dropping his shoulder underneath his father's arm.

"I don't need all this help, you know," his father said. "I've been practicing walking with this splint"—he leaned over and knocked on the wooden rod that was wrapped tightly around his lower leg—"and despite what your mother thinks I've been pitching in around here. I'll be walking and running and jumping and dancing in no time."

"Sure, Pa," Samuel said, repressing a grin.

"Isabel," Samuel's mother said as Samuel set his father down at the end of the table. "Get Edward and Eva Marie ready for dinner, would you?"

Without a word, Isabel wiped her hands on her apron, untied it, and hung it from a hook on the wall. With the ease of youth, she walked over to her three year old brother Edward and picked him up by the armpits. Edward giggled at the swiftness of it. After wiping his freckled face and hands clean, Isabel set him down at the table.

"I'll get Eva Marie," Thomas said, which surprised Samuel.

As Thomas carefully placed Eva in her high-chair, Samuel's mother swung around with a steaming pot of potatoes and placed it on the table between the bread and a tea kettle of hot cider. Finally, the family was all seated at the table, Samuel's mother on one end with Eva Marie at her side and Samuel's father at the other. On one side Samuel sat next to Thomas and on the other Isabel sat next to Edward. All of them stared expectantly at their meal of sliced potatoes layered with dollops of goat butter and hunks of day-old wheat bread. It was by no means a grand meal, but a meal nonetheless.

"I've got some bacon saved up special for tomorrow," Alexandra said, breaking the momentary silence.

"Shall we say grace?" Samuel said.

With their heads bowed, Samuel's father led the prayer, saying thanks for another day and another meal, and asking blessings on his family.

"Let's eat!" Thomas said with the enthusiasm of a child at play.

Happily, the family scooped up mounds of potatoes and broke hunks of stale, but warm bread. The tea kettle let off swirls of steam as hot water was poured into wooden cups. For a minute or two jaws were exercised in chewing rather than talking and the mood was calm.

"Thomas. Isabel. What did you learn at school today?" Samuel's mother finally said as she wiped Eva's mouth with a red and white plaid handkerchief.

"Um," Thomas thought, "in history they taught us all about the Revolutionary War."

"What about it?" Randolph said.

"Well, the teacher said this country started out as a British colony, you know, from England." Thomas struggled a little to explain, but continued. "She said the English people left England to gain more freedom but they still had to fight for their freedom here, in America. So they declared themselves free and then fought to keep it that way."

"Do you think they were right?" Samuel said to his brother. "Do you think they were right to fight back?"

"Yeah they were right," Thomas said, turning his head confidently toward Samuel. "They were being told what to do by a King thousands of miles away that didn't have nothing to do with them. They had all their rights taken away and the teacher said they had to pay taxes that weren't fair. They just wanted to be free to live in their own way in their own communities with their own rules. Everybody deserves that."

Samuel's father supported Thomas saying, "That's right. If a big and powerful government is telling you what to do and where to live, eventually you have to fight back. And because they fought back we now enjoy the freedom to live and work as we please. It's something to remember." Samuel's father shoveled a spoonful of potatoes in his mouth and then continued. "In fact, that's why we live here in Vermont. Your great grandfather was given this land as a reward for fighting in the Revolutionary War. We can all be grateful for that."

"Let's not be too grateful," Samuel's mother said, a hint of sarcasm in her voice.

Everyone's heads turned.

Samuel's mother brought her head up and pulled her shoulders back noticing the attention she'd drawn. "I'm sorry. We ought to be grateful for your great grandfather and this homestead. I'm just concerned because the doctor's assistant stopped by today—while you were resting."

"And?" Samuel's father said.

"And, as I said, he's the doctor's assistant, Randolph." She spoke clearly and audibly, trying to make a point without mentioning specifics. Tension crept across the table. After a long pause she said, "He came with another bill. It's more than we can afford, Randolph, and winter is still early."

Samuel's father straightened in his chair as if to defend himself. "We still have that maple syrup to sell, and the goats are still producing milk."

"Barely," Samuel's mother said. "The syrup won't pay for half the bill and the goats are partly starved and only giving enough milk for us and the children. Plus, we're still behind on the barn payments. I told you we couldn't afford to rebuild that barn. This land just doesn't produce enough."

"Well how could I know I would break..." Samuel's father paused and looked at his children who sat in stunned silence. With a change of tone he said, "We'll make it work. It'll be hard for a while but we'll make it work."

Samuel looked across the table and saw fear in the faces of young Isabel and little Edward. Even Thomas' normally pleasant attitude appeared broken by the harsh reality of their family's situation.

"You can't just wish this away, Randolph," Samuel's mother said, pressing her hands against the table. "Taxes have gone up and our income has gone down." She paused and took a deep breath, looking with concern over her five children. "I think it's time we sell the oxen, it might be the only way we make it through this winter."

"Don't!" Samuel said, surprising himself. All eyes turned toward Samuel and he felt a rush of nervousness. "I mean, before we think about selling the oxen I have another idea." Samuel reached into his pocket and pulled out a crinkled, folded piece of paper. He handed it to his father.

Samuel's father unfolded the paper and slowly read it aloud. "Land. Opportunity. Adventure. The new state of Minnesota."

Samuel's father then held it out for the rest of the family to see.

Samuel's mother said, "You want to move to Minnesota?"

Samuel could feel everyone staring at him. "Well... I... now might be the time for a change. And the man, Mr. McPherson, he told me the land is practically free for the taking. Acres and acres of it."

After a moment, his father broke in. "I think it's a great idea."

Samuel felt a sudden burst of pride. "You do?"

"Once my leg is better, after spring arrives... it'll be the perfect opportunity to start over. To give us a fresh start. An exciting start. Maybe put this trouble behind us."

"Yeah!" Thomas said. "It'll be an adventure."

"Hold on a minute," Samuel's mother said. "Adventure is one thing, but we have to think about what is safe and possible—about what is best for the family. Our home is here in Vermont."

"I wasn't sure at first," Samuel said, trying to persuade his mother. "I picked up that flyer months ago. But the more I think about it, the more I like the idea. Like I said, the land is cheap and open. It's not like it is here with hills and trees that need to be cleared and land that's all used up. Plus, we can start over and build a new home, a better home with more space. If we sell enough crops, we can have a two-story house with more than one room. I get more and more excited the more I think about it."

"That all sounds wonderful, Samuel," his mother said, "but—"

"The Murrays did it," Samuel's father said, interrupting. "Remember, Alexandra? And the Donnellys, too. Jared wrote back about a place called Spirit Lake—called it the Eden of the West. The timber is thick and tall he said, and the lakes are quiet and filled with fish."

"But how would we get all the way out there?" Samuel's mother said. "Trains are too expensive. We'd have to load everything in the wagon. And," she paused, "it's not safe. Traveling all that way. And once we get there, isn't that Indian country?"

Samuel shook his head quickly. "No. Mr. McPherson works for the land management office, and he said the Indians sold the land. He said they all moved west opening the land for settlement for families like ours. Plus..." Samuel paused as he glanced at Thomas, "the air is fresh and invigorating. Good for the lungs." Samuel made the last part up.

Samuel's mother took a deep, measured breath, shaking her head. Just then a gust of wind howled outside, taking hold of the door and shaking it violently against its latch. From the corner the wood burning stove flickered, its light and heat slowly abating in a ceaseless effort to fight the cold seeping in through the chinking.

"We'll hold on to the oxen for now," Samuel's mother finally said.

The family smiled in unison as Thomas said, "Minnesota here we come!"

"Hold on. That just means we'll think about it," Samuel's mother said. "Don't get so excited." Then she looked across the table at her husband.

"We'll see," Randolph added. "I'm excited, too, but your mother's right that we should take some time to think about it. That's a mighty big change."

"I know," Samuel said as he lowered his eyes back to his cooling bowl of potato hunks. As he took another scoop he felt an incredible sense of relief followed by a moment of happiness. For the first time since he could remember he wondered hopefully about what the future might bring.

Chapter 9

WasabishkiMakwa
Mooniingwanekaaning-minis
Binaakwe-giizis
(Madeline Island, October 1854)

Rain fell softly from a perpetually gray sky that hung over Mooningwanekaaning. No one on the island stirred. They just sat in quiet contemplation while listening to the patter of the raindrops against the roofs of their lodges and wigwams. Four winters had passed since the tragedy at Gaa-mitaawangaagamaag, the memory of it still haunting their dreams.

Days earlier, the island had been a deluge of activity and energy. Thousands gathered from all ends of Ojibwe country to negotiate a new treaty—a treaty that would ensure the Ojibwe who lived near Gichigami would never again be asked to remove from their homeland. In the end it was a great victory, especially for those like Waabi who had lost loved ones at Sandy Lake because of the U.S. government's cruel, manipulative attempts to force the Ojibwe off their land. But like the rain that fell that day, it was a somber victory. For Waabi, nothing would heal the hole in his heart left by his father's death. For the Ojibwe, who may have saved their homeland but had agreed to live on reservations, they knew nothing would ever be the same.

Inside the wigwam a warm fire glowed while Ogimaa carved new arrow tips, Memengwaa patched holes in the makaks, Nokomis brushed Star's hair, and White Cloud played with a spinning stone. Waabi, sitting cross-legged and covered in warm blankets, stared into the glowing fire. His fifteenth winter approached and he was almost past the age of the vision fast—a time in the life of every Ojibwe boy when he would journey alone to a hidden place, abstain from food and water, and wait for a dream or vision to be revealed. Sitting there, watching the flames, Waabi didn't know if he was

Colin Mustful

ready or not. Most boys his age had gone through the fast and had seen their vision. But Waabi, who was still mourning the death of his father, was given more time to prepare. By this time he knew, with the treaty signed and the move to a reservation assured, he no longer had the same allowance for waiting. Now, everyone was in mourning. Though they gained a reservation, they lost the island.

While Waabi stared into the fire, his uncle got up, filled a cup with ash and water, and stirred it into a black paste. He sidled up to Waabi, dropped to his knees, and held the bowl forward. Looking Waabi directly in the eyes he whispered, "Are you ready, now?"

Waabi felt a spark of nervousness. His breath shortened and his skin tingled. Slowly, he calmed his nerves, kept his eyes fixed on his uncle's and said, "Yes." With that Waabi closed his eyes and felt the warm paste pressed against his face by his uncle's fingers, firm but gentle. First, he applied the paste under Waabi's eyes, dragging his middle and pointer fingers down the curve of Waabi's cheeks. Then, being less gentle, he dabbed the nose and forehead, spreading the black paste all the way to Waabi's temple and hairline.

"What are you doing, father?" Star asked as she looked on.

"I am preparing Waabi. It is time for his vision fast."

"Where will he go? When will he come back?"

With his eyes still closed, Waabi listened carefully, wondering the same thing.

"I do not know," Ogimaa answered. "Waabi must be led by the Great Spirit to a place only he knows. He will return when the Great Spirit reveals his true path in life—when he sees his vision."

Silence followed. Waabi opened his eyes. Everyone stared at him, straight-faced and calm. Ogimaa held out his hand offering Waabi a gift. "They are leaves of wintergreen," Ogimaa said. "You may wish to chew on them after several days. They will help during the darkest times of your fast."

Waabi nodded, taking the leaves in his palm. Then he stood, shedding his warm blankets. He could wait no longer. It was his time to go on a vision fast—to face himself and his future—the moment was upon him. He gathered a bear-skin robe for warmth and a tobacco pouch for offerings. As he stepped past his aunt and

79

uncle, he looked back at his grandmother and cousins and said, "Gigawaabamin."

Waabi stepped outside and took a deep breath of the cool, wet autumn air. He didn't know where to go, so he just started walking. He moved past the lodges and wigwams, watching puffs of smoke slowly escape each birch-bark roof. Then he came upon La Pointe and the wood-frame buildings. First the trader's store, then the Catholic church, then the schoolhouse. He continued through the town and finally past the small, wood-frame homes of the white and métis residents. Looking at the scattered one and two-room cabins, he saw silhouettes of people through the dark, weather-worn windows. He imagined the people inside—happy families with warm stoves, ovens filled with baking bread, and fathers reading stories to their children. He wondered which home belonged to Agnes and her family. Was it a happy day for them—knowing a new treaty was signed? Or did they feel the same as Waabi did: confused and torn over the results. When the Ojibwe were gone from the island, would Agnes leave too? Would he ever see her again?

Waabi continued northeast past trodden foot-paths and out of sight of the settled areas of the island. The forest grew dense as rain continued to softly patter the green, red, and yellow leaves that clung to the trees. Water gathered on Waabi's fur-lined robe and soaked his moccasins, making them heavy and cold. Small drops of water pelted his hood, echoing loudly in his ears. He wiped his eyes and cheeks until he finally gave up and just let the water roll down his nose and drip from his face. He thought of collecting the water on his tongue, but his fast had already begun and he knew he had to abstain.

Hours passed. He grew cold, hungry, and weary. Darkness was arriving and he still wasn't sure where he was going. Through the trees he saw the endless gray waters of Gichigami. The hard ground softened as dirt gave way to sand. He had reached the north-eastern edge of the island. As Waabi looked out over the water he shivered violently, clutching himself to try to stay warm. He needed shelter.

Waabi looked left and right. To the east he saw a rocky out-cropping and limestone dunes. Quickly, he made his way toward the dunes. The yellowish rock was worn smooth from countless seasons of waves battering their surface. Waabi edged his way along the rocks looking for some protective cave or inlet. Finally, he saw it. A break in the rocks, wide enough for him to fit through. And inside was a dry, flat, walled area large enough for him to be comfortable. This would do. This was perfect.

Waabi settled into his small, dark space, hunching his shoulders and pulling his knees in for warmth. Through the opening in the limestone walls he watched the last glimmers of daylight melt away until the final trace of light on the horizon was gone. He thought of building a fire, but he was exhausted. No longer able to keep his eyes open, Waabi fell into a deep, restful sleep.

A day passed. Then two. Then three. Waabi wasn't sure what he was supposed to do to obtain his vision. He only knew that if he returned home without a vision, he would have to attempt the vision fast all over again...and again...and again...until his vision was received.

Waabi passed the time observing the sky, the water, the shore, and the world all around him. He watched as day transitioned to night and night to day and saw the sun and stars move across the sky in a circular pattern. He admired the tan and brown walls of his rocky enclosure. He marveled at that layers of rock that carried a story of years gone by, long before his ancestors migrated west and settled in the land where food grows on water. He watched the trees bending over the shore, their trunks curved and broken, battered each day by the wind and rain and sun around them.

Waabi rarely felt hungry, or thirsty, or tired. He enjoyed the peacefulness and solitude of his temporary home. He didn't even have many thoughts about his past: his father, his mother, his life at Mooningwanekaaning. He didn't think about his future either. What reservation life would be like. What would happen to his people. For three days, he just existed.

On the fourth morning, the sun quickly broke through the fog that covered the horizon and melted away the lingering clouds. The sky was a bright, clear blue, and the air was warm and inviting. But as he looked out across the calm lake waters, he found himself longing to drink the cold, crisp water. He dragged his tongue across his upper lip suddenly realizing it had become dry and cracked. Moments later, he felt hunger pangs in his abdomen that were strong enough to bend him over. His body convulsed and he started coughing. He went down to his hands and knees and began dry heaving. His stomach was now completely empty and he wished to do anything to fill it.

Thankfully, the pain subsided. Waabi took a few deep breaths through his nose, rose up off his hands, and then sat back against the limestone wall. This was the pain he would have to endure if he were to have a vision.

"Waabi!"

Agnes appeared at the opening. Turning herself sideways she entered the enclosure. She carried a knit pouch and had a look of concern on her face.

"Waabi, are you all right? You look... you look awful." She kneeled down so she was eye-level with him. She reached out her open hand but did not touch his face.

Waabi straightened his back and lifted his chin. He was shocked. How had she found him—and why? In the past four years they had become good friends, speaking to each other each day at school, visiting with each other at every island event, even meeting at the edge of the water to skip rocks. He felt calm in her presence, happy even. But he didn't know what to do with that feeling. He was a Native and she was the daughter of a white minister. And now here she was. She had sought him out, which seemed like the actions of someone more than a friend.

"I am fine," Waabi said, hiding the surprise from his voice. "How... how did you find me? Why?"

Agnes' expression quickly changed as she smirked, tilted her head, and shrugged her right shoulder. "I saw you. A few days ago. You stopped and stared like you didn't want to go wherever it was you were going. I knew you'd be going on your vision fast. I knew you hadn't done it yet."

"But... how did you find me here?"

Agnes smiled and looked away, blushing. "The island isn't that big, Waabi. There are only a few places a person can hide."

Waabi felt flushed with embarrassment. He tried to respond but could think of nothing to say. He caught her eyes and for a few moments was no longer thinking of anything.

"Listen," Agnes said. "I was worried about you. I would have come sooner but I had to wait until my father left. If he knew, he wouldn't let me come see you. I know your vision fast is important, but I also know you need to take care of yourself."

"I will be all right, Agnes."

"No. Look at you. Your lips are dry and cracked. Your skin is pale. You're thin as a birch tree!" Agnes paused and looked away. Then she opened her bag and reached inside. "I brought something to share with you. I wanted to bring you some berries and water, but I know how important it is to keep your fast."

Pulling her hand from the bag she revealed a small book. "It's called *La Vita Nuova* by Dante Al-igh-i-eri," she said, stumbling over the pronunciation. "It's Italian—it means 'The New Life.' It's a book of poems I found on my father's bookshelf, and I know how much you enjoy the poetry lessons in class." Agnes spoke quickly, and her freckled face began to redden. "It's actually more of a story written through poems. My father says it's about discovering the beauty of the soul. Anyway, while I'm here, I thought I could read a little to you?"

Waabi nodded as he straightened his back and sat back against the stone wall.

"Oh, good!" Agnes said with a glint her eye. After a moment, she shifted her weight so that she was no longer sitting on her knees. She opened the book, held it in front of her, cleared her throat, and began to read.

The words flowed freely from Agnes' lips. Her voice was soft and clear. Waabi watched as her lips moved together then apart, wide then narrow, emphasizing some sounds and softening others. Waabi did not understand all the words, but he didn't have to. It was the rhythm, like the rising and falling of waves, that caught his attention—that made his heart fill up with joy.

Agnes paused and looked up at Waabi. "I'll read one last poem, then I'll be on my way so you can return to your vision fast."

She offered a reticent smile and Waabi nodded in return.

She read:

In that book which is
My memory...
On the first page
That is the chapter when
I first met you
Appear the words...
Here begins a new life

Agnes lowered the book, her eyes now carefully searching Waabi's face. "What do you think?"

"It was... It was beautiful," Waabi said, feeling both grateful and anxious. "You read so well."

Agnes blushed. "I'm so glad I found you here. And that I could get away for a moment."

"Me too."

"I should head back. Just don't stay out here so long that you hurt yourself, all right? Are you sure I shouldn't bring you any food?"

Agnes continued speaking before Waabi could answer.

"And I know you're worried about the new treaty—the new reservation—we all are. But my father says it's in God's hands now. Your ancestors, too. They must be watching out for you from the Spirit Path. Your father with them."

Agnes stood, returning the book to her knit pouch and brushing the sand from her knees. She reached down to help lift Waabi to his feet so they were eye to eye.

"Be careful Waabi," she said. Then she leaned forward and kissed him on the cheek. Without waiting for his response, she turned and left the rocky enclosure.

Waabi, stunned, brought his hand to his cheek, touching the spot where her lips landed. It tingled, like a gentle pinch against his skin. For a moment, Waabi just stood there enjoying the warmth of the sun on his face.

Another day passed, and still Waabi had no vision. He

slept sporadically, waking up to fits of hunger, headaches, and discomfort. He had memories of his mother, his father, his life in the maple groves or ricing beds but nothing that spoke to him or offered knowledge of the future.

He drew words in the sand to stay occupied—English words, for practice. He imagined writing to Agnes or to his own father. Then he imagined writing to Agnes' father. What might he say to gain his daughter's hand some day? Strength. Care. Love. He wiped the words away. What could he possibly say to change the way a white man looked at an Indian; even a kind white man like Pastor Hall?

It was the second day since Agnes' visit, the beginning of the sixth day since he left his wigwam. The clouds grew thick and gray. The wind became cold and strong, causing the waters of Gichigami to churn and swell. Specks of snow flew horizontally through the air. Winter was arriving.

Waabi grew desperate. He clung to his robe, pulling it tight while wrapping his arms close to his chest. He shuddered, leaning back and forth, shivering, trying to stay warm. He cried out in pain from the stabbing, relentless hunger in his belly. Vision or not, he would have to return soon. If he didn't, he might die out there.

Waabi's eyelids grew heavy. He wanted nothing more than to sleep, but he could no longer be sure if he did, that he would wake again. He shook his head, fighting the urge to sleep. He clenched his teeth to bear the pain in his stomach. He screamed out once more; angry, tired, uncertain. The sound of it echoed off the rocky walls, ringing in his ears.

Waabi wasn't sure if he should stay or go—quit or keep waiting for a vision. As he debated himself, he remembered the mint leaves given to him by his uncle. He felt his pants pocket. There they were. With a cold, unsteady hand, he removed the leaves from his pocket and laid them on this tongue. He was startled by the strength of their flavor. As he swished the leaves around his mouth, he closed his eyes and enjoyed the sensation of them against his teeth. His mouth became moist with saliva, a sensation he never knew how much he had taken for granted.

His senses calmed. He is body stopped shaking. The pain in his stomach faded. His head felt light and comfortable. He no longer felt afraid or angry or uncertain. He felt nothing. Was it day or night? Was it winter or summer? Waabi didn't know because he had slipped into a vision.

Waabi is surrounded by white men, women, and children. They're eyeing him like a pig to be slaughtered. They edge closer to him, one step at a time. Waabi feels stuck in place. He can only watch as they get closer and closer. Their faces grow more intense. Their mouths begin to drool. They raise their arms, ready to strike. Waabi's heart is racing with fear. "Gaawiin, gaawiin gegoo!" he shouts. Suddenly the whites turn into Bwaan. They are painted for war—red, black, and vermillion. Their bodies glisten with sweat. In their hands they carry javelins and hatchets. They draw back ready to strike. Waabi closes his eyes tight, turns his head, and raises his arms to shield himself from their blows.

Nothing. It's black; silent. Slowly, he lowers his arms, turns his head, and opens his eyes. The Bwaan are gone. He's in a rolling field with tall grass on a warm, sunny day. A white bear comes along and drops a fish at his feet.

"Eat," the white bear says and then sits back on his hind legs to watch.

Waabi takes the fish in his hands and raises it to his mouth. He opens his mouth, but before he can sink his teeth into its flesh, it turns into a book. The Bible. Shocked, he looks up to see that the bear is gone.

Instead, in the distance, he sees a man nailed to a wooden structure. His arms are outstretched, his feet are crossed, and his head hangs down to his chest. He appears to be dead, but fresh blood drips from his hands and feet. It is Jesus, the Christ, Waabi realizes. It is the man that white men revere as the son of God, the one who died on the cross and rose again.

Waabi was struck with fear and wonder. He got up and began walking toward the man—toward Jesus. But then the wind grew strong. Dark clouds rumbled overhead. The storm grew quickly. Waabi leaned into the wind pushing himself forward. He raised his arms to his face to protect himself from the strong winds, but as he did the world went black. When he lowered his arm again he found that he couldn't move. He was looking out across the field where he'd been walking. He was looking down on it. He was looking down... Waabi was filled with fear. He looked to his right to see that his arm was nailed through the wrist against the cross. Then he looked to his left to see that his other arm was nailed through the wrist to the cross. Then he looked down to see his legs were crossed and nailed through the feet to the cross. Waabi lost his breath. He panicked. He shook himself, trying to break free, but he was completely immobile. He raised his head to the sky, took a desperate breath of air, and screamed out in horror.

When Waabi woke up, the sun was hidden behind a tall, white cloud. There was a chill in the air, but the warmth of the daylight made it comfortable. Birds hung in the air enjoying the breeze off the lake. Waabi looked down at his hands and wrists, opening and closing his palms. They were free. He looked around to see that he was back in the rocky enclosure. He was free. He had his vision.

Chapter 10

Samuel
Londonderry, Vermont
April 1860

When winter finally broke in central Vermont, the snows melted, the rivers flowed swiftly, peaks of green could be seen on the hills, and the fresh air smelled of wildflowers. It was spring, a season that normally brought with it a sense of optimism. But even with Samuel's father's leg finally healed, the brightness of the spring sun could not overcome the weariness of Samuel and his family's homestead.

"It's time you went back to work," Alexandra said to Randolph one April morning. "The rivers are flowing again and they'll need the extra hand. Don't you think you should head to the mill with Samuel? Your leg is strong enough?"

Samuel looked on from the front door where he kneeled to tie his boots. Nothing more had been said about the move to Minnesota and Samuel wondered if it were still a possibility. Seeing his father hesitate he believed it was.

"Maybe...maybe I don't go back to the mill," Randolph said, almost stumbling over his words.

"What!" Alexandra said, straightening at the waist. "We haven't any choice, Randolph."

Samuel added, as if automatically, "But we do. Remember the flyer, Ma?"

Samuel and his father acknowledged each other with a glance and then both looked toward Alexandra who shook her head.

Moments later, Thomas came in through the door holding an envelope in his hand. "Found this in the post box," he said. Not recognizing the tense mood he walked swiftly over to their father and handed him the envelope.

"Aren't you supposed to be out feeding the oxen?" Samuel said, upset his brother suddenly stole the attention.

"Relax," Thomas answered, "I'm just bringing in this letter somebody dropped off. It didn't take me but a second."

"You two fightin' again," Isabel said from her seat at the table where she was feeding Eva and Edward.

"All right, all right," Randolph said, as he opened the letter.

Looking over his shoulder at the unfolded document in her husband's hand, Alexandra let out an audible groan.

Randolph grunted and bit his lip to keep from cursing.

Samuel stood after tying his boots and took a step forward. "What is it?"

With a soft voice Alexandra said, "It's nothing," but the strain on her face told another story.

"It's not nothing," Thomas said, rather boldly.

Isabel leaned forward with curiosity while Edward and Eva sat still, somewhat frightened.

Randolph glanced at Alexandra who was still turned away from the family, then looked back toward his children. With a sigh he said, "It's just...it's just the latest doctor bill. It's more than we can pay."

Alexandra turned back toward the family. "You don't need to tell them that," she pleaded.

"Nah, it's all right. It's best they know the reality."

"Another reason, maybe, to think about that move to Minnesota," Samuel said, now just as bold as Thomas.

"No," Alexandra said, extending the word as long as possible. "But it is a good reason for your father to go back to work."

"But you said we would think about it," Thomas said. "That's why we didn't sell the oxen."

A moment passed. Then another. No one spoke.

"It's now or never," Randolph said looking up at his wife from his seated position.

Alexandra shook her head again. "It's too dangerous. It's too risky."

"It'll be worth it though," Samuel added as his mother shot him a disapproving glare.

89

"Listen, honey," Randolph said taking his wife's hand. "Like Thomas said, we would think about it, and I have been thinking about it. I've been lying in bed thinkin' about it for months now. And this doctor bill finally put my mind over the edge. It is now or never if we want to make it in time to build a decent shelter before winter comes. We can sell the goats, the homestead, the extra wood and pelts I've still got stored in the barn. It'll be enough money to get us to Minnesota by wagon. We can start over. With more land and no debts. We can work for ourselves and eventually build a real house instead of just a rickety little homestead."

"But it's not safe," Alexandra said. "I know it's hard here, but did you ever stop to think how hard it'll be starting over? In a new place, so far away?"

"There's nothing left for us in Vermont," Randolph pleaded. "We have no sheep for wool. We can barely grow more crops than we can eat. You and Isabel have spent all winter turning flax into linen and for what—a few dollars?"

Alexandra stared down at her husband, biting her lip.

Randolph stood and placed his hands on his wife's hips, looking into her eyes intently. "You've taken such good care of me while I was laid up. I saw how hard you worked. I'm just sayin' that maybe there's a better life out there somewhere else. This was never our homestead anyhow. They gave it to my great grandfather, and it's been passed down so many times there's nothing left. Let's make our own homestead. Let's make something better to pass down to our children."

Samuel watched as his mother tapped her foot against the floor, turning thoughts over in her mind.

"And the doctor bills?" Alexandra said. "The money we borrowed for equipment? We have debts to pay. We can't just ignore them."

"Why not? They won't follow us cross this country. Forget the bills. Forget the sawmill. Forget the potatoes. Forget all of it. Let's start new! Build a better life for us—for the children."

Randolph moved his hands from his wife's hips to her shoulders and pulled her in close. With her chin resting on her husband's shoulder she looked at Samuel. In return, Samuel offered a silent look of hopefulness.

Subtly, almost imperceptibly, Samuel's mother nodded. Then, pulling herself away from her husband's embrace and staring him straight in the eyes, she said, "All right. We'll follow this promise of land and opportunity—this notion you and your son got for a better life. But you have to work harder than ever. No more jokin' around or layin' about. And you, Samuel. You got to keep this family safe and work real hard to build this future you're foreseeing."

"Of course, darling," Randolph said as he grabbed his wife by the hips, lifted her off the ground and twirled her through the air. She gasped in surprise, but then laughed at the joy of it. Samuel joined in, laughing and smiling and throwing his hands together. Edward jumped up and down mimicking his older brother and Isabel ran over from her seat at the table to embrace her mother. Finally Thomas ran over and joined in the jubilant scene.

"So this is it?" he asked, looking at Samuel.

"I think so," Samuel answered. "We're doing it. We're moving to Minnesota!"

Two weeks passed as the family made arrangements for their big move. They sold the goats, wood, pelts, and anything they couldn't take with them. Besides saying goodbye to a few friends and neighbors, they did it all in secrecy so they wouldn't alarm their creditors. But Samuel could tell that people knew. It had become all too common for families to pack up and leave.

In early May, with one wagon hauled by two oxen, they loaded all their earthly possessions in a heap held together by coarse manila rope. With Randolph, Alexandra, and young Eva Marie on the bench of the wagon, Edward and Isabel sitting on the tailgate, and Samuel and Thomas walking, they took one last look at their Vermont homestead. Then, with a crack of the reins and the exclamation *Ya!* from Samuel's father, they began their long journey west.

As the oxen edged forward and the wagon wheels began to turn, Samuel felt a sudden sense of caution and dread. This was his plan, his great scheme. As he watched the homestead fade away in the distance behind him, he was flooded with doubts. Then he remembered the words of a poem—a poem he had read in *Leaves of Grass*.

"And will never be any more perfection than there is now, Nor any more heaven or hell than there is now."

Samuel turned his head forward, putting the homestead forever in his memory. But he wondered, were they chasing a dream that would never be?

Back when Samuel was still in school, while sitting in geography class, he learned about the vastness of the country. He learned about the snowy heights of the Rocky Mountains and the endless stretches of prairie in the middle west. He knew of California and the gold rush and the Pacific Ocean. But it was not until he and his family headed west in an ox-driven wagon, that he began to understand how extensive the country really was. Before then, he had never left the town of Londonderry. He was like a fish in a bowl.

After three weeks the family had yet to cross the entire state of New York. Whatever excitement they felt for their new adventure was quickly washed away by the tedium and exhaustion of daily travel. Up by 4 a.m. each morning, breakfast had to be prepared, the camp had to be packed, the oxen hitched, and often repairs had to be made. Once everything was ready they continued west at a slow but steady pace following a winding wagon trail through the eastern hills, often encountering obstacles such as rain, mud, frozen temperatures, river fords, boredom, sun stroke, and exhaustion.

After resupplying in the town of Buffalo, New York, they headed south and west along the southern contour of Lake Erie. Shortly after entering the state of Pennsylvania they came across a dangerous river ford.

"The crossing point is clear," Samuel's father said as he surveyed the rushing water. "You can see where the wheel ruts lead right into the river. But the water is moving too fast. It looks to be three or four feet deep."

"What should we do?" Samuel asked, trying to sound like his father's buddy instead of his son.

Ignoring Samuel, his father held his flattened hand against his brow and peered left and right looking for another crossing.

"We just need to take it slow," Thomas said, as if he had solved a great puzzle.

Samuel turned his head down to look at his little brother. "Yeah, but we need a plan. Or maybe we should head up river, look for another crossing."

"We can't do that," Randolph said. "That could take us a hundred miles out of our way. Let me test it first."

Randolph looked around until he found a large stick. "I'll walk into the river using this stick to measure the depth in front of me."

"Be careful," Alexandra said from the bench of wagon cradling young Eva close to her chest.

Randolph entered the water moving quickly at first, then more slowly as he neared the center of the river. He poked the stick up and down to determine the depth as he took one slow, deliberate step after another. The water reached his knees, then his thighs, then his hips. He buckled, but held strong against the water. Then he returned.

"The water's high, but the wagon will hold," Randolph said, breathing heavy and soaking wet.

"Are you sure?" Samuel said. "It looks too high. Maybe we should wait and see if conditions improve, or maybe caulk the wagon and float it across."

Randolph paused, but then shook his head. "It's really not so bad. And the bottom is smooth, not rocky."

Alexandra added, "I agree with Samuel. I think we should we find another crossing."

"There ain't going to be no other crossings," Randolph quickly responded as he began walking toward the wagon.

"Are you sure it's safe?" Alexandra said, her normally pale cheeks reddened by the sun.

"It's safe. Besides, we haven't got much choice," Randolph said, now standing next to the wagon and looking up at his wife. Isabel and Edward sat on the ground near the wagon playing with each other and using sticks to draw pictures in the dirt. "We'll unload some of the materials that can't get wet like the flour and gunpowder. Then, I'll take the wagon across along with you and Eva. After we've crossed, I'll tie a rope to my waist and come back to help the children across one at a time. Then, Samuel and I can carry the flour and gunpowder ourselves."

Alexandra tilted her head, doubtfully. "This isn't going to be like last summer when that tree fell on your leg, is it?"

Randolph smiled instantly. "No, darling. Everything's going to be just fine."

"Boys," Randolph instructed, "grab the coffee, flour, and gunpowder and wait here with your little brother and sister. I'll be back across to get you one at a time."

"Yes, Pa, you can count on us," Thomas said.

Randolph whirled around and hoisted himself back atop the wagon bench alongside Alexandra and Eva Marie.

Samuel and Thomas removed the items quickly; the flour and coffee being held in barrels and the gunpowder in a powder horn.

After waiting for the go ahead from Samuel, his father cracked the reins forcing the cumbersome oxen forward. Slowly, the oxen entered the water which flowed easily around their thin legs. By the time the wheels of the cart entered the river, the water had reached the low hanging chests of the oxen, but it did not deter them.

"Yah!" Randolph yelled as the oxen hesitated but continued forward, water crashing against their rib cages and forcing their noses upward.

The wagon began to shake and bend against the strength of the rising water. Samuel's mother raised Eva to her shoulder and held her tightly. The oxen edged forward as Samuel, Thomas, Isabel, and Edward watched anxiously.

The water nearly covered the tops of the wheels and splashed continuously against the thin wooden rails. Suddenly, it swayed with the force of the water, causing the oxen to stop and bellow. "Yah!" Randolph called with another crack of the reins. The uncovered wagon, with all their earthly belongings, nearly tipped but recovered. Samuel's heart jumped in his chest.

Moments later the oxen began emerging from the water with the cart emerging too. The fast flowing water could no longer cause harm as ox and wagon moved closer to the opposite shore.

"They made it!" Thomas exclaimed with a joyful leap. Isabel and Edward imitated the celebration. Samuel, however, had to take a deep breath to calm his wiry nerves.

On the other side, Randolph jumped spryly from the wagon, took off his hat, and wiped his forehead. "Give me a few minutes," he shouted looking across the river, the light of the sun glinting off the waters between them. True to his word he tied one end of a rope to the wagon and the other to his waist, then waded carefully across the river. The water reached his belt, but made it no further. With his pants heavy with water and his face dripping with sweat, he stood on the shore, rope nearly taut and looked with grace on his children.

"Good job, Pa!" Thomas said.

"Thanks, Thomas," he said, patting Thomas on the shoulder. "I'll carry Edward across," he said to Samuel. "Then I'll come back for Isabel. Thomas will come with the powder as I lead him, then we'll both come across with the barrels."

Samuel nodded.

"All right, Edward," Randolph said and he knelt down to his youngest son. Edward reached up and grabbed his father from behind the neck. "I'm ready, Pa!" he said excitedly, unable to understand the danger of crossing the river.

The two crossed without incident and Randolph returned for Isabel. Meanwhile, as Isabel was carried across, Thomas grew impatient.

"We don't need to wait for Pa," he said, slinging the powder horn over his shoulder.

Samuel reached out, halting his brother. "Yes, we do," he said.

"Let go of me," Thomas said, squirming free of Samuel's hand. "You can't tell me what to do."

"Those were Pa's instructions," Samuel said as he tried to grasp his brother by the arms. Thomas moved too quickly and started racing toward the river.

Samuel tried to catch him, but his foot struck a root, cat-apulting him to the ground. By the time he got up, he saw that Thomas was waist deep in the stream. "Thomas!" he called. "Come back before you get swept away."

Thomas leaned into the current, bracing himself against its force. Determined but naive, he continued on, one step at a time. For a moment, it looked like Thomas might make it safely across. Then, like he was hit in the legs by a charging boar, Thomas was thrown horizontal and was immersed by the rushing water.

Samuel was struck with fear. He was certain his brother would be drowned by the rushing water. But, moments later, Samuel's father appeared, leaping from his position mid-river and grabbing Thomas by the shirt. Together they were carried down river until the rope forced them to a halt. Regaining his footing, Samuel's father carried Thomas to the shore where they both sat exhausted and wet, but breathing and alive. Alone on the eastern banks of the river, Samuel bent over in relief.

"I told you not to cross, Thomas!" Samuel said fifteen minutes later once everyone and everything had been carried across. "Why would you do something so dangerous!"

Thomas just hung his head as he sat in the warm sunshine with their mother caressing him.

"There's no need to scold him now," Samuel's father said as he sidled up next to him. "The boy's been scared half to death and your mother's already given him a dressing-down." He paused, then said, "She gave me one too."

Samuel turned away from his traumatized little brother and tilted his head, squinting into the endless rays of April sunshine. With a pat on the back his father said, "We got a long way to go. But it'll be worth it. We'll make it just fine."

Chapter 11

WasabishkiMakwa
Mooniingwanekaaning-minis
Abitaa-niibino-giizis
(Madeline Island, July 1855)

Waabi's heart swelled with pride. He had located the roost, waited quietly for the sun to rise, and released his arrow straight through the heart of his target sending it flailing to the ground. It was a large, beautiful turkey with golden-brown feathers, white tipped wings, and a bright red waddle. This time, unlike the rabbit he had let scurry away years earlier, he captured his gift. But this gift was not for Agnes, it was for her father.

Waabi did not take the time to dress and clean the turkey, he just removed the arrow and lifted the dead bird by its thin legs. Carrying it like a mashkimod at his side, Waabi walked casually through the wooded terrain of Mooniingwanekaaning-minis on his way to the wood frame homes that stood just north of La Pointe. As he walked he grew more and more nervous, wondering what he might say to Pastor Hall; wondering if he'd be turned away or if Agnes would reject his gift—his intent of courtship.

He had not seen much of Agnes since that day she laid a kiss on his cheek. Winter came, sending him and his family to their winter lodge. Spring was spent in the sugarbush and when they resettled for the summer, they did so at their new reservation at Miskwaabikaang located on the mainland west of Mooniingwanekaaning-minis. Those Ojibwe who didn't resettle at Miskwaabeking, did so at Mashkii-ziibi, located on the mainland just south of Zaagawaamikong-wiikwed that was established as a settlement for Christian Ojibwe years earlier. Still, Waabi felt a connection to Agnes he couldn't understand. He was drawn to her and, he thought, she was drawn to him too. They had reached the age of courtship; he need only gain the approval of her father.

Waabi arrived at the grouping of wood-frame homes where he knew Agnes lived. Weeks earlier, after a day spent fishing with Agnes and her brother Edwin, he had walked her home but stopped short of walking her all the way to the door because he feared being chastised. Pastor Hall had been a fine teacher and showed a depth of compassion for the Native people that Waabi had rarely seen in a white man, but he wasn't sure he would allow his daughter to take up with one.

With the turkey in tow, and his heart beating like a painted drum, Waabi walked up to home of Pastor Hall and rapped his knuckles against the door's wooden frame. Waabi waited, then knocked again. He heard commotion from inside. His chest tightened, his feet stung, he thought of turning and running... but then the door swung open.

He stood facing a green-eyed woman with gray and white streaked hair, wearing a blue and red plaid calico dress and white apron. The woman, who Waabi presumed to be Agnes' mother, opened her mouth to speak when her eyes darted to the blood-dripping turkey hanging upside down in Waabi's right hand. She snapped her mouth shut as her eyes grew wide with surprise. She looked back up at Waabi, raised one finger, and then turned and receded back in the home. "Sherman," Waabi heard her call. "There's a young man here to see you."

Moments later Pastor Hall appeared in the doorway, a pair of spectacles pinned to his nose and a well-worn Bible in his hand. "Waabi," he said in a cheerful tone. "It's nice to see you again."

Over his shoulder Waabi saw that Agnes and her sister Sarah had gathered behind their father.

"Boozhoo," Waabi said. "I..."

"You've brought us a turkey," Pastor Hall said, his tone going from cheerful to plain.

"Yes, it is a gift. It is..." Waabi struggled to calm his nerves.

Pastor Hall stepped outside, closing the door behind him as Agnes and Sarah both craned their necks to catch their last glimpse of the conversation.

Pastor Hall took off his spectacles and leaned in closely to Waabi. "I understand why you've brought the turkey, Waabi. I've lived among your people for twenty years, and I understand your customs. I respect your courage for coming here today, but I cannot have you courting my daughter. I cannot have her with an Ojibwe, especially one that does not profess to be Christian."

"I can provide for her," Waabi said, raising the turkey forward. "I can protect her. I can raise our family in Ojibwe country, living off the land, living close to our people and your people. I can raise a happy family."

"No, son," Pastor Hall said, shaking his head. "You're a kind young man but you're not fit to care for my daughter. Your way of life is nearly gone from this world and I can't send my daughter backward into a place—a way of life—that will be soon be gone."

"But, Pastor Hall..."

"Go back to your reservation, Waabi, and don't return."

Waabi could feel all the life, all the hope, draining from his body. He stood there, waiting for wisdom from beyond—from his father, his mother, his ancestors.

"Go!" Pastor Hall said, pointing over Waabi's shoulder.

Waabi dropped the turkey and marched quickly away, feeling angry and hopeless. He had made a mistake.

As he dashed away he heard the door open. "Waabi!" Agnes yelled out. He turned his head and saw Agnes as she reached out for him while her father held her back. "Waabi, I'm sorry!"

Waabi ignored her cries and walked on into the woods and out of sight of the settlers' wood-frame homes.

**Waatebagaa-giizis
(September 1855)**

A stiff wind blew, picking up brown and yellow leaves and sending them through Waabi's wide, bent legs. In his hands he held the shoulder blade of a moose. It was narrow at the base, wide at the end, and concave in the middle—perfect for digging. With a grunt he slammed the edge of the shoulder blade into the dirt, piercing the earth. Using the strength of his legs he forced a piece of hard dirt to separate from the ground, then tossed it aside. He repeated this, again and again, stopping only for short breaks to chew some dried berries and enjoy the solitude of an autumn day.

Several moons had passed since Waabi was turned away by Agnes' father. He had not been back to the island. Fueled by heartache and resentment, Waabi dug hard and strong, creating a hole that was as deep as a young sapling and as wide and long as a small canoe. The hole was needed as a food cache for the wild rice his aunt and cousins had harvested and processed. Once the hole was dug, Waabi lined it with birch bark and then rested in the short, yellow grass while looking up at the thick gray sky, day-dreaming of how life might have been. With his ankles crossed and his hands clasped across his belly, lying just a stone's throw from the great Gichigami, Waabi's eyes became heavy and he drifted off, napping peacefully.

"Boozhoo, Waabi!" said his now adolescent cousin Star, startling Waabi from his nap. Star leaped from her canoe and splashed into the water, then pulled the wide and heavy birch bark boat ashore towing her mother and numerous makaks of wild rice along with her. "There is no time to rest. We have enough rice this year for the entire winter lodge."

Waabi regarded his younger cousin who smiled brightly above her blue and cherry colored front piece. "Where are Uncle and White Cloud?" Waabi asked as he rose to his feet.

"They have already gone to the island for the coming payment," Meme answered as she bent over to lift a heavy makak of wild rice from the canoe. "They will set up the wigwam and we will join them tomorrow."

The annuity payment may have been good for the Ojibwe people, but it reminded Waabi of his father's death and the years of hardship that followed. And of Agnes. "I would hardly call it a payment," Waabi said with uncharacteristic scorn. "What we get lasts barely longer than a rainstorm, the rest goes to the traders... or whiskey sellers."

Meme huffed impatiently. "We are fortunate for what we get. At least now they are finally coming to us, instead of forcing us to travel long, hard distances during the icy hard moon."

"Do you really believe that?" Waabi said. "That we should be grateful? The government that gives you rations also forced you from your home and now asks you to live stationary, like a rodent in the talons of an eagle. We are not rodents."

Meme set down a full makak of rice and glared at Waabi like a bear deterring her cub. "That's enough," she said in a cutting, but not harsh tone. "We gave you time to mourn, but your mourning turned to anger. We have all been hurt, Waabi. We have all lost someone. Anger will not bring them back. You have to move on and be at peace, or live in pain forever. We are your family, Waabi," she said, nodding her head toward Star, "and we love you. But if you want to live with hate in your heart, you must do it somewhere else."

Waabi stood completely still, listening to the rhythmic clapping of the lake water against the back of the canoe. With the sun setting behind him and the air turning cooler, he stepped forward to take a full makak of rice from his cousin's arms. The rest of the evening was spent in silence, filling and covering the cache, where the food would wait for lean winter days.

The next day, after a warm morning meal of fish and rice, Waabi, Star, and Memengwaa loaded the canoe with supplies, shoved off into the bay, and headed for Mooniingwanekaaning-minis. The air was crisp and felt pleasant against the skin. The water was calm and reflected the orange hue of the rising sun in the eastern sky. The bay was scattered with canoes all directed toward the southwestern tip of the island. Along with the canoes were several Mackinac boats, their white sails flat in the calm, almost windless environment. Waabi paddled steadily from the rear of the canoe while his aunt paddled from the front. Star sat comfortably in the middle on top of some folded beaver hides that they intended to trade.

"What is that?" Star said, pointing to the southern edge of the island.

From behind the tree lined shore of the island emerged the largest vessel Waabi had ever seen. Its bow alone rose higher than even the tallest sail. The hull was colored red, and the ship had a huge sidewheel and two gray tubes, like branchless trees, rising toward the sky. Plumes of white smoke escaped from the tubes, dissipating gradually in the opposite direction the ship traveled.

"How does that vessel stay afloat?" Waabi said. "It is larger than the largest canoe. It is like fifty canoes."

As they got closer to the island, Waabi saw people exiting the large ship and then being taken to the island on small row boats. There were scores of people, all on one ship and all of them going to Mooniingwanekaaning-minis.

"They are not Ojibwe," Meme said of the people being rowed ashore. "They are white, but they cannot all be traders. What business do they have on our island?"

Hundreds of canoes lined the shore of the island and still more were traveling in Waabi's wake. He saw an opening on the shore and directed the canoe up onto the grassy beach. Pulling the canoe securely on land, Waabi, his cousin, and aunt removed their supplies and headed toward the trading post.

To Waabi's astonishment, the island was a flurry of activity. Countless Ojibwe—some painted and dressed in full regalia, others in pantaloons, calico shirts, and wide-brimmed hats—crisscrossed the open center square traveling between storage buildings and merchant shops. White traders and French voyageurs set up kiosks for the selling and buying of furs, blankets, flour, trinkets, and implements of all kinds. They shouted commercial statements and conducted business in all types of languages not limited to English and French, but including Ojibwe, Menominee, and various other Native tongues.

If all this wasn't remarkable enough, there was another kind of people on the island. They were not of any Indian tribe nor were they white traders, sellers, government agents or business people. They were men, women, and children with carefree smiles and happy demeanors. They wore elegant, patterned and formal clothing—the women in colorful skirts and dainty shawls and the men with buttoned up vests and shiny leather shoes. They walked around unencumbered without purpose or concern. These were the people Waabi had seen getting off the humongous boat.

A small boy with red hair like the cape of a rooster pointed at Waabi and then started bouncing his flattened hand against his open mouth while making sounds similar to a patterned drum beat. "Look, Ma," he exclaimed, "real Indians!" His mother pulled him close, whispering some rebuke.

"Who are these freckle-faced people?" Star said, mesmerized by the sea of white faces on their island. "Why are they here for our payment?"

The three of them continued past the trading post until they reached the outskirts of the village, a semi-wooded area interspersed with tepees and wigwams. Like the trading post, it too abounded with activity with Ojibwe families gathered around fires, children chasing each other around trees, blankets and rugs hung to dry over basswood twine, women beading, and men fashioning arrows out of bone. It might have been serene if not so overrun with people. Lodges stretched from the shore to the forest without so much as a canoe length separating one family or clan from another.

A wave and shout came from Waabi's uncle who was seated outside a small wigwam smoking a pipe alongside two other men and Waabi's cousin, White Cloud. One man had a small drum between his legs and the other held a flute. "Meme," Ogimaa said, speaking above the activity of the camp around him. "Join us for song and friendly communion."

As Waabi, Star, and Meme approached, the two men stood up and nodded politely. With their long black hair pulled back and blankets covering their shoulders they smiled and said, "Boozhoo." Ogimaa introduced them as Ishkode and Nagamo from the Crane clan.

"We have come from Gakiiwe'onaning," Ishkode explained as everyone found a comfortable place to sit atop the dirt and grass. "It is two days travel to the east."

As pleasantries continued to be exchanged, Waabi could not shake the images of the great boat and the small red-haired boy. He hardly heard a word that was said while he continued to ponder the strange visitors.

After a pause in the conversation, Waabi broke in. "We saw a very large boat in the bay. It was filled with white faced people. Do you know who they are or why they are here?"

Ishkode and Nagamo looked at each, silently debating who would explain. "They come from the east," Nagamo said. "They traveled on the big boats all the way from the Great Salt Water Sea."

"Why?" Waabi said with honest curiosity. "They have not come to trade."

"They are called tourists," Nagamo said using the English word. "A lock and dam was built at Baawitigong that allows their big boats to come through from their cities in the east. The people there are so numerous they are like ants in an ant hill. They come to escape their crowded cities. They say they are only here to visit. To see our islands and witness our way of life."

Waabi's head was filled with confusion. He knew of the eastern cities. The chiefs and elders of La Pointe had been there to council with the American government leaders. But he could not imagine traveling such great distances for pleasure and recreation. "I hope they will not stay long," Waabi said.

"They seem to be enjoying themselves very much," Ishkode said. "I'm afraid they will tell others and then more will come."

"More!" White Cloud exclaimed. "How could there be any more?"

With a straight face Ishkode said, "There are always more white men. Always."

Before the conversation ended a boy dressed in leggings and a beaded sash came walking up to their group holding an abalone shell and eagle feather. "Smudge?" he said. White smoke fluttered slowly from the bowl along with a comforting scent of sweetgrass and sage.

"Daga, daga," Meme said.

The boy proceeded to hold the bowl in front of each member of the group as he wafted the smoke toward their faces. With eyes closed, each of them accepted the cleansing white smoke using their hands to move it around their cheeks and forehead. As Waabi took his turn, he could feel the heaviness being lifted from his heart as the smoke curled around his head and lifted into air.

"Miigwech," Ogimaa said as the boy continued on to the next group of people. "Enough about tourists gathered here. Let's play some music together."

With smiles all around, Ishkode put his hands to his drum and Nagamo put his lips to the flute. Together with Ishkode and Nagamo, the group created an effortless melody, all of them swaying and singing, clapping and moving. They passed the afternoon in joyful fellowship.

Clouds passed slowly overhead on an unusually warm late September day. Hundreds of Ojibwe gathered outside the long red storehouse owned by the Bavarian landowner, Julius Austrian. After several weeks of waiting and some negotiation, the day of the payment finally arrived. Many of the Ojibwe were unhappy because the traders claimed for themselves the majority of the money that was promised as a result of the treaty that was signed a year earlier. The Ojibwe disagreed, but after a long council and an impassioned speech by the Ojibwe leader Makade-binesi, the government officials handed the money over to the traders anyway.

A long line formed at the pay table for members of the Miskwaabikaang band. Waabi and his uncle Ogimaa patiently waited their turn to approach the agent and collect their annual ration of goods and cash. It was a small amount—each family receiving just ten dollars a head—but every little bit helped, especially as the value of furs dropped and the hunting grounds became depleted.

From a distance, Waabi caught the eye of Agnes. He froze nervously. He wanted to feel angry, but he couldn't. What happened was not her fault. Looking at her now, Waabi was struck by the gracefulness of her movements. The ease of her stride. The way her hair, tied back, bounced nimbly off the blue shawl that covered her swaying shoulders. Getting closer, she raised her hand and smiled. Dumbstruck, Waabi waved back.

"Your maiden?" Ogimaa said, leaning into his nephew's ear and chuckling.

"A... a schoolmate," Waabi stuttered without looking away from Agnes.

"Ha!" Ogimaa laughed, slapping his nephew on the back.

"Waabi!" Agnes said reaching her arm out for an embrace. Hesitant, Waabi opened his arms and leaned forward. The embrace was firm and lasted longer than he expected.

"I'm so glad I found you," Agnes said, finally releasing him. "I never did get to apologize for my father."

Waabi hesitated, his eyes glancing to the side.

"Well, I'm sorry," Agnes said, her voice filled with tenderness. "My father, he..."

She reached out her hand, touching Waabi on the forearm. Waabi looked up at her gleaming blue eyes. A gust of wind blew her hair back, revealing the bean-shaped birthmark above her temple. She quickly brought her hand off Waabi's arm and drew her hair back down to cover the birthmark.

"I understand," Waabi said, somehow comforted by the embarrassment he saw in her face. "It was not your decision. Was it?"

With her chin held toward her chest, Agnes smiled. "Thank you for understanding." She paused and looked up. "It wasn't."

Silence passed between them despite the commotion of the scores of people moving about the island around them.

"Ah, this is my uncle," Waabi said, motioning to Ogimaa who was standing beside him like an affectionate pet.

Agnes gave a small curtsy. "Boozhoo, it is nice to make your acquaintance," she said, speaking fluent Ojibwemowin.

"You speak very well," Ogimaa said. "You must have grown up on the island."

"I have. My father is the Lutheran minister."

"Oh," Ogimaa said. "A saver of souls."

Agnes smiled, meekly, her round, dimpled cheeks turning red. "Well, we did our best. "

"Did?" Waabi said. "Has something changed?"

Agnes bit her lip and nodded. "Yes. I'm afraid I won't be here much longer." Agnes' pleasant expression shifted. "That's why I am so glad I found you among all these people. I didn't want to leave without saying goodbye."

Waabi's heart dropped like an anchor, deep and heavy in his chest. "Why are you leaving? Where will you go?"

"A place called Crow Wing," Agnes said, looking at Waabi intently. "It's a small agency among the Mississippi bands of Ojibwe. My father will open a new mission there. He has become frustrated with the mission here because he didn't feel like it was having much impact."

"When will you leave?"

"In a few days. As soon as the payment is over. We'd like to get settled in before winter comes."

Waabi was silent, unsure of how to properly reply.

"Look," Agnes said, pulling a rectangular object wrapped in white paper from her bag. "I have a gift for you."

"What is it?" Waabi said, taking it in his hand.

Agnes laughed. "You have to open it!"

Holding it in his hand, Waabi took a moment just to enjoy the mystery of what it could be. Then he ripped open the paper to find a small, green, leather-bound book. "The Bible?"

"No," Agnes said with a giggle. "It's poetry. Like what I read to you. But different. I want you to have it."

Waabi held it closer to his eyes and read the title aloud. "Leaves of Grass," he read, admiring the gold lettering and textured, leafy pattern on the cover.

"It's new," Agnes said. "I bought it off of one of the tourists from New York City. I think you'll really like it."

Waabi flipped through the pages pretending to read various lines. "Miigwech," he said, looking back up at Agnes. "But, I have nothing to give you."

"Oh, I didn't expect anything. Just promise to keep that close and think of me when you read it."

Waabi nodded, and they embraced again. As they let go and looked at each other to say a final goodbye, Waabi could see the strain in Agnes' face.

"Goodbye, Waabi," she said. "It was nice to meet you Ogimaa."

Agnes attempted a smile, but then dropped her head and turned to walk away.

Ogimaa nudged Waabi on the shoulder. "You like this girl?"

Waabi looked at his uncle, whose brow was folded waiting for a response. Then he looked toward Agnes, then back at his uncle.

"Young nephew, if a bird stopped pursuing its mate the first time she flew away, in a short while there would be no more birds. She clearly has affections for you. If you ask to court her, perhaps she will stay."

107

"Her father... her father said no."

"A father cannot forever decide what is best for his young. Eventually they leave the nest. You have had your vision fast. You have shown you can hunt. Perhaps it's time you left the nest together."

Waabi felt frozen in place. He could see Agnes getting farther away, mixing among the crowd. Would he see her again? If he did nothing, would he ever know how she felt?

Waabi lifted his foot from the ground and began walking quickly in Agnes' direction. He could still see her blue shawl among the crowd of white tourists that had invaded the island. "Agnes!" he yelled, holding his hand high. She didn't hear. "Agnes!" he yelled again, still pursuing her. He lowered his head and walked faster. Should he continue after her? What would he say? "Agnes!" he called one more time as he raised his head. He stopped in place suddenly realizing he had lost sight of her. He looked left and right but the crowd had thickened and she had disappeared among them. She was gone. Agnes was gone.

Chapter 12

Samuel
The Trail
May 1860

Lying under the stars, after more than a month of travel, Samuel began to feel an irrepressible pain in his feet and legs. Weeks earlier it had only been a numbness. Going to sleep was a comfort, and he often woke up refreshed and ready for another day of travel. But with each day and each mile, the numbness became pain and the pain became constant aggravation. He turned himself onto his left shoulder. Then he turned onto his right. Then he laid straight on his back with his eyes open and his hands clasped. The pain resonated in the soles of his feet and up the inside of his calves and thighs. It was like a tremor emanating from his big toes all the way up to his hips. Attempts at sleep were futile.

He began to loathe the nighttime. Rather than a period of rest, it had become a long, unbearable period of discomfort and frustration. If he did sleep, he woke up feeling heavy and always less and less eager to start a new day. But he did not complain or show any signs of weakness. He wanted to look strong in front of his father, and he wanted to set a good example for his siblings. After all, this cross-country adventure was his idea.

"Pa," Samuel said early one morning. "Can I drive the wagon today?"

"You drove the wagon all day yesterday," Samuel's father answered.

"Did I? Well maybe I can just drive the wagon for a little while."

"We'll take turns, how 'bout that? I'll drive us now, but we can switch in an hour or two."

Samuel nodded, offering a trace of smile. Then he closed his eyes and braced for hours of walking.

The trail wasn't all hardships. Samuel and Thomas would play games and sing and challenge each other, like they did when they were younger. Even chores felt like an exciting part of the adventure. Samuel helped by fetching water when needed, scrubbing clothes, gathering wood and buffalo chips, and, of course, driving the oxen. At night he enjoyed the cool, fresh air. On Saturdays, he helped his mother bake bread. He helped care for his little brother Edward and little sister Eva. When given the chance he swam and fished in the rivers. He hunted rabbits and other small game. The trail offered Samuel so much more freedom and joy than his daily regimen at the sawmill and homestead. At times, Samuel felt happy.

But happiness, he found, was a brief distraction on the trail. The wagon road was bumpy, causing constant hard jolts to Samuel's rear, back, and shoulders. When the sun was out, its rays were relentless, causing his skin to redden and itch. When the sun wasn't out, it was often cold and rainy with no indoor escape from heavy raindrops or the occasional hailstorm. Food was scarce and hunger was constant, sickness struck the family more than once, mosquitoes and horseflies were everywhere, and dirt and dust clung to the skin like cocklebur. Mile after mile passed with eternal slowness. Rarely, if ever, was there a change in scenery or a break from the tedium, discomfort, and misery.

One evening, as the sun began to set beyond the seemingly unreachable western horizon, Samuel was sent to a nearby creek to fetch water. He took two pails in hand and went alone while his father set the fire and his siblings gathered kindling. It was a short distance, but each step felt like a trial by fire because of the blisters on his toes and heels. After walking through the tall prairie grass he turned himself sideways to balance down the creek's embankment. There he found the peaceful rush of water that sounded as beautiful and soothing as a hymn. He rested for a moment, soaking up the solitude.

With a deep breath, he scooped water from the creek, filling the pails with as much water as they could hold. He turned to move back up the embankment one small step at a time. The added weight of the water was agonizing on his feet and it caused a great strain to his shoulders. But he dug in and forced his way up the incline relying on the strength of his legs. With one last step to go, he lifted his right leg and brought it forward. Before it could land, his left foot slipped out from under him and he twisted, falling hard against the pail in his right hand. The water splashed, and the buckets tumbled down the embankment all the way back down to the creek.

Lying in the dirt, Samuel looked himself over, realizing he suffered no serious injury. Looking down at the empty pails Samuel broke. How could he possibly continue? How could he go on for another day, week, month, second? Samuel started to cry. He felt so weary and hopeless, he just needed to let it out. He laid there and sobbed, silently, so his family would not overhear. It felt good. It felt like a release, as if someone had loosened a rope that had been tied around his chest.

Not wanting to draw attention to himself by being gone too long, Samuel stood up and brushed the dirt from his pants and forearms. Walking back down the embankment he picked up the pails and filled them again with water. He took a moment to admire the bright orange and yellow sunset, then he trekked back up the embankment and brought the water into camp. No one noticed his long absence or his wet clothes, except his mother.

"Are you all right?" she said with a tenderness only a mother could provide.

Samuel sighed. "Yeah, I'll be just fine."

As the days passed the weather warmed and the countryside became verdant and green. The sun rose early and set late allowing for long hours of travel, but bringing with it rising temperatures that didn't subside until all shadows faded and blackness enveloped the landscape. There was solitude on these nights—pure, unbreakable solitude. Looking up at the stars with the soft rustle of blowing grass being the only sound, Samuel pondered his new life and the decision to leave Vermont behind.

"Psst," Thomas whispered, breaking Samuel from his wonderings. "Psst," Thomas whispered again, poking Samuel in the shoulder as he lay next to him on the hard ground.

"What? What is it?" Samuel said in hushed and bothered tone.

"I can't sleep."

"Yeah, me neither."

The distant but constant chirp of crickets surrounded them.

"I'm gonna do better, you know," Thomas said.

"Better? What are you talking about?"

"I mean once we're in Minnesota. Once we start over. I'm gonna help you out more. I'm gonna help the family out."

"You been helping plenty," Samuel assured him.

"No, I haven't," Thomas said, speaking in a whisper.

A gentle breeze swept over them bringing with it inviting, cool air.

"I know it's time I grew up," Thomas continued. "And I know how much we risked—how hard this journey is. I know how much you want this to work out. Heck, you're even looking out for me so I can breathe better in the frontier air."

"That's not why..."

"Just listen, Samuel. I'm gonna do real good in Minnesota because I know how important it is. I'm gonna do real good for Ma, for Pa, for everybody. I'm gonna do good things, things you would have never expected back in Vermont. You might have to remind me once in a while but you won't have to watch after me."

"All right, Thomas, all right," Samuel said, the words so quiet they barely escaped his lips. "I believe you."

"Good," Thomas said.

The crickets continued chirping as the first wisps of light could be seen on the eastern horizon. Not another word was said between them until the full light of dawn announced a new day.

It was late June when the family finally arrived in Dubuque, Iowa, a settlement of westward travelers called the "Key City"—a place that opened the door to a better life.

"Look at that," Randolph said as he stopped the wagon on a bluff overlooking the vibrant frontier settlement.

"Wow, Pa," Thomas said, rushing in front of Samuel to get a better view. "Is that Minnesota? Did we make it all the way to Minnesota?"

"No, not quite," Samuel's father said, through his long,

dark beard. He looked worn but undaunted from months of travel. "That's Iowa."

"It's beautiful," Alexandra said with Eva Marie seated next to her clutching her hand.

Samuel, too, looked on in admiration. The frontier city was larger than he had imagined and even more picturesque than he could have hoped. The river was wide, like a lake, and was filled with schooners and steamships. At the basin of the river, two and three-story buildings gathered like marbles toward a drain all vying for access to the port. The city center was framed nicely by rolling hills covered with trees and scattered with wood-frame houses. Carriages moved up and down the wide streets, and from a distance Samuel could see people scuttling about like fish in a pond. The city was alive and bustling. Looking at it, Samuel felt renewed—emboldened—like he had the day Mr. McPherson gave him the flyer.

"We'll rest in Dubuque for a few days," Samuel's father said, "then we'll push on to the northwest. To Minnesota."

"Couldn't we just stay here, Pa?" Isabel asked. "How much further is it to Minnesota?"

Standing still and looking out over the bluff Samuel responded, "This is the city, Isabel. I admit it's beautiful, but nobody's free in the city, and we would have gone all this way for nothing. We need to make our own way. We need to seek out our own land and build it up ourselves. It's our manifest destiny."

"Destiny?" Thomas said. "What's that supposed to mean?"

"It means that all the land, from Vermont to California, has been set aside by God for American settlement. It's meant for people like us, and the people here in Dubuque, to settle and tame the land. To build towns and till the soil and to be prosperous and happy."

Samuel was surprised by his own statement. Though he had read of Manifest Destiny, the actual sentiment had not sunk in until that moment, standing on the bluff and looking down at the product of the American frontier spirit.

There was a brief silence before Samuel's father said, "I think Samuel's right. We have to make our own way; our own prosperity. Just like my great grandfather did years ago when he took up the homestead in Vermont."

Samuel felt a burst of pride hearing his father agree with him, then turned his eyes toward his father hoping for a nod or smile. But his father gave none and Samuel's pride quickly fell away.

"Destiny or not, I'm starving," Thomas said. "Can we head into town and get something to eat?"

"Yeah," Isabel and Edward agreed.

"All right, all right," Randolph said. "Let's take the ferry across the river into Iowa and get refreshed and re-supplied."

Randolph got back on the wagon and took up the reins. With excitement and uncertainty, the family moved down the road toward the ferry. Taking one last look from the bluff, Samuel saw a hawk swoop down. With incredible swiftness it grasped a mouse in its talons and flew up and away just as quickly as it had come.

As the family came off the ferry and rolled slowly into town, the clouds parted revealing a vast and inviting blue sky. Dust rose up from the streets and the chatter of pedestrians could be heard on every corner and in every alley. Men and women, busy with their chores and labors moved by with a quickness unfamiliar to people from the hills of Vermont. They moved about paying no attention to the newcomers.

After a satisfying and hearty meal at a local cafeteria, the family settled into a hotel—the first roof they'd slept under since leaving home. While Alexandra bathed herself and the younger children, Samuel and his father went to the trading post to sell what was left of their pelts and resupply for the remaining trek to Minnesota. Thomas and Isabel stayed back to help their mother.

"Do you sell maps of Minnesota?" Samuel's father asked the white-haired clerk.

"Yes, sir, we do," the clerk said, slowly bending down to reach for a map from underneath the counter. He placed it on the shiny, brown lacquered counter and smoothed out the paper with his weathered-looking hand. Samuel leaned in to see the map.

Minnesota was much bigger than Vermont. In fact, as far as Samuel could tell, it was the same size as all of New England. Flat and mountainless, stretching from the Mississippi to the Dakota Territory, Samuel began to understand just how much land there was to claim, to use, and to live upon. There were numerous counties drawn out—some in perfect squares, others cut in half by the jutting St. Peters River. They covered the eastern and southern portions of the state, looking like a shadow behind a rock the way they were drawn out on the map. The northern and western sections were filled with numerous rivers and lakes, but not many settlements.

"Where are you folks headed?" the clerk muttered. "Are you frontiersmen?"

Samuel couldn't help but smile at the term.

"Yeah. Yeah, I suppose we are frontiersmen," Randolph said as he turned and winked at his son. "We're looking for free and open land," he said, looking back at the bespectacled clerk. "Though we ain't exactly sure where."

"Well, there's plenty of that here," the clerk said pointing to the empty spaces on the map. "Thanks to a pre-emption act, all you gotta do is lay claim to a section of unsurveyed land and later, after you've settled, you can file your claim to buy it."

Samuel felt a tempered rush of excitement.

"But you folks might want to settle in town first," the clerk continued. "Get your feet wet. The frontier takes some gettin' used to, and a lot of grit."

Randolph raised his eyes from the map. "We aren't exactly afraid of hard work, we just want it to finally pay off. We want to build something for ourselves."

The clerk nodded. "That's a sentiment I can definitely relate to."

Dragging his finger across the map, Randolph said, "What do you think Samuel? This was your idea. Where should we start our new lives?"

"We can just pick anywhere?" Samuel said.

"Just about," Randolph said, his sun-worn face tightening with a smile.

"All 'cept the reservations," the clerk broke in, "and the land already been claimed. But there's still plenty left. Minnesota only been a state for 'bout two years."

"Indian reservation?" Samuel asked.

"Yeah, the Winnebago been moved here," the clerk said,

pointing at a spot just below a dot on the map labeled Mankato. "And the Sioux, they been moved here along the St. Peters." The clerk dragged his crooked pointer finger along the St. Peters River in the direction of the empty western plains. "The Indians won't be much of a bother. You'll find some roaming the region, but if you do, they're just out looking for food."

Samuel had never seen an Indian, and he was curious. He also wanted to appear brave in front of his father and the clerk, so he spoke quickly without thinking. "We can handle any Indians."

"I'm bettin' you can," the clerk said with a chuckle.

Looking back down at the map Samuel was mesmerized by the vastness of it all. "How about here, Pa?" Samuel said, pointing below the crook in the St. Peters River.

"Blue Earth," Randolph said, reading the name of the county. "I like how that sounds."

"I like it too. It sounds... like a poem."

"Well, Mr. Clerk," Randolph said looking up while placing his finger down on the map. "That's where we're headed. Blue Earth."

Chapter 13

WasabishkiMakwa
Miskwaabikaang
Onnaabaw-giizia
(Red Cliff, March 1862)

At the farthest edge of the wigwam, the flickering firelight illuminated Ogimaa as he rested on his shoulders against his cattail filled pillow. In his hand he held the counting stick which was used to mark the passing of days. Already it was Onnaabaw-giizia, the Snowcrust Moon, but it did not look or feel it outside. The snow piled high and the wind was like ice-water against the skin. Months earlier, before the harshness of winter set in, the community was struck by the disease that left pox marks on the skin. In response, groups isolated themselves, moving their wigwams to separate corners of Ojibwe country hoping to stop the spread of the disease. It did not save Waabi's aunt, Memengwaa, who was among the first on the Miskwaabikaang reservation to show signs of sickness. She was given hot water to clear her throat and cold water to break her fever; she was visited by the Mide who sang and prayed over her, giving her herbs and tobacco; she was given the utmost comfort, but aunt Meme did not recover. Her body and belongings were brought out to the deep woods and wrapped in birch bark, and she was laid down with her face toward the west so she could continue her life on the spirit journey.

Seven winters had passed since Agnes said goodbye to Waabi. Seven winters since the island was rushed upon by scores of white tourists seeking an exotic adventure. Since then, hundreds—thousands—more white men and women and their families pushed into the area, laying claim to the land, and putting up their wood frame businesses and dwellings wherever it suited them. The Ojibwe were hemmed in on every side. Slowly, season by season, the open spaces were scooped up, the forests were struck down, and

117

the traditional livelihood of Waabi and his people was made almost impossible to sustain.

That evening, while watching his uncle whittle another mark in the counting stick, Waabi dropped a few fresh cedar boughs on the fire. The crisp aroma of cedar filled the air, touching his face like a pelt that had been warmed in the sun. Ogimaa caught the eye of his nephew and motioned him over with a twitch of his eyebrows. Waabi stepped around the fire, moving gently toward his uncle. Reaching him, he crouched down and leaned forward.

"Yes, Uncle?"

In a steady, hushed tone Ogimaa said, "Do you remember how you got your name?"

Waabi looked up and watched the smoke of the fire billowing out through a hole in the ceiling. He shook his head. "I have been told the story. I do not remember the incident."

Ogimaa laughed, his teeth glimmering in the firelight. "It was in the spring," he said. "The chicory was blooming, the streams overflowed their banks, and the forests were teeming with new life. You had passed but ten seasons, having barely had any time unstrapped from the cradleboard." Ogimaa smiled again, his dark brown eyes shined. Waabi smiled back, listening with pleasure to his uncle's story.

"Your father and I were out checking the trapline, not far from the wigwam. We heard your grandmother cawing like a wild eagle, and she came running. We found her outside of the wigwam fighting off a white-furred bear with a stick. It was quite comical to see her meager figure shewing at a full size bear with only a stick in hand."

Waabi chuckled at the thought of it.

"Yes," Ogimaa said, seeing his nephew's smile. "You find it humorous now, but you found it more humorous then. We did not realize it at first, but you were behind Nokomis, laughing and pointing like you wanted to play. Then you tried to walk past your grandmother to get to the bear. You were unafraid! Poor Nokomis was bouncing back and forth like a ball trying to ward off the bear while trying to capture you. Your father acted quickly, striking the bear in the shoulder with a blunt arrow but it did not run off. Your father and I ran toward the bear, hoping to scare it away. When we did, you skipped through your grandmother's legs and continued toward the bear laughing and smiling, waddling as fast as you could. But your father scooped you up while I struck the bear in the ribs with a large stone, causing it to bellow in pain. Still you were unafraid, reaching for the bear from within your father's grasp. Finally, your grandmother found two sticks to knock together. The loud sound of the slapping sticks frightened the white bear enough to make it turn and run away into the woods. That's when you started crying—when the bear ran away! You were so sad to see your friend go. Once the shock of the moment passed, we could not help but laugh. You wailed like a baby fresh from the womb. It was the funniest thing we ever saw."

"And so I am called WasabishkiMakwa, White Bear."

"Yes, a sacred bear," Ogimaa said, barely above a whisper. Then he lowered his eyes, altering his expression. In a calm tone he said, "I can feel a fever coming on."

Waabi swallowed hard and stared at his uncle with anxious silence.

Ogimaa held out the counting stick, giving it to his nephew. Hesitantly, Waabi accepted.

"After I've left I want you to burn my blankets in the fire," Ogimaa said, plainly.

"You can't..." Waabi began to say before his uncle shook his head demonstratively.

"Sooner or later we all must take the spirit path."

With each loss of his family, Waabi felt the hole in his heart growing bigger. His chest tightened as he held back his emotions. He stood and nodded accepting the role his uncle had given him. A moment later Nokomis and his cousins entered the wigwam.

"The stars are beautiful tonight," White Cloud said. "The creator has painted them in a brilliant path."

"Very good," Ogimaa said. "I will look upon them with gratitude."

Ogimaa said no more, and for the rest of the evening he lay peacefully, enjoying the comfort of the wigwam. At some point in the night he slipped away and was lost to the darkness—lost to the wretched pox.

When spring arrived, it came abruptly. Ice receded from the lakes like a snake slithering away in the grass. Snow turned to puddles, soaking the earth and muddying the dirt. The skies turned blue, the grasses greened, and the trees were once again filled with orange-breasted robins.

Under the warmth of the spring-time sun, only Waabi, his grandmother, and his cousins emerged from the winter wigwam. Despite the loss of his aunt and uncle, nature spoke of life that would inevitably go on.

"Noozhis," Nokomis said to Waabi, shielding her eyes from the dazzling sun. "It is Iskigamizige-giizis and the trees are flowing with sap. Your cousins and I will go to the maple groves to fill our makaks. But we need more than sugar. The harshness of winter has left our stomachs empty and our bones brittle. You must go to the falls where the fish are spawning. When you catch your supply we will have plenty to eat."

"Yes, Nokomis," Waabi said with willingness.

"Also, take your pelts and your uncle's pelts," Nokomis continued. "Go to the island and exchange them for some bread and bullets." She smiled as if undeterred from the recent and continual losses in the community.

"Game was scarce this winter and we only have a few pelts," Waabi said. "But I will exchange them for what I can."

"That is good, grandson," she said in a kind but grating voice, showing her age. "We will meet you again at Miskwaabikaang when the warmth of niibin will bring pleasure and life back to our lodges. We are all sad now, but we must go on."

Waabi nodded, encouraged by his grandmother's endless optimism, but discouraged by his own continued sense of resentment. After the cold winter, and the disease that took so many, his grief felt like a bow-string wrapped tight around his heart.

Waabi walked alone to the mouth of Mashkiigiminikaaniwi-ziibi carrying a heavy pack of furs on his back while mud covered his moccasins. But he enjoyed the solitude. He took relief in seeing no one else wandering through the filtered sunlight of the birch tree forest. When he arrived at the river, he found two dozen other members of the Miskwaabikaang reservation gathered in makeshift lean-tos near the mouth of the river where the water flowed rapidly.

"Boozhoo, Waabi," Chibines exclaimed, Waabi's former classmate. He had grown into a formidable, stout armed man. "I'm glad to see the smallpox disease did not claim you this winter."

Waabi lowered his head, unable to return the enthusiasm. "Boozhoo. Sadly, my family did not go unharmed. The disease claimed my aunt and uncle, orphaning my poor cousins, though they are older now."

Chibines pursed his thin lips, frowning. "No family has gone untouched. I lost a sister and a grandparent. You will notice that many are missing from the gathering to collect spawning fish."

Waabi answered with a cold look of despair.

"Come," Chibines said, putting his hand on Waabi's shoulder. "Let us get that heavy pack off your back. We can clean the mud off your moccasins and fill your belly with warm water and cooked fish."

Waabi nodded gratefully and followed Chibines to the river where the rest were gathered. They welcomed Waabi, energetic and fearless as they did.

After exchanging pleasantries and eating fish, Chibines told Waabi he might be leaving Miskwaabikaang. "Reservation life is not for me," he said.

"Where will you go?" Waabi asked. "Will you join our northern clans in Canada?"

"No, if anything I may go south."

"South?"

"There is a war between the states—between the white farmers in the south and white businessmen in the north."

Waabi didn't understand what Chibines was telling him. "Why get involved? Why not just let them kill each other?"

Chibines paused a moment. "I don't feel like myself. I haven't for a long time. It's too late to go back to the old ways, and the changes to reservation life have me feeling empty. As a soldier, there is another way. Another way to learn the way of life they want for us."

"But that's not right, friend. You must not leave at their calling."

"But I cannot stay either. Besides, the money will be good."

"What money?" Waabi asked with interest.

"They will pay you to fight—pay you to kill. Thirteen American dollars every month. That is more than I'm given at the annuity payment each year. And one of the traders told me he could get me an extra fifty American dollars if I mentioned his name when I sign the papers. I can bring that money back home to the reservation. I can bring it to my family. It's too good to pass up. You should think about it, too, Waabi. They won't let us be warriors, like our ancestors, unless we pick up their guns and fight against their own."

Waabi answered with silence. It was yet another big change to his once much smaller world.

The catch was scarce, unlike the days of Waabi's youth when the spawning fish were so numerous one could hardly distinguish the fish from the water. Waabi caught and cleaned what he could then laid the meat in a basket and covered it with salt for drying. He gave the basket to Chibines and asked him to carry the fish to Miskwaabikaang. Waabi, instead of going to the reservation, went to Mooningwanekaaning-minis like his grandmother had instructed. On his way to the ferry, he passed through the town of Bayfield—a new and growing village filled with white miners, fishermen, lumbermen and their families. He saw wood frame buildings where he once saw wigwams and lodges. He saw wide and muddy streets where he once saw narrow paths. He saw men in hats and vests and women in bonnets and skirts instead of men in breechcloths and leggings and women in buckskin dresses. Looking at himself in his calico shirt and long pants, he realized he didn't look much different than the newcomers to his land. He shook his head, confused by the sudden and drastic changes.

Using a beaver pelt to pay his fare, Waabi boarded a ferry to the island. Arriving there it appeared just as foreign as Bayfield. There were no longer wigwams and tepees covering the edges of the forest. They were replaced with a strange emptiness—void of feeling and life, as if the island had not, for more than two hundred fifty years, been home to his family and ancestors. Only the small cemetery, with its spirit houses, now rotting, and tall Christian crosses, remained as a reminder that Mooningwanekaaning was the home-land and center of all Ojibwe life. Waabi felt lonely, like a foreigner on his own soil.

He proceeded to the trading post, which looked to be the same as it ever was. The middle-aged clerk softened his bored expression once he saw Waabi approaching the counter. "Boozhoo," he said, greeting Waabi in Ojibwe. "How can I be of assistance?"

Waabi nodded politely, not recognizing the clerk, and laid his pack of muskrat, beaver, and rabbit pelts on the counter.

"I'd like to trade these for flour, wheat, fish hooks, and ammunition," Waabi said, speaking English. "What is the cash value?"

Without speaking the clerk unwound the basswood cord surrounding the pack and began examining the pelts. He lay them one by one in a pile, moving his hand across the fur and skin while searching for any flaws or blemishes. After every second or third pelt he grunted and made a note in his ledger.

"Do you have any debts to settle?" the clerk asked.

"I have none," Waabi said without hesitation.

The clerk paused, then pulled a black leather ledger out from underneath the counter. Paging through it he asked for the spelling of Waabi's name. Moving his finger across ceaseless pages of carefully written records the clerk looked up and said, "You're right. You're all paid up. That's quite unusual these days."

Waabi was relieved. The Ojibwe often found themselves in debt, and they had no way to check the claims made by the traders.

"I can give eleven fifty for the pelts," the clerk said.

"Eleven fifty?" Waabi said, raising the pitch of his voice. "That is hardly enough for a pound of gunpowder and a pound of flour. One beaver pelt used to pay for a pound and half of gunpowder."

"That's true," the clerk said, standing straight and unbothered. "But their value has dropped quite a bit. I can give you a pound of flour and a pound of powder and maybe twenty fish hooks, but I can't give you much more than that."

Waabi felt hot with anxiety and anger. "I can't return to the reservation with just..." Waabi stopped himself and took a deep breath to calm down. Looking at the gray bearded clerk, he realized that the man behind the counter had little if anything to do with the price of furs. "Yes," Waabi said almost inaudibly.

"Yes?" the clerk repeated.

"Yes, I'll take a pound of flour, a pound of powder, and some fish hooks."

Without a word the clerk laid a piece of parchment paper on a scale and then leaned over to scoop some flour. Taking his time, he measured out exactly one pound and then dumped it into a paper bag. The clerk paused while looking at Waabi who had his head down.

"You know," the clerk said, "there are lots of industrious men in Bayfield looking for young laborers like yourself."

Waabi looked up, meeting the strained blue eyes of the clerk.

"I met one just last week," he continued, "who said I should send anyone looking for work his way. A miner, I believe he was?"

Waabi thought for a moment. Certainly his grandmother and cousins would have some maple sugar and syrup from the sugarbush, and they still had a cache of wild rice, but game had become so scarce that it was almost impossible to find. Without meat, his grandmother and cousins would have to rely on what they could gather.

"What does it pay?"

"Fifty cents a day, I think's what he said. You can earn in two weeks what took you all winter to earn through the fur trade." The clerk paused, waiting for a response. "Here," he said, searching his pockets. "I've got his business card somewhere."

The clerk pulled out a small, brown card and handed it to Waabi. In dark, cursive lettering it read, *Cyrus Mendenhall, Mining Entrepreneur, Lake Superior Mining Company, Bayfield, Wisconsin.*

"Stop and see him on your way back to the reservation," the clerk said pointing at the card in Waabi's hand. "I'll bet he puts you to work straight away."

Waabi placed the card in his bandolier bag and waited patiently as the clerk collected the rest of his supplies. He knew of other Ojibwe who had taken labor in recent years and he had few other options—except perhaps the U.S. Army, like Chibines planned to do.

"Voilà," the clerk said, putting Waabi's goods together in a larger paper bag and sliding it forward on the counter. Then he smiled warmly, like a well-meaning grandfather.

"Miigwech," Waabi said, trying his best to return the warm smile but only managing a polite grin. Without saying more he continued out the door and into the cool spring sunshine.

Chapter 14

Samuel
The Trail / Blue Earth County, Minnesota
July 1860

The oxen tired, but dug on over the soft dirt of the endless prairie. Samuel's father directed the wagon north and west by compass, cutting deep ruts in the earth, forging their own path. For days they traveled without seeing a single inhabitant or sign of life.

Throughout the long, hot summer days, Randolph and Thomas tried to keep up a sense of optimism. They were like puppets on the same string. "This is quite an adventure!" Thomas would say. "We're real frontiersmen, aren't we Thomas!" Randolph would answer back. Meanwhile, Alexandra grew increasingly exhausted from the relentlessness of the summer sun and round-the-clock care she provided Eva Marie. Isabel and Edward did their best, but they often squabbled and complained of fatigue and boredom.

After four days of travel without encountering a single living thing but prairie grass and mosquitoes, there appeared on the horizon a curious makeshift scaffold. Made of four upright branches and located atop a rise in the prairie, the scaffold held a horizontal figure covered with a blanket. As the wagon drew closer it became clear that the scaffold held a dead body.

"Indians!" Thomas said, the first to mention the curious structure. "That's an Indian burial, isn't it?"

"I don't really know," Randolph answered, unable to take his eyes off the object that lay atop the scaffold.

"Take a wide berth," Alexandra said, holding Eva close. "Whatever it is and whoever it belongs to, we don't want to cause a disruption."

Randolph did exactly as his wife asked, and before long the scaffold faded into the distance, the wind causing the prairie grass to wave around its makeshift beams.

After a much needed stop in a small settlement called Albert Lea, the family continued on to the last portion of their journey. Excitement and adrenaline overcame fatigue causing the last few days to pass quickly and with relative ease. As they continued, Samuel noticed a slight change in the landscape. What had been flat, endless prairie that was the dull color of flaxen had changed to a more varied, rolling landscape that was much greener, dotted with trees, creeks, and lakes. Whereas there had been no inhabitants, they now began passing small homesteads and log cabins where clean laundry hung on cords, and where fields of corn, potatoes, and peas grew.

"So this is Blue Earth. It's beautiful here," Alexandra said, showing a smile for the first time in days. "The land looks so perfect. So wide and open. It's like every family has a hundred acres."

The wind blew back Alexandra's bonnet as she squeezed her eyes, continuing to admire the vast landscape. "What do we do now?" she asked. "How do we get a plot?"

"Look there," Isabel said, pointing to the northeast. "I see some folks."

About a half-mile in the distance a woman hung laundry just outside a large wood-frame cabin. In a field not far from the cabin a man and two children tended crops. They looked so free, Samuel thought, like they hadn't a care outside their vast and open homestead.

"Let's go talk to 'em," Thomas said looking back at Pa from his position ahead of the wagon.

"That's probably a good idea," he answered as he whipped the reins and yelled, "Haw, haw!" turning the oxen right.

As they grew closer to the homestead, the man in the field picked his head up and peered forward from beneath the brim of his hat. After a few moments, he left his task in the field and beckoned the children to follow him as he walked forward to meet the group of oncomers.

"Hi there, folks," he said with a hand raised as he continued walking forward to meet them.

"Whoa!" Randolph called, halting the oxen.

"Hey, mister," Thomas said as he continued ahead of the

wagon so that he was the first to meet the strangers. "I'm Thomas and this is my family." He rattled off everyone's name pointing at everyone as he did. "We came all the way from Vermont and we're lookin' to start a new life here in Minnesota."

"That's a long way," the man said, his sun-darkened face no longer hidden by the shade of his hat. "Well I'm pleased to meet you all. I'm George Maxfield and these are my children Jules and Willie." He gestured toward the teenaged boy and girl that stood behind them. They nodded but did not speak. "We came here from Ohio—mine and my brother's family. It was tough at first, but it's been real nice ever since."

"Looks like you got yourself a nice home," Randolph said as he scanned the homestead with his eyes.

"Bet you're looking for a place to settle, aren't ya," George said as he removed his hat and wiped the sweat from his brow.

"That's right Mr. Maxfield," Samuel said as he sidled up next to Thomas. "We came all this way after receiving word that there was free and open land in Minnesota. Now we just want to settle down. You know how we can stake a claim?"

The teenaged boy, Willie, spoke up. "Pa, tell 'em about that place just north of here."

The man smirked, "I'm getting to that." He turned his toward Randolph on the wagon. "As my boy said, there's a lovely spot just north of us beyond the creek. It's open and unsettled. Just continue north and you'll see it."

"And the claim?" Randolph added. "Do we head to the land office first?"

"No need for that," George said, putting his hat back on. "As long as the land is unsurveyed, you just set your things down and claim your spot. At some point you gotta head to town—Mankato that is. They'll give you land scrip as long as you intend on improving the land."

"That's sounds real nice, real easy," Samuel said.

"Well, we'll be pleased to have some new neighbors."

"Thanks Mr. Maxfield," Thomas said.

"No need to call me Mr. Maxfield, I'm George to you all now. Me, Willie and Jules, my wife Martha, we know how tough it was getting here and we're happy to help anyway we can. We even got a cow if you folks need milk."

"Thank you, George," Randolph said, "we really appreciate that."

As George, Jules, and Willie started heading back to the field, George turned and said, "Don't worry about the Indians neither. They might come around once in a while, but they're harmless." He tipped his cap and then continued walking back toward the field.

"What could that mean?" Alexandra said.

"It don't mean nothin,'" Randolph said as he struck the reins again. "Yah, yah!" he hollered, pressing the oxen forward and turning them back toward the north.

The wagon bumped along as it had before. After a few minutes, as the Maxfield homestead began receding in the distance, ahead of them appeared a creek and grove of trees that looked to be without a homestead. "I think I see our new home," Randolph said, leaning forward and squinting. He pointed ahead to the creek and grove.

"That's it, Pa! That's it. The place Mr. Maxfield told us about," Thomas said, moving ahead of the wagon. Samuel continued to walk behind the wagon, watching Isabel and Edward giggle as they sat on the longboard enjoying the bumpiness of the prairie.

The wagon continued forward, crossing the shallow creek. Cool shade engulfed them from the wide canopy of honey locust and maple trees. The song of sparrows filled the air and yellow ambrosia grew along the edges of the creek. As they moved ahead, beyond the shade, they found an expansive opening that was flat and covered in golden stemmed grass swaying in the gentle summer breeze like waves in the ocean.

Isabel hopped off the longboard and ran forward into the long grass. "Is this our new home?" she said, twirling in her new surroundings.

Randolph stopped the wagon and took a long look around. "Yes, little darling, I believe it is."

"Truly?" Alexandra said. "We can just set up our home here?"

"This is the spot just beyond the creek," Randolph said, "and seeing that it looks unsurveyed... yeah, I think it's ours."

Thomas was the next to run forward letting out a giant yelp skyward. He was followed by Edward who began chasing Thomas through the tall grass. Then Isabel joined in the chase and they all began giggling and smiling and playing a game of tag-n-run.

Randolph, who was standing from the bench of the wagon, hands on hips, turned to Samuel. His face was soiled from the long trip but the gleam in his eyes never faded. "You're never too old to play with your brothers and sisters," he said. "Go have some fun."

Unable to repress his smile, Samuel took off into the fray catching Thomas first. "Tag! You're it!"

"Not for long!" Thomas said, spry as a fox as he took chase.

Long days of walking were replaced by even longer days of labor. First, a temporary shanty had to be built. Samuel, Thomas, and Randolph immediately went to work stacking logs to create a small, one room structure they covered with dry grass and chinked with moss. When it rained, water seeped through, and when the temperature dropped there was no escape from the cold, but the excitement of their new home and new land overcame their temporary burdens.

"We've already built a shanty; that was the first step," Randolph said one evening as the family huddled together for bed. "Then we build a log home. Then, in a few years, after we've made money selling crops, we can build a permanent frame home with room to spare."

It was a pleasurable thought, and one that kept the Samuel and the family going even during the cold fall rains and the endless daily labors.

By November, just before the first winter chill had arrived, they had built a nice log home with a slanted roof and a roughhewn floor covered with rags to act as carpet. It was nestled among the trees; the back of the home was just fifty yards from the creek with the front overlooking one hundred acres of tillable land. Food was scarce, but the family received much support and goodwill from the Maxfield family and other settlers living in homesteads to the east and west. And, much to their excitement, Randolph located a cranberry marsh that provided sufficient fruit for the winter with enough left over to send to market in the spring.

"That's awful fortunate," Alexandra said when Randolph brought home news of the cranberry patch. "Are you certain we can just help ourselves? Someone else must have discovered these cranberries before?"

"It was untouched," Randolph said, "except for the deer. I think we can claim it just like we did the homestead. And besides, we don't have much choice—not if we want to make it through the long winter. We need all the good fortune we can get."

"I suppose we do," Alexandra agreed.

"We'll ration throughout the winter," Randolph said, "and take the cranberries to market in the spring in exchange for seed. Then we'll plow and plant the field and by this time next year we'll have enough food to last ten winters."

Alexandra looked at him with skepticism. He returned her look with a playful smile.

As the family sat down to their first meal after finishing the new log home, Samuel felt a great sense of pride. Though they sat on log stumps, the table was filled with the most decorated meal they had had since leaving Vermont. There was cranberry sauce made fresh from the nearby cranberry patch. There was bread made from the wheat flour given to them by their neighbors to the east and sweet potatoes given to them from their neighbors to the west. A kettle of baked beans steamed in the center of the table and a plate of salted pork sat on the end. Each of these was bought in the nearest town, Mankato, with the last of the family's savings. They also had hot green tea made from the Camellia leaves that Isabel had found one afternoon while out for a walk. Finally, there was water sweetened with molasses. It was a meal, as Thomas put it, fit for a king.

"It is fit for a king!" Samuel said with delight. It was his idea that led them to Minnesota. It was the flyer that he found and he kept. Now, finally, after months of strain and hard work, he felt happy—secure in recommending that the family take a risk and move halfway across the country.

"Pass the potatoes," Isabel said across the table at Thomas.

"You forgot to say, *please*," Thomas chided, grabbing hold of the bowl and pulling it closer to him.

Isabel smirked, shaking her head melodramatically, her long hair tail swinging back and forth. "PLEEEASE," she said.

"No!" Thomas said, laughing.

Samuel, who was seated next to Thomas, pried the bowl from his hands. "Stop being a brat," he said as he handed the bowl to Isabel.

In that moment, Samuel's attention was caught by the sight of movement outside the window over Isabel's shoulder. He stood and leaned over to get a closer look.

"What is it?" Samuel's mother asked.

Samuel stiffened. It was almost impossible to see through the greased paper window, but he was certain he'd seen the movement of a large group of people coming toward the cabin. "Shh," Samuel said, and he pointed toward the window.

Everyone was silent, listening intently. Voices could be heard as the group neared the cabin. They did not speak English nor any other recognizable language.

"Indians," Samuel said in a low whisper.

Randolph turned to Samuel. Steely-eyed he said, "Get my gun."

"No!" Alexandra said mutely, holding out her hand as a gesture to stop. Speaking in a whisper she said, "There must be two dozen of them. What good would your gun do but get us all killed? Besides, George told us they were harmless, remember?"

The silhouette of a man appeared outside the greased paper windows as he raised his hand to his eyes, trying to glance inside. Isabel and Edward began shaking.

"Stay calm," Thomas said.

Samuel was surprised by his little brother's show of courage.

As Randolph and Alexandra looked at each other, silently contemplating what to do, the door swung open.

Isabel shrieked.

In the doorway stood a middle-aged man with dark, wanting eyes and long black hair braided neatly over his ears on each side of his head. A reddish-brown blanket hung over his shoulders reaching all the way down to his moccasin covered feet. He held his right arm close to his body as if it were injured. Behind him, several other Indian men looked over his shoulders trying to get a look inside the cabin. The man walked through the doorway, stepping lightly as his wandering eyes silently investigated the people and contents of the home.

There were now four men inside the cabin, with more men, women, and children gathered outside. All of them appeared somewhat destitute in their dirtied blankets and worn moccasins. Some also wore head bands and had various trinkets and furs. They did not appear to Samuel like he had imagined Indians to be—powerful and intimidating with painted faces and long spears and tomahawks.

The first man turned toward Alexandra and began motioning toward his mouth with his thumb and forefingers pinched together. Samuel's mother, still frozen with fear, did not understand.

"I think he wants food," young Edward said, innocently.

"We don't have any food to give," Randolph said as he stood up from the table, prepared to defend his family. "We've barely enough for ourselves."

The man turned toward Randolph and continued motioning toward his mouth. "We would just like a little food," he said, showing that he could speak English.

"No, no," Randolph said, shaking his head over and over. "We have no food for you or your people."

The man stopped motioning toward his mouth and pointed at the cranberry sauce, furrowing his brow. "The berries," he said as he looked again at Randolph who was still shaking his head. Then the Indian man, who appeared to be the leader of the group, turned and began speaking with the men gathered behind him. After a short conversation in hushed tones, one of them moved toward the door and communicated something to those outside. Before long, he was handed what appeared to be a hand-woven basket which he then handed to the man with the injured arm.

The man with the injured arm held the basket toward Alexandra. It was a large, flat, round basket made of grass, neatly woven with a geometric pattern of alternating brown and tan squares. Samuel's mother looked at it with curiosity as the Indian man thrust it in her direction.

"Take it, Ma," Thomas said, now unafraid of the strangers. "I think they want to trade."

Alexandra looked toward Randolph who shrugged and nodded. Looking back toward the Indian, she took hold of the basket and said thank you, pulling it slowly from the man's hand.

"The boy is right," the Indian stranger said. "We've offered you a fine hand-woven basket, will you offer us something in return?"

"I think you'd better give him some food, Ma," Thomas said.

Hesitantly, Alexandra rose to her feet and walked toward the corner of the cabin. There, she gathered the remaining sweet potatoes that had been given to them from the neighbors and placed them in a burlap sack. With the bag in her hand she walked back to the Indian man and held out the sack. The man smiled like a child in awe and took the sack.

"Wopida, wopida," the man said, backing away.

"You're welcome," Alexandra said, but she was too shaken to return his gracious smile.

The strangers walked out the door, closing it behind them. Within moments the sounds of their feet through the grass faded until all that could be heard was the trill of the birds.

"They seem friendly," Thomas said as everyone's nerves settled.

Samuel said, "Friendly but hungry. That worries me."

Alexandra glared at Samuel narrowing her eyes as if to say, *don't frighten the children.*

"At least we know who our neighbors are," Randolph said. "Maybe, in time, we'll make friends."

"Do you suppose they'll come back?" Thomas said.

"I suppose they will," Randolph said as he scooped a heaping spoonful of mashed sweet potatoes in his mouth. "But as long as we treat them good, they'll treat us the same. There's no need to worry."

The family ate the rest of their meal in silence. Outside, a cold breeze swept down the river valley, a sign of the coming winter.

Chapter 15

Samuel
Blue Earth County, Minnesota
March 1861

Heavy, wet flakes of snow fell from an endless gray sky landing silently across the open landscape. In the cabin, the family huddled closely around the stove watching their natural light being siphoned by rising piles of snow along the windows. The roof creaked with the growing weight of the frozen precipitation. With her arms clutching her knees, Isabel shivered. Samuel warmed his sister, rubbing her blanket covered back with his hand.

"How long's this winter goin' to last?" Thomas moaned as he bounced a ball repeatedly against the wall. "I'm bored sick!" He looked toward the rest of the family, expecting them to commiserate, but all they gave back were long, dreary faces.

"We could use some more wood," Alexandra said, sitting in a chair that Randolph had recently built.

"Or you could hunt for more acorns," Randolph said, smirking like a schoolchild.

Thomas squeezed his face tight like he'd been kicked in the shin. "I swear! If I have to eat another acorn or cranberry tart I'll just stop eatin' all together."

Everyone laughed.

"Don't worry," Samuel said after the laughter died down. "Pa and I will be headed to Mankato soon with those bushels of cranberries and be returning with fresh supplies. Right, Pa?"

Randolph tilted his head offering a crooked glance. "Soon?" he said. "There's three feet of snow out there. How do'ya expect we'll get there?"

"What choice do we have, Pa?"

Randolph rolled his eyes and curled his lip as if to suggest the idea was ridiculous.

"Randolph!" Alexandra snapped. "Samuel's got a point. We can't wait another month for the snow to melt, can we? We have nothing left but a few potatoes and those cranberries. I can't ration anymore."

"Well," Randolph said, "what about tapping the maple trees? Once the weather warms, even a little, we can tap trees and go to town with more than just cranberries."

Samuel asked, "Can we wait that long? Can we wait a few weeks to collect and boil maple sap before going to town to get supplies?"

"Maybe waiting would be best," Alexandra said in a dry, accepting tone. "Going to market with maple sugar and cranberries will provide us a lot more supplies than just cranberries alone. We just have to hope and pray this weather warms up real soon."

"What about the Indians?" Thomas said, catching the ball in his right hand and turning his head.

"What about 'em?" Samuel said. "They seem harmless. Besides, you were the one encouraging us to make friends with them."

"I wasn't encouraging us to make friends," Thomas said, taking a defensive tone. "That was different. They were in our home. Once we get out there, how do we know they won't ambush us or something? Scalp us and take all those berries?"

"Thomas!" Alexandra said, like a sudden bolt of lightning. "Don't talk of such horrible things. We did not come all the way from Vermont for such a fate. Besides, the Indians have shown themselves to be friendly and kind."

Samuel thought back to what McPherson told him. The Indians were gone, all living on reservations now. But he'd also seen them now. He'd seen them in his own home. "Ma's right, Thomas," Samuel said. "We don't need to worry about them."

Samuel's response was followed by silence. The low crackle of burning wood from the stove filled the small cabin. Moments later, Thomas began to bounce his ball again.

"How about that wood, Thomas?" Alexandra said. "It might be more interesting than that infernal ball."

Thomas caught the ball again and offered his mother an empty stare. "Ah," he moaned, "I don't want to get all dressed up and go out in this snow. Do I have to?"

Before Alexandra could say anything, Samuel volunteered. "I'll do it, I'll do it. I need to get out of the cabin anyway, no matter how much snow is falling."

"Thank you, Samuel," Alexandra said, speaking loud and clear to make sure Thomas heard.

Samuel didn't need to do much to prepare for going outside since he was already wrapped in a wool scarf and thick sweater. He shed his blanket and put on his long winter coat. After lacing his boots tight, he tied cedar boughs to his feet to act as snowshoes and then put on his wool gloves and hat.

"You look downright silly bundled up like that," Samuel's father said in his usual carefree manner.

Samuel looked back, pretending to be annoyed, but under his scarf he was smiling.

He opened the door to a white wonderland. Snow covered every inch of the prairie and weighed down every branch of every tree. The snow flew thick and fast making it difficult to distinguish the ground from the air. But Samuel pushed ahead, one step at a time along the previously shoveled path. Not far from him was a snow fence that Samuel's father had the foresight to build back in October—it shielded the wood pile which was covered by a large muslin sheet.

Reaching the wood pile, Samuel steadied himself against the snow fence. Because it was nearly spring, the temperature wasn't bad, but the wind was strong and the snow was persistent—almost unbearable. He kneeled down to lift the muslin sheet and began gathering split logs. He took as many as he could carry, piling them in his arms up to his nose knowing he would need to return for a second trip. As Samuel lifted himself and turned to go back to the cabin, he noticed a dark spot in the distance of otherwise unbroken white landscape. He squinted and leaned forward trying to determine what he saw. What or who could possibly be out in this winter storm?

For a moment, Samuel thought it was nothing, but then the

object moved. It bobbed up and down moving closer to the cabin. It was a person.

Samuel thought it might have been a neighbor that needed help or a stranger that was lost. He dropped the wood at his feet and began waving his arms. But as he did, the object became clearer and Samuel was suddenly filled with a sinking feeling of dread. The man was hunched under a bear skin coat and in his hand there appeared to be a hatchet. It was an Indian, and though Samuel didn't know his intentions he felt strangely uncomfortable at the sight of the man.

Feeling frightened by the stranger, Samuel decided he should hurry and bent down to pick up the wood. He gathered it, piece by piece, in his arms. When he stood and looked back across the field, the man was gone. Samuel looked left and right, peering through the thick snow but he saw no one. He trudged back to the cabin wondering if he should say something or not. He didn't want to upset his younger siblings. The Indians hadn't given them any trouble before. Entering the cabin he laid down the logs and said only, "I'll be back with another load." He decided not to speak a word of the unknown stranger.

Three weeks passed and the weather warmed. It was April and the sunshine was deceptively warm—like a blanket against the skin. Mud filled the shoveled paths to the wood pile, outhouse, and wooden shelter for the oxen. Samuel had to put down wooden planks just to make it traversable. Another two weeks passed and the family had collected a decent amount of maple sap. Things had turned around quickly. But despite rationing all winter, and the generosity of neighbors, they were entirely out of food with the exception of seven bags of cranberries and a half dozen jars of maple sugar they intended to sell. Thomas had tried fishing in the creek, but it was too shallow for anything but minnows and tadpoles.

As Samuel and his father walked the planks toward the wooden shelter that housed the oxen, Samuel said, "Pa, we can't wait any longer to collect more maple. We've got nothing left to eat."

Randolph bent down and grabbed a handful of wet snow.

"I know, but the snow is still a foot deep. How are we supposed to get there?"

"The snow could last until nearly May, Pa. We'll have to move slow, but the settler's road is only a mile north. Once we reach the road, it'll be muddy but I'm guessing there's no snow on it. Besides, if we wait too long the cranberries will thaw and go bad."

Together they entered the oxen's shelter which was nothing more than a frame and a few boards. Randolph paused while looking at the half bale of hay that remained from what they purchased in the fall.

"Is this all the hay we got left, too?"

"That's all we've got, Pa," Samuel said, grasping a load of hay with both his hands. "And I've been giving them less and less each week, tryin' to make it last."

Randolph shook his head. "Yeah, you're right. We can't wait any longer. We'll go tomorrow, come what may."

Samuel dropped the hay down for the oxen to chew. "It'll be hard getting there, Pa, but it's the only way we'll get through to spring."

The next morning began with cold sunshine that quickly warmed and became almost pleasant. The songs of birds filled the early morning air, and the blue sky was dotted with wispy, white clouds. The sound of trickling water could be heard all around as the snow melted steadily. It seemed so long ago that the family hunkered next to the stove day after day trying to outlast the frigid temperatures.

As Randolph hitched the oxen, Samuel began loading bags of frozen cranberries into the wagon. With a grunt, Samuel heaved the first heavy bag into the bed of the wagon. Then, with another grunt and a swing of his arms, he heaved another bag into the wagon. It landed with a percussive thud against the wooden slats. Samuel continued until all the bags were loaded and then grabbed the crate with jars of maple sugar and placed it in the wagon, nestling it in the corner and held in place by the weight of the cranberries.

"Ain't Thomas coming with?" Samuel asked.

"Nah," his father answered. "I told him to stay home and

help his mother. Besides, I thought getting this wagon to the road might be too hard on his breathing."

Of course! Samuel thought. *Thomas wouldn't be asked to do any of the hard labor.* "Some things never change," he said under his breath.

"What?"

"Nothing," Samuel said. "Let's get going."

With that, Samuel and his father set out toward Mankato for much needed supplies and seed. It was an exciting moment because the seed was the key to the future they imagined. It represented the hope that brought them all the way from Vermont to Minnesota. Rich and arable land, combined with a little hard work and a few sacrifices—it would all pay off. But it was also a difficult moment. The snow layered the ground like paste and, being a new homestead, there was no well-worn path to the road. Because of that, Samuel found that he often had to unhitch the oxen and take them out-and-back, fifty yards at a time, just to tramp down a path that the wagon could be pulled through. Luckily, the ground beneath the snow still had some firmness despite the melting temperatures. In no time at all Samuel was soaking wet from his toes to his thighs, as if he'd been walking through dew covered bushes. Finally, after two hours of trudging through the snow, Samuel and his father made it to the tree line just beyond view of the homestead.

"The road will be a lot smoother," Randolph said from behind the wagon as he tried to help push it through the snow. "I'm sure some of the nearby homesteaders have made the trip to town since the weather warmed."

"Giddup! Giddup!" Samuel said, as he pulled the oxen by the halter and slapped them with the prod pole.

Randolph slipped and nearly fell as he continued to push with both hands against the tailgate. "Ooof," he groaned. "Anything would be better than this snow."

"Haw! Haw!" Samuel yelled as he tapped the closest ox on the rear and steered them left to move the wagon around a tree. "It'll sure be nice to get some supplies."

"Sure will," Randolph said. "We'll be working our own land instead of puttin' all our time into a sawmill owned by somebody

else. With all that land we got we might be able to get some horses...
if we can save up."

"You really think?" Samuel said, excited by the thought.

"Yeah. In a few years we'll build a frame house, too. With a
bedroom and an attic. And it'll all belong to you someday."

Samuel relished the thought as he closed his eyes and raised
his face toward the warm sun. A moment later, as he continued
to knock the oxen with the prod pole, they suddenly stopped and
bellowed in discomfort.

"Giddup! Giddup!" Samuel shouted. "Get movin'!"

"It's stuck, Samuel," Randolph said, walking out from
behind the wagon to examine the wheel. "Looks like some rocks."

Randolph leaned over the rail of the wagon to grab a shovel.
As he did, Samuel saw a group of five Indians, on foot, coming up
from behind them. They did not look like the ones that had visited
the homestead the previous fall. These men had faces streaked with
red and black paint. Their hair was adorned with tall feathers and
on their chests they wore colorfully beaded sashes. In their hands
were hatchets and rifles.

"Pa!" Samuel said, hushed but serious. "There are some
Indians coming."

For a moment Randolph froze, but then he slowly moved
his hand to the family's 1812 Springfield Musket that lay in the back
of the wagon. Without lifting the musket, he turned and faced the
oncoming men.

The Indians stopped about fifty feet away standing in the
tracks of the wagon. The intermittent shadows of the trees accentu-
ated their already intimidating appearance.

Samuel stood firm beside the oxen, but fear rattled his body
as he looked back and forth between his father and the unknown
men.

The Indian man who stood out in front of the others began
to speak, saying something in his native language. Another man
translated. "What do you carry in your wagon?" he asked without
any hint of anger.

With his voice wavering, Randolph answered, "We're carrying cranberries to market. We haven't any other food but these.

We need to sell them to get supplies to support our family after the long winter."

The head man spoke again. His face looked hard and worn. His cheeks were sunken and his eyes piercing. Even from a distance, Samuel could see a gash in the man's right nostril, disfiguring his nose.

"That cranberry patch does not belong to you," the translator said. "It feeds our families and it fed our fathers and mothers before us."

Randolph hesitated, his hand still clutching the musket. "We were told you sold this land by treaty, didn't you? It does not belong to you anymore."

After receiving a translation, the head man answered. He spoke quickly, with urgency in his voice. The translator said, "We made no agreement with you or your people. Now you all come, like blackbirds to the fields taking everything. You cannot have everything. Someday soon, when we take it back, you will have nothing."

Samuel, shivering with fear, said, "We've done nothing to hurt you."

The Indian men stood there, stone faced and silent.

"Pa, I think they want their cranberries back," Samuel whispered. "We should give them the cranberries."

Randolph whipped his head around toward Samuel, a hard look on his face. "Then what? Like you said, we need these cranberries. And we've got as much right to them as they do."

Samuel's heart was racing, his knees were weak. He felt flushed and anxious. He knew how important the cranberries were but he was afraid that if his father didn't offer them, the Indians would take them by force. "You can have the cranberries," Samuel called out.

The head man nodded.

"What are you holding onto in the wagon?" the translator asked Samuel's father. "Remove your hand from the wagon so we know it's safe to approach."

But Randolph still clutched the musket with an unsteady hand.

Let go! Samuel screamed in his mind. The musket will do no good against five Indians!

One of the Indian men raised a shotgun.

The head man said something in a demanding tone pointing at Samuel's father and looking toward the translator.

"Remove your arm from the wagon," the translator commanded. "We'll take the cranberries from you if we have to, and leave your bodies in the snow."

"Pa!" Samuel yelled, almost in tears. "Just let them have the cranberries."

Randolph turned toward Samuel, a look of sheer terror on his face unlike any Samuel had seen before. After taking a deep breath, his father mouthed the word *run*.

Fear shot up through Samuel's body, tightening his throat so he couldn't say, *No. Don't. Stop.* He just froze there unable to speak or raise a hand in protest.

Before his father could turn back one of the Indians fired his shotgun, striking Randolph in the leg, causing him to let out a barbaric scream. Startled by the noise, the oxen pulled the wagon hard freeing it from the rocks.

Flushed with fear, confusion, and desperation, Samuel took off running as fast he could.

He heard another gunshot as shotgun pellets struck the back of the wagon. He looked back and saw an Indian in pursuit. In his right hand he held a hatchet, and he moved with amazing quickness. Moments later, the wagon broke free of the harness, splintering into pieces and launching dark red cranberries across the snowy forest floor. Samuel looked back again and saw that his pursuer had been struck by the wooden debris of the wagon. He felt a trace of hope before it was extinguished by a wave of despair.

Behind the now hindered pursuer, he saw his father on his knees. Clutching his father's hair was the gaunt faced Indian with the disfigured nose. With a large knife that glinted in the scattered sunlight, the man tore off his father's scalp.

Samuel forgot everything. Where he was. Why he was running. What he was running from. He felt only emptiness as if the earth and sky had melted together forming a bubble of nothingness.

Samuel was brought back to reality by the sight of a hatchet striking the tree in front of him, just missing the back of his head.

He ran harder now, desperate to get away. He continued running behind the oxen who started pulling away. Samuel didn't even know if the Indian was still pursuing him. But then, just a few feet ahead, the road appeared. There was a wagon on the road!

"Help! Help!" Samuel yelled. "Help! Get your guns!"

Samuel stepped out onto the muddy road waving his arms. Within a few seconds three men came rushing from the wagon, each of them with a musket in hand. One of the men he recognized as his neighbor, Mr. Maxfield. "I'm being chased by Indians. They scalped..." Samuel choked on his breath.

Mrs. Maxfield rushed to Samuel's side putting her arm around him and guiding him to the opposite side of their wagon. Mr. Maxfield and the two other men moved down the road in the direction Samuel had come, each of them with their muskets ready to fire. Willie, the neighbor boy, settled the frantic oxen.

A few seconds passed. Then a few more. The men looked into the wooded area, but there was nothing. There was no one.

"He's not hurt," Mrs. Maxfield said as she looked him over for injuries. "Just real startled."

The men returned to the wagon. "They're gone. There's no one coming. Whoever was chasing you has gone back into the woods."

Samuel's whole body convulsed, his teeth chattered, and his face was streaked with tears and snot. He cried out loudly, wailing like a baby.

Mrs. Maxfield embraced him, putting her arms tight around his back, and just let him cry.

Chapter 16

WasabishkiMakwa
Bayfield, Wisconsin
Iskigamizige-giizis
(Bayfield, Wisconsin, April 1862)

A thick, yellow mud covered the streets of Bayfield. Carriages moved slowly through the sludge, many getting stuck, forcing their drivers to dig their wheels out while their passengers stepped out cautiously to continue their journey on foot. Waabi found it humorous to watch young ladies in their hoop skirts and prim hats step around cloudy puddles only to land on a spot of sinking mud. The whole town, Waabi thought, was strange and contradicted the natural order of things. Why would people build an unmovable station sealed off from the lakes, lands, and forests that sustained them?

Nevertheless, this had become Waabi's new reality, all of it coming so quickly after the treaty was signed a few years prior. Waabi brought the supplies he purchased on the island to his grandmother and cousins at Red Cliff, but stayed with them for only two days before departing again. He told Nokomis, and his cousins, who continued traditional gathering and hunting practices, that he may have found a new way to hunt for what they needed. They did not ask questions, instead they took a moment to smoke tobacco as an offering to the manidoog.

Walking along the boardwalk, avoiding looks from nervous white residents, Waabi saw a window with the words *Lake Superior Mining Company* painted in large white lettering. Looking at the business card between his thumb and index finger, he knew that it was his destination. Hesitantly, he opened the door and poked his head in before stepping completely inside. The office was small, only about the size of a wigwam, with a desk on each side. Papers, folders, envelopes, and pencils covered the brown wooden desks, but their chairs were empty.

On top of one of the desks, Waabi noticed a jagged gray rock that twinkled with speckles of a metallic reddish brown. The rock seemed alive with freckles of dancing light reflecting the natural sunshine that came in through the window. It was copper, Waabi realized. Moments later, he heard the sound of splashing water and a man came out of the door in the back of the office wiping his hands on a towel.

They regarded each other.

The man was slim, middle-aged, with a full beard, spectacles, and a thinning head of black hair. He wore a buttoned blue vest, belt, and trousers. "Good day," he said with only the hint of a smile. "You're from Red Cliff?"

"Boozhoo," Waabi said. "I am."

"And you speak English, then?" the man said.

Waabi nodded, feeling unsure of himself in a city office. He held out the business card. "The trader at La Pointe said you were looking for laborers. He said you would pay."

The man dropped the towel from his hands onto the corner of his desk and then spun around and lowered himself onto his chair. Without responding he started sorting through papers until he found the one he was looking for. "Ah ha!" he said, as he pulled it from the stack.

"Are you the man on the card? Are you... Mendenhall?"

The man's yellow teeth showed as he looked up at Waabi. "Indeed. And you are?"

"I am called WasabishkiMakwa, but most call me Waabi."

"Well you're in luck, Waabi," Mendenhall said, wasting no time. "I *am* looking for laborers. Especially men of your..." he paused, looking Waabi up and down, "caliber. It's fifty cents a day, with your lunch included, Monday through Saturday. You just show up at the docks each morning, 6am—around sunrise—and a keel boat will take you out to the work site. You understand?"

Waabi thought for a moment, surprised by the ease and quickness of the arrangement. He didn't want to give up his way of life, and the way of life of his father and ancestors. He didn't want to join the prison of daily labor in the white man's world. But the annuities were nothing more than bones that had already been picked clean, and the furs, what could still be gathered, had lost almost all value. Though he continued to fish and hunt and gather, it was only just enough to keep from starving.

Mendenhall leaned forward, sliding the document he had found earlier forward on the desk. "Just sign here," he said, pointing to a solid line on the bottom of the page.

With a silent lament, Waabi grabbed the pencil and wrote his name on the line.

"Very good," Mendenhall said leaning back in his chair. "Tomorrow morning. Bayfield docks. Sunrise, no later."

Waabi nodded politely and turned to leave, feeling his stomach churn with apprehension.

"Don't worry, young man," Mendenhall said. "It's good work and you won't be the only Indian out there."

Waabi stopped and turned his head to his new employer. "I'll be there at sunrise," he said and continued out the door.

The keel boat took Waabi and seven other men to a small, uninhabited island northwest of Mooningwanekaaning-minis. The men spoke fast and had accents that made them difficult to understand, but they said little to Waabi besides the casual introductions. One of them was Ojibwe—a Christian named Dewe'igan who said he lived at the Bad River Reservation.

"Is mining worth the money?" Waabi asked him as the boat cut smoothly through the dark blue waters of Gichigami.

Dewe'igan just shrugged, a look of somber acceptance on his face.

When they arrived on the island, the men unloaded their heavy equipment and climbed the craggy, cliff-lined beach to a spot on top of a low bluff. There, they walked to a small wooden structure that stood above a hole in the rock. Waabi was handed a hard round hat that was scuffed and dirty. On the brim was a half-melted candle. He was also given a wooden-handled metal tool with a sharp point on each end of its curved head.

"That's a pickaxe," the red-haired foreman explained. "Once we're down there, you'll use it to strike the walls of the cave, breaking loose the minerals and copper."

Waabi nodded and followed the men through the hole in the rock and down a set of moving steps. The light from the surface slowly faded away until it was nothing more than a dot, like the moon on a starless night. Finally landing at the bottom of the hole, the men lit the candles on top of their hats revealing a narrow, dusty space littered with rock fragments. The air was cool and wet and had a pungent, earthy smell.

"Now we dig," the foreman said to Waabi, his face completely obscured by the shadow cast by the brim of his hat. "Strike the rock here," he said, pointing to a jagged crack in the wall. "The other Indian will load the debris into a bin to be taken up the man car. When you get tired, you can switch positions with each other. Understand?"

"Yes," Waabi said, though he felt quite uncertain of himself.

"Good. If you see any copper—anything shiny at all—try to hammer around it so that the copper stays in one piece." The foreman paused. "There'll be a break for lunch."

The foreman departed, his lighted head bobbing like a glowing frog in the darkness. Waabi turned and faced the rock as he began to hear echoing thuds of metal striking rock from other corners of the cave.

"Time to begin," Dewe'igan said. "There are no herbs or traditions down here. No Mide. Only you, the rock, and the darkness."

Dewe'gian's words felt cold and harsh.

Waabi turned to face the rock, breathed in the cool air, drew back, and swung forward. The metal point landed hard causing an insignificant dent in the rock wall. He drew back and swung again, and again, and again, each time removing only bits and pieces of rock. Before long his hands became sore and his arms grew heavy and weak. He paused to take deep breaths, almost choking on the thick, dusty air. The light from his candle dimmed and darkness seemed even more suffocating than the dust. Waabi felt afraid as if he were trapped by a winter storm with no hope for escape. He coughed between each swing of the pickaxe, feeling lost in the dust and darkness.

Waabi bent over in a fit of coughing. Dewe'igan placed his hand on Waabi's back, which helped his racing heartbeat to settle.

148

After a few moments, Dewe'igan relit the candle on Waabi's hat. "It takes some getting used to," he said in English, then took Waabi's pickaxe and continued the work of striking the unshakable wall.

Waabi regained his composure and then started to pick up the loose pieces of rock and load them into the bin. When it was full, two other men pushed it toward the moving steps where it was loaded and then began moving slowly up toward the distant dot of light at the surface. Waabi watched for a moment, in curious awe, and he thought of Agnes, wondering where she was and what she might be doing. Then, as he watched the heavy bin slowly rise toward the surface, he recalled the words of a poem in the book she gave him: "Eternity lies in bottomless reservoirs... its buckets are rising forever and ever, They pour and they pour and they exhale away."

Is this Eternity?

A dull rain landed softly on Waabi's head as he walked back to the reservation after one of the countless days in the mine. His long hair became heavy and wet, sticking to his cheeks and neck. His hands bled and his back ached. He had never felt such exhaustion—such shame.

Day after day he repeated the same routine until spring became summer and summer became nothing. He spent most of it in the dark, hammering at the rocks in the bottom of a pit. His lungs became weak and his hands calloused.

As he continued to walk through the light rain, a few coins jingled in his pocket acting as a reminder of his labor. He scooped them out and examined them in his palm. The penny was made of copper and had the head of a Indian on its surface. How strange, he thought, to take the very same copper he cut from the rock and to place upon it the image of a Native. While the penny and its Indian head had value, he did not.

Returning home Waabi found Nokomis alone in the summer lodge cooking wild rice soup over the fire.

"Boozhoo, young one," she said as she stirred the thick broth with one continuous stroke.

"Where are my cousins?" Waabi asked. "Have they gone to another lodge for singing and storytelling?"

Nokomis, in a tender way, motioned for Waabi to sit beside her on a folded red blanket. Waabi did and then he waited patiently as she scooped up a bowl of steaming soup and handed it to him.

"Miigwech, Nokomis."

Blowing on it first, Waabi took a spoonful in his mouth, enjoying its comforting warmth, its creamy texture, and its rich flavor. Like a thick bear-skin robe it soothed Waabi's cold, tired body.

"Your cousins, Star and White Cloud have gone away," Nokomis said, her expression plain.

"I do not understand. Have they gone to hunt? When will they return?"

Seated cross-legged and hunched, Nokomis repositioned herself away from the iron kettle of steaming soup and toward her grandson. "They became tired of life on the reservation. They could no longer live like otters in a small pond. They want to live like sturgeon in a great lake."

Waabi closed his eyes and leaned his head back, accepting the sudden blow.

"You are hurt," Nokomis said, seeing her grandson's response. "You live with anger that you carry within a warrior's heart."

Waabi nodded and opened his eyes. He was looking, unblinking, at his grandmother. For a moment he admired her golden-brown Ojibwe eyes and wondered what the world looked like the first time she opened them generations earlier. "Enya'," he said faintly.

"You have lost your mother, your father, your aunt and uncle, and now your cousins have gone away. You have lost the way of your ancestors, too. Everything has been taken from you. Everything has been taken from us."

A tear formed in Waabi's eye and rolled down his cheek, landing in his bowl of soup. He wiped his face and held the soup tighter to his chest.

"Do you know of..." Nokomis paused, as her eyes turned to the ground. "Wiindigo?" she finally said.

Waabi shook his head, "Gawiin."

Nokomis arched her back and looked toward the top of the lodge. She took a deep, satisfying breath and brought her head and eyes back down, level with Waabi. Her falling jowls and sunken eyes gave her a bleak, grim appearance. "The Wiindigo is a tall, hideous monster with rotting purple flesh that hangs loosely from its dry, hard bones. He lives deep within the collective dreams of our people, waiting to come out and feast upon our weakness and fear. When he does, his shadow is so large it blocks out the sun and his breath is so ghastly it causes disease and death. He haunts the Ojibwe from one generation to the next. First he came as hunger. Then he came as disease. Then he came as war. Now he comes as the white man—the one who takes our land, our way of living, and our lifeblood."

Waabi sat silently, his mind fully engrossed in the imagery of the story.

Nokomis paused to sip some water. She held the wooden cup in both her hands with her head down. Gray streaks of hair bunched on the crown of her head. She continued: "One day, an Ojibwe named Weniboozhoo was called upon to kill the Wiindigo. He failed many times, but each time he learned from his failure. He loved his people—he loved the Anishinaabe—so much that he kept trying, each time a little more successful. But the people did not love Weniboozhoo back, and they stopped telling his stories. Because of this, Weniboozhoo got into a canoe with his grandmother and paddled away. That is why our people suffer. Our protector departed long ago and the Wiindigo has returned, stronger and more devilish than ever. That is why our people grow sick and die and why our way of living is being strangled. Wiindigo is alive and well."

Waabi sat there silently, keeping his hands on his bowl of soup. He didn't know how to respond.

"You are in pain," Waabi's grandmother said, reaching out her aged hand. "You have been since you were a boy, when your father left for the spirit world. But you are no longer a boy."

Waabi looked up at his grandmother. She appeared to be at peace, like a dog bathing in the sun. "What do you mean, Nokomis? How can I ever overcome this pain and loss?"

"You have served your family well," she said, "but there is no one here left for you to care for. Meanwhile the Wiindigo continues to feast on your people. There is a place for you, beyond the island, beyond this reservation, where you can challenge the pain in your heart, face your own spirit, and serve your people well."

Waabi first thought of Agnes, but too many years had passed. Certainly, she had started her own family by now. Then he recalled Chibines' plan to join the army. This could be the opportunity his grandmother spoke of. "Do you wish me make revenge for my father's death?" he asked. "Do you wish me to fight in battle like our ancestors?"

Nokomis answered with a curious smile. "You see only what is in front of you," she said. "You may wish to seek revenge, but you will not find it. The Wiindigo knows revenge and he feasts upon it like a cannibal. You must keep your heart open, even in the battle for your life. You must go armored with mino-bimaadiziwin, the life-giving way of our ancestors. It will restore you and give you power. Use it to protect, not to destroy."

Waabi nodded, looking at his grandmother with reverence and awe. Putting down his bowl he examined his hands. They were calloused and scarred from months in the mine. They looked dirty and hard and felt coarse to the touch. His heart sank and he felt a lump in his throat. Looking at his dear grandmother, he knew the time had come for him to leave the reservation and with it, his homeland—to walk away from the place where he was born and where his mother lay. He didn't know if he would ever return.

Chapter 17

Samuel
Blue Earth County
Summer 1861

For two months after their father's death Thomas wouldn't speak to Samuel. He wouldn't even look at him.

"What happened out there? How could you..." Thomas finally said, speaking just above a whisper. "How could you let Pa get killed?"

The question filled Samuel with shame as he turned his head, barely able to look his brother in the eye. Behind Thomas, as they sat side by side outside the homestead, the sun was setting over the trees spreading an array of orange and yellow light across the family's freshly plowed field.

"It happened so quick, Thomas. I..."

"You ran! You ran like a coward while Pa got scalped."

Samuel closed his eyes tight, feeling the deep pain and grief of the moment. Ever since their father's death sorrow was ever-present. Despite it all, the family decided to press on with plans to plant grow crops and build a life for themselves in Minnesota.

"You brought us out here," Thomas continued. "You brought us to Minnesota and said life would be better. But then... Then you just let Pa die and ran away instead of defending him!"

"It wasn't my fault!" Samuel answered quickly. "I told Pa to let go of the gun, to give up the cranberries. I told him to let the Indians have what they wanted. But he didn't listen. He just told me to run. He TOLD me to run, Thomas."

Thomas shook his head demonstratively. "No. No. I don't believe you. You hated Pa. You hated that he liked me more than you, so you let him die." Thomas glared hard at Samuel, his jaw clenched, his cloudy eyes lined in red. "You wanted him to die!"

153

"No, Thomas..." Samuel breathed heavy, almost sobbing.

Thomas shook his head again and got up with a flurry. As he walked away he said, "I'll never forgive you for this."

The Indians left Randolph's body where it fell. It was a gruesome sight—bloody scalp exposed, gunshot to the leg, hatchet wound to the chest. Most of the snow around him had melted from the warmth of his spewing blood. The snow that remained was a dark, almost rust colored brown. "He bled out quickly," the coroner assured Alexandra. "It was probably painless."

The burial was simple. Only the Maxfields and a few other neighbors showed up. They buried him right there on the property, about a quarter mile from the homestead. Isabel was old enough to know that their father wasn't coming back, but Edward and Eva had many questions, none of which could be answered with any real honesty. Alexandra remained practical, tending to daily chores, writing letters back home, and occupying her mind with the responsibilities of taking care of the family. But she wore her sorrow on her face which was in a permanent state of puffy redness. She never talked about Randolph's death and Samuel wasn't sure if she blamed him the same way Thomas did. The only time she even acknowledged his death out loud was when she would ask about the depredations claim. According to the Sioux treaty, any citizen that received injury or property loss because the actions of Indians, was entitled to, as the wording went, "full compensation."

"No, Ma," was Samuel's practiced response. "Compensation hasn't been made." Then she would return to whatever chore she was doing as if life were normal.

Samuel knew why the claim wasn't paid, and he was sure his mother knew why, too. War had broken out in the United States. Civil War. News of it in the paper was unrelenting. First was the defeat at Fort Sumter, then President Lincoln called for the enlistment of 75,000 troops. As spring turned to summer, the news only got worse and more calls were made for troops, including several regiments in Minnesota.

"I think I'll join the Union Army," Thomas told Samuel one hot July afternoon as the two of them were checking for weeds in the cornfield.

Thomas had spoken to Samuel so little since the death of their father that the sound of his voice startled Samuel. What was more startling were the words that he spoke.

"You can't be serious," Samuel said, standing up from his crouched position in the dirt.

"But I am serious. 'Course I'm serious."

"You're only fifteen years old. And the army won't take someone with your..."

"My what!" Thomas said looking at Samuel with hard, narrow eyes. He'd changed over the past few months. He no longer joked or laughed or acted at all like he had before their father's death. "My asthma? You think they won't take me because of my asthma?"

"Yes, exactly, Thomas. You can't join the army because of your asthma."

"That won't matter," Thomas said. "They're just looking for soldiers. They won't ask me how old I am and they don't have to find out about the asthma."

Samuel stopped to bend down and pull a tall, prickly weed. Grabbing the stem carefully he pulled with just enough strength to remove the roots and not tear the base. "Even so, why?" Samuel said as he pounded the roots against the ground to loosen the dirt. "Why would you want to leave us and risk your life out there? You might just get yourself killed."

"What, like Pa?" Thomas replied.

A cloud covered the sun casting a cool dark shadow over the field as Samuel accepted the blow his brother just delivered to his gut. Samuel did not want to talk about Pa. "Boys who go to war don't come back," he finally said. "And besides, we got enough problems of our own trying to manage this place."

Samuel bent down to pull another weed. It looked almost like a flower with small white petals and vibrant, green leaves, but he remembered his mother telling him, "Anything that wasn't planted should be picked." Samuel struggled to pull it out by the root. Blood

155

rushed to his forehead as he dug his fingers into the dry dirt and pulled hard. "Ouch," he said, putting his hand to his mouth after getting pricked by a thorn. Frustration bubbled in his chest. He brought his hand back down to continue digging at the roots. He could feel the dry dirt under his finger nails and no matter how he tried he could not get a grip on the flowery weed.

"Ahh!" he yelled out suddenly. "Are you just going to stand there?" he said, turning to Thomas. "And why are we doing this anyway? It should be Isabel's and Edward's job. We've got a fence to build and more land to till."

Thomas stared at Samuel, appearing detached from their task. "You know what, you can do this all by yourself," he said dropping the weeds he had picked and walking away with long, purposeful strides.

Samuel took a few deep breaths. He could feel his blood pulsing in his neck and forehead. He lowered his head, shielding it from the hot summer sun and leaned forward on his hands and knees saying quietly, "Smile O voluptuous coolbreathed earth!" quoting *Leaves of Grass*.

Just then a breeze picked up dirt as it swept through the waist-high cornstalks and a cloud of dust swirled overhead.

Summer passed quickly—quietly. The harvest was better than Samuel expected. Even without much knowledge about tending big plots of land, they grew enough corn, beans, and potatoes to last the winter with a surplus to sell at market. Fall breezes ushered in changing colors and colder temperatures. Winter descended on the landscape like a vise that couldn't be moved or loosened. The creek stopped flowing, the ground froze hard as rock, and the air became still and empty without so much as a bird crossing overhead. The cold days went by in quietness and solitude for Samuel, like it did for the rest of the family. Thomas said almost nothing and just kept to himself as each day collided with another, and another. Samuel couldn't help feeling guilty, that it was his fault Thomas had turned so bitter toward him. That it was his fault their father was killed. It was true, he brought them to Minnesota and he insisted they go to town with the cranberries.

Throughout the winter there were occasional visits from hungry Indians. Samuel wished he could turn them away, but his mother knew better. "Do you want to get us all killed, too?" she said one cold winter morning as a few blanket-covered Dakota approached. "We'll just give them some food and let them be on their way. The Indians are not long for this world, but my children will be." That hurt Samuel immensely to know that even his mother blamed him.

Spring arrived and Samuel set about his work with vigor and pent up energy. He cleaned out the stove, repaired the outbuildings, cleared the path to the creek, picked up sticks and debris from the field, re-dug the drainage ditch, and, when the ground was soft enough, began the plowing. He knew he needed to get a head start if they were to pay off the debts they took on, not to mention the gifts they'd accepted from their neighbors. He also wanted to expand the farm by bringing chickens, goats, and horses—something that his father had envisioned. The work would be something he could be proud of, but more importantly it was something to occupy his mind—to hide from his pain, anger, and shame. It was the least he could do since he couldn't bring Pa back.

A string of wet days followed by warmer than average temperatures made plowing easy as Samuel took to work one day in late April. The metal point of the plow dug in, readily moving the rich, black dirt to the side like a canoe through water. Samuel kept his arms raised leaning on the handles while watching his line carefully and urging the ox forward. "Giddup! Giddup!" he commanded. The work was pleasing and he enjoyed the feel of sweat on his brow and the softness of the earth beneath his feet. It was such a welcome break from the endless monotony of chopping wood over the long winter months. He felt like he was back in Vermont, pushing logs through the mill pond.

"Whoa," Samuel said, bringing the single ox to a halt so he could take a break and look up at the blue sky. He wiped his forehead and then turned around to look for Thomas. It was nearly midmorning, and he had expected Thomas to be out tilling the fallow field like he'd been asked. Looking back at the house he saw his mother, along with little Eva, raking the garden.

"Ma," he said, cupping his hands around his mouth. "Where is Thomas? He's supposed to be out tilling this field."

"He didn't tell you?" his mother said, straightening up and leaning against her rake. "He went into town."

"By himself? What for? How's he getting there—he didn't take the wagon."

Alexandra shook her head causing the brim of her white bonnet to wave back and forth. "He didn't say what for. He said he'd be taking a ride into town."

Samuel tilted his head and turned back to the plow. Thomas had never gone into town by himself before. He couldn't imagine what for. "Giddup," Samuel said, pushing the ox forward to continue plowing. An uneasiness settled over him.

That evening while Samuel was finishing up with the plowing, Thomas came walking out from the path through the trees. When Samuel saw him, his heart sank. Thomas was dressed in a gold buttoned navy blue wool coat and sky blue trousers with a forage cap on his head and a bright smile on his face. He strode forward, excited as a dog at dinner time and just as naive.

Samuel unhitched the plow and brought the ox back toward the barn pretending he hadn't noticed Thomas. He seethed, worried that Thomas would lose his life but also angry that he had gone and enlisted without his permission.

"Well, Samuel. What do you think?" Thomas said, standing with his hands on hips at the entrance of the ox barn.

For a moment, Samuel ignored him while he led the ox into its pen, removed its halter and closed the gate. He turned his head toward Thomas. "I think you're a fool. I think you'll die out there."

Thomas rolled his eyes. "I thought you'd say that. But you lost the right to tell me what I can and can't do a long time ago."

Samuel didn't answer. He could feel Thomas glaring at him, waiting for a response as he hung up the halter and then picked up a pail of water which he set down inside the pen.

"I wanna protect you," Samuel finally said. "I'm your big brother."

"Ha!" Thomas bent over in feigned shock. "You still think you can protect me, after what happened? After what you did?"

Samuel didn't respond. He couldn't.

"Besides," Thomas said, lightening his tone. "They're not sending me south. They said they're going to keep me here at Fort Snelling. I won't be in any battles. I probably won't ever have to shoot a gun."

"And what about the farm? What about the family?"

Thomas snickered. "None of that matters now, does it?"

Samuel stared at his little brother, baffled by the sight of him in Union blue. "Of course it matters, Thomas. We can still make this work. We can still have the future that Pa wanted."

Thomas just shook his head, hands still on hips. "I'll send money home," he said. "And I'll never be in danger. I might even learn some discipline. You and Ma can use the money for supplies to make the farming easier. Maybe get some new clothes; maybe pay to send Isabel and Edward to school? It'll help, just not the way you thought."

Samuel grabbed a towel and wiped the dirt from his hands thinking hard about what he ought to say next. "You know I loved Pa, too. I didn't want that to happen. I might have been jealous sometimes about your relationship with him, but I never, never wanted to lose him. And now...now you think you can just join the army and make things all right? It's true, Pa made life easy for you and now you think you can do what you want. But the fact is that Pa ain't here and you're going to have a hard time in the army having people tell you what to do and how to do it."

As the words left his mouth, Samuel felt a lump in his throat that he couldn't swallow. Standing there, he waited, anxiously, for his little brother's response, the rustling noise of the oxen eating hay filling the silent gap between them. Behind Thomas, the orange glow of twilight framed his still boy-like figure.

"You never did think too much of me, did you?" Thomas scoffed. "And now you still think you know what I am and ain't capable of?"

"No, that's... that's not it. I love you, Thomas. You're my brother. I just think you're making the wrong choice for the wrong reasons. And I think your goin' to regret it."

Thomas hardened his face. "You don't love me. And you

sure as hell can't protect me. I'm joining the army no matter what you think. I might even kill some Indians while I'm at it."

Thomas' words were like a knife to the heart—like a wound ripped open. Samuel felt the life pouring out of him, but he didn't want Thomas to see how much his words hurt—how deep they cut. "Go then!" he said, with all the anger and shame he had built up inside of him. "We don't need you here, we never did."

As Samuel was about to march past Thomas, he stopped and leaned forward until their faces were inches apart. "This is more than a risk, you fool. It's a lot more than a risk. It's a God damn death sentence."

Samuel then walked on, out of the barn. Holding back tears of fear, shame, and anger, he said to himself, "I was trying to give us all a better life. I was trying"

"Is that it then?" Thomas called as Samuel faded into the twilight.

Samuel stopped and turned. "Don't expect me to say goodbye."

Three days later, early in the morning while there was still frost on the grass, the family gathered outside the homestead to see Thomas off. With a hug and a kiss for Alexandra, Isabel, and Eva, and a firm salute from Edward, Thomas slung his haversack over his shoulder and took one last look at Samuel. A cold, expressionless stare was all Samuel offered. The same was all he got in return. Thomas did an exaggerated about face and then began his walk across the fallow field of unplowed dirt toward the trees. "Goodbye! Be safe!" Isabel yelled, with tears streaming down her face. When Thomas reached the tree line he turned around and gave one last wave before disappearing down the shadowy path. As Alexandra returned to the cabin, she gave Samuel a disapproving glare and mouthed the words, "We'll talk later."

That afternoon, while Samuel was planking wood, he kept shaving too much which forced him to start over again and again. Then, while repairing holes in the ox barn, he missed the nail and hammered his thumb. Later, while digging a stump out of the ground, Samuel let out his pent up frustration by hacking at the roots with his spade like it was a demon he had to kill. He stabbed and dug and then pulled the shovel back with all his strength to pry it free from the ground. No matter how hard he pulled he could not get the stump loose. With one final gasp, Samuel used all his weight, all his strength, to pull back at the stump when the metal tip of the spade broke free of the handle sending Samuel backwards to the ground where he landed with a thump. Lying there, enduring the sudden pain, he wished he was back in the mill pond in Vermont sorting logs. It was a simple life but at the time he knew of no other. To him, back then, Minnesota wasn't even a word let alone a place. He should have never taken that flyer.

As he lay there, never wanting to move again, he turned his head to the side and there, like it were happening all over again, he saw his father with his back to him, on his knees. In front of his father was the vile Indian, his left hand holding his father's head by the hair and his right hand drawn back ready to bring forward the hatchet. "No!" Samuel yelled, stretching out his hand, but the image faded away as Samuel's father fell like a heap to the dry earth.

That evening at dinner no one said much. Afterward, there were no night time stories or conversations. Once Isabel, Edward, and Eva were put to bed, Alexandra sat across from Samuel at the table with only the light of a candle between them.

"You're angry," she said, the dim light of the candle revealing the deep, permanent lines on her forehead. Much of her red hair had dulled or whitened, her eyes were sunken, and her skin was creased. "I'm angry, too, Samuel. And tired. God, I'm tired. But you know I couldn't stop him from joining the army."

"Yes you could..."

She interrupted Samuel. "When he said he was heading into to town, I didn't know he was going to enlist. He never mentioned it. He never said a word."

Samuel felt the sudden weight of shame, remembering what Thomas had told him almost a year earlier.

"But you could have stopped him. You could have told him to return that uniform and cancel his enlistment."

"He's too headstrong," Alexandra said, raising her voice for a moment before realizing she needed to speak quietly while the children slept. "He's too headstrong, Samuel. Just like you. I couldn't stop him any more than I could stop the wind from blowing."

Samuel shook his head, realizing the truth of it and feeling guilty for not having stopped him himself.

Silence passed between them. It was so quiet, the flame of the candle could almost be heard as it consumed the wick.

"Ma?" Samuel said as if he were still a boy instead of a man now of eighteen years.

"Yes?"

"I still feel like I like I need to protect him," he said. "He's still so young and he has no idea what he's getting into."

"Do you?" she asked, suggesting Samuel was the same way, not knowing what he was getting into.

Samuel let out a quick exhale, realizing the irony of the question. "No, I don't, do I."

Samuel's mother reached her hand out and placed it over his as she looked over the flame of the candle at her eldest son. "I am angry. I was angry. But, I've had time to grieve now. I've had time to think. Listen to me carefully. I want you to know that it wasn't your fault. It wasn't your fault, Samuel."

Samuel was struck with a wave of relief and pain as he lowered his head and squeezed his eyes tight enduring the sudden emotion. He took several deep breaths, his chest convulsing. "I'm sorry," he said, looking back up at his mother.

"It's all right, it's all right," she answered, stroking the back of Samuel's hand. "You couldn't have prevented what happened."

"Thank you, thank you for saying that," Samuel said through heavy breaths. He took a moment, collecting himself. "But what about Thomas?"

"What about him? He's made his choice."

"He hates me," Samuel said plainly. "And I didn't leave him much choice the way I behaved. The way I just yelled at him. I don't want to leave it like that. I don't want to leave him out there on his own."

"What are you saying?

"I think... I think I have to join too." Samuel said, forming the idea for the first time as the words left his mouth.

His mother pulled her hands back. She opened her mouth to speak, but instead looked away.

"I have to," Samuel said. "If I join now, I'll be stationed here, with him. I couldn't protect Pa but I can still protect Thomas. And maybe... maybe he'll stop hating me."

"And leave us? Just like Thomas did? How will we raise any crops without you? How will *we* survive?"

Samuel nodded. "You're right, but... But I think I have to." Samuel brought a hand over his face, closing his eyes tight and rubbing his temples and forehead. As he brought his hand down and opened his eyes he said, "It won't be long, Ma. A year most. Mr. Maxfield can help you harvest what's already been planted and if we're not back by spring, I'm sure he and his family will help out just like they've already been. It can work and everything will be better again when we get back."

Alexandra looked at Samuel, her head tilted, eyes tired but kind. "I won't stop you Samuel. Same way I didn't stop Thomas after he made his decision," she said. "It'll be hard without you, but if you think that's what you have to do, then that's what you have to do. I don't want you to live feeling like you let Thomas down."

"I know it will be hard on you, Ma. I know it'll be hard on all of you, but I think I have to. I really think it's what I have to do."

The dim light of the candle was reflected in Alexandra's watery eyes as a tear rolled down her cheek. She blinked and two more tears fell. "All right," she said. "I can take care of your younger siblings while you're away and the neighbors will help me with the farm, I'm sure of it. I know you're hurting and I know how much you love your brother. I know how much you want him to be safe and happy—how much you want all of us to be safe and happy. You've always been so considerate and thoughtful, even since you were a little boy." She smiled at the thought as she brought her hand to her face to wipe away the tears.

Samuel laid out an open hand on the table. Recognizing the gesture, Samuel's mother dropped her hand in his palm. He squeezed gently and said, "I'm sorry things happened this way, Ma."

"I know you're sorry, Samuel," she said. "I know."

Chapter 18

WasabishkiMakwa
Gaa-mitaawangaagamaag / Gaagaagiwigwani-ziibi
Abitaa-niibino-giizis
(Sandy Lake / Crow Wing River, July 1862)

As Waabi walked through the scattered sunlight of the familiar wooded terrain, he felt the firmness of each step against the softness of the forest floor. The early morning summer dew that clung to the sage leaves soaked his torn and muddied moccasins and spread cold water up the tattered hems of his pant legs. Without the benefit of a canoe, he was guided by a natural bearing ingrained in his lifeblood from years of living off the land and centuries of ancestral heritage. His feet hurt and his stomach rumbled, but he thought only of his father who had done nothing to deserve the bitter, lonely death he experienced merely by following the orders of the American government. His father, who died when he was still just a boy. His father, who was not here now to give him wisdom or direction.

Waabi arrived at Gaa-mitaawangaagamaag after a five-day journey from Miskwaabikaang. It was not his final destination. He sought Gaagaagiwigwani-ziibi where it intersected with Misi-ziibi, since he knew this was the nearest agency that was enlisting Indians for the white man's war. It was also the place that Agnes had left to—a place called Crow Wing. But that is not what propelled him forward. Agnes was an infatuation of childhood remaining only in the back of his mind, perhaps even the longings of his heart. But at the front of his mind were grief, anger, and a desire to find himself.

The lake was crystal clear and shone with a brightness that forced Waabi to shield his eyes. Walking north and west along the shore while sidestepping moss-covered birch trees that reached toward the clear blue sky, he found a camp of scattered summer lodges. The people there, about half a dozen families, were drying meat, scraping furs, and resting in the sprinkled sunshine.

"Boozhoo, I am WasabishkiMakwa," he said, meeting a camp of Ojibwe who lived near the lake. "You may call me Waabi." He then asked his fellow Ojibwe where he might find the burial location of those who perished at the annuity incident half a generation earlier. They responded with looks of despair, as if their loved ones were killed only days earlier. "We will show you," one of the clansmen said, "but you must take your mourning elsewhere."

"Where shall I mourn?" Waabi asked with the sincerity of a child.

The man shook his head. "Our fallen kin were not shown the spirit path. We do not know where they shall be mourned. We know only they are not here."

Waabi followed the man, an elder who wore the traditional clothing of leggings and breechcloth, to a small hill on the north end of the lake. It was treeless, covered in crimson clovers and lush green grass. The elder pointed, looked Waabi in the eyes, said nothing and walked away.

Emotionless, Waabi stood there admiring the pristine look of the mound. After a few silent moments, he felt a rush of sadness and fell to his knees as if struck by a blow to the gut. Short of breath he gasped for air and felt a heaviness in his stomach. Reaching out to steady himself Waabi began to sob. He remained there for a close to a minute, hunched over and weeping. Slowly, he regained his breath and raised his head from the ground. In his hands he clung to his father's bandolier bag, admiring its beautiful floral design and remembering the day his father had given it to him—the day his father had departed, never to come back.

Waabi reached in the bag and removed a pinch of tobacco. He stood now, cleared his eyes and steadied his breath, then released the offering of tobacco, watching as a light gust spread the dry leaves across the mound. With the story of the Wiindigo still fresh in his mind, Waabi slung his bandolier bag over his shoulder and began walking southwest.

It had been eight days since Waabi left his grandmother at Miskwaabikaang and three since he laid a pinch of tobacco at the mound near Sandy Lake where his father was buried. In that time, the Halfway Summer Moon had become the Ricing Moon. Without a canoe to traverse the lake speckled landscape he had grown tired from long treks around marshes and inlets. He survived on small rations of rice and berries and drank lake water he boiled every night. He did not carry a lodge and slept under the infinite night sky, swatting at mosquitoes that landed on his arms and cheeks. Though the journey was unpleasant and lonely he felt like he had a purpose, something he hadn't felt since his father's death.

When Waabi finally reached the Misi-ziibi, where the Upper Mississippi Bands of Ojibwe resided and the great Bagone-giizhig reigned, he knew he was close. He needed only to follow the banks of the river south until it met with the Gaagaagiwigwani-ziibi. His feet were soft from days of constant wetness, and they had become torn and blistered. Each step was agony, forcing him to walk in different manners, alternating placing pressure on one part of his foot and then another. Still, he moved forward admiring the lush green landscape, the powerful flowing river, and the large, shade-giving oak and elm trees. Trekking over the land, with its abundance of flowing rivers, deep lakes, and rich hunting grounds, he understood why his ancestors forced their enemies, the Naadowens, to the south and claimed the territory for themselves.

As the sun reached its apex on a warm afternoon, Waabi discovered what could only be the place known to the whites as the Crow Wing Agency. In a clearing on the west bank of the Misi-ziibi was a row of freshly painted wood-frame buildings with slanted roofs. It looked quaint and comfortable, set as it was with the river in the foreground and layers of spruce in the background. To Waabi's surprise, the agency was a flurry of activity. Young Ojibwe men crisscrossed the grounds, most appearing jubilant and care-free. They laughed and shouted and danced like a niimi'idiwin was taking place. Crossing the river in a canoe ferry, Waabi asked the operator, a white-skinned boy who apparently worked for the agency, what was going on.

"They been influenced by spirits. Liquor," the boy said as he casually paddled the canoe across the wide and lazy river.

"Are they here to enlist in the white man's war? I did not expect so many. I did not expect them to be so excited."

"Yea, that's what they're here for," the boy said with a nod. "The excitement... that's just the liquor. And the liquor... that's just a little extra persuasion."

"Persuasion?"

The boy just shrugged his shoulders as the canoe slid gently onto the sandy shore. "Let's just say, I wouldn't risk my life for $13 a month."

Waabi thanked the boy and proceeded to the agency building which was not hard to find because it overflowed with young Ojibwe men and boys who crowded the entrance. Once inside, he stood shoulder to shoulder with those waiting to reach the enlistment table and make their mark. Most, if not all of the Ojibwe alongside Waabi appeared as he did—thin, tired, dirty, and wearing government issued clothing that had long since worn out.

At one end of the crowded room was a bearded white man with a pen and paper laid out on the table before him. The man sat straight-backed with a collared gray shirt that made him appear refined. When each young Ojibwe approached the man, whom Waabi assumed to be a trader, he wrote their name on the paper in front of him, and then pointed to the paper and handed the pen over so the Ojibwe could make their mark. It was not unlike the process of receiving annuities.

Standing next to Waabi, a young man with braided hair and an innocent face took particular notice of him. "How far have you come?" he asked, looking at Waabi's muddy moccasins.

"I have come from Miskwaabekong," Waabi said, speaking his native tongue. "It was an eight-day journey. From where have you come?"

"I am Binishii. I have come from Gayaashko-zaaga'igan, only a half day's walk, and home to the powerful leader Bagone-giizhig."

Waabi offered a look of interest. "Doesn't he wish violence upon the whites?"

"Not violence," Binishii said in an inspired tone. "Retribution. We share a common loss and we seek a common result. Don't you seek retribution?"

Waabi thought for a moment. The loss of his father was no mere coincidence. The loss of his land and his ways of life were done intentionally by the white government. They took everything quickly and willfully. Yes, he thought, he did seek retribution.

"Then why are you here?" Waabi asked in response. "Why join the white man's war instead of joining Bagone-giizhig in a fight against them?"

Waabi was honestly curious. He was drawn by the promise of monthly pay. And he knew he sought some form of revenge, some form of healing. Would killing a white man give him that? Would it matter who he was fighting for?

"I am not here to sign up for the white man's war," Binishii replied with a determined glare. "I'm here to recruit."

Waabi stood there blocking out the commotion around him, curious to know more.

"Don't fight for the white man, fight against him. With Bagone-giizhig's leadership we can reclaim our lands. We can return to our traditional ways of living. We can have the lives our ancestors knew and punish the white man in the process. Will you join us?"

Before Waabi could even consider his response, the door swung open.

All chatter stopped. As if drawn by a single thread, every man turned his head to see who entered. Standing in the doorway was an elder wearing a beaded floral sash along with two eagle feathers that rose high above his farmer's hat. In one hand he held a long-stemmed pipe and in the other he held a leather glove filled with moss and tobacco, a symbol of war.

The man spoke slowly and deliberately. "I am Niskigwun, an elder from Gaa-zagaskwaajimekaag. Many years ago, when my mishoomis was still a warrior, our people defeated our enemy, the Naadowens, at Misi-zaaga'iganing and forced them south onto the prairie. Over the years we have exchanged with the Bwaan times of peace and times of war—sometimes changing as often as the seasons. But now, as land is taken from us just as it is taken from them, we share a common enemy. Sitting before you," he said, speaking of the trader at the enlistment table, "is a representative of our common enemy—a man who gives you poisoned water and paper bills in exchange for your lives. He asks for you to fight for them; for the agents and traders that took your land, your lakes, your language and religion. Some of the elders—they say it is not time to fight. They say a war against the whites is vain, like hunting a bear by going inside his den. But this is not what Taoyateduta of the Bwaan, and his band of Mdewakanton soldiers say. They say the time to fight is now, while the white soldiers fight amongst themselves way far off. And that is why I am here. Our leader, Bagone-giizhig, is ready to fight alongside Taoyateduta and the Bwaan against our common enemy. Do not trade your lives for more broken promises from foreign invaders. Join now with Bagone-giizhig and fight to save your land and your ways of life. Fight for what you have lost— for what has been taken from you. Fight for those who are buried in the ground beneath your feet and who can no longer fight back."

The speech was met with strained silence. Looks of confusion marked the faces of the young Ojibwe. They had come to enlist in one war and were now beckoned to another. Was victory against the whites possible? Could an alliance with the Bwaan really happen? Waabi felt nervous and hot, crowded between two apparent inevitabilities, both so far away from his tender youth.

The trader stood in front of his table to give a response. "I understand their reticence," he said, speaking to Niskigwun, the elder in the doorway. "The days of Indian fighting are over. You are farmers now, living on land that is allotted to you. Your people are now dependent on the United States government. To fight against us would finally destroy your entire race. But if you fight for us, we will train you, give you weapons, give you money—you'll be fighting a just war."

Moments later, one of the men from among the crowd turned and hurled a knife toward the trader's head. The spinning silver blade gashed the trader's right ear before striking the wall behind him and landing with a clink against the floor. The man immediately raised his hands to his ear as droplets of blood spilled out.

As the trader was bent over shouting curses, the man who threw the knife said, "We no longer wish to listen to your lies. Lies that leave our wives widowed and our children orphaned. Never again."

The trader straightened his back, hands still covering his

ear while blood trickled out between his fingers. With his head low and eyes up, he looked with disdain on the gathered Ojibwe. Finally lowering his left hand he gathered his papers and walked quickly through the crowd, past the old messenger, and out the door.

The men and boys gave out a unified cheer, slapping each other on the backs, and whooping with enjoyment.

Niskigwun raised a hand to silence them. Once there was silence, he held his pipe forward. "There is no turning back. That man will go to St. Paul and tell the white officials what happened here. The choice has been made, now you need only smoke from the pipe, dedicating yourselves to the war effort. Who will be the first?"

The man who hurled the knife at the trader walked forward and took the pipe in his hand. The men watched with a sort of patient but frightened awe. Taking his first puff, the crowd finally responded in unified roar, raising their voices and slapping their chests. Waabi did the same, compelled by the energy of the room. The pipe was passed, sealing the fate of every young Ojibwe. Taking his turn on the pipe, after years of heartache, after a lonely and grief-stricken journey, Waabi realized that now it was time to take back what was lost.

Chapter 19

Samuel
Fort Ridgely
August 1862

Standing in the barracks at Fort Ridgely, Samuel admired his navy and sky blue army-issued uniform—a drastic change from his opinion months earlier when he saw his brother Thomas dressed the same. From head to toe he wore a tall shako Albert cap with a short angled bill and head strap, a single-breasted, dark blue wool frock coat, a gray flannel shirt, trousers of sky blue wool, and ankle high boots of black polished leather. His cap and coat were trimmed in sky blue indicating his position as an infantryman, and on his right and left arms were the classic gold three-lined chevrons. He was a soldier, for better or worse, he figured. While battles raged in the South, he was safe at Fort Ridgely and Thomas was safe at Fort Snelling.

He was also pleased to know the family was getting along well. In his mother's letters, which she sent frequently, she did not complain. She said that Isabel had taken to working in the field with the help of the neighbors Jules and Willie. Edward, who was seven now, became quite handy around the house and Eva, who was four, was quite helpful in cleaning up after meals. His mother even wrote that she'd earned enough extra money to hire a teacher to come to the homestead once a week to give lessons to his younger siblings in reading, writing, and arithmetic. Once Samuel got his first leave, he couldn't wait to go back home and visit.

As Samuel stood there, looking into the dented metal mirror, he actually appreciated the cleanliness and professional appearance of his uniform. Usually, he wore a white calico shirt that scratched at his skin along with thick, rugged combat boots and a floppy crowned forage cap. Also, he was rarely clean. In most cases he was covered in dirt and sweat and carried either a shovel or ax as he tended to chores around the fort. But on this day, Samuel was prepared for dress parade when the officers called upon every soldier to dress in full uniform and line up to ensure that the ranks were tight and orderly.

With his long, wavy brown hair tucked neatly under his cap and his face cleanly shaven, Samuel straightened his jacket and brushed off his insignia when he heard the bugle call. A nervous spark shot through his body as he grabbed his rifle and rushed to the parade ground for inspection.

"Fall in!" First Sergeant Findley shouted while pacing back and forth on the north end of the parade ground.

From every direction men came running, their freshly shined boots pattering the dry grass. Within seconds they arrived in neatly lined rows, perfectly spaced, chins held high and arms at their sides.

"Atten—tion!" Sgt. Findley called.

The men clipped their heels in unison and pulled their shoulders back. Samuel smirked at the joyous discipline of it all, but managed to put on a straight face before inspection.

He watched as Captain John Marsh, dressed in a long coat, cinched at the waist, and tall boots, walked slowly up and down the ranks. All was quiet but for a few cawing ravens pecking at the ground nearby.

Samuel felt a lump in his throat as the captain walked by, his green eyes moving up Samuel's uniform like a bug crawling up his skin. Captain Marsh had never reprimanded Samuel before, but a single loose button could mean latrine duty for a week. Silently, Samuel breathed a sigh of relief when the captain moved on to the next soldier.

A strong, dry breeze came in from the west picking up dust and dry grass, swirling it high through the air above Samuel and the other soldiers. Men twitched their heads but refrained from craning their necks in curiosity. The sound of the rustling grass and swirling dirt was quickly replaced by galloping hooves coming from the west. This the men couldn't ignore.

A mounted soldier came darting onto the parade ground. Behind him was the sentry, a boy of not more than sixteen, running as fast he could. "Sir!" the sentry called while running. "I couldn't stop him. He says he has an urgent message."

The mounted soldier pulled up beside Captain Marsh who was now standing in front of his neatly arranged rows of soldiers.

"I am Private Peters of the Third Minnesota," the mounted soldier said. "I come with an urgent message from Lieutenant Sheehan at Yellow Medicine."

Captain Marsh glared up at the soldier as if disturbed during his dinner. Then he held out his gloved hand, "Very well. May I have the message?"

Fumbling nervously, Private Peters reached into his breast pocket and pulled out a folded piece of paper. He handed it to Captain Marsh. Opening the paper, the captain tightened his lips expressing a look of concern.

"Thank you," Captain Marsh said, handing the letter back to Private Peters.

"What shall I inform the lieutenant?" Peters asked.

Keeping his eyes fixed to the ground, Marsh answered, "Tell him we shall arrive post haste."

Private Peters saluted the captain, spun his horse, and then, digging his heels in, galloped away in the direction he had come.

Samuel and the soldiers of Fort Ridgely looked on in desperate curiosity.

The captain held his hands behind his back and took one long look at his soldiers. "Gentlemen," he said with the American flag whipping in the wind above him. "I will require fifty men to accompany me to the Yellow Medicine Agency. A large and armored group of Sioux have caused a disturbance there by surrounding our guard and breaking into the storehouse. While the agent has avoided violence by handing out some provisions, the Sioux remain unsatisfied. We are to report there immediately to quell any threat of violence and do our duty to protect these frontier settlements. If your name is called you will ready yourself for combat and gather at the parade ground for departure at 1700 hours. You can remain at-ease while I draw up a list."

The men were enlivened by this announcement and looked at each other with hopeful grins. Many, like Samuel, had never experienced combat and were excited for the opportunity to take part in their first skirmish.

"An Indian fight!" Private John Magill said, leaning toward Samuel. "I guess the frontier ain't so boring after all."

Samuel offered a polite chuckle, but didn't respond. His mind rushed with memory of his father's death at the hands of Indians.

After a few minutes Sgt. Findley returned to the parade ground and called the soldiers to attention. Without preamble he started reading the list of names.

One by one the men were called. With only eighty soldiers stationed at the fort, Samuel knew he'd likely be called, but he wasn't sure if that's what he wanted.

"Copeland, Samuel, Private First Class!"

Samuel was startled upon hearing his name and rank. In that moment he didn't feel happy or scared, he felt hollow. Would he face the Indians in battle? Would he be able to take a life? He thought he could, but as he hurried back to the barracks to prepare for the march to Yellow Medicine, he wasn't sure.

The men marched in three columns, about fifteen rows deep. It was a long and tedious walk, split in half by a quiet night on the prairie. The following day, as they approached the Yellow Medicine Agency, the sun was high in the sky and the grass was dry and brittle, crunching beneath their leather boots.

"Keep your rifles on your backs, boys," Captain Marsh said, peering forward at the agency buildings.

The scene was not what Samuel expected. The broken wooden doors of the two-story brick storehouse lay on the ground, but that appeared to be the only indication of tension or violence. There were a handful of soldiers who stood guard outside the store-house while scattered groups of Sioux Indians were camped on the prairies west of the agency buildings. There was no indication that a fight had ensued or that one was imminent.

"Halt and hold your position," Captain Marsh announced from atop his horse, his shaved cheeks glistening with sweat. "I will go confer with Agent Galbraith."

As the captain rode off, Samuel took a moment to look over the landscape. He had never been to the Upper Agency. It was the second of two agencies created as a result of the 1851 Sioux treaties. Looking around he saw rolling plains of golden prairie grass dotted with groves of oak and elm. To the south was a meandering ravine cut by the slowly flowing muddy waters of the Minnesota River. The agency itself consisted of several modern wood frame and brick buildings occupied by the missionaries, traders, and storekeepers. The roads were beaten and well-worn especially at the center of the agency where one road could no longer be distinguished from another. To the west, beyond the temporary Sioux camps, were more permanent camps—large tepees with thick wooden poles reaching high in the sky as pillows of smoke escaped their openings. There were so many tepees they could not all be counted. Samuel estimated that thousands were gathered; most likely they had come from the western plains and gathered in anticipation of the coming annual payment. These were the Reservation Indians, the Farmer Dakota. They were the ones who came to the homestead in winter, looking desperate and in need of food. They were not the ones who had murdered his father. In his mind he knew this, but in his heart Samuel wasn't sure he could distinguish them.

Captain Marsh rode back to the company at a trot. He was stone faced but appeared unconcerned. "A council will be held to-morrow," he announced as he came to a halt. "Set up camp past that knoll to the east." He pointed to a rise in the prairie. "But keep yourselves ready if something should happen."

Camp was set up quickly and easily. Having departed in haste and expecting to be gone briefly, the men brought no tents, only bed rolls and a few other necessary provisions.

When evening arrived the men ate a meal of hardtack and salted pork while they drank coffee, sat around the fire, and complained about their lots in life.

"I haven't had a decent meal in months," Private Thomas said just before his teeth clasped down on a stale piece of hard-tack. He grimaced as he chewed, and the men looked on with expressions of mild amusement. "What are we doin' out here on the prairie anyway? I never thought I would actually miss the barracks."

The men chuckled in unison.

"A roof and a bed would sure be nice," Private Magill said, "or, at least some beans to go with this hardtack, but we ain't even get that."

Chuckles were replaced by frustrated grumbling. Samuel paid little mind as he sat back, held a tin cup of coffee tightly in his hands, and enjoyed watching the dancing flames of the bonfire in front of him.

"It's all cuz of them Indians," Private Rabenski said. Rabenski was a young, ill-tempered soldier with dark hair and a thin mustache. "That's the reason we're here and not fightin' the Rebs. Rather than save the Union we gotta save some Indians."

The men let out another chorus of dissatisfied grumbles, sounding more like children than soldiers.

"I don't know why we don't just let 'em starve to death," Private Taylor said. "They don't do nothin' but take federal money and waste it on liquor. They're downright drunks."

"Kinda like you," Magill said, the teeth behind his smile flickering in the light of the fire.

Samuel couldn't help but laugh—a deep, gut-aching laugh. The rest of the men laughed with him.

"Shut up!" Taylor said. "I'm serious! We're out here risking our lives for some Redskins? Don't make no sense. Let them fend for themselves."

"C'mon, Taylor," Private Ellis said, a red-haired Irishman from St. Paul. "They're people too ya know. Just like the slaves we're fightin' to set free. And besides, these Indians never hurt nobody."

That caught Samuel's attention. His heart jumped and his muscles stiffened. He never confided to the men that it was an Indian who killed his father.

"Did you already forget about Spirit Lake... what, five years ago?" Taylor said raising his voice. "I guarantee those folks down there didn't. Damn Indians musta killed fifty settlers, women and children, too, for no reason."

Ellis, leaning forward with his elbows to his knees, replied, "That was Inkpaduta. Scarlet Point. He's long gone now and so are his followers. Any Indian who still believes in tradition and warfare is on the western plains."

176

Taylor grunted disagreeably. "Well, I don't know about that. I'm just sayin' we ain't responsible for some Indian folk. Whatta we care if they starve or not?"

"Ah, come on, Taylor!" Rabenski said, flinging his arms through the air. "Don't give in so easily to that goody-goody Ellis. You're right, man. The Indians are wasting good land. They're useless. They're the last thing standing between America and our future. They should either be civilized or moved outta the way."

"Don't listen to Rabenski," Ellis said. "He's talking about being civilized and he don't even know how to read!"

The men laughed, tilting their heads back and slapping their knees.

"I do too!" Rabenski shot back, his face reddening in the orange fire light.

"Most of those Indians *are* civilized," Ellis said. "They farm and speak English and attend Christian service. The only reason they are poor and in need of help is because of what this country did to 'em."

"What do you mean *this country?*" Magill said, a born and bred American who took offense to the Irishman's words.

"I don't mean it like that," Ellis said. "I came here because this is the land of opportunity and I still believe it is—even if there's a war going on."

"What do you mean then?" Magill said.

Ellis straightened his back and uncrossed his legs, leaning forward, "I mean that the government took all the Indian land and forced them to live on smaller and smaller plots. Then the traders and bankers and other people looking to make a quick buck came in, took all the money we gave them for the land, and convinced them to buy on credit. Now, they can't even get that. That's why they broke into the storehouse. That's why they're gonna start a war. Right here. Where families have settled and cities have taken root. And they don't just want their land back, they want their dignity."

Rabenski tilted his head to the stars and let out a bellow of a laugh. "Ah, whadda you know," Rabenski said, slapping his knee. "If they knew better they wouldn't be in this situation."

There was a brief silence as tensions reached a high point.

"You been awful quiet," Taylor said, peering through the embers of the fire at Samuel. "What do you think we should do with the Indians?"

"Yeah, Cope?" Rabesnki pressed, referring to Samuel by his military-given nickname.

Samuel wanted no part of the conversation. He felt too conflicted, too confused. He wanted the Indians to pay for what they did, but he knew that wouldn't bring his father back. Samuel pursed his lips and shook his head with a slight shrug of the shoulders.

"Ah, you can't just answer with a shrug," Taylor urged. "You ain't said more than two words this whole expedition."

Thoughts swirled through Samuel's mind. Memories. Decisions. Visions of his life before everything changed.

"I think it's not up to us," he said. "I think we should just follow orders, do what we're told, and let the officers and politicians sort it all out."

"Man!" Rabenski said as he bent toward the flickering light. "That's no answer. Just tell us what you think."

Samuel stood up and looked at each one of his fellow soldiers. Then he looked hard at Rabenski. "I don't have to say a damn thing." Samuel paused, released his stare, then tipped his cap. "I'm going to bed," he said as he walked away into the darkness of the camp. In his stomach he felt a churning worse than hunger; worse than sickness.

The next day began cold and dreary with low, gray clouds and a slight chill that was unusual for August. Samuel spent the morning by himself sipping coffee and reading from *Leaves of Grass*. He had already read the book of poems five or six times, but he continued to read it, looking for new meaning in each line. This particular morning he pondered over the words, "All truths wait in all things. They neither hasten their own delivery nor resist it." All truths, he thought.

At 1100 hours the men were called to order and soon after they marched a short distance to the agency. When they arrived they were met by Lt. Sheehan and about one hundred men of Company C who were assembled neatly outside the storehouse and standing at attention. Samuel and the men of Company B assembled along-side them and waited for the Dakota to arrive.

Outside the open door of the storehouse stood Agent Thomas Galbraith, a young man with a brimmed hat, chestnut brown goatee, and a golden buttoned vest. He was a politician assigned to manage affairs with the Dakota people. Samuel could not make out the words of his conversation, but he was speaking adamantly with the Reverend Riggs, a tall, thin, older man who preached Christianity to the Dakota believing he could somehow save their souls by instructing them in the ways of civil society. Samuel recognized him because he had come to the fort on several occasions to preach to the soldiers.

Off in the distance stood the Dakota camp. It was filled with hundreds of tepees scattered about with all sorts of smoking fire pits, buckets, wagons, and various indistinguishable implements. Samuel could see the camp was stirring but no one had yet marched from the camp to the agency.

"What's takin' so long?" Private Taylor said, as he stood at attention next to Samuel. "My feet are tiring, and this breeze is starting to give me the chills."

Moments later, a large assembly of mounted Dakota appeared from behind a hill riding steadily toward the agency. Each man had long, smoky-black hair that streamed behind him like a flag on a pole. Most of the men were dressed in buckskin pants, moccasins, and wore colorful sashes across their chests and mid-section. Though they rode vigorously, they did not appear to have violent intentions.

Behind the horsemen was a horse-drawn buggy that bumped along steadily. It appeared unusually formal among the Native Dakota. Upon reaching the front of the storehouse, the mounted Dakota soldiers parted allowing the buggy to roll past. It came to a halt front and center of the storehouse just a few steps from where Galbraith and Riggs stood.

"Who is that?" Taylor said as two Dakota men stepped out of the buggy, one dressed formally, the other in a traditional style. "I didn't expect an Indian dressed in a suit."

Samuel hesitated. He had seen the man before. Though he

looked different now, the man in the suit carried his right arm like it was injured in the same way as the Indian who first came to his family's home.

Taylor said, "You know, I think that's Little Crow. The leader of the Sioux down by the Lower Agency. But, I thought he was a blanket Indian?"

"He was," Samuel said, amazed that the Dakota leader had stood in his family's home.

"Well, can't trust 'em whether they're blanket or farmer."

The agent, reverend, and two Dakota leaders exchanged handshakes while their faces remained stern and serious. The driver of the buggy, who wore a farmer's hat and calico shirt, got down off the buggy and stood alongside the four men. As they spoke, he interpreted.

While the council took place, hundreds of Dakota from the camp began to gather on the opposite side of the soldiers. They looked peaceful but anxious. Their faces were bleak and their clothes were soiled and torn. Some of the younger men wore breechcloths and carried javelins and rifles, but the majority were women and children quietly observing the negotiations. For a moment, Samuel took pity on them.

"Look at 'em all," Taylor said. "They must outnumber us ten to one. If they really wanted they could destroy our whole company—start a war right here and now."

"Nah," Samuel said, brushing aside Taylor's concern.

"You don't think so? Imagine if they joined forces with the Chippewa—or Ojibwe, whatever you call 'em—they could wipe us all out before the federal government even had a clue what was goin' on."

"Aren't the Chippewa enemies of the Sioux?"

"Yeah, but if they just wised up. Got together against a common enemy, you know?"

"Nah, the Sioux and Chippewa hate each other, don't they? And besides," Samuel said looking at the thousands of Sioux gathered across from them. "They're all just reservation Indians. They're like mice looking for a morsel of food, not a fight."

"I reckon you might be right. But if they ever combined

forces and really put together a plan of attack, I bet they could wipe us out—even with our artillery."

"They're just beggers now," Samuel assured Taylor. "They can barely take care of themselves let alone fight a war."

Taylor shook his head. "I wouldn't be too sure. Lord knows they have every right to fight back against the treatment they receive. If I was them, I'd kill every white man I saw."

The statement struck Samuel deep. He didn't want to think about it. He didn't want to think about who was to blame or why or what the right course of action was. He was trying to move forward, he just didn't know how.

After an hour of negotiations an agreement was reached. The four men: Riggs, Galbraith, Little Crow, and the other Dakota leader, shook hands and went their separate ways. Captain Marsh announced to the men that they would stay at the Upper Agency to supervise the safe distribution of annuity goods before returning to Fort Ridgely. Company C, he said, would head north to Fort Ripley.

"Company C is leaving?" Taylor wondered. "Shouldn't they stay here until the gold is paid out?"

Agent Galbraith, who overheard Taylor, craned his neck toward the men and replied haughtily, casting his voice over the entire group, "The payment trouble is over for the year. There is no more threat of an outbreak."

Taylor looked at Samuel, folding his brow.

Samuel just shrugged.

Chapter 20

WasabishkiMakwa
Gayaashko-zaaga'igan
Manoominike-giizis
(*Gull Lake, August 1862*)

After following the messenger from Crow Wing to Gayaashko-zaaga'igan, Waabi and the new Ojibwe recruits arrived to a great and glorious feast. Tawny skinned, tender girls carried birch bark baskets filled with beef, corn, wild rice, squash, potatoes, berries, and hard sugar. They invited the men and boys to sit and relax in the shade of the elm trees and the calm and sunny shores of the lake. Children ran playfully while elders smoked and passed their pipes outside of their lodges. Dogs laid in the green grass, lounging in the summer sun. Men carried pitchers of sweet tea and cold water, offering a drink to each new soldier who arrived. The entire scene was one of peace, tranquility, and togetherness.

In the distance, beyond the lodges and wigwams, was a large, two-story wood-frame house—the largest house Waabi had ever seen. It had clear, pane glass windows and a neatly finished double door. It was painted in rich and vibrant shades of walnut and hickory. It was like the great buildings he heard about from those who had traveled east, into the white man's world.

"Is that Bagone-giizhig's home?" Waabi asked one of the many strangers near him.

"Yes," the man answered with energy. "Bagone-giizhig lives like a white man in a big house, but leads the People with passion and wisdom. He's learned their ways and he knows their tricks. Under his leadership we'll take back our land, ways of living, and our language!" The man raised a fist and ran away with boisterous yelp, spinning and hopping, enjoying the celebration.

For a moment Waabi stood there, wondering if this could be true. Could an Ojibwe leader reclaim what had been lost? Would it matter—without his father, his uncle, his aunt, what did he have left? What about his vision? Why was he the man on the cross? Why was he the man with nails in his wrists? Waabi closed his eyes and shook his head, wiping the thoughts from his mind.

For more than an hour Waabi enjoyed pleasant banter with Binishii and several other Ojibwe who, until recently, had intended to enlist in the U.S. army. Sitting in the sun he rubbed his belly and stretched his chin to the sky. He hadn't felt so relaxed and satisfied in years. He had no labor to do and no family to protect. He let go of all his worries. It was a moment of bliss in between everything that had been lost and everything he had yet to encounter.

As afternoon turned to evening, with the calm and quiet lake reflecting the orange glow of the horizon, several men stepped out from the large house. The man leading the way could be none other than Bagone-giizhig. His appearance was striking. Though dark-skinned with long braided hair ornamented with feathers and beads, he wore a long, black, double-breasted suit coat in the style of a white man. On his legs he wore trousers, but on his feet were moccasins adorned with red and yellow beads. On his white shirt collar he wore a dark neck tie, and around his neck hung several gold and bronze medals that bounced methodically off his trim figure.

A hush fell over the crowd of chattering young men as they turned to behold the influential leader.

"Gather in close," the Ojibwe leader said, his voice projecting effortlessly across the camp. In response, hundreds pushed forward, squeezing together.

"Some of you may know my father, Bagone-giizhig the Elder," he began. "My father, at a time when the white government was swooping in and claiming our land and our ways of life, consolidated our power and protected our rights against their incursions. Though not a leader by blood, he was a leader by necessity. That leadership has fallen on me, Bagone-giizhig the Younger." He paused, looking over his captive audience. "I've seen the ways of the white government. They come with pen and paper and wish to negotiate. But they take everything and give nothing. They watch as our people die and our homeland shrinks giving nothing in compensation but drunkenness and shame. Now, after killing us with starvation and sickness, they come to claim your lives in a war against their own? They promise you money, but what good is money to those on the spirit path? What good is money when they control the prices? I have met the white man at the negotiating table. I have traveled through concrete forests of white marble and met with the man who claims he is our father and we are his children. Negotiation leads to nothing but suffering and loss. Our time is slipping away. Like the buffalo of the plains or the timber of our woodlands. Soon they will be gone and we will be gone with them. That is why the time for negotiation has passed."

He paused again. Steely-eyed, he looked over the audience and then turned his eyes toward the darkening sky.

"Tomorrow, a council of white men from St. Paul will come to talk with us. I have stolen their cattle and taken some of their people captive. These men believe they can save their captives and punish me for the theft of cattle. But there will be no more negotiations. For we cannot get what we want through peaceable means. Unsuspecting, we will fall upon them like lightning from a storm cloud. This will be our declaration of war. It will be the day your children and grandchildren remember as the moment we reclaimed our land and our lives and secured forever what is rightfully ours."

The men cheered, but Bagone-giizhig put up both hands to silence them.

"You are right to be excited. Today marks the end of an era. An era of retreat. Tomorrow we begin anew, taking back our sovereignty, defending our rights, protecting our children, and saving the land where our mothers and fathers, grandmothers and grandfathers are buried."

Waabi was reminded of his father, who was among those buried, left for dead because of the negligence and greed of the white man. Perhaps this leader, Bagone-giizhig, with his confident stance and tone—his uncompromising attitude—could actually do what he said.

"This is our home and if we do not fight back now we will never retrieve it. Our children will never forgive us. Our future generations will become captive, and they will look back with tears in their eyes and ask, 'How could you do nothing? How could you agree to their demands over and over again, seeing what it did to you and knowing what it would do to us?'

"I can no longer stand idly by, like a baby eagle helpless in its nest, only taking regurgitated food from its mother's mouth. I'm telling you the days are numbered. The days we still have a chance to fight back. It's already happened to many great eastern bands. The great Haudenosaunee and Cherokee, the Sauk and Potawatomi—defeated and confined, they are now left with virtually nothing and have no way to earn it back. These once proud nations—nations of great warriors—are but wounded elk in a barren valley."

Bagone-giizhig paused again and took a deep breath. It was nearly dusk and lanterns were being lit by the women of the band.

"I may speak in clichés and elaborate metaphors," he said, continuing, "but it is not out of ignorance. It is out of real true knowledge of our circumstances. The white government is a vast, powerful enemy with resources far beyond our own. We would not be the first to fight back against their incursions, lies, and treachery. I know we cannot do it alone. It begins here today, with you. But our effort must be a unified one. Some of our chiefs have denied their support for this war effort. But there is another who sees the necessity and wisdom of attacking the enemy while he is weak; while he is occupied. I speak of Taoyateduta, called Little Crow by the whites. Though he belongs to our hereditary enemy the Mdewakanton Bwaanag, he and his soldiers are ready to give their lives for a cause we share. While they attack from the south, we will attack from the north. Once we join forces, no white militia will be able to stop us and no army will act quick enough to defeat our cause. Messengers have been sent west, in search of Inkpaduta, the Wahpekute leader who eluded the white armies and who waits in longing to reclaim our traditional way of life. Do not be afraid or hesitant. Do not wait for another moon; another season. The longer we wait, the more they take, the more they destroy. Even our hearts and minds they take and crumple like dry leaves in their hands. Join me. Join us. Take back your land and your lives. It's time to free our land from foreign rule."

The crowd responded with a frenzy of shouts, jumping like fish out of water and howling like wolves at the moon. Without thought, Waabi beat his chest and raised his voice. Caught up in the excitement of the moment, he leaped in the air, smiling ear to ear.

A drum beat sounded. It boomed over the exuberant young men. It became quick and rhythmic and was joined by several other drums. More lanterns were lit, then fire pits flourished with flames. A circle formed and inside the circle dozens of young men hopped and twirled, moving quick and free to the beat of the drums. Voices began wailing, low and then high, harmonizing with each other. On and on they continued in unison until the outline of the horizon was shaded black and the sky twinkled with starlight. After many happy hours, spirits free and unburdened, the young men collapsed where they stood, and welcomed a dreamless sleep in the cool grass of Ojibwe territory.

Chapter 21

Samuel
Fort Ridgely
August 1862

Samuel leaned against the stone corner of the mess hall sipping a steaming cup of fresh, black coffee. Its pungent aroma stung his nostrils, giving him a pleasant wakeful feeling. He watched as light from the rising sun began to touch the grass at the western edge of the parade ground and the long shadows of the barracks shortened. Birds swooped up from the ravine of the Minnesota River Valley, briefly circling overhead, and then swooped back down in a cycle of freedom.

Though he tried to relax, his body was shaking with nervous energy. He tapped his foot against the ground and tried unsuccessfully to hold his coffee steady. It was Monday, August 18, the day his brother was coming to Fort Ridgely. As the assistant quartermaster at Fort Snelling, Thomas was entrusted with escorting the Indian payment between the two forts. Thomas, his obnoxious and often irresponsible little brother entrusted with such a duty. Samuel couldn't believe it. Nevertheless, the Indian payment was scheduled to arrive that very evening and the two of them hadn't spoken since their argument and silent goodbye. Samuel had written letters, but received no reply. Samuel wasn't sure what he would say when his brother arrived—if he would ask for forgiveness or expect an apology—he just knew that they needed to reconcile.

As the warm sun melted the dew on the grass, Samuel went to the magazine where he was tasked with cleaning rifles. It was a pleasing, solitary task that involved taking the rifles apart, wiping them clean of grime and powder, and putting them back together again. He even polished the wooden butt of each rifle to make them look shiny and new, though most were relics of wars past. As he sipped his coffee and settled into his task, he heard a soldier calling for a medic. He stepped outside the magazine and saw a soldier walking up the ferry road with a civilian clinging to his side and limping. The civilian's face and thigh were stained with blood.

"Medic! This man needs a medic!" the soldier cried as he led the civilian through what would be the sally port if the fort had walls. Worried and curious, Samuel rushed through the prairie grass and past the guard house until he reached the parade ground where he found Privates Ellis and Magill. "What do you think happened to that farmer?" Samuel said through quickened breath.

"Somebody got'em good," Magill said. "But it's too early to get into a drunken brawl."

"Nah, it's never too early for that," Ellis said, drawing a smile from Magill.

"What if it was Indians?" Samuel said.

Magill, with a manure fork at his side, turned and gave Samuel a questioning look. "That mess was smoothed over when we opened the storehouse for 'em. Now they're just waitin' for their payment and they wouldn't do anything to risk losin' it."

"If it was Indians," Ellis said, "it was only one or two of 'em that probably got hungry and tried to steal from that farmer."

Moments later, the trill of drums echoed off the buildings as the long roll was sounded, calling all soldiers to the parade ground. Samuel, Magill, and Ellis quickly fell in line along with about eighty-five others who had been stationed at the fort. "It *was* Indians," Samuel said to Ellis. "They wouldn't gather us up if it wasn't."

"Could be. This all seems too familiar to the near outbreak a few weeks ago. You ready for a fight?"

Samuel's mind wandered to thoughts of battle. He'd been trained now. He knew how to handle a rifle and he'd been drilled in hand-to-hand combat. But was he ready to take a life? Maybe then Thomas would forgive him.

Captain Marsh strode out in front of the soldiers who stood at attention. Turning to face them he paused and threw his hands behind his back. With the sun glistening off his golden shoulder pads he began. "Soldiers of Company B, we must act quickly. I am told there has been an Indian outbreak at the Lower Agency, the extent of which we do not yet know. We know only that some of the Sioux Indians there have violently attacked the civilian population. We must quickly organize a defense and march along the ferry road to the agency to defend our citizens and engage the enemy if necessary. I am calling for a force of fifty men to join me and our interpreter, Mr. Quinn, to quell this outbreak. First Lieutenant Bishop will call the names of those I've assigned to this expedition. Those assigned should gather forty rounds of ammunition and one day's rations. We'll depart at 0900. Those remaining will stay in defense of the fort. We expect more injured civilians to be arriving soon."

Captain Marsh stepped back and the lieutenant stepped forward. He held a fresh sheet of paper close to his face as if he needed spectacles and began reading. Most men reacted with silent joy, hardly able to suppress their smiles at the promise of action. Some, less brave but more discerning, audibly huffed in reluctant acceptance of their duty. When Samuel heard his name, he fell somewhere in between.

When all the names had been called and the captain dismissed the men, Ellis, who had not been called, turned and offered his sympathies to Samuel. "It's probably nothing. Probably just a few hotheads who decided to kill for their next meal. They'll be no match for fifty armed soldiers."

At 0900 sharp, fifty-four men, along with a six-mule team carrying supplies and ammunition, marched out from the shadow of the stone barracks and down the sloping ferry road into the Minnesota River Valley. In rows of three the men marched in cadence, stepping right to left in unison. The steady rhythm of boots along the dirt road was pleasant and calming. Coupled with the slowly flowing river and the large, shade-giving cottonwood trees— on any other day it would have been easy for a soldier to drift away into a soothing day dream. But this was not any other day. Samuel felt tense and eager. He clutched his rifle with shaking hands while his eyes darted back and forth, searching the landscape. A part of him wanted to face the Indians in battle, but he wondered if he was bold enough to kill one—even in defense of his life.

The soldiers walked for several miles without encountering

anything unusual or alarming. "This is some march," Rabenski said to anyone who would listen. "Maybe I should have invited my girlfriend!"

A few of the men chuckled. "I thought you did, Rabenski," Magill said. "If your girlfriend's imaginary, you can invite her just about anywhere."

The men laughed again when the march was suddenly halted. Samuel expected a rebuke from Captain Marsh but none came. Instead, on the right side of the road he saw a body. It was an older white man who had his throat cut and his guts spilled. The site of it was revolting. "Be on the ready, men," Captain Marsh said. "Expect an ambush." Then, as the line continued, panic-stricken civilians—women, children, and a few men—hurried past them on their way to the fort seeking safety. "Indians!" they cried. Their faces were colorless and their eyes were wide and red. For the soldiers, it was a dismal and frightening reality.

After assuring the civilians that the Indians would be captured, Captain Marsh ordered the men forward. Before long, they found more bodies, most of them struck in the back with arrows and tomahawks as they attempted to flee. Their lifeless bodies, still warm, had looks of terror on their faces, eyes wide and faces contorted in desperation. "Oh, my God," the soldiers said under their breaths as they walked past body after body. Some brought handkerchiefs to their mouths to keep from vomiting. Samuel could not believe what he was seeing. The frontier was not so peaceful anymore.

By noon the fifty-four men of Company B reached the ferry crossing opposite the agency. It appeared uneasily calm as if a storm had recently passed through. On the north bank, along with the soldiers, was the ferry boat. On the south bank, was the mutilated body of the ferryman, Mauley. Samuel was suspicious that the ferry had been sent over to bait them across. As Captain Marsh evaluated the site, an Indian dressed in farmer's clothes appeared on the opposite side. He had his hands raised and open to show he carried no weapon and began speaking calmly in the Dakota language.

"He says there has only been a little trouble," Quinn, the interpreter said. "He wants us to come across to have a council."

"It looks to be more than a little trouble," Marsh shouted back across the river, his voice amplified by the ravine.

The Indian replied, calmly again. "It was some of our young men who caused the trouble. We wish to apologize and make peace."

Before Marsh could respond, Magill leaned toward Captain Marsh explaining that he recognized the Indian as White Dog, a farmer Indian from the Upper Agency.

After a moment, Marsh called across the river, "Why have you come all the way from the Upper Agency?"

He answered quickly and Quinn translated. "He has only come to visit for a few days."

While Marsh stood contemplating the situation, Samuel, secretly doing reconnaissance, went down by the river to scoop out some water. As he leaned over and looked downriver, he saw the swishing tails of several ponies in the bushes along the south bank. Samuel decided to climb atop a sand hill to get a better look. "Captain," Samuel said. "I see some ponies downriver. This could be an ambush."

"What are the ponies doing there?" Marsh asked the Indian across the river, pointing. "Are there many more of you?"

White Dog answered by pulling a gun from his belt, shrieking loudly, and firing across the open water.

Quinn yelled, "Look out!" Then he fell to the ground with a bullet to the chest.

Before the men could raise their rifles, Indians came rushing down from the top of the ravine behind them, screaming and firing shotguns. Others, from the top of the ravine on the other side of the river, rose up and fired into the crowd of U.S. troops.

Samuel, panic-stricken, swiveled his head back and forth witnessing the ambush like it was theater. At least a dozen men fell injured or dead after the initial assault. Coming to his senses, Samuel raised his rifle and aimed at the group of oncoming Indian soldiers. Before he could fire his left arm was grazed by a bullet fired by the enemy on the opposite bank. The bullet tore through his jacket and broke his skin causing him to drop the head of his rifle and grasp his arm. He expected pain but there was none. Seeing that it was only a deep cut, he leaped off the sand hill so he was no longer an easy target, but before he could gather himself to fire again, he could see that his company had been overwhelmed. Those that remained standing had turned their rifles horizontally, using them as bars to shield themselves from swinging tomahawks. Others withdrew their scabbards ready to kill or be killed. The fighting had turned to hand-to-hand combat.

Samuel slung his rifle over his shoulder and pulled out his out his own scabbard, prepared to fight. An Indian, who looked fierce as a devil, drenched in sweat and blood, faced him head on. Samuel took a deep breath and readied himself for a life-or-death struggle. But, as the Indian enemy approached he was shot through the side of the head. His body flung swiftly to the ground, his head gushing with blood.

Samuel almost retched at the sight of it. He looked up and saw Rabenski with his rifle still pointed, smoke pouring out of the barrel. "Get to the hazelbrush!" Rabenski yelled, looking at Samuel. Together they ran for the thick hazelbrush just upriver. Before they could make it, an Indian appeared with his shotgun raised. He fired. The explosive sound it was deafening, paralyzing his senses. Dirt and gravel erupted into the air, pelting Samuel in the head and chest. The shot had landed short.

"Are you loaded?" Rabenski said, his face showing no fear.

Samuel nodded and raised his rifle, ignoring the gash in his left forearm. He fired but the Indian dove away. "Come on!" Rabenski said, and together they streaked toward the hazelbrush.

All the men who remained alive had escaped to the thick hazelbrush along the bank of the river, though Rabenski and Samuel were separated from the larger group. The Indians surrounded them, firing indiscriminately into the brush. Rabenski and Samuel found some cover behind two thin trees while firing back as quickly as they could. Shotgun pellets whizzed passed them like a hail storm as the firing continued for ten minutes.

"God, won't they ever stop?" Rabenski said while reloading his weapon once again. Samuel had managed to cover his wound with cloth, but he felt weak and dizzy. It was not from blood loss, it was from shock. His head pounded, and his mouth was sticky and dry. Still, he fired and reloaded as quickly as he could.

The shooting continued. Dirt and bark exploded off the trees sending chunks of debris in every direction. The air smelled of burnt powder, and gray smoke covered the area like fog. Back on the landing, the painful groans of men nearing their last breath could still be heard. *This is it,* Samuel thought, his life would soon be over. But seeing Rabenski bravely fire back again and again, Samuel swallowed his fear and calmed his nerves. He had to keep living.

Finally, after what felt like hours the firing died down. Rabenski turned toward Samuel and leaned his back against the small tree he had been using as a shield. "You don't look so good," he said.

Samuel rolled his eyes and shook his head, no longer fully comprehending their situation.

Rabenski reached for his canteen. It was empty. Then he looked over both shoulders and appeared to be listening intently for signs of the enemy. Seeing and hearing nothing, he moved slowly down the slope toward the river.

"Where are you going? What are you doing?" Samuel said.

"I'm getting you some water."

"It's too dangerous," Samuel pleaded.

"They're gone now," Rabenski said, stretching his neck to peer through the brush.

As Rabenski proceeded to the river and leaned into the water, urgent shouts of the enemy came from the road above. Rabenski whirled around but it was too late. The Indian soldier fired his shotgun, pelting Rabenski in the side of the face and slinging him into the river. There was no way he could have survived. Samuel rose up and fired back, hitting the Indian in the stomach. Instinctively, Samuel darted away, knowing his position was compromised. He looked back to see Rabenski lying face down in the river, blood staining the water around his face.

Samuel moved quickly up the river bank staying low under cover of the hazelbrush. Shots ripped through the brush, none finding their target. Weaving through the tall grass and thick brush he found a downed tree. He hurled himself over the heavy log and laid low on the other side. Bullets whizzed through the air as Samuel curled his body tight, closed his eyes, and begged God for mercy.

"Please, please, please," he said over and over again.

Samuel cradled the back of his head with his hands while the firing continued. But, luckily, the shots were sporadic and landed nowhere near Samuel's position. After a few minutes, the firing ceased. Exhausted. Terrified. Ashamed. Samuel merely lay there, knees curled into his chest, thinking of the terrible encounter. That morning it was just another day, but now, many of his friends were dead. Samuel was stunned. His company was shattered. And the sight of Rabenski, tattered in the face with enemy fire while trying to help him, made Samuel nauseous. He just lay there, huddled behind the downed tree, listening to the songs of the birds and the chirp of the grasshoppers until darkness finally covered the river valley.

Though he felt more exhausted than at any time in his life, the arrival of night did not mean it was time to rest. He knew he had to return to the fort if he was going to survive. Darkness offered safety.

Samuel finally calmed himself, ate some rations, and crawled down to the river for several frantic gulps of water. Then he splashed his face. The cool water felt invigorating. He shook his head, blinked his eyes, and was ready to move. With the strap of his satchel on one shoulder and the strap of his rifle on the other, Samuel moved up the ravine and onto the road. He walked slowly, constantly surveying the darkened shapes out in front of him. Occasionally, he lowered himself to a knee and raised his rifle, thinking that he saw shadowy movements, but there was nothing. Everything was quiet.

After many hours of his slow, cold, and lonely march, a pale glow finally appeared on the eastern horizon. As the brilliant orange sun began to rise, it was framed perfectly by the river valley. Its growing light painted the lazy waters of the Minnesota River orange and made the world appear sanguine and new. But, with light came visibility, which meant danger. Samuel stepped off the road and settled into a low lying area, covered nicely by some tall dogwood. Hungrily, he ate his last bit of hardtack and settled in for a nap. He drifted off easily, exhaustion overcoming his pain, shock, and fear. He slept for what could have been hours or days. When he awoke, the sun was high and he heard the distant sound of cannon fire. The Indians were attacking the fort.

Chapter 22

WasabishkiMakwa
Gayaashko-zaaga'igan
Manoominike-gizis
(Gull Lake, August 1862)

After a restful night, Waabi awoke feeling refreshed and in-vigorated. He sat up, took a long, deep breath, and admired the morning sunlight as it cut through the forest canopy. Looking around he saw the camp was a whirl of activity. Some of the young men leaned against trees and ate their breakfast while others bathed in the lake or did stretching exercises. Others applied streaks of vermillion and blackberry to their faces in preparation for battle.

"Good morning!" said a tall Ojibwe soldier who then gave Waabi a piece of venison. Waabi took a bite of the fresh, seasoned deer meat and looked up at the soldier with curiosity.

"It's me," he said, smiling, "Chibines!"

Waabi shook his head in surprise. He did not recognize his old school mate dressed as he was in a breech cloth, leggings, head-dress and warpaint.

"I wasn't sure you'd come after I saw you last," Chibines said, his smile bright as the morning sun behind him. "I came to join the white army, to earn some pay, but when I heard Bagone-giizhig was joining the Bwaan to reclaim our land I could not turn away."

He paused and offered Waabi his hand, lifting him from the ground.

"I do not hate the whites," he continued. "Many of them are our neighbors and friends. But their traders and agents have taken so much from us. We only want a little back."

"When I left Miskwaabikaang, I never expected this," Waabi said, looking around at the activity of camp. "But, now that I'm here I feel renewed—full of life—in a way I haven't since I was a boy. I feel a sense of unity unlike any I've known since I was very young and

196

there doesn't seem to be any..." he considered a moment, "despair."

"It feels good to be free of their rules," Chibines said, grab-bing Waabi by the shoulder. "Soon I hope all of the Ojibwe and Bwaanag will know that feeling. We will live like our ancestors again."

Waabi smiled in return, but quickly dropped his smile as he remembered visiting Sandy Lake.

"What is it?" Chibines asked, seeing that Waabi's expression had changed.

"I don't need to live like my ancestors," Waabi said. "I've lived at peace with the whites my whole life and I don't wish for that to change. I just want to protect the land where my father is buried. Where our ancestors lie in rest."

Chibines lowered his eyes and gripped Waabi's shoulder tighter as a sign of comfort. "You cannot have both, that is what I told myself."

Moments later, a crier came rushing by on a horse. "White soldiers are nearing the sentry," he called. "Take your positions!" The crier paused next to Waabi and Chibines. "Take a position with the rear flank," he said matter-of-factly, pointing to a group of armed Ojibwe to the southwest. Then he continued on, his loud and clear call reaching every corner of the camp.

Waabi, Chibines, and a group of about sixty Ojibwe took a position in the woods, southwest of the meeting place. Many of the men carried rifles. Waabi, who was given a quiver and bow, filled the quiver with arrows and held the bow firmly in his right hand. Over the years he had become a skilled marksman, but he had never aimed his arrow at a human being.

The Ojibwe hunched low in the brush, grass, and trees as they heard the rickety lumbering of the oncoming wagons. Soldiers appeared out ahead dressed in blue coats with gold buttons. They walked in unison at a steady, moderate pace. Waabi felt his body shaking as he eyed each soldier that passed, wondering which one might be his first kill. This was not like hunting deer with his father. There would be no offering of tobacco.

Chibines put his hand on Waabi's shoulder and looked at him reassuringly. "We will make our ancestors proud," he said.

The soldiers that marched past were followed by three empty wagons. Apparently, they were brought as a means to take the captives from the camp. Waabi had still not seen the captives, nor knew how many the Ojibwe held. After the wagons, came the negotiators. They arrived riding on shiny brown horses, but the men did not appear particularly powerful or imposing.

"Is that them?" Waabi said in a low whisper. "Is that the Americans?"

He expected men of regal bearing with tall hats, brass buttons, and long, gold-handled swords. What he saw were unshaven, pot-bellied men with snuff in their mouths and loose fitting, drab clothing. The soldiers, too, who followed the wagon train looked nothing like the ones who preceded it. These soldiers, though quite numerous, had no uniforms. Instead they wore straw hats and torn pants as if they'd just been taken straight out of the farmer's field.

Chibines chuckled. "Now I know why the Naadowens decided this is the time to fight back. The white man can barely field an army."

The American caravan finally halted at a creek connecting Gull and Round Lakes. On the other side of the creek was Bagone-giizhig and several other Ojibwe leaders looking far more regal than their American counterparts.

"When Bagone-giizhig gives the signal," one of the Ojibwe soldiers said, "we spring out and hem the Americans in, like beavers in a pond."

An exchange took place between the Ojibwe and American leaders, but Waabi could not hear what was being said. He only saw that Bagone-giizhig was emphatic like he was the day before, raising his arms and showing a determined expression. Then, he thrust his javelin into the ground.

"That's it! Move out!"

Waabi and Chibines, along with the other Ojibwe, sprang out from their hidden positions. They moved quickly toward the American soldiers, raising their voices as they went. From the opposite flank came another large group of Ojibwe soldiers, also moving quickly and raising their voices to instill fear in their enemy.

The Americans clustered close together feeling the mounting pressure, then took defensive positions and raised their weapons. The Ojibwe, now just several long strides away, also stopped and raised their weapons.

One of the American commanders yelled, "Steady, men. Hold your fire!"

Bagone-giizhig began to laugh as the American negotiators turned their attention away from the potential violence and back toward their counterparts. Bagone-giizhig explained to the Americans that they were outnumbered and outmaneuvered. Realizing the truth of the matter, the American soldiers were ordered to lower their weapons and stand at ease. The Ojibwe, keeping the Americans tightly surrounded, lowered their weapons as well. Waabi could feel his heart pounding through his chest as the commotion settled.

"What is it you want?" the American negotiator asked Bagone-giizhig.

With his feet planted firmly in the ground, the Ojibwe leader took the opportunity to address his grievances. He spoke of a treaty in 1825 that established peaceful boundaries. He spoke of treaties in 1837 and 1842 that promised the Ojibwe they would never be moved from their land if they only allowed the U.S. government to use the land's resources. He spoke of the treaties in 1854 and 1855 that moved the Ojibwe people onto reservations with promises of wealth and services. "Those promises were broken," he said. He spoke of the traders who inflated their prices, of the lumber companies who stole trees from their land, of the government appointed farmers, doctors, blacksmiths, and teachers, who accepted their salaries but never once set foot on the reservations. And he spoke of the constant pressures to give up their way of life—to retire their hunting practices and pick up the plow, to cut their hair and put on a suit coat and jacket, to deny their gods and mark themselves with the cross of Christ, to raze their wigwams and replace them with permanent buildings, and to cut out their tongues and the tongues of their children so they never again speak a Native word.

"Can't you see?" he pleaded, speaking in fluent English. "We've done all we could to let you wipe us off the face of the earth.

Like an endless snowfall your people keep coming and keep taking more and more until the snow is impassable and our people are crushed under its weight. But it is time for the sun to come out. It is time for the spring rains to lighten our loads and renew our paths. I did not want war. We," he said, motioning his arms to the Ojibwe soldiers that surrounded them, "did not want war. We wanted only our rights, but could not get them through peaceable means."

The American negotiators, appearing withdrawn and angry, huddled together and discussed their response. After little time, the largest of them, a man with sagging eyes and an untrimmed beard, stepped forward from the group. "You are quite foolish to believe that a violent response will end with anything but defeat, and perhaps, utter annihilation for your people. But seeing that we are in no position to negotiate, we only ask that you release those captives you've taken earlier. They served their purpose by leading us into this trap, but holding them now can serve no further purpose."

Bagone-giizhig, with his shoulders back and head held high, turned toward the group of leaders at his back. Like the Americans, they discussed their response.

"We are at war," Bagone-giizhig answered minutes later. "And whether you acknowledge it or not, you are facing a powerful and determined enemy. We are not alone in our indignation. The Naadowens have already made plans for an attack and we will be joining them. Because we are at war, we cannot release our captives. But, we will show you that they are safe and being treated well."

The bearded American put his hands on his hips, then nodded.

Bagone-giizhig turned and motioned to someone in the distance behind him. "Have them come forward," he said.

Slowly, from out of the shadows, came several armed Ojibwe soldiers with a line of six white prisoners. They held their heads low, but appeared unharmed. Among them were an elderly man and woman, two middle-aged men, one middle-aged woman, and a young woman—a young woman with blond hair and a familiar gait.

Waabi felt his heart jump. "Chibines!" he said. "I think that is Agnes."

"From school? The pastor's daughter?"

"Yes, I think that's her." Waabi's excitement, as he realized the tragic circumstances, was quickly replaced by guilt and confusion. How could Agnes be held captive? She had never done any harm to anyone.

"She's just leverage," Chibines said, likely sensing Waabi's worry.

Waabi understood, but he wasn't sure how he felt. He knew the whites and their government were treacherous. They had to be punished for his father's death—his aunt's and his uncle's deaths. He did not want it to be Agnes, but he also didn't want to give himself over so easily; for one person, for one soul. He wanted to hold on to his resentment—to slay the Wiindigo.

Bagone-giizhig addressed the Americans again, "Now that you have seen that they are safe, you must join them. Tell your men to lay down their guns."

The negotiators, who had come expecting to scold the Ojibwe like children, were livid, scorning each other as they discussed their options.

"Let us send a messenger to St. Paul," one of them pleaded.

"There will be no messenger," Bagone-giizhig said. "Lay down your guns now, or I will order my soldiers to fall upon you like hungry wolves."

The large, bearded man fumed. "All right!" he said, his face red as a chokecherry. Then he turned to his soldiers, lifted his arms, and brought them down slowly. "Lay your guns in the grass and then take a step back."

Moments later, the Ojibwe rushed forward, confiscating the weapons and forcing the soldiers to their knees. Waabi followed along, hardening his face to look as fierce as he could. As he pointed his taut bow at the soldiers, he took a furtive glance toward Agnes. She had her head low and shoulders slumped like a mother in mourning. Waabi, standing there with his weapon aimed at the enemy, struggled with conflicting emotions of resentment and compassion.

The American soldiers were shaking with fear, some even cried. They were easily led away and brought to an old mission house where they could be held and monitored. The American negotiators were less docile than their soldiers, as one spat on the ground at Waabi's feet before being forced to go to the mission house. But eventually, the soldiers and officials were all packed inside the house, helpless in the struggle that would soon ensue.

The Ojibwe celebrated briefly, dancing on the shores of Gayaashko-zaaga'igan like school children at play. Waabi, however, did not join their joyous celebration. He sought out Agnes. As he walked hurriedly through the creek, his moccasins splashing in the cold water, he heard the crier announcing that all men should be ready to march south in a matter of minutes. "It's time to earn your war feathers!" the crier shouted.

Waabi warned himself that he shouldn't talk to Agnes. He knew it would only cause him a deeper pain and confusion. But his feet moved automatically and his body felt pulled by a string. As Waabi reached the wigwam where the captives were held, two armed guards barred his entry.

"I want to speak to one of the captives," Waabi said. "She's... a friend of mine."

The guards, whose smooth faces and soft shoulders exposed their youth, looked at each other. Turning his head to Waabi one of them said, "No one is allowed entry without the permission of the chief elders."

"Please, I only wish to say goodbye. We are readying to leave and I don't have time to seek permission."

"Waabi?" came a tender voice from inside the wigwam. Then, out stepped Agnes. Her floral patterned dress was torn and dirty. Her hair was tangled and coarse. Her face looked sullen and cold. Only her bright blue eyes, like two shiny agates from the shores of Mooningwanekaaning, remained the same.

The guards thrust their javelins in front of Agnes. Waabi appealed with them to let her out for only a moment, but they would not pull away their javelins. Then, a powerful voice sounded at Waabi's back.

"Let the boy speak to the girl," the man said. "Even war cannot deny our humanity. Besides, she is his sweetheart."

Waabi turned to see that the speaker was Bagone-giizhig. Waabi nodded his thanks and Bagone-giizhig, now wearing a plume of feathers on his head, nodded back.

The guards drew back their javelins and Agnes sprang forward. She opened her arms ready to embrace Waabi, but she held up at the last moment. "Waabi," she said in a strained voice. "What... what are you doing here?"

Waabi swayed as his legs buckled. "I... I left... I left Red Cliff," he mumbled. "My aunt and uncle passed away, my cousins left, I was mining copper; hammering rocks in a hole deep in the earth." Waabi struggled to express his grief.

With upturned eyes, Agnes peered at Waabi. "I'm so sorry. I'm sorry for everything that's happened to you. I know how much it hurt you to lose your father. And I've seen how quickly things have changed. But..." she stuttered, "but you can't go to war, can you? You can't kill. Thou Shalt Not Kill. Surely you remember the lesson of the Ten Commandments?"

Waabi stepped back and thought to respond harshly. Though he attended their Christian school, he was not a Christian. He grew up in the tradition of the Midewiwin, yet another thing the whites were taking away. Rather than respond with anger he said, "Are you hurt? I just came to see that you're all right."

"I'm not hurt," she said, lowering her head and eyes. She paused. "My mother and father escaped to Fort Ripley and I have not been harmed. But..." She paused.

"But what?" Waabi asked.

"I just want this to end," she said, bringing her eyes back up. "Don't you want this to end?"

"Of course I do," Waabi said without hesitation. "That's why we are going to fight. To finally put an end to the suffering and loss. To regain our land and traditions. To live at peace with nature like we once did. Like we did when I was still just a boy."

"Waabi," Agnes pleaded, "violence will not end anything. It will only create more violence. And besides that, you are not a warrior. I know you. I know you would not shed the blood of another."

"Stop!" Waabi said, surprised by his own reaction. "How many of *our* people have to die before we fight back? If we don't fight now, someday soon, there will be no one left! I may not be a warrior, but we are a warrior nation. War is in our blood; it's in my blood."

Waabi could not look Agnes in the eyes. He did not want to see her disappointment. He did not want the shame of his anger reflected in her face. He turned to walk away.

"At least ask them to release me, Waabi," she said, calling after them. "Let me be with my parents at Fort Ripley where it might be safe."

Waabi paused, still fighting his conflicting thoughts and emotions. "Nowhere is safe for the whites. Not after today."

"Wait," Agnes yelled, her voice choked.

Waabi walked with purpose toward the Ojibwe soldiers at the lake, chastening himself to ignore Agnes. As he did, he heard the cries of a young child from inside the wigwam. "Mamma!" the young child sobbed. He turned his head to see Agnes bending low to embrace the child—a blond-haired child with pink cheeks and freckles.

Waabi stopped in his tracks, feeling both sympathy and regret.

"You...you married?" Waabi said, looking back at her.

Agnes was crouched holding her son close and stroking his curly hair. "It's been seven years, Waabi. Of course I married." She looked at her boy, tears now rolling down her cheeks, then back at Waabi. "But... but he was killed—killed trying to protect us."

Waabi was struck with sorrow and despair. Before he could speak, Chibines called to him. "Waabi! The soldiers are departing. The march begins." Chibines waved his arm frantically, urging Waabi to join them.

Waabi looked at the soldiers, then back at the wigwam. Agnes' face was red and streaked with tears, her son's face buried into her shoulder as she stroked the back of his head.

She looked at Waabi peering back at her. "His name is Everett. Won't you help him? Won't you help us?"

Waabi didn't know what to say, so he said nothing.

Instead, he turned and ran to join the soldiers marching south.

Chapter 23

Samuel
New Ulm
August 1862

Samuel winced, grabbing his throbbing left arm. The blood had dried up and hardened, but a stinging pain permeated from the gash left behind from the bullet that grazed him. He needed the wound to be cleaned out. It had been a day and a half since leaving Fort Ridgely to investigate the Indian raids, about a day since Rabenski died trying to offer Samuel some much needed water, and an hour since he found the bloated body of Captain Marsh floating upside down along the banks of the river. How quickly one reality became another.

The sky was clear and the sun felt warm as Samuel wandered slowly down the fort road. He must have been close by now. He thought of his mother and younger siblings and feared the Indian attack had reached beyond the agency and fort. Were they safe? Had they been attacked? Were they alive? The sight of dead bodies along the road, gutted and fly-ridden, made Samuel fear the worst. His family, poor as they may have been, were safe when they lived in Vermont. They were alive. Why had he dared bring them to Minnesota!

Samuel looked at the river and noticed how nicely the waters reflected the color of the sky. It was a perfect mirror, like one could not be separated from the other. Samuel was tantalized by the glassy waters when he heard the faint rumbling of a wagon coming from behind him. With a few quick steps he withdrew from the road and hid among the thicket. The wagon rumbled along slowly and he heard no voices—Indian or White. It must be settlers, he thought. Indians would not have traveled so quietly. As the wagon neared, Samuel saw that it was indeed filled with settlers. Most had absent, tired looks on their faces. Walking alongside the wagon were several young men carrying rifles and scanning the area carefully in all directions. Much to Samuel's surprise, the wagon was driven by a Dakota man—a Sioux Indian. Though his skin was dark, his hair was cut short and he wore a farmer's hat and pants.

Carefully, and with his arms raised, Samuel rose up from the thicket. "Whoa there!" he said.

The men lifted their guns but immediately recognized him as an injured soldier and rushed to his side.

"Where you all headed?" Samuel asked, as two young men—boys really—with faces younger than his brother's assisted him toward the wagon. "I'm not sure the fort is safe. I've been hearing cannon fire coming from that direction."

"You think the Sioux got the fort?" the young man on Samuel's right asked. His youthful face was covered with dirt and sweat. He looked pained, like he'd been working in the field all day and couldn't take another minute.

Samuel turned his head toward the people in the wagon. Their harrowing, frightened appearances struck him. They resembled beggars, hunched over and cold. Physically they appeared unharmed but their eyes showed a fear Samuel had never encountered. They stared back at him, faces empty and detached, waiting for a response. Samuel knew that whatever fear or heartache he carried, he had to push it aside.

"I can't say for sure," Samuel finally said, trying to remove of any lingering cowardice from his voice. "But if they haven't overtaken the fort, I'm almost certain they're surrounding it. I say we head for the settlement of New Ulm."

"But that's another ten miles!" said a boy who couldn't have been more than twelve years old. "We'll be out here all night and that's when they'll come get us."

Several of the young women gasped, clutching their children tighter.

"Keep your voice down," commanded a tall, older gentleman who sat in the front of the wagon next to the Indian driver. Samuel recognized him as Reverend Riggs, the same man who had negotiated at the agency a few weeks prior. "I know you're scared, but we needn't arouse attention to ourselves. It's best we listen to this soldier. If the fort's been overtaken, then there's no purpose continuing to it. We should press on to New Ulm. If we stay quiet and stay awake, we'll be just fine. The Lord will protect us."

Reverend Riggs, who wore a dark suit and preacher's collar, nodded at Samuel as he was hoisted into the back of the wagon. The settlers scooted tightly to every edge and corner to make room. Looking at them more closely, Samuel could see that their faces were red and puffy from hours of crying.

Once Samuel was safely inside the wagon, Reverend Riggs turned to the driver. "John," he said, "continue past the fort and down the river valley until we reach the German settlement."

"John? What kind of name is John for an Indian?" Samuel said, a touch of animosity in his voice.

"That's John Other Day," said the young man seated next to Samuel who was examining the makeshift wrap on Samuel's left arm. "Does that hurt?"

"Mildly," Samuel said, pulling his arm away. "Why you got an Indian driving the wagon? Aren't we running from Indians?"

"He saved us," the young man explained.

"Saved you? An Indian?"

"John is a member of my father's Hazelwood Mission," the young man said, pointing to the reverend. "I'm Alfred and that's my father, Stephen Riggs."

"I know," Samuel said. "I've seen him preaching at the fort."

The young man nodded. "These other folks are my brothers and sisters and other people from Yellow Medicine. John Other Day warned us of an attack and now he's leading us to safety."

Samuel thought once again of his family, who lived not more than twenty miles away. "They attacked Yellow Medicine, too?"

"I'm afraid so," Alfred said, his head bobbing up and down with the bumps in the road. "A large group of angry Dakota led by Little Crow spread out across the river valley and places south. Now they're attacking the settlements and taking captives."

Samuel was stung by the realization that the Indian attack was not limited to the Redwood Agency or the soldier's fort. His family must have either fled or been killed.

"We're all in shock right now," Alfred said. His demeanor was calm, as if he'd already fully accepted their new circumstances.

Samuel grimaced and clutched his arm at a sudden tinge of pain.

Alfred placed his hand gently on Samuel's shoulder. "We'll get you a doctor in New Ulm. For now just lay back and rest."

Samuel winced, holding back tears. A mother seated behind him gently rubbed his back and shoulder, saying nothing. Taking a moment to collect himself, Samuel looked up at Alfred.

"Get some rest soldier. I know you've been through a lot, we all have. But the fighting isn't over."

Samuel took a deep breath and closed his eyes. He imagined his family by the warm stove before everything had changed. He imagined a life that could have been, but never was, and tried to fall asleep to the constant, rhythmic bumping of the wagon.

After a long and tense ride over the prairie and through the dark, Samuel and his motley crew of settlers, missionaries, and one very helpful Dakota arrived safely at New Ulm. The burgeoning town was a large German settlement at the confluence of the Minnesota and Cottonwood rivers. Samuel had never been to New Ulm, but knew it equaled Mankato and St. Peter as a hub of population and resources for the ever-growing frontier. The town was a flurry of activity as frightened residents began barricading themselves within the city center using anything and everything at their disposal—tables, desks, wagons, mattresses, plows, even hay bales. The wagon was allowed passage through a barricade protecting the town's main road and then directed to a house near the center of town. The three-story, Victorian-style house had been turned into a hospital for injured settlers to find medical care.

Samuel was welcomed by a nurse on the porch with bright eyes and a ready smile. Samuel judged her to be in her fifties and wondered if she had grown children who were soldiers fighting in the South. The woman led Samuel to a small room that appeared to be a closet, though it had a small window. The bed, which was only a few inches smaller than the room, was just a wooden table with some sheets and pillows on top of it. "You can rest here," she said. Her tone was direct and urgent. "I'll be back to clean your wound."

Samuel did as he was told, and he found the bed surprisingly comfortable. The sheets were clean, and the room was cool despite the rising heat of the August sun. As he lay there, he could not help but notice the din of noise and chaos that marked the house. He heard grown men screaming in agony, young children crying, and women sobbing, probably at the loss of their husbands. Footsteps moved throughout the building, both above and below him, with incredible quickness and purpose. Nurses and doctors shouted commands while volunteers directed incoming patients where they could find help and rest. Alfred was right, Samuel thought, this fight is much more than an outbreak at the Lower Agency. It's much more than a few aggrieved Indians.

The nurse returned with a tray of supplies and a bowl of steaming hot water. She said her name was Margaret and that she had no medical training, but that she would take good care of Samuel anyway. She also brought some toffee and bread which Samuel gobbled up quickly.

"I have three boys," she said while wiping Samuel's arm of dried blood. "They're men now, I suppose. But growing up they got hurt about as often as the sun rises and sets. That was all the medical training I needed."

Samuel listened, but wasn't in the mood to talk. He was more tired than he thought—more shaken by the battle that took the lives of his friends and might just have easily taken his own. He thought he'd be safe if he were assigned to a post in Minnesota. He thought he could protect Thomas. How wrong he was.

Margaret went on talking as she applied antiseptic. Her boys were in the war, she said, but were assigned to positions away from the front. She spoke of their eventual return and their plans for the future. It all sounded so picturesque and promising. "We came from New York," she said, "where rents were high and jobs were sparse. We were told of a place that was like the Garden of Eden. And so we came, chasing the American Dream. Nobody told us that the land wasn't ours to take."

Margaret finished cleaning the cut on Samuel's arm and wrapped it with a fresh bandage. As she got up she brushed her hand against Samuel's hair. "You rest easy now," she said. "I've got to attend to others with more serious wounds."

Samuel was already half asleep and did not notice when Margaret left. The pain in his arm had turned to numbness and his stomach felt satisfied, if not full. Beside him were his belongings, including *Leaves of Grass* which he carried in his army satchel. He felt confident Thomas, for the moment, was safe at Fort Snelling, an impenetrable fortress high atop the Mississippi River bluffs. Surely they had turned around with the payment and returned to the fort once they heard of the outbreak. He still wasn't sure about his mother and siblings, but he could do nothing about that now. As he succumbed to sleep once again, he knew he had to be prepared for more. He, and the town, would not avoid an attack. He would have to be a soldier again.

When Samuel finally woke up he had a dry mouth and an agonizing headache. He didn't know how long he'd slept, but the dim light coming through the window suggested it was dusk. He picked up his head from the pillow and leaned forward peering through the half-open door of his small room.

Seeing the fleet-footed nurse scamper by, he said, "Miss... um, Margaret."

She stopped in her tracks and poked her head inside the doorframe. "What is it, deary?" she said, eyebrows raised.

"Could you please show me to the latrine? And perhaps some fresh water? My mouth is about as dry as the sun is hot."

"Of course," she said, gently, a welcome difference from the urgency in her tone earlier. "You must be quite thirsty." She moved to enter the room, but then turned at the sound of an agonizing scream coming from down the hall. She looked back at Samuel and held up her finger to indicate she would be right back, then quickly departed toward the source of the scream.

Samuel leaned back on his elbows and sighed. He pivoted, dropping his feet to get up. As he bent down to put on his boots he heard the voice of a man just outside his room.

"I've got some water for you soldier," the man said, holding out a dented bronze canteen. The man had a thick goatee that was well trimmed and was long enough to hide his neck. His dark brown hair was slicked back across the top of his head. He was a tall, lanky man with greenish-brown eyes who was dressed formally, in the style of a business man with a suit coat and vest. He was no workman or farmer.

Samuel reached out his uninjured arm to take the canteen the man offered. He unscrewed the lid, tipped it back, and drank the cold, refreshing water. "Thank you, sir," he said, barely able to catch his breath before tipping the canteen back and taking another swig. Feeling satisfied, Samuel handed the canteen back and wiped his wet lips.

The man twisted the cap back onto the canteen and spoke. "I'm Major Judge Charles Flandrau, Indian agent to the Sioux. Now I am organizing the defense of this town."

Samuel nodded, unsure what he was expected to say.

There was an awkward pause. Screams and urgent yelling could still be heard in the background. "How's your arm feeling?" the judge said.

Samuel looked at his arm as if it were a tool, not a body part. "It's just a cut. I should be fine now that it's been cleaned and wrapped."

"Good," Flandrau said with a hesitant smile.

"What is it?" Samuel said.

Judge Flandrau drew his shoulders back, taking a deep breath. "To be honest with you, young man, our circumstances are dire. We have very few men with any military training in town."

"I can surely help," Samuel said, "if that's what you're asking."

Flandrau looked at Samuel's arm. "Can you fire a rifle?"

"Of course," Samuel said with enthusiasm, though he was suddenly struck with the chilling memory of the attack at the ferry.

"Are you sure?" Flandrau asked. "I don't want to send you back into battle if you're not ready."

Samuel paused as memories darted through his mind—the trip west, the hard winter, the day his father was killed, the day

Thomas showed up in Union blue, the ambush that nearly took his own life.

"Soldier?"

Samuel shook his head free of the memories. "Yes, of course. I'm ready. I'm ready to fight the Indians and protect this place. To protect our future."

"All right then," Judge Flandrau said with a nod. "For now, gather your strength. When you're ready, we'll need you on the front lines. As I said, we have very few men with any military training. Your assistance will be invaluable to these farmers and city folk."

Flandrau lowered his hands at his side, still holding the canteen. He gave Samuel a look of gratitude and turned to leave.

"Wait," Samuel urged, reaching out his hand.

Flandrau paused and looked back at him.

"Can you tell me what's really happening?" Samuel asked, thinking of his mother and siblings. "I mean, I know we're in for a fight, but since the battle at the ferry I've been in the dark here. I lost my company. The fort's been under attack. The town is frantic. What exactly is our situation?"

Straightening his suit coat, Flandrau turned back to face Samuel. Without hesitating he said, "We expect an Indian attack and we need all able-bodied men ready to defend the town."

"You're not telling me much, Major," Samuel said. "*Did* we lose the fort? Exactly how many Indians are on the attack? How far do their forces extend?"

Flandrau raised his eyes to the dirt streaked window on the side of Samuel's makeshift bed. As he looked back at Samuel his expression shifted. He released the facade of confidence and calm he'd been expressing. He nodded. "The Sioux overran the fort. The soldiers held them off for as long as possible, but they were too greatly outnumbered. The Indians set fire to the barracks and took another two hundred captives on top of the two hundred fifty they already held."

Samuel gasped, struck by the realization that the fort had truly been overrun. Deep down, he felt a tinge of relief that he had not been there.

Flandrau continued. "They've attacked numerous

settlements, some as far away as Lake Shetek. The entire state is in a panic. People have fled to the towns for safety. Right now, there is no way to know how many settlements the Sioux have attacked or how many are engaged. We know that there is division among them, and we doubt they have the strength or resources to make an attack on St. Paul."

Samuel put his head in the palms of his hands. He worried, not knowing if his family was still alive or had found safety. He calmed himself and asked, "Reinforcements? What about reinforcements?"

"Messengers have been sent to Fort Snelling. We've telegraphed Washington as well. But help won't arrive in time for us, I'm afraid. Plus, there are disturbing rumors that Hole-in-the-Day—Bagone-giizhig—intends to join the fray."

"The Chippewa? The enemy of the Sioux?"

"The rumors are that Little Crow and Hole-in-the-Day have been conspiring for some time—that they have been planning a combined war effort for more than a year."

Samuel thought back to their first encounter with the Indians—with Little Crow, standing there in his home acting like a friend; like a needy child. He had no idea a needy child could mount such a vicious attack—could change their world.

"My family," Samuel said. "What about my family?"

Flandrau's posture softened and his face fell. "I don't know of your family, but I know many reached safety before the Indian assault spread. Others are being held captive, but they are unharmed."

Flandrau paused as he stepped forward and glanced down at Samuel solemnly. "Listen. Frontier settlers are vigilant, determined people. We will defend our homes against all odds—your family, too. We just need to take this one step at a time, adjusting to the circumstances as they come. Before long, we'll get this under control and the Indians will be punished. They will never be allowed, not in a million years, to do something like this again. Not in America."

Samuel struggled to understand the major's assurances. He felt anxious and tense, but didn't want his fear to show. Hiding any cowardice he answered, "We have to brace ourselves for the next fight, not worry about the one that may never happen."

As the major left his side, Samuel turned his head to the window. Looking down from the second story he saw a man in the street teaching a boy how to reload a musket. Probably a father with his son.

Chapter 24

**Samuel
New Ulm
August 1862**

It was early morning when the alarm was sounded. "*Indians! Indians!*" Samuel heard from outside his temporary hospital room. He jumped to his feet and nearly tipped over with dizziness, unable to balance himself because of a sudden rush of blood to his head. After recovering, Samuel grabbed the flint-lock rifle he was issued at Fort Ridgely and his Union-blue army jacket. Looking around he found his satchel and flung it over his shoulder. Samuel ran quickly out the door and down the steps. Several other injured men were also rising from their beds and makeshift cots, taking up weapons and heading outside. Others—men, women, and children—watched helplessly, their faces flushed with fear.

Stepping outside, Samuel saw throngs of men rushing northwest along the main road, clouds of dirt rising in their wake. "Form a defensive position on the outskirts of town!" he heard a man shout. "Both sides! They're coming from both sides!"

Both sides? Samuel thought. *How could that be? Were their forces that large?*

Looking to his right Samuel saw that it was Major Flandrau who shouted orders from atop his horse, directing men to their positions. Flandrau paused, turned his head, and made eye contact with Samuel.

"Get to the front of the lines on the northwest end of town," Flandrau said. "Seeing you in your army fatigues will give the folks confidence."

With a nod and salute Samuel watched as Flandrau whirled around and galloped in the opposite direction. Shedding the bandage from his arm and putting on his army jacket, Samuel joined the crowd of men heading past the barricades and toward the front lines. There were men of all ages among them, some appearing as old as eighty and others still just teenagers. They were farmers, most of them, wearing tattered and threadbare cotton shirts. Their bearded faces were darkened by the sun or whitened by age and most wore wide-brimmed hats covering their thinning, unkempt hair. But they appeared determined and resolute, perhaps unaware of the tragic and grisly reality that awaited them. Samuel had seen his first taste of battle at the ferry before anyone really knew the intentions of the Dakota. They actually waved from across the ferry as a sign of friendship, before springing their ambush and killing his friends and comrades.

Samuel was afraid. He did not want to die or have the town overrun and destroyed by Indians—a people of a bygone era. But necessity overruled emotion. Whatever fear he had or need for revenge remained hidden while he thought only of what he had to do to protect himself and the people of the settlement. They deserved death no more than his father had. And stopping them now meant stopping them from getting to Thomas.

Weaving his way through the crowd of defenders, Samuel reached the front where bags of flour, corn, and sand had been laid as a battle line. Looking out over the rolling prairie Samuel could see Indians gathering. They were still far off, but they appeared like a great and powerful storm their numbers were so large.

"We'll meet them here," said a young man who was already kneeling and waiting, his rifle resting against his shoulder. "They aren't getting past us. They aren't taking our town."

Samuel recognized a German accent in the young man's voice. He looked with curiosity at the resolute settler.

"I'm Karl," the young man said with a subtle nod. "It's nice to see a real soldier with us. What happened to your arm?"

"It's nothing," Samuel said. "A bullet grazed me at the ferry, first day of the attacks."

Another man came forward, speaking with urgency to the young man. He spoke German.

"Rolf," Karl said, interrupting the man. "This is..."

"Copeland. Private Samuel Copeland." Samuel shook hands with the man. His eyes were a deep blue that shined like gems amidst his white hair and beard. His face was withered and worn, and his once powerful chest and arms were deflated by age.

"Ja, I'm Rolf," he said, sounding more like a young man than an old one.

Turning to Samuel, Karl said, "Rolf was just saying that he thinks those are Chippewa out there, not Dakota."

"Then it's true what the Major said, the Sioux and Chippewa are coming together to fight us."

"Pff," the old man scoffed. "It's just another uprising— another damn uprising."

"Another uprising?" Samuel said.

"Ja," Karl said as he looked out across the prairie at the Indians who had now halted. "We're forty-eighters, Rolf and I. Fought against the Austrian aristocracy for the rights of the working class, but lost. We had to flee or risk losing our heads."

Samuel knew Germans in the army, but he never asked them much about their pasts. "That's why you're here?"

"That's why we came to America. That's not why we came to New Ulm."

Samuel stared back, inquisitively.

"You ever heard of the Turner Movement?"

"No."

Seeing the Indians were not advancing, Karl lowered his rifle at his side. All around them was the commotion of men moving to position, loading their guns or praying to the heavens for good fortune and courage.

"Turnerism is all about good exercise, national pride, political and religious freedom, education, and equality. We believe in sound bodies and minds, fellowship, and the common good. But we couldn't practice these beliefs anywhere, so a community of Germans established New Ulm as a sort of German sanctuary. A place with good soil and lumber, where we wouldn't be persecuted or called squareheads."

Samuel chuckled, remembering a few times he called Germans squareheads. "Sorry," he said, realizing Karl didn't find it funny.

"Now we have to fight to protect what we built. What we made for ourselves."

Samuel realized how fortunate he was to grow up in Vermont. They may have left because of hard times, but not because they were being persecuted. "Do you ever regret coming here? Are you angry that you had to fight the government back home and now you have to fight the Indians here?"

Karl shrugged. "It won't be like this forever. It's only a matter of time before the Indians are gone for good. Then my children and grandchildren will have this whole vast and beautiful countryside. And nobody's going to call them squarehead anymore."

"They're movin'!" a voice shouted clear as a bell.

Samuel's body shook as he looked out over the open prairie. Coming toward them was an endless horde of Native Indians armed and dressed for war. Their skin shone bright and their metal hatchets glistened in the morning sun. In front were half a dozen riders on painted horses. Their faces were blackened and their heads were decked with red and yellow beaded headbands. Behind them were scores of infantry. Some carried rifles, others carried javelins, bows and arrows, and blunt mallets. Their approach was steady and determined. It was terrifying yet somehow majestic, Samuel thought, like admiring the destructive power of a tornado while it was heading straight at him.

Samuel lowered himself to one knee and rested his musket atop the siege line and pointed it toward the enemy. Only his gray kepi was visible from behind the fortification.

"Hold your fire!" Major Flandrau commanded as his horse nervously plodded at the rear of the line. "Let them come closer, men!"

Shots rang out in the distance, but they did not come from the approaching enemy. A commotion rose from the nervous defenders.

"They're attacking from two fronts," Samuel said to no one in particular. "The other side of town is under siege."

"Steady men!" Flandrau shouted. "Focus on the task at hand."

The commotion lightened, but the tension was thick as

218

water. Men looked on with hardened faces now dripping with sweat, their eyes filled with uncertainty.

"Für Freiheit und Zukunft," Karl said, sensing the moment was near.

"They can't have New Ulm!" Flandau shouted, trying to instill determination into his men. "Remember your wives and children. Remember your farms and homes. Don't give up the fight!"

A shot rang out, piercing the air. It was followed by a sudden hush and a cloud of smoke that floated, ghost-like, from the barrel of one of the farmer's guns. The echoing sound of the shot was all that could be heard. The moment stood still.

"Fire!" Flandrau shouted.

Like falling dominoes an array of cracks and pops sounded as men fired toward the oncoming enemy, few actually hitting their mark. A thick cloud of smoke obstructed the defenders from seeing the reaction of their enemy. But, from behind the smoke, they heard the shrieking of hundreds of Native soldiers scampering forward in a rush toward the siege line.

"Faster! Faster!" Samuel said to himself as he reloaded his rifle. For a moment, he noticed the quickness with which Rolf reloaded, impressed with the old man's dexterity.

Once Samuel had his rifle loaded, he lowered it atop the barricade and aimed through the sight. His heart sank. The Indians were already upon them. Samuel fired into the crowd now just a few yards away and then reached for his Bowie knife and braced for hand-to-hand combat.

The defenders began to turn and run, but many were cut down. They fell to the ground one after another with an arrow, tomahawk, or bullet to the back. Some men continued firing, others parried blows from Indians leaping over the line. The sound of screams of pain, shouts of bravery, and explosions of gunfire meshed together to create a horrible din of noise.

Seeing that their position was immediately compromised, Major Flandrau called for a retreat. "Fall back!" he shouted. "Fall back to the barricaded town center!"

With Karl still beside him, Samuel fended off a leaping attacker catching him by the throat with his knife. Warm, salty blood splattered across Samuel's face causing him to gasp, almost throwing up. With the sleeve of his uniform he wiped the blood from his eyes and mouth.

Seeing Karl pinned to the ground by an Indian who held a knee to his throat, Samuel, acting instinctively, grabbed his rifle by the barrel and swung the butt down hard against the Indian's skull. The attacker winced in pain, putting his hand to his head and releasing Karl's throat. Seeing his opportunity, Karl pushed the Indian aside and stabbed him through the chest with his knife.

Karl looked up at Samuel. His eyes were wide with terror and he was panting furiously.

Seconds later, an arrow pierced Karl's temple. The sound of torn flesh was sudden and clear. Karl fell, lifeless as a rock, eyes still open.

Turning forward, Samuel saw an Indian rushing toward him with a javelin aimed at his heart. Acting automatically, Samuel glanced the blow aside with his rifle and then leaped on top of the Indian who had fallen with his stomach to the ground. Having dropped his knife, Samuel feverishly beat the back of the man's head with one blow after another. But the Indian managed to move his head, putting Samuel off balance and allowing the Indian to force Samuel off of him. With his javelin still in his hand, the Indian thrust it forward catching Samuel in the thigh.

Samuel, from the ground, arched his back in pain. Reaching his hands back to support himself, Samuel's right hand came in contact with his knife. The Indian pushed the javelin in harder causing Samuel to scream out. But, as he did, he grasped the handle of the knife tightly in his hand. From his hips Samuel launched his upper body and arm forward plunging the knife into the side of the Indian's neck. Like a hammer to a nail it caught perfectly. The Indian brought his hands to his neck and started coughing up blood. Samuel inched back in horror as he watched the life of the Indian pour out through his mouth and neck. Moments later the Indian convulsed violently, then dropped his head and was motionless.

Samuel held his breath and gritted his teeth as he pulled the sharpened wooden tip of the javelin from his leg. Luckily, it had missed the bone, but blood spurted from the wound. Acting quickly, Samuel emptied the contents of his satchel which included cloth and rope. He stuffed and wrapped the wound and then tied the rope above his knee to slow the flow of blood. The pain had passed and Samuel realized he was alone. Looking around he saw that all of the Indian attackers had moved beyond the original siege line and toward the center of town. Karl lay dead beside him along with a few other unfortunate settlers. He did not know if Rolf had survived or not.

There seemed to be nothing he could do now. Injured as he was, if he re-entered the fight he would surely be killed. If he stayed put he would be captured and likely killed. For a moment, Samuel sat there listening to the rushing waters of the river in the distance while noticing the warmth of the rising sun. It was a peaceful moment amidst unthinkable chaos. But if he was to survive he knew he had to move.

Using his rifle as a crutch Samuel stood, putting all his weight on his left leg. He limped forward, surprised he could walk at all, and started heading for the trees at the edge of the river valley. Enduring pain with each step but moving as quickly as he could, Samuel reached the cover of the trees unnoticed. Grateful to be alive, he weaved through the empty forest as the sounds of war cries and gunfire dissipated. The smell of blood and gunpowder was replaced with the pleasant aroma of ferns and flowers. But as Samuel neared the river he began to feel dizzy, and then he began to stumble. Catching himself against a tree, he felt determined to make it the river where he could be refreshed. He moved forward but could barely take a step without stumbling. Now, just yards away, his legs went numb and he collapsed. The world went black.

Chapter 25

WasabishkiMakwa
Marching south to New Ulm
Manoominike-giizis
(August 1862)

The land looked different as the Ojibwe marched south. What had been quiet lakes and streams surrounded by tall, deep green coniferous trees changed to dry, golden plains marked by groves of oak, maple, and cottonwood trees. They had gone to a place Waabi had only heard of. A place beyond the Big Woods where the Lakota once hunted buffalo. A place fought over by his ancestors where the Ojibwe made revenge raids followed by the Naadowens making revenge raids of their own. The land was open and free of barriers. There were no places to hide—for an animal or a man. Waabi felt a small but distinct discomfort being so far from home. He felt out of place.

He found encouragement, though, in the procession of Ojibwe gathered around him—walking with him, all moving toward the same goal; the same destiny. They were not like the white soldiers who walked side-by-side, row-by-row, in unison across the land, like one giant slow-moving target. The Ojibwe were free to move about; to talk, to sing, to run, to rest. They did not have to prove how disciplined they were. Each one had already smoked the pipe and dedicated himself to the purpose. Their women came along, too, hauling wagons filled with dried fruits, herbs, potatoes, and drinking water. Even some dogs and children came along ready to set up camp wherever a fight took place.

Waabi traveled with his bandolier bag bumping at his hip. It was frayed at the edges and had lost some beads from years of use, but it was heartening to have his mother and father with him in that small way. He also thought of Agnes and the fear she had in her eyes when he spoke to her—when he spoke in such an unforgiving tone. He did not want Agnes to suffer or hurt, but this was bigger than her, he told himself. This was bigger than any single white man or woman he had met over the years. Wasn't it? This was a collision of his people's past and their future. Even if it was a mistake and the Ojibwe were defeated, Waabi had a responsibility to fight—to take revenge for his father's life and to follow in the path of his people's traditions.

After several days of marching, the large Ojibwe procession neared its destination—a settlement called New Ulm by the whites. They had met with several white militias along the way who were so daunted by the vastness of the Ojibwe army that each retreated without a fight. It drew laughter from the Ojibwe soldiers and spurred confidence in their ability to destroy the white army. The night before the scheduled attack, they camped at the farmstead of a settler who tried to flee from the Bwaanag. He did not survive, and the body of the farmer along with his wife and two children lay dead in the field behind the house. For many of the Ojibwe, it was the first time they had ever seen a dead white man. Some found it amusing, others found it difficult to look at.

"Back on the island I never thought I would take up the war-cry against the whites," Chibines said to Waabi as they lay in the tall grass underneath the moonless night sky. "I was angry at times, but many of the whites had become our neighbors and friends at Mooningwanekaaning. I would never attack my neighbors and friends."

"Do you think you will be able to take a life?" Waabi asked with honest curiosity.

Frogs croaked somewhere in the distance. The air was unusually warm and heavy.

Chibines was slow to answer. After a few silent moments he said, "I have a younger brother named Waatese. You did not know him. He did not attend school with us. Waatese was not born of my mother.

"One day, while my older brother, Migizi, was out on a fall hunt, he found a boy who was a few years younger than him. Apparently, the boy had been lost for many days because he was very thin, weak, and acted strangely. My brother offered the boy some deer meat from his hunt. The boy ate it, hardly taking a moment to chew, but when my brother offered to lead the boy to our village he refused to go. That night, when my brother slept alone in the woods, the boy snuck up on him and killed him so that he could take all the meat.

"When my brother did not return home my family became very worried. My father tried to calm my mother by saying he was probably picture writing in the woods, and that he would return when he was satisfied and left his totem mark. A few more days passed and still my brother did not return.

"Then a heavy rain came and my father told my mother that he would go out looking to see that my brother was safe. But as he took his first step, a boy appeared from the woods. He looked like a spirit who was neither alive nor dead.

"The boy, seeing the grief and worry in my father's face, immediately recognized him as the father of the person he had killed over some deer meat. He walked up to my father, barely able to open his eyes through the pouring rain, and told him what he had done. He then lifted his head toward the sky, closed his eyes, and waited for my father to cut his throat. My father gripped his knife so tight that his hand became white and his forearm bulged like a snake that had eaten a rabbit. Then, behind the boy, somewhere in the woods, lightning struck, followed by the immediate clap of thunder. It was my brother's spirit, telling my father to spare the boy's life. My father dropped his knife in the mud and embraced the boy. 'You will never go hungry again,' my father said. 'You will be called Waatese and you will be adopted into our family to take the place of the one we lost.' The boy embraced my father and was welcomed into our wigwam. He has been my adopted brother ever since."

"I did not know this," Waabi said. "But why have you told me this story? How does it answer my question?"

"We cannot adopt every white man to take the place of all those we've lost," Chibines said. "For justice, there must be an exchange. A life for a life. I am prepared to kill so that we shall find this balance."

Waabi stared at the night sky, feeling a certain sense of relief wash over him. The sound of the frogs had dissipated, and only a soft breeze remained rustling through the grass like a serpent. The heavy air was lifted and finally a coolness settled in, lulling Chibines and Waabi to sleep.

The march to New Ulm began early, while the light on the eastern horizon was a soft glow and the dew on the grass was thick and cold. The women stayed behind in camp ready to provide support to injured soldiers. The young men prepared their souls through quiet chants and meditation, then they applied natural colors, created by ground-up roots and leaves, to their faces and bodies. It was all done quietly and routine-like.

By the time the march started, the top of the sun had begun to show, covering the horizon with a rich, brilliant orange that made it look as if the prairie had caught fire. The day would be clear and warm. Waabi put aside his fear and doubts and focused on the words of his grandmother. He would not be slaying the white man, he would be slaying the Wiindigo. He would be creating a future for his people to thrive again—a place for them to stand and look in all directions and see only Ojibwe country.

The men followed Bagone-giizhig who urged them forward, a bow slung over his shoulder and a rifle in his hand. He sat atop a white, brown-spotted horse. Being a woodland people who traveled by canoe, it was unusual to see an Ojibwe soldier on a horse, but it was visually appealing to the young men who, like Waabi, looked to Bagone-giizhig for confidence and bravery.

They moved steadily, as a single unit now, knowing that they, along with the Dakota, outnumbered the defenders of the town. While it was still early in the day, the town appeared in the distance. It was much larger than Waabi imagined. There were buildings, too numerous to count, and roads that were wide and well-traveled. For a moment, it appeared abandoned, until they drew closer and could see men with guns huddled behind piled objects. Before long, Waabi could almost make out the faces of the men behind the barriers. They were old—many of them—their faces lined with age and their hands held unsteadily on the barrels of their rifles, muskets, and pitchforks. Waabi didn't know these men,

225

but he assumed they were little different than the white men near Gichigami, set on progress and motivated by paper money.

"Be brave," Chibines said, sensing the battle was near.

"Be merciless," Binishii said, the Gull Lake Ojibwe Waabi had met at the enlistment building. "Carry your scalps on your belt and bring them back for the women who grieve over the loss of their land and ways of living."

Waabi, seeing the fire in Binishii's eyes, was startled, but then he remembered his father and the place his father was buried. He wished to take at least one scalp and lay it at the grave of all those who died at Sandy Lake.

The Ojibwe halted, now just a short sprint from the defenders of the town. Waabi thought he could hear them breathing.

Out front, Bagone-giizhig and several other soldiers on horseback paced back-and-forth. They offered no instructions or impassioned speeches. They just looked on, waiting for a signal from the Dakota who planned to strike the opposite side of the town.

The dew had evaporated, and the grass was dry and brittle. A single shifting step made a loud crackling sound like bark being torn from a tree. The soldiers were tense and reacted to every sound and movement with heightened awareness. It was a natural instinct most of the young men had experienced only while hunting animals during the dead of winter, when their survival was at stake.

A plume of smoke rose up from the hills to the south of town. Seeing it, Waabi felt a jolt of nervous energy pass through his heart and all the way through his feet and hands. For a moment he was numb.

Then, like an unexpected bee sting, Binishii was struck by a bullet directly between the eyes. A drop of blood trickled down the bridge of his nose and he fell dead before he even knew he'd been hit. As his body toppled forward there was a moment of pure stillness. But when his lifeless figure landed against the dirt with a thud, it acted like a spark on a loaded cannon. The men raised their voices in some strange unison of dissonant sounds as they charged the town. Startled by the suddenness of Binishii's death, Waabi hesitated. Being bumped as more and more men ran by him, Waabi, who hoped some kind of warrior instinct would kick in, felt only fear and confusion.

"The Ojibwe is brave before his enemies!" a soldier shouted while staring intently at Waabi, the soldier's face painted with streaks of black and red. "Advance!" he commanded, pointing toward the town.

Waabi burst forward, his hatchet held out in front of him like some generic Indian brave he'd seen in the white storybooks. As he drew nearer the line of engagement, he could see men, both white and Ojibwe, toppling over, bloodied and lifeless. He was bewildered by the instantaneousness of death followed immediately by its permanence. This was nothing like killing the deer or bear which surrendered its life for the survival of his family and people. Gifts of herb and tobacco were not spread in gratitude over the lives of men. Instead, war gave life a whole new meaning. Kill or be killed. There was no gratitude nor sacrifice, only passion, fear, and rage—men in their most primitive, primal forms.

Waabi raised his hatchet, prepared to slam it down on the skull of the first white defender he encountered. But, by the time he reached the barricade where the settlers once knelt, he was too late to engage in combat. The settlers had retreated and were sprinting toward the safety of the town center. To his surprise, Waabi was relieved. He stood there for a moment, watching the Ojibwe soldiers chase after and cut down the retreating whites when his foot began to feel wet and warm. He pulled his foot back and looked down to see that his moccasin had been soaking in a shallow pool of blood. Waabi heaved forward, almost vomiting. Beside the pool of blood was an old man who lay prone on the ground with the top of his head missing and blood pouring from his chest. The man's mouth was open and his tongue was out. He appeared irredeemably dead. Looking around he saw more bodies, their faces contorted into portraits of rage, shock, and terror. There were old men and young, none of them dressed in army uniforms. They were ordinary; they were plain.

Waabi straightened himself and looked off to the north, away from the town. He saw a line of trees that bordered the river and led down into a secluded ravine. He turned his head forward and saw his comrades firing guns and shooting arrows from behind the cover of the numerous buildings. The defenders fired back, preventing them from charging. Clouds of smoke rose up from their rifles and the pop and crack of shooting littered the air. The battle was in full force now and there would be no one to notice if he just slipped away. He looked down at his forearm, painted with lines of black and glistening with sweat. In his hand he clutched his hatchet, clean of blood and sparkling in the early morning sunshine. A gurgle and a moan startled him. He raised the hatchet to defend himself, before realizing it was an Ojibwe soldier who had caught a bullet in the eye. The Ojibwe, who was just a boy, had only enough energy to turn his head and look at Waabi with his one remaining eye. The boy's eyelid fluttered as if he were trying to stay awake, and then it closed forever. Waabi looked back at the hatchet in his hand and remembered the final words his father gave him: "Never let hate enter your heart." Then he tucked his hatchet into his belt, turned away from the battle, and ran north toward the river.

Without looking back, Waabi reached the safety of the wooded river basin. It was cool and quiet, the only sound being the burble of the flowing river. The sounds of battle were distant and indistinct. His new environment completely contradicted the one he had just left. The bushes were thick and green, dotted with flowers and berries. The trees shaded the ground and housed the birds and rodents. The river flowed smooth and gentle. It was a place of peace, solitude, and life, not death, hate, and revenge. It felt so much more natural and soothing to Waabi than the conflict inside him.

As Waabi made his way toward the river to get a cool drink, he saw what was, unmistakably, a blue uniform. Quickly and silently, he darted behind the trunk of a tree. Like the first time he killed a deer, his heart raced. He took a few deep breaths and focused on listening. He heard nothing but the subtle and constant sounds of the forest. Apparently, the man in the blue uniform was not moving. With his back to the tree, Waabi rolled his weight to his shoulder and tilted his head around the trunk peering toward the spot where he saw the uniform. It was indeed a soldier, but he appeared to be dead. The soldier's head was flat against his shoulder and his eyes were closed. Taking his hatchet firmly in his hand, Waabi stepped forward from behind the tree and began walking toward the soldier. The soldier was on his rear with his back to a tree. He could just be sleeping. He looked young. The sleeve of his army coat was torn and his right pant leg was soaked in blood. Now, Waabi was close enough to touch the soldier as he leaned forward looking for any signs of life. Cautiously, Waabi put the back of his hand in front of the soldier's mouth. He was breathing.

This is it, Waabi thought. This was his chance to take a scalp, to kill a white man, to take revenge for the death of his father. Waabi unsheathed his knife and planted his feet on each side of the soldier's legs. He leaned down, pulled back the soldier's hair, and pressed his blade against the top of the soldier's forehead. His heart pounded hard and fast causing his eardrums to pop. His hands perspired and his breathing quickened. It was finally time to take a life for everything he had lost. Waabi grunted and groaned, holding back his pain and sadness and fear. He remembered the decaying scalps he saw as a boy blowing in the wind. He remembered the words of his mother who said that before doing harm, he must first judge the consequences. And then, as if his father were there beside him, he heard the words, "Never let hate enter your heart." Waabi dropped the knife and fell backwards landing hard against the forest floor. Tucking his head into his knees Waabi heaved and cried like he had when he learned of his father's death.

Chapter 26

Samuel
Outside of New Ulm
August 1862

Greeted by a pulsing headache, Samuel groaned in pain. He opened his eyes to find his vision blurred. He blinked quickly, several times, and squeezed his eyes tight before reopening them while gasping for breath. He licked his dry, cracked lips and sniffed the air. It was rich with the smell of smoke as if a campfire were right in front of him. As his vision cleared he suddenly remembered what happened. He turned to his left, looking over his shoulder and saw huge plumes of dark smoke rising up to the sky. New Ulm was on fire. It was unlike anything Samuel had ever seen. Smoke poured into the air like water and gathered into one massive cloud that spread over the western prairie, slowly dissipating toward the south as the wind tugged on its tail.

"Oh, my God," Samuel said aloud, his voice cracked and broken.

Samuel coughed. His throat was dry and he felt hot flashes, like he had a fever. He needed water. He looked to his right at the clear water of the river, almost salivating at the sight of it. But he couldn't move. He felt heavy as a rock and his leg throbbed. Looking down he was startled to find that the wound on his leg had been wrapped. He jolted backwards not realizing he was leaning against the trunk of a tree. The hard, course bark stung his backbone. Recovering from the pain, he reached for his gun, but it was gone! Worrisome thoughts tumbled through Samuel's mind. Who had taken his gun? Who had dressed his wound, and what did they intend to do with him? Would he be tortured and scalped?

He heard a splash upriver. He looked through the trees and saw a young Indian man, a few years older than him, spearing for fish. Fear rose up through his body, but he told himself not to panic. If the Indian intended to kill him, he would have been dead already.

The Indian stood up from his knees and, with several fish in tow, began walking toward Samuel. He wore moccasins and dark trousers along with a beaded, deer-skin vest hemmed with lines of red and black. His skin was smooth, without blots or scars, and he had no feathers atop his long, tied-back hair, nor any war paint on his face. He did not resemble a Sioux.

As the Indian drew closer, Samuel tried to get up so he could prepare to defend himself. He brought his feet in close and placed the palms of his hands against the cold dirt, but as he tried to leverage his way up, he realized he had been tied by the waist around the tree. He groaned and sat back down. His movements had caught the Indian's attention.

"Stop!" Samuel said, holding his hand out in the universal gesture.

The Indian froze in his tracks, staring at Samuel like he had just seen a wild animal and didn't know whether to run or play dead.

Sensing an advantage Samuel said, "If you come any closer I swear on my father's life I will choke the life out of you with my bare hands!" Samuel spoke with such vigor that he spit as the words escaped his mouth.

The Indian slowly lowered his spear which was merely a stick he had fashioned himself. Then, he held out his empty hands and said, "I mean you no harm." His voice was gentle, almost motherly.

"We're at war," Samuel said, "I can't trust you." Followed by, "You speak English?"

"Yes," the Indian said, nodding. "The missionaries taught me as a boy. I attended the white man's school."

Samuel began shaking and he felt a sudden chill. Anger mixed with confusion and fear. He was not well. "Why did you wrap my wound? What do you intend to do with me?" he said, trying to sound stronger than he was.

"You are thirsty, aren't you?"

Samuel didn't answer. His mind raced. He saw an Indian—dark skin and eyes, straight mouth and narrow lips, round face, buckskin and moccasins—not much unlike the man who killed his father, or the horde that just attacked New Ulm. An enemy was an enemy.

"I thought of scalping you," the Indian said. "I held my knife to your forehead. I thought of returning to my people with honor. I thought of carrying the scalp to the graves of my family. But there would be no honor in scalping a man who could not defend himself." He paused and looked away. "And I found out, even with the tradition of war that runs through my blood, even with memory of everything I have lost, I am not a killer." He paused again and looked Samuel straight in the eyes. "I am not a killer, and you have done me no harm."

Samuel was filled with uncertainty, but found relief in the Indian's words. Strangely, the Indian reminded him of himself, before all of this—before enlisting; before his father was killed and his family was broken. He longed for a return to the simplicity of life even in its labors.

"Yes, I am thirsty," Samuel said, giving in to the Indian's generosity.

The Indian man's eyes brightened, but his mouth quivered, hesitant to smile. He picked up Samuel's canteen which lay beside his satchel on the ground. Slowly, the Indian brought the canteen to Samuel and handed it to him. Samuel, allowing himself to take his eyes off the stranger, drank it greedily. He took several quick gulps, paused to breathe and then took several more.

After satisfying his thirst, Samuel placed the canteen in the dirt beside him and said, "What do you call yourself?"

"I am called Waabi. I am of the Loon Clan from the La Pointe band of Ojibwe at Mooningwanekaaning-minis."

Samuel shook his head, unaware of such a place.

"It is several days travel to the north and east, on an island in Gichigami, the lake your people call Superior."

"And what brought you all the way down here?"

"It is a long story," the Indian named Waabi said. "And besides, I could ask the same of you. But for now, you should eat something. You need some food and more rest."

Waabi began collecting sticks and branches and arranging them in a pile to build a fire. While he was doing this, Samuel tried to reach around the tree to loosen the vine that held him to the tree. He found it was impossible.

"Aren't you going to untie me?" Samuel said.

"I cannot trust you, yet," Waabi answered, now preparing the fish over a fire. "And I know that you do not trust me."

"You can't just keep me here."

Waabi sat down in the scattered grass, making himself comfortable. "Your leg is injured. You're sick with fever. Even if I untied you, you are not well enough to go anywhere. Just try to rest."

The fire crackled while the fish sizzled atop the tin that held them. Darkness had slowly begun to fall over the landscape. Smoke still billowed from the town of New Ulm but it had died down significantly. The sounds of war had all but disappeared.

Samuel sighed heavily. He could think of nothing worth saying in response to the Indian. Minutes later, Waabi handed him a plate of fish. Eyeing each other, Samuel grasped the plate and brought it quickly to his chest. The smell of cooked meat rose up from the plate, tantalizing Samuel, causing him to forget his discomfort. Like a starved animal, he ate. They both ate, never speaking but listening intently to the burble and eddy of the river and the ever-loudening chirp of crickets. As the evening became darker, the dancing light of fireflies entertained them until, eventually, they set down their plates and both drifted off to sleep.

Samuel, being in pain and discomfort, spent much of the night awake. His thoughts meandered as he thought of ways to escape while at other times mourning his situation. His back ached and his legs had become numb—not from his injury, but from being unable to move. He was stuck there, helpless. But, at some point before morning, exhaustion overtook his discomfort, his head fell to his chest, and he slept dreamlessly.

When he awakened, the sun had just begun to show through the trees and its amber light dappled off the water of the river. Samuel let out an involuntary moan as he stretched his upper body as best he could. When he had finally become alert, he saw the Indian, Waabi, boiling water over a small fire.

"Are you making some kind of Indian potion?" Samuel said, half-sarcastic, but genuinely curious.

"I'm making coffee," Waabi said, turning his eyes up but not his head.

Samuel smiled, "You are more white than Indian."

"We are not as helpless as your people seem to think."

Samuel thought of responding harshly—of challenging the Indian's statement—but he thought better of it since it would not do anything to improve his situation. "You can't keep me here, you know," Samuel said. "I am quite uncomfortable against this tree and I need to..." Samuel paused, "...relieve myself. Really, I do."

Samuel could see that the Indian was thinking deeply. Waabi answered, "That may be true, but as I told you yesterday, I cannot trust you."

"And should I trust you?" Samuel said, his voice more clear than before.

"I know you do not, but you have no choice," Waabi said.

Samuel felt his muscles tighten. "You and your people just leveled an innocent town of settlers and immigrants. Your men nearly wiped out my entire company in a surprise ambush!" Samuel's pale face turned red.

Waabi regarded the captive soldier. His expression remained plain and emotionless. "But I spared you, and wrapped your wound," he said as he poured coffee grounds into the boiling water. "I saved you. Isn't that reason enough to put some trust in me?"

"Ha! You spared me because you are a coward. Isn't that right? And besides, you admitted that without a scalp you can't return to your people with any honor. I just can't trust you. I can never trust you."

Waabi had no response. His hooded eyes were blank.

"Besides," Samuel continued, tamping down his emotions, "if anything, we saved *you*. And now your people want to throw it all away by attacking us—killing us."

"You saved me?" Waabi said, speaking softly while tilting his head and furrowing his brow.

"*We* did," Samuel continued, remembering the conversation among his fellow soldiers that night on the prairie. "We civilized you. Gave you an education. Taught you how to farm, how to work. Taught you how to contribute to society. I never met Indians before coming to Minnesota, but when I did I found that they were nothing more than beggars. Hungry for scraps and desperate enough to steal and harass and live like animals in the wilderness."

Waabi changed his tone. "Civilized!" he said, glaring at Samuel like he were an ungrateful child. "Saved?" He paused. "Tell me... how long have you lived here?"

"Only a few years, but what difference does that make? Our government negotiated the sale of this land, and I have as much a right to it as you do."

"If you want the land that was counseled for by your government, then you also accept the years of theft and greed that caused this war. You have no idea what happened here. You just showed up."

"You know nothing of me."

"And you nothing of me!" Waabi said, maintaining a heavy stare. "You and *your* people have destroyed everything I know—that my people have known for generations: My language, my land, my family, my ways of living. You have taken everything from us. Everything."

Samuel felt his own anger rising. "You are not so innocent."

Waabi responded quickly, "We have tried to live at peace with the whites. We have tried to make agreements but your people break their promises faster than their ink dries on paper. We have done you no harm."

Samuel widened his eyes and stuck his head forward. "No harm! The Sioux killed my father. Scalped him over some cranberries! And now, for all I know, they've killed my mother and siblings. We had done nothing to you. We settled on land that had been given up by your people and we lived as good neighbors. My father did not deserve to die!"

Samuel felt his anger turning to grief.

"Your father?" Waabi said.

"Yes," Samuel said, his tone now somber. "We were merely headed to market with cranberries that the Sioux claimed belonged to them."

Waabi looked away from Samuel. He looked back and forth

at the ground and then looked back at Samuel. "What happened to your father—to your family—was set in motion many seasons before when your people placed us on reservations and took away our rights. Stole our land. Stole our lives."

Again Waabi looked away, almost quivering with emotion. Samuel just watched as the Indian squeezed his face tight, his countenance marked by anger and sadness at the same time.

A few silent moments passed while the coffee continued brewing. Its strong aroma filled the air.

Regaining himself, Waabi asked, "Do you have a cup?"

Samuel bit his lip, swallowing any lingering resentment. "In my satchel. I've got a tin cup in my satchel."

Waabi turned and reached for the leather bag. Throwing the flap open he reached inside and felt for the cup. While he moved his hand through the bag, Samuel could see a look of curiosity forming on the Indian's face. Pulling his hand out he did not hold a cup, he held a book.

Samuel was immediately defensive of his possession. "That's my book," he said. "Put it back."

But the Waabi did not put it back. He appeared mesmerized by the book which he turned over and flipped through, examining it carefully. "*Leaves of Grass*," he said, reading the title aloud. "Where did you get this?"

"That's none of your business. Just put it back."

"I have the same book."

"You? An Indian!"

"Do I contradict myself?" Waabi said, quoting a poem in the book. "Very well then, I contradict myself."

Samuel interrupted, completing the line. "I am large, I contain multitudes."

They regarded each other silently.

"That book was a gift from my little brother, Thomas," Samuel said. "It is dear to me."

"Mine was a gift from a schoolmate. A girl... the missionary's daughter, Agnes," Waabi said. He took a few steps back where his father's bandolier bag lay on the ground, then reached in and pulled out his copy of *Leaves of Grass*. It looked identical to Samuel's copy—the green cover had faded and turned yellow along the bend of the spine, the edges were frayed, and the corners were bent.

"You told me the Sioux killed your father. I lost my father, too," Waabi said. "That was many winters ago now."

Samuel looked at Waabi, offering no sympathy, but he was not callous either. He was amazed to find a man with Native blood—an enemy—whose story was so similar to his own.

"It was during the annual payment at Gaa-mitaawangaagamaag, a place you call Sandy Lake. I was too young to go, but they made our people travel many days—far from our homes. When they arrived, no one from your government was there to greet them and provide them with the food or supplies that they were promised. They waited and waited. Many became sick and died. One of them was my father." Waabi paused, holding back tears. He rubbed his eyes and continued, "The Indian agent didn't arrive until all the leaves had fallen from the trees and snow had started to fall. When he did, he had nothing—no promised payment for our people. By this time the snow covered the ground and ice had overtaken the lakes and rivers. My people had to leave their canoes behind and walk home. They had nothing but the clothes that covered their backs. Many more died of sickness and hunger, or they froze to death. They were misled—we were misled—being told to expect one thing, but given another."

Samuel nodded at Waabi, acknowledging that they had each lost people they love.

"Where is your brother now?" Waabi said.

"Fort Snelling. He is the assistant to the quartermaster there."

Before Waabi could respond Samuel said, "And Agnes? Where is she now?"

Waabi shook his head and lowered his eyes, his face filled with sadness. "I saw her just a few days ago. She was being held captive by the Ojibwe at Gull Lake. She is all right, I think, but I should have done more to help her."

"Your sweetheart is being held captive by your own people?"

"She... was not with me," Waabi said. "We are not courting. A mistake, perhaps."

Silence again, but this time much softer than before. Inviting. Comforting.

"What now?" Samuel asked.

Waabi placed the two copies of *Leaves of Grass* on the ground and then pulled the knife from his belt. The steel blade flickered, reflecting the rays of sun that found its way through the trees.

Samuel swallowed hard, unsure if he should be afraid or relieved.

Waabi stepped toward Samuel with the knife at his side, his cheeks now streaming with tears. "I fled from battle," he said. "I am not for this war."

As Waabi drew closer, Samuel closed his eyes, accepting his fate. The next thing he heard was a snap, and the vines around his waist loosened. He realized that Waabi was behind him, cutting loose the vines. He opened his eyes.

"Do what you wish," Waabi said. "You are free."

Slowly, Samuel got up off the ground, but dropped to one knee. "I can barely move, anyway. I need time to heal."

Waabi bent to Samuel's side and took him by the arm, helping him to sit back down.

Samuel groaned in discomfort, but felt grateful to be alive. "We haven't got much time," he said, "before the Indian army is on the move again."

Waabi handed him a steaming cup of coffee.

"I'm betting they'll head to Fort Snelling," Samuel said, speaking of the Dakota and Ojibwe alliance that had destroyed New Ulm.

"I know," Waabi replied, sighing. "It will be old world versus new. Nation against nation."

Chapter 27

Outside of New Ulm
August 1862

Samuel grimaced as he peeled away the cloth that had been wrapped over his injured right thigh. The blood had turned the white cloth brown and it clung to his skin like glue. Days earlier, after Waabi had cut him free, he applied stitches himself from the supplies in his medical kit. To his surprise, the stitches held and the redness around the wound had significantly diminished.

"How does it look?" Waabi asked.

"As good as I could expect. Hand me another wrap." Samuel pointed to his open kit that lay on the forest floor nearby.

Waabi picked up the entire box and handed it to Samuel. As Samuel rewrapped the wound, there was a silent discomfort between them.

For the previous two days they exchanged few words. Waabi graciously provided Samuel with fresh fish to eat and clean water to drink, while Samuel gratefully accepted his captor's generosity. But they both knew the fleeting and precarious nature of their circumstances. There was a war going on. Samuel was in enemy territory, and Waabi was a deserter without much hope for redemption among the Indian Soldier's Lodge.

"We cannot stay here much longer," Waabi said, sensing that the time had finally come to move on.

"Are we allies now?" Samuel said.

"We are like two leaves fallen from separate trees but blown by the same wind," Waabi said. "We are not friends nor enemies, but we are linked."

Samuel laughed. "That sounds like something my father would say if he were an Indian."

"Your father sounds wise." Waabi smiled at his own joke.

Samuel turned his head left and right, admiring the

greenness of the late summer forest. "You could just go home, couldn't you? Back up to... what did you call it... Red Cliff... and forget any of this ever happened?"

Waabi raised his head to the sky, remembering for a moment what the cool breeze off Gichigami felt like. "There is nothing left for me there. Even if I did return, it is not the same."

"But you can't rejoin your army," Samuel said.

Waabi shook his head. "Before I left Red Cliff, my grandmother told me about the Wiindigo, an evil spirit that feasts on the souls of my people—that destroys us. When she told me the story, I thought that the Wiindigo was the whites. I thought it meant that I should destroy them in order to save my people from the Wiindigo. But I don't think so anymore. The evil spirit cannot come from without, it comes from within. It may have come on the backs of the whites, but it burrows in our hearts. The Wiindigo is not what happens to us, but how we respond. I will not fight this war, but I will not return home either."

Samuel felt a momentary tinge of respect for Waabi's honesty and wisdom. Since his father's death he did not think he could see an Indian that way.

"And what will be your path?" Waabi said.

Samuel thought for a moment. He thought about the death and violence he'd seen; about the ambush at the ferry; about the Germans at New Ulm; about the hot blood of the enemy that he spilled across his face. He was no longer innocent, but he did not feel guilty either.

"Well," he said. "I figure I have two options. I can head south to see about my family, or I can head north to see about my brother. But the war..." He shook his head. "There is no good in killing each other."

"The only way south is across the ferry at the agency," Waabi said. "You'll be caught and killed."

Samuel thought about his mother alone with his younger siblings and what might have happened to them. His emotions bunched in his throat, tightening. If Thomas hadn't been so stubborn and naive, he told himself, they might all still be together, with the exception of their father.

"I should go north," Samuel said, suppressing his fear and regret. "I joined the army to protect my brother, Thomas." He paused and took a deep breath. "And besides, there is nothing I can do for my family now. They are either captive, safe, or dead."

"Let me go with you," Waabi blurted. "Let me help you save your brother."

Samuel looked up at the smooth faced Ojibwe. "You want to help me?"

"As I told you, I have no place anymore. Instead, I will follow the creator by looking in all directions. Right now, that direction is with you."

Samuel lowered his head, contemplating Waabi's willingness to help. "You must have other motivations."

Waabi looked away, then began nodding before turning his head back to Samuel. "My friend, Agnes. She pleaded with me to help her and her son, but I walked away. Maybe I can help her now."

Samuel probed Waabi's dark, glassy eyes. He still did not want to trust an Indian, but Waabi guarded him and saved his life. He appeared and sounded sincere. Confusion reigned in Samuel's heart.

Waabi continued his heartfelt admission, "I thought we would marry—Agnes and I. I thought it didn't matter that we came from separate worlds, but her father had other ideas."

Samuel pursed his lips, trying to offer condolences.

"She has a bean-shaped birthmark above her right eye," Waabi said as his mood suddenly became joyful. "She always tried to hide it and I liked that about her. But then, seeing her with her blond-haired son, my heart fell. The boy's father was killed protecting them and I am the one who felt hurt. I am ashamed of it now."

"It's all right," Samuel said, knowing there was nothing he could say.

After a long pause Waabi brought his head up, tears rolling down his cheeks, and said, "I will help you protect your brother, the one you carry with you... who gave you the words found in *Leaves of Grass*. And you will help me protect the one I carry with me, and who gave me the same wonderful words found in *Leaves of Grass*.

Agnes. It is fate that we found each other and fate that will lead us north."

Samuel allowed himself a moment to accept what now seemed inevitable. They had both lost so much already. The only thing left to do was try to gain some of it back—to make sure they each had a future. "All right," he finally said. "I think you're right. I think we can help each other, and maybe stop some bloodshed in the process."

Seconds later, a low rumble permeated the ground beneath them. It began as a subtle, almost imperceptible vibration, but before long the branches of the trees started to shake.

"They're marching," Samuel said.

Waabi reacted quickly by pushing their things behind a bush, and then he lowered himself behind a tree. Samuel did the same. With the river at their backs, it was only fifty yards to the prairie as they hunched low looking on through the trees.

"They have reorganized quickly," Waabi said.

Samuel drew his fingers to his lips, "Shh."

Keeping still and silent, Waabi and Samuel peered through the filtered light of the forest. Outside the tree line, scattered columns of Dakota and Ojibwe soldiers were marching north. Most appeared happy and carefree—energetic even—hopping and singing as they went. Row after row after row passed by, followed by wagons filled with supplies, horses dragging *travoises*, and even some oxen pulling artillery.

The rumbling parade of soldiers continued for thirty minutes before the procession finally ended.

Samuel spun around to face the river. "They must have a thousand armed men... and artillery, too!"

"They will beat anyone they meet in the field," Waabi said, "but your fort at Zaagiwakiing, the place the Dakota call Bdote... I have heard that it is impenetrable."

"That may be, but they can't hold out forever against a thousand men. They'll need reinforcements from the Union, and right now they're having enough trouble protecting Washington from a bunch of southern farmers."

"What do we do?"

242

Samuel tightened his fists and bit his lip, agonizing over their choices. "We can do nothing here. We have to outpace them and reach the fort before they do. At least we could provide a warning."

"I am not a soldier," Waabi said. "But my ancestors were always prepared for a fight in case the enemy came by surprise. Your army must know what's coming."

Samuel looked at Waabi, his face filled with fear. "They may know that Fort Ridgely and New Ulm have fallen, but they aren't expecting what's coming. They're sure to underestimate the Indian forces."

Waabi looked to the ground, silent.

"You don't have to come," Samuel said, recognizing Waabi's hesitation. "You can leave here today, forget all this happened."

"Forget? I can't forget. My people will never forget. Remember, I lost my father too. But now that I've seen war, I know that it's not the answer. It will not bring back my father or yours, it will only cause more suffering. I've seen the Wiindigo and he lives in our own hearts. Maybe, if we stop this war, we can chase him out for good."

Samuel saw a deep sadness in Waabi's being, the same sadness he held in his own.

"Can you ride a horse?" Samuel asked.

Waabi tilted his head. "I've ridden work ponies, never a horse, but I could manage."

Samuel got up and quickly began collecting his things, then grabbed his rifle. "All right. Think you can find us two horses?"

Waabi hesitated. "Yes."

Chapter 28

Between New Ulm and Fort Snelling
August 1862

The trail north required no tracking skills to follow. The combined Dakota and Ojibwe forces, along with their carts, animals, and some family members, left a path that was about as wide and destructive as a river of lava. Their horse-drawn wagons tore ruts in the ground, their campsites flattened the grass and left piles of smoldering wood, and their stamping of feet—row after row—killed the vegetation in their path. Even a cloud of dust could be seen rising up above the trees like a tail at the end of their procession.

"We can't stay behind 'em," Samuel said, halting his unsaddled horse. "We have to find a way around."

Waabi came up from behind, struggling to keep his horse moving straight. "I don't know this country. My people travel by canoe through the lakes and rivers in the north. I know only that the river flows to the fort."

Samuel nodded, "Yeah, I know."

"We will have to find a way around them, to the west. But we must stay close enough to see their direction."

"They are moving slow enough," Samuel said. "And they aren't concerned about making themselves visible, that's for sure."

Waabi stared ahead, watching the dust cloud behind the procession penetrate the blueness of the sky. As he did, black smoke started to filter through the dust. "Look," he said to Samuel.

"Oh, my God!" Samuel said, stunned and frightened.

The smoke grew darker and thicker, reaching higher and higher into the sky, until it looked less like smoke and more like a heinous shadow over the landscape.

"They're burning the towns along the way," Samuel said.

Waabi looked on in silence, dozens of thoughts and memories bouncing through his mind. He wanted justice for his people, for his family. But he did not want this. He did not want destruction. He did not want annihilation.

Samuel turned toward Waabi. "We need to keep going," he said, his voice straining.

With his calves and inner thighs, Samuel squeezed the robust ribs of his horse commanding it forward. The horse trotted on, waving its tail to scatter the gathering mosquitoes. Waabi followed, sitting straight and doing his best to remain steady atop the large animal.

As they increased their pace, moving west of the Dakota-Ojibwe Alliance, a large and continuous line of green and yellow-leaved trees obstructed their view of the Indian army, but the smoke remained clear, like an anchor in the sky. After several hours they knew they had not yet passed the Alliance but couldn't be sure how far they would have to travel before they could cut in front.

As darkness slowly gathered, Samuel suggested setting up camp. "Surely they've stopped by now," he said. "I am famished, and my leg is throbbing."

"We should move toward the trees," Waabi said, "where we can find cover."

Samuel agreed, and together they went east toward the forested area that separated them from the Dakota-Ojibwe Alliance that was moving up the river valley. As they neared the trees, a man armed with a musket stepped into their path. He appeared to be a Dakota, but wore a farmer's hat, cotton shirt with a blue kerchief around his collar, and trousers. He was diminutive but stood firm. "Show hands!" he commanded, as his right eye guided the muzzle of his musket at Samuel's head.

Caught by surprise, Samuel and Waabi did as they were told, raising their open hands high.

"Throw your weapons to the ground... far away, where you cannot hope to reach them," the stranger said. "Then dismount."

Without question, Samuel and Waabi threw their weapons aside and got off their horses.

Within seconds of dismounting, several more men appeared from behind the trees and bushes. All appeared to be Dakota, but wore the clothes of white men. They approached Samuel and Waabi and checked them for any concealed weapons. Satisfied that they were now unarmed, one of the men said something in Dakota to the man holding the musket. In response the man walked closer to Waabi and Samuel.

His hard stare lightened. He lowered his gun revealing a round, friendly face. "Strange pair," he said. "Like a fox with a rabbit."

The men laughed.

Samuel and Waabi kept their hands raised, both of them still somewhat uncertain if the Dakota men were friends or enemies.

"Red and white together," the man with the musket said. "You know you are at war? You should be killing each other, not riding together."

"We began as soldiers," Samuel said, looking over at Waabi. "But... but..." Samuel wasn't sure how to describe their agreement. "But we decided not to fight."

"Why haven't you fled?"

"My brother," Samuel answered. "Our loved ones. We share a certain... grief, and we don't want to grieve anymore."

The Indian leader, whose hair was cut short, a sure symbol that he had accepted the requirements forced upon him by the whites, looked at Waabi to confirm Samuel's statement.

Waabi acknowledged the truth by lowering his hands to show they were not enemies. "Peace is better than war," Waabi said.

"Yes," the man said. "Killing leads to more killing."

Seeing they were friendly, Samuel also lowered his hands.

The man smiled. "We gave you quite a scare," he said, his smile widening. "I am Paul Mazakutemani," he said. "Some call me Little Paul. I am a farmer Dakota from the mission called Hazelwood. We are part of a new republic of Christian Dakota. Men who follow the word of God and live at peace with Indian and white."

"With Reverend Riggs?" Samuel said. "Stephen Riggs is your preacher?"

"Yes," he said, his eyes shining. "Come, you must be hungry. Let us take you to our camp for food and rest. And perhaps some care for that leg," he added, looking at Samuel's bloodied powder blue army pants.

Samuel took a deep sigh of relief knowing he and Waabi would not be alone in their efforts. Stepping forward he looked over the trees and could see that the cloud of dust in the distance was beginning to settle.

Little Paul turned to observe the same thing. "They have halted for the night. You will not lose any ground. Come now," he said, ushering them forward with his forearm. "There is much for which to talk."

As twilight fell over the Minnesota River Valley, the heat from the summer sun lifted and the air cooled until it was perfectly comfortable. An amber glow filled the horizon, and the brightest stars began to show themselves high in the sky. It was a calm and quiet evening, as if war did not exist; as if life had not been forever changed.

"Your stories are filled with sorrow, but they are also redeeming," Mazakutemani said, as he and several other Hazelwood Dakota ate dinner around the fire with Waabi and Samuel. "They are expressions of our shared experience as people in this world. It is good to find common ground."

"What is your story?" Waabi asked. "You do not wish to fight to save your land and return to your ways of living?"

Mazakutemani looked up at the brightening stars. Taking a deep breath he said, "I grew up knowing very little about the white man. As more and more of them came to our land, I learned to hate him. I hated him for taking our land and forcing us to live on a reservation. But one day I was given a book." Mazakutemani held his hands together in front of him as if holding an open book. "A white man began to teach me how to recognize the words in that book and their meanings. Slowly, I began to read and understand. The book was called the Bible and it told of a man named Jesus who taught his followers forgiveness and gratitude. This message touched my heart."

"But do you not miss your old ways?" Waabi said.

"I do. We all do," Mazakutemani said. "But we still practice many of the sacred ways of our Dakota ancestors. We carry red stone pipes quarried from the sacred ground at Inyansa K'api. And we always have with us the medicine wheel symbolizing the four directions with the colors red, white, yellow, and black. Just because we have learned and accepted some of the ways of the white man, we have not stopped being Sisseton Dakota of the Seven Council Fires. We have come to welcome a new way, one that speaks of forgiveness of sins and everlasting life. One that adds to what we already know—what we already are."

Waabi nodded, finding Mazakutemani's statement profound.

Mazakutemani continued, "We also see it as a path forward. A way of peace. A way to exist with the white people as neighbors, not as enemies."

"I do not wish for war," Waabi said, "but when will they take enough? Peace does not satisfy them."

"Ask the one next to you," Mazakutemani said, gesturing toward Samuel.

Samuel and Waabi looked at each other, but neither spoke.

"Surely not every Indian is the same," Mazakutemani said. "Whether he be Sisseton, Mdewakanton, Anishinaabe, or Ho-Chunk. So too is it with the whites. Many whites are our neighbors and friends, sharing their resources with us in times of need, protecting our children in times of fear. There are also those among them that wish us harm. Those who have risen to positions of power and now control our fate. These are the men we are fighting against."

"Then we should fight," Waabi said.

Mazakutemani smiled, his round face becoming even rounder, illuminated by the light of the fire. "We all experience sorrow. I have lost many loved ones over the years—to the whites, and to the Ojibwe. And I have been on the warpath, taking a life for a life. But I have learned that we do not heal through hate or anger. A child pouts when he experiences loss, but a grown man must learn acceptance and forgiveness. Once we forgive, we free ourselves from the heavy burden of hate. Perhaps you feel it now."

Waabi lowered his head and let the words sink into his heart.

Samuel was equally moved, thinking of his father, but also still thinking about his mother and siblings... still thinking about

Thomas and the argument they had the last time they were together.

After allowing the moment to settle, Samuel decided it was best to move on to more practical matters. "So, what do you know about the alliance now headed to the fort?" he asked. "Have tried to talk with them? Before the outbreak, did they ask you to join them?"

A few of the men gathered around the fire shook their heads. "No," Mazakutemani said. "They did not seek our council or ask us to join. But yes, we did confront them shortly after the attacks at Redwood."

"What happened?"

"After the first day they had with them many captive women and children," Mazakutemani said.

Samuel felt a sudden shock of both hope and fear, reminded that his family may be among them.

"This made our hearts very sad," Mazakutemani continued. "I asked them to release the captives, but they said no. I told them they were foolish to think they could defeat the Americans. Taoyateduta, their leader, said that at one time he would have agreed with me. He said that now the time was ripe, and that they had formed an alliance with the Ojibwe. That is when they asked us to join them. We said we would not be a part of any killing."

"They are determined," Waabi said. "Bagone-giizhig carries much influence over the young Ojibwes. I joined them, believing in their mission and believing in his words."

Mazakutemani nodded. "Taoyateduta and Bagone-giizhig are powerful leaders. We've seen their influence grow and feared they may organize a joint attack. But when we warned the white agents they would not take us seriously."

"Have you spoken to Little Crow...Taoyateduta...since the war started?" Samuel insisted. "Are the captives safe?"

"Yes," Mazakutemani answered plainly. "The captives are safe for now. But when I asked for the release of the captives, the Dakota Soldiers' Lodge would not listen. They told me that if they are to die, they wish for the captives to die with them."

Samuel slunk down fearing the worst.

"How many men do you have with you now, in this camp?" Waabi said, looking through the darkness at the scattered tepees.

As Waabi said this, Samuel looked up at the fire-lit eyes of the men and women surrounding the campfire. They appeared sallow and worn, like they'd been laboring without end. Their vacant stares and tired faces expressed a deep sense of loss.

"I have not yet been completely honest with you," Mazakutemani said.

"What do you mean?" Samuel said, drawing his head back.

"They are growing larger—the Alliance," Mazakutemani said. "As they win more battles and burn more white towns, they are gaining support from the surrounding bands. Some believe a great victory is coming and they want to be a part of it, too. But we are also growing larger."

"What are you saying? Are you going to challenge them?" Samuel said.

"We started with only a few dozen men in a mission for peace, to act as protectors to the captives," Mazakutemani explained. "Many—more than we expected—have joined us." Mazakutemani paused and drew his hand across the landscape of scattered camp-fires behind him. "Take a closer look at the faces of the men sitting around those fires," he said. "We are the resistors."

Samuel and Waabi leaned forward, straining their eyes to get a glimpse of the men and women throughout the camp. Within a few moments it became clear—there were bearded men sitting with the Dakota. White men. Settlers. Farmers.

"You have white men with you," Waabi said.

Mazakutemani grinned coolly. "They are from the white militias."

Samuel was confused. "They are friendly to you?"

"We started growing unexpectedly. First it was the Sissetons. Then some of the Mdewakantons and Wahpekutes. They wanted to join our camp. After the Indian Alliance began destroying towns on their way north, we understood that we may also have allies among the whites. We sought the white militias and have convinced some of them to join us."

"Join you for what?" Waabi said, though he knew the answer.

"We want peace. We wish no violence upon the whites or the Natives. But, peace cannot be found as long as one group

250

takes authority over another; as long as one group forces its way on another. We wish for all of us—White, Red, Black—to share this place of beauty and abundance. And we believe we can. We can share this land. And once we restore peace, we may also restore our ways, whether they be Christian ways, Dakota ways, or the ways of the Midewiwin. That is why, when we've grown strong enough, we will attack the Alliance. Not in the open field, but from the rear while they attack the fort. This way, we can defeat them and bring peace back to Mni Sota Makoce. The whites will acknowledge our efforts and someday, they will acknowledge our humanity, too."

"But," Waabi said, "I cannot fight my own brothers. I cannot fight my own clan. Then I become what I am against."

"And how can I join forces with the Sioux?" Samuel said. "Waabi is an Indian, but I've learned that he is an Ojibwe and he spared my life, but the Sioux killed my father."

Mazakutemani pointed at Samuel. "You," he said. "When you told us your story, you said you have a brother to save. And you," he said looking back toward Waabi. "When you told us your story, you told us you have a friend to save whose tenderness has affected your heart. I ask you now, what good can you do by yourselves? What purpose would it serve to run to the fort? The only way to save your friends, your family, your beloved, is to win the fight against the Dakota-Ojibwe Alliance that threatens to take over. I see two options for you—to flee or to stay and fight with us."

Waabi was quiet in thought. He pulled out his book, *Leaves of Grass*, and etched his finger over its textured surface. He thought of his past on the island, of his vision quest, of his grandmother's words. What would any of it mean if he walked away now?

Samuel, looking at Waabi's fingers tracing the title, recalled a line from one of the poems. He said, "For every atom belonging to me as good belongs to you."

Waabi said, also quoting a line from the book of poems, "I will not have a single person slighted or left away."

They looked at each other—Waabi into Samuel's blue eyes, Samuel into Waabi's brown eyes—then turned their heads back to Mazakutemani. In unison they said, "We will join you."

Chapter 29

The Minnesota River Valley south of Fort Snelling
September 1862

Daybreak brought cold temperatures, a reminder that fall came early in the northern regions. It reminded Samuel of life in Vermont where some of the trees began changing their colors before the first of September. He lived in blissful ignorance then. Though he slept on a bed of hay in a small one-room cabin, he slept well. Now, his nights were restless and his bed was the hard dirt.

After rubbing the sleep from his eyes, he saw that either the camp had grown overnight, or the light of day exposed its vastness. Behind every tree was a tepee, tent, tarp, or bedroll. Men gathered around morning fires with coffee or tea in their cups and hardtack or jerky in their hands. There were Indians, like Mazakutemani, dressed in farmer's clothes. There were also Indians wrapped in colorful wool blankets with feathers extending from their long, braided hair. And there were white men, old and young, with jackets of brown leather, button-up pants, and wide-brimmed hats shielding their eyes from the rising sun.

"Mino Gigizhebaawagad," Waabi said to Samuel, meaning, *it is a good morning everywhere.* He handed him a plate with oats and a large red apple.

"An apple!" Samuel said, like it was a birthday present. "Where did you get an apple?"

"There is an orchard nearby. It has been abandoned by the farmer so I helped myself."

"I haven't had an apple since..." Samuel thought for a moment, "since my first full year in Minnesota." Samuel rubbed the apple against his breast and took a large bite.

"Messengers were sent out," Waabi said. "They return now with more men and women willing to fight against the Alliance. That is why the camp is growing."

"Last night, I had no idea there were this many," Samuel said, speaking through a mouth full of chewed apple.

"Mazakutemani says we have two hundred, with more on the way. He says we will remain here one day, even though the Alliance is already on the move."

"Why wait?" Samuel said, tensing his face.

Waabi raised his hand as a gesture of calm. "They are slow moving and will not outrun us. We will wait here so others can find us and join the effort."

"Sorry," Samuel said, nodding. "I'm uneasy. I haven't slept well."

Waabi sat down beside Samuel. "I am uneasy, too. The elders used to speak of war as if it were heroic, but I believe we all live in fear during war, even the brave."

"It's not the fear, exactly," Samuel said. "What I've seen... it makes me sick. But it is my brother; my family. I don't know whether they are alive or dead. I don't know if they will survive. I know you lost your family, too, but they are not in danger now, not at this moment."

Waabi watched the strain on Samuel's face. His eyes looked tired and heavy.

"Perhaps I do know," Waabi said, reaching his hand back to steady himself as he sat cross-legged on the ground.

"What do you mean?" Samuel said, calm enough now to take another bite of his apple.

"Your father—you say he was killed over some cranberries?"

Samuel shrugged, a sign of innocence. "Yes, while we were bringing them market."

"You needed them to survive," Waabi said. "Your family needed them to make a living here in this place—in Mni Sota."

Samuel nodded, searching his mind for the point Waabi was trying to make.

"My friend, no matter what you were told about this place—by your government, your neighbors, your father—those cranberries were not yours to take. This land was not yours to settle on. The Dakota live here. They raise their families here. They bury their mothers and fathers in this dirt." Waabi scraped the ground with

253

his fingers. "Imagine taking to the air and telling the birds they must move out to the sea. Imagine taking fish out of the lakes and telling them they must learn to walk."

Samuel continued nodding, but the confusion never left his face or his mind.

Waabi continued, "I know loss. I know fear. And I sympathize with you and what you're going through. It's the reason I am here with you, to fight against the Dakota-Ojibwe Alliance. But what you feel is temporary. What the whites lose they always regain and ten times as much. What the Native loses, he loses forever." Waabi paused, enduring the heaviness of the moment. "Your father was not killed over some cranberries. Your family was never a target. You. Me. We're merely part of a struggle that began long before us and will continue long after we're gone."

Samuel closed his eyes imagining everything he had gone through. Everything *he* had gone through. But then he realized, Waabi had sacrificed as much or more than he had. And now here they were together with the same circumstances. As painful as everything had been, Samuel realized that it wasn't about him. It wasn't about what he gained or lost or thought about his right and his family's right to a happy and abundant life. Waabi was right. It was about everyone.

"My life has changed a lot since coming here," Samuel finally said. "In a bad way, mostly. In a way I would never wish to relive. But I am glad that it brought us together. And I'm truly sorry for the loss you and your people have experienced. You have given me something I didn't think I needed, and I am glad for that."

Waabi stretched his mouth into an uncertain smile. Seeing Samuel begin to smile back he let his grin grow wide and unrestrained.

Samuel stood and held out his hand. Waabi grasped Samuel's hand and was lifted off the ground. The two embraced.

"Thank you," they said to each other.

With a sigh of relief Samuel released his embrace. From behind Waabi he could see the activity of the camp had increased. "It's time we should start our day," he said.

Turning toward the rest of the camp and letting out his own sigh Waabi said, "Yes, it's time."

The day was marked by various councils. Some were held among the white militias who had been displaced from their small but flourishing communities on the route between New Ulm and St. Paul. Some were held among those Dakota from the Hazelwood Mission and other practicing Christians. Other councils were held between those Sissetons and Wahpetons who continued to pour in from the western plains anxious to stop the war and prevent the further displacement of their people that would result from a military loss to the U.S. government. Throughout the day, all the various groups met to discuss their tactics and resources. The discussions continued into nightfall.

"We must encircle them to hold them in place while the artillery from the fort decimates their lines," the leaders of the white militia argued.

"We must strike them by surprise," the Sisseton leaders said, "hitting them with quick blows from alternating positions to create confusion and chaos."

"We don't have the cavalry for that," the white militiamen countered. "And they could scatter and attack the unguarded cities."

"If they scatter, they can be defeated in the open field."

The arguments continued this way late into the night. It was finally decided that they would strike by surprise, but that it would be done in one fell swoop. They would also wait until the Dakota-Ojibwe Alliance had dug in and forgotten somewhat about the danger of being flanked.

The council then began as it ended, with the passing of the pipe and a sacred smudging ceremony—a ceremony even the whites agreed to participate in.

"We will depart just as the sun is rising," Mazakutemani announced at the end of the ceremony. "Pray to your gods, call upon your ancestors, and dream of the world you long to create for the generations yet to come."

A smooth, thin layer of dreary gray clouds covered the entire sky as the camp of resistors gathered their things and continued their march north. There were several hundred of them marching in packs of ten and twenty. The soft, southwesterly breeze was cool and rich with moisture. It smelled of dirt and vegetation from the hundreds of farms now abandoned just to the south and west. All was calm and comfortable despite the path of destruction they followed—the path left behind by the Dakota-Ojibwe Alliance.

"The river looks cold and gray," Waabi said. His face was sober even as it was painted with streaks of azure and crimson. Over his shoulder he carried his bow and quiver, and across his chest hung his floral patterned bandolier bag. "The Dakota call this the Land Where the Waters Reflect the Clouds. Now I see why."

"Is that what Minnesota means?" Samuel said, still marching in his Union blue though it was torn and stained with blood.

"Yes," Waabi said.

"Vermont, where I am from," Samuel said, "is French for Green Mountain. As a boy growing up, I never thought about the conflict that region must have gone through before my birth. You know... of the fight to protect or claim the land. But I see it now because I am living it."

"Yes, and as you've learned my people have known this for one hundred years, and we will know it for one hundred more."

They continued walking, step-for-step, headed toward the inevitable battle. After some minutes of silence between them Waabi said, "I had a dream last night."

Samuel turned his head to listen.

"I saw my grandmother," Waabi explained. "She was on the shores of Mooningwanekaaning. There were no boat launches or agency buildings like there are today. I saw only bright green pine and poplar trees next to birch bark wigwams and lodges. Berries grew on the trees and squash grew in the gardens. But behind her was the Wiindigo."

"Wiindigo, the evil spirit you spoke of?" Samuel said.

"Yes, a hideous monster. An evil that stalks our people like a hunter stalking its prey. The Wiindigo was devouring everything. The wigwams, the berries, the trees, the earth. I was in a canoe paddling toward her, pushing the water as fast as I could, until my shoulders burned and my hands cramped. But my grandmother stood there unafraid. She was waving me away, pointing at the opposite shore. I turned and looked at the mainland. I saw my father, my mother, my cousins, my aunt, and my uncle. I saw my family. And I saw Agnes, too, though she did not look the same. I only recognized her because of the birthmark on her temple. They were gathered around a fire. All of them together except Agnes who was also watching me from the shore. When I turned back to my grandmother she was swallowed up by the Wiindigo. I called out to her but suddenly the water turned to ice, and I fell through. I was trapped and unable to breathe. But you—you reached your hand in and pulled me out. The Wiindigo was gone and the sun came out, melting the ice and turning the land green and lush. Then I awoke."

"What do you think it means?"

"When I left my home, I left to fight the Wiindigo and to protect my people. To seek revenge. To kill those who were killing us. But I understand now that that was not what my grandmother was telling me. She was not telling me to fight the Wiindigo, she was telling me to fight for something else."

"For what?" Samuel asked. "For Agnes? For your family?"

Hearing the pine needles of the forest floor crack beneath his feet as he walked Waabi answered, "I don't know. I still don't know, but I believe I am on the right path."

"I think you are, too," Samuel said, putting a hand to Waabi's back. "I admit now, I took my family for granted. My father... my brother... they seemed a nuisance to me. But I need them. I love them."

Moments later lightning struck in the distance, catching Waabi and Samuel's attention. A second bolt cut through the darkening sky. In the burst of light Fort Snelling revealed itself, high upon the bluffs, looming king-like over the vast region.

Chapter 30

Rain soaked the region overnight, cold and steady. The determined group of resistors clung to their knees shivering, both from cold and from fear. Few, if any, slept. They camped only a half mile from the Dakota-Ojibwe Alliance and there was no doubt a full scale attack would be launched in the light of dawn.

Throughout the long night more councils were held and battle plans were laid. Despite numerous disagreements between the various groups, all previous differences—religion, culture, language—became irrelevant. Everyone involved, Indian or white, wanted to protect Minnesota from the severe consequences it probably deserved. Or—like Samuel, like Waabi—they sought to protect friends and family.

The rain finally let up with the first light of day as a streak of sunshine broke through the clouds on the eastern horizon. The light illuminated the Mississippi River Valley along its meandering route northeast to the city of St. Paul, where thousands, perhaps tens of thousands, of refugees gathered for safety.

"Move out!" one of the white militia leaders commanded. "Stay with your company and be ready for anything."

Samuel and Waabi went together along with a company of about thirty-five others; some white, some Dakota. They were one of eight companies who planned to strike the Dakota-Ojibwe Alliance unsuspecting from the rear. As they marched through the wet, wooded terrain, the ominous sound of cannon fire pierced the air. Samuel immediately recalled his loathsome walk along the fort road the day after the war began. He swallowed hard. "The battle's started."

"Your brother, Thomas, he will be all right," Waabi said.

"And you will find the direction you seek," Samuel said, attempting a smile.

The sounds of war grew louder and more distinct as the group of resistors neared the battle ground. The screams of men and the war-cries of Indians could be heard over the whiz and plunk of bullets. Gray smoke from the powder of guns and the explosion of artillery rose up over the fort joining the dissipating clouds. Soon the sounds gave way to sight. Waabi and Samuel gasped when they saw the overwhelming numbers of the Dakota-Ojibwe Alliance. They were more than a thousand strong, and they surrounded the fort on both its exposed sides, the north and east sides being protected by the high bluffs. The fort, of course, had the decided advantage of a tall, limestone curtain, but they would not be able to hold back the larger force of the Dakota-Ojibwe Alliance forever—not without reinforcements.

The Dakota-Ojibwe Alliance, using artillery confiscated from Fort Ridgely, shelled Fort Snelling, lobbing mortars over the walls and pounding them with twelve-pound field guns. Close up now, the sound of the exploding guns was deafening. Foot soldiers fired bullets and arrows at the fort from the safety of the tree line, while men in feathered headdresses atop painted horses darted to and from the round tower throwing exploding gunpowder into the loopholes. The screams of the burning soldiers inside, like shrieking bats, was agonizing to hear.

"Hold here!" said the company leader, a Sisseton Dakota dressed in a breechcloth and leggings.

Waabi and Samuel regarded each other once more.

"This is it," Samuel said.

Waabi nodded. "This is it."

As the group awaited their cue, the chaos of battle increased. The fort fired several cannons from the tops of the wall all aimed at their crowded enemy. The cannon fire dispersed the crowds, but the attackers continually regrouped all while their own field guns pounded the limestone walls causing them to break and crack. Large stones, as big as carriages, fell from the walls like pieces of shattered pottery.

What are we waiting for? Samuel asked himself, worried and wondering what Thomas was doing in the fort—wondering what his little brother was going through. It seemed like only moments ago they were back on the Vermont homestead, still just kids without a single care. Without a single worry. So much had changed so fast and now they were fighting for their lives and the future of the place they thought they'd be calling home.

Explosions rang out, vibrating the ground beneath Samuel's feet. While Samuel looked on at the grim circumstances, their Sisseton commander shouted something in Dakota, waved his hand, and sprang forward quick as a fox. All the separate companies of resistors did the same, raising their voices and surprising their enemy.

Indian men with bows and arrows dropped to their knees and let off numerous arrows in quick succession. White men with rifles stood firm amidst the smoke and noise, aiming and firing toward the artillery.

Samuel took aim at one of the riders scampering toward the fort. He focused on his target and took a deep breath, feeling his heart slow. One... two... He fired, knocking the rider from his horse. Samuel turned to share his success with Waabi, but he was nowhere to be found.

A cheer rose up from the untrained soldiers of the fort when they saw their reinforcements take action. Samuel waved a fist to his fellow men in uniform before quickly reloading. He looked around for his next target, but hand-to-hand combat had ensued. He could not risk shooting, or he might hit one of his own.

Samuel raced toward one of the field pieces, ducking a hatchet aimed for his head. His reaction was swift and automatic. Before the Indian attacker could unsheathe his knife, Samuel dropped to a knee and fired, hitting the enemy in the chest, catapulting him backward. Blood spurted into the air like water splashing from a pond. The Indian's death cry made Samuel feel both sick and grateful.

Samuel turned to check his back. It was free, but he noticed the entrance of the fort had been opened. Seeing their advantage, the U.S. soldiers were ordered out into the fight. The men quickly formed lines making them easy targets. Before they could even fire they were hit with a barrage of arrows.

Looking to find where the arrows had come from, Samuel

took cover behind an unmanned field piece. He reloaded his weapon and found a large group of Indian soldiers who were still unchallenged. Out in front of them was a charismatic, boisterous leader dressed in full regalia and urging his soldiers on. *It's Bagone-giizhig*, Samuel realized.

Samuel reloaded as quickly as he could, pouring powder into the barrel and pulling back the ramrod. He aimed at the Indian leader and pulled the trigger, but it didn't fire. "Not now!" Samuel said, realizing his weapon had jammed.

He worked quickly to repair the jam when a white militiaman came to Samuel's side. His bearded cheek was covered in blood, but he appeared unharmed. With a grave but determined look he said, "Forget that old rifle, we need to turn this fieldpiece toward that group."

"We're going to need more men to turn it," Samuel said, shouting above the gunfire.

"God damn it! We don't have time for that," the man said. "They're advancing on the fort."

Moments later, Waabi came running toward them. The white militiaman raised his rifle, but Samuel screamed, "He's with us! He's with us!"

Waabi stopped in his tracks.

The man lowered his gun. "All right then," he said. "Let's turn this field piece."

Working as one unit, the three of them grabbed hold of the tail of the field piece, lifted it off the ground and started to edge the right wheel forward, turning the field gun to the left. Bullets and arrows whizzed in every direction, some from friends and some from foes. But they ignored the danger and concentrated on moving the gun. As they did, more soldiers came out of the fort and it appeared like, despite still having superior numbers, the Dakota-Ojibwe Alliance was starting to fall back.

"One more push," the militiaman grunted.

Once the field gun was in place, Samuel exclaimed, "This will force them back!"

"Do you know how to work this big exploding tube?" Waabi said, keeping his eyes open for any potential snipers.

"Yeah, I think so," Samuel said. "They drilled us on it at Fort Ridgely. First we have to clean the barrel."

Samuel moved to pick up the field gun's sponge which was attached to a long wooden stick.

"I'll cover you," Waabi said, taking an arrow from his quiver. "Throw my bandolier over your shoulder." Waabi handed the well-worn bag to Samuel who took it hesitantly.

"I can fire quicker," Waabi said, noticing Samuel's hesitation.

Putting the strap of the bag over his shoulder, Samuel then took the sponge and rammed it down the barrel of the field gun. As he worked feverishly to clean the barrel, he noticed a strange silence. He looked around the field, which extended hundreds of yards, and saw that the fighting and shooting had stopped. Then he looked at Waabi and the militiaman who were frozen in place as they stared off to the west.

Samuel's eyes widened, his jaw dropped, and his body went numb.

"The Lakota," Waabi said softly.

More than a thousand painted soldiers, all on horseback, rode swiftly in the direction of battle. Their staunch, muscular figures were covered in tints of red, blue, and black. Their horses looked fierce and powerful, thrusting forward in full gallop with colorful beads and streamers waving from their manes and tails. The soldiers whooped and hollered, carrying rifles, javelins, spears, and bows that they began to point and aim as they drew closer. The ground rumbled and the trees shook.

"Retreat!" a U.S. army soldier called. "Retreat! Retreat!"

The militiaman turned and ran toward the wooded terrain southeast of the fort.

Waabi turned and looked at Samuel.

"We have to go!" Samuel said, and together they sprinted from the oncoming enemy reinforcements.

The soldiers of the Dakota-Ojibwe Alliance bellowed and cheered and then resumed their attack, chasing down soldiers before they could retreat to the fort.

Samuel and Waabi were one hundred yards from the relative safety of the forest. Samuel paused to raise his rifle and fired at an enemy soldier who was engaged with one of the U.S. army men. The enemy soldier was hit in the side and went down in a heap. The U.S. soldier tipped his cap before his face filled with terror as he looked over Samuel's shoulder. Before Samuel could turn around, the army soldier was hit in the chest with an arrow, then hit again in the stomach. The soldier's look of fear changed to a look of shock as he curled over and fell to the ground.

Samuel turned around and saw that the Lakota were upon them, cutting and slashing men as they went by; shooting arrows and guns at every retreating soldier and Indian defender.

"Go! Go!" Waabi insisted. He was ten yards in front of Samuel now.

Samuel continued running but was slowed by his still-injured right leg. Fifty yards now... forty... thirty. Samuel felt a wave of sudden and unimaginable pain. He yelped and grabbed his hamstring where an arrow had pierced his flesh.

Seeing that Samuel had fallen, Waabi stopped. He looked back at Samuel grimacing in pain. Then he surveyed the field. For a moment time seemed to slow down and he could see everything clearly. He could see guns firing. He could see cannons exploding. He could see arrows spinning and knives slashing. He could see fear in the eyes of men running for their lives. He could see bloodthirstiness in the eyes of his Ojibwe brethren as they cut down white men. He could see chaos, death, and savagery reigning supreme. And he could see Samuel—injured, in pain, and desperate to live.

This was it. This was the moment he'd seen coming. He was the man on the cross. He was the one falling through the ice while Agnes watched from the safety of the shore. And he was the one pulled up by Samuel's guiding hand. There was no place in his heart for cruelty. There was no place for vengeance or hate. War was always coming. It was always coming to Minnesota. The only thing left was his choice in this moment.

As fast as he could, Waabi ran back to help Samuel. As he did, he sent his hatchet hurling through the air at an oncoming Lakota. He missed, but the Lakota fell from his horse to avoid the spinning metal ax. Helping Samuel to his feet he pushed him forward. "Move! Get to the trees."

"What about you?" Samuel begged, clutching his right leg.

Waabi breathed deeply, his heart slowed, the morning sun warmed his face. He felt at peace.

"Go!" he said, as the chaos of war re-entered his senses. "Go now! We won't make it if I go with you." Turning, he unsheathed his knife to face the Lakota attacker.

"What are you doing?" Samuel said. "We have to find cover right now!"

"I won't let you die like your father. I won't let your family lose another part of it. You will live on."

Meanwhile, the Lakota soldier rose to his feet and smiled. "You defend the white man," the Lakota said.

"No," Samuel pleaded. "I can't leave without you."

Turning his head to Samuel, Waabi softened his tone and said, "I'll be right behind you."

Hearing the calm in his friend's voice, seeing the peace that had overcome him, Samuel knew he had to continue on to safety without Waabi. With a grunt of displeasure, Samuel willed himself toward the tree line pulling his right leg like an anchor behind him. Without further incident he reached the safety of the trees where he found numerous other defenders taking cover behind the trunks of trees.

One of them, a medicine man he said, told Samuel to lay prone to the ground. The medicine man took hold of the shaft of the arrow protruding from Samuel's leg. He whispered several words in Dakota and then, without notice, pulled the arrow from his flesh. Samuel groaned in agony, tightening his face and lifting his shoulders from the leaf-covered ground.

With his head held up, Samuel looked over the battlefield. The Dakota, Ojibwe, and Lakota attackers were everywhere, many of them now crawling up the walls of the fort. Then he saw Waabi. He had dispatched the Lakota soldier and was racing toward the tree line. He was going to make it.

Samuel's pain was overcome by relief, when... Waabi was struck in the back and tumbled to the ground.

Samuel tried to get up but the medicine man held him down.

"Hey!" Samuel yelled. "Let me go!" He looked back trying to wriggle free, but the medicine man would not relent.

"No," he said, softly, almost remorsefully.

Samuel looked again at Waabi who was on his back, leaning on his elbows, facing an Ojibwe who stood over him with a knife in his hand.

"Shoot him!" Samuel yelled at the other defenders.

But the Ojibwe soldier—once a compatriot to Waabi, now an enemy—thrust his knife into Waabi's chest.

"No!"

Samuel reached out, pain and anger shooting from his eyes, saliva spitting from his open mouth.

Moments later the Ojibwe who had stabbed Waabi was hit with a barrage of bullets, falling backward and landing hard to the ground.

Waabi lay flat against the grass, his left arm extended out, his right arm curled in and resting on his chest, his eyes facing the clearing blue sky. With one final movement his head drooped, turning to the left, and he was dead.

Samuel lowered his chest to the ground, held his face in his hands, and sobbed. The sounds of battle faded until all Samuel heard was a shrill ringing in his head. He felt the grass between his fingers and the hard, cool ground against his forehead. He remained there, crying, visions of his father's death infusing with visions of Waabi's death.

He felt a hard pull on his shoulder.

"We have to go, now!" he heard a voice say.

The sounds of battle seeped back into Samuel's consciousness. Bullets stung the trees around him. Screams, yells, and commands jumbled together in confused disarray. The smell of exploding gunpowder filled the air.

"Get up," the voice said. "If we don't fall back now they will cut off our retreat."

Samuel wiped his eyes, turned his head and saw that it was Mazakutemani urging him to move. His hand was out and his face looked kind even though it was stained with dirt and smoke.

Samuel took his hand, got up from the ground, and wrapped

his arm around Mazakutemani's shoulder. Together, they moved south while the men around them held off the oncoming attackers.

Samuel took one last look back. The field in front of the fort swarmed with Dakota, Ojibwe, and Lakota soldiers. Many of them were scaling the shattered walls of the fort. From inside the walls, black smoke poured into the sky.

Many of the defenders had stopped returning fire and started running through the trees toward the south hoping to avoid being outflanked. Samuel clung to Mazakutemani's shoulder dragging his injured right leg along.

"Leave me be," Samuel said. "You won't make it carrying me like this."

"No," Mazakutemani said, "God will see us through."

God! Samuel thought. *Where is God in this?*

"Just let me be," Samuel said, pulling his arm away. "I have caused so much death already, let me not cause yours, too." Samuel stepped back and put his hands to his knees.

Mazakutemani stopped and placed his hand on Samuel's head. "We all make choices," he said. "And we cannot know the outcome. But whatever comes and goes, it is neither your flaw nor your strength. The world will change, with or without you. The only sin would be to give up."

Samuel breathed heavily, almost choking. He was reminded of the words from *Leaves of Grass*: "Something long preparing and formless is arrived and formed in you. You are henceforth secure whatever comes and goes."

Lifting his hands off his knees, Samuel put his arm back across Mazakutemani's shoulder. "Whatever comes and goes," he said, and together they moved with quickness through the trees.

As they continued they found that they were no longer being pursued, nor were they among their own men. Still, they forged ahead.

After a few minutes, Samuel saw a large group of defenders who had stopped moving south. The trees had given way to an open valley that spread out like a serene and tranquil dream, the wide and flowing river to the east and green and grassy undulating knolls expanding endlessly to the west. But as Samuel and Mazakutemani grew closer, they could see it was no serene dream.

Scores of Lakota soldiers, armed and mounted, surrounded the hopeless defenders. They peered down from their decorated horses with sly, satisfied grins while pointing their guns and arrows toward the defeated group of white, Christian, and Dakota defenders.

"Our retreat has been cut off," Mazakutemani said.

Chapter 31

Small icy specks of snow sliced through the gray, colorless November landscape. Samuel admired the glinting specks of ice before blinking rapidly and turning his head away from the early winter onslaught. As he tucked his nose into his shoulder, he was startled by the rank odor of the soiled blanket he had wrapped around his seated body.

"Samuel," his mother, Alexandra, called. "Come inside the tent where it's warmer. There's no sense being out in the snow."

Samuel lifted his eyes from his shoulder, peering back at the blue army tent that held his mother, his sisters Isabel and Eva Marie, and his brother Edward. "No thanks, Ma. I heard they're bringing in new captives today. I want to see who they're bringing in." Samuel turned his head forward again, squinting against the icy pellets.

Two and a half months had passed since Samuel's capture. Two and a half months since the Native Alliance of Dakota, Ojibwe, and Lakota had toppled Fort Snelling and surrounded Samuel and his group of assorted defenders. Two and a half months since Waabi died saving Samuel's life—for the second time. Immediately after the fall of Fort Snelling, the Alliance established an internment camp for their captives just below the fort on the place formerly known as Pike's Island—the same place, fifty-seven years earlier, Lt. Zebulon Pike negotiated the first treaty with the Native people of the region. Samuel and hundreds of others were brought there, including Samuel's family. It was a surprising and tearful reunion. Until then, Samuel was unsure if his family had survived the initial attacks. "Where is Thomas?" his mother asked him moments after they were reunited. "I—I don't know," Samuel answered, looking with sadness at his younger siblings.

Day by day the camp grew as the Alliance spread through-out Minnesota, capturing and taking prisoner anyone who had failed to flee the region or attempted to put up a defense. Not even the highly populated cities of St. Anthony or St. Paul were able to save themselves from what quickly became an inevitable defeat. There were no Federal reinforcements—no hope of turning the tide. The Alliance only grew more powerful as the days carried on. By November, the camp of captives had grown to more than two thousand persons, most of them white, but there were also some of the Dakota defenders who did not join the war effort.

A fence was built around the encampment, and hundreds of tents and tepees were packed closely together. Food and water were provided just once a day. The food was taken out of the Fort Snelling commissary and was usually rancid. Long, open pits were dug for people to urinate and defecate. The smell of it was unbearable.

On this icy cold November day Samuel stayed outside the tent, staring ahead, swaying his upper body back and forth, occasionally breaking out into fits of coughing. A sarcastic smile came to his face as he thought of Mr. McPherson, the eccentric land management officer who had promised him land and opportunity. How foolish that seemed now.

Finally the wooden gate began to open. Scores of ragged and confused-looking settlers were ushered in by Lakota and Dakota soldiers on horseback. Samuel wasn't sure if the captives were recently taken prisoner or if they were being brought in from some other camps in the region. They walked in slowly, hesitantly, assessing their new surroundings. There were men, women, and children among them, carrying their meager belongings clutched closely to their chests.

"The new captives are here," Samuel called, turning his head halfway around to the tent. "I'm going to go greet them."

Samuel got up from the stump where he sat and limped forward, crouching under his blanket and looking more like an old man than a young one. His leg had never healed properly, and he was utterly malnourished.

Samuel approached an elderly-looking man. His gray and

white beard was long enough to cover his neck, and his sun-worn face sagged heavily around his cheeks and eyes. "Greetings," Samuel said. "Where have you all come from?" Samuel looked behind the man and saw that there must have been about thirty of them. As he peered across the small, huddled crowd, the gate behind them closed.

"Gull Lake and Crow Wing," the man said. "We were held three months at Fort Ripley after it was overrun."

Samuel nodded.

"What are they going to do to us?" the man said with a look and tone of acceptance.

Samuel felt a surge of grief in his chest, but took a deep breath and ignored the question. "Come," he said, "let me show you all around."

"At what?" a woman in a soiled bonnet and tattered dress said. "At the mud and tents? At the vermin and filth? At this wasteland? At our hopeless prison?" Her voice rose with panic.

The woman nearly started crying before another, younger woman rushed to her side, gently stroked her back and whispered words of calm. The young woman also clung to the hand of a small boy who had gleaming blue eyes, a head of curly blond hair, and light, freckled skin. The boy was a curiosity to Samuel.

"I'm sorry," the older man said, breaking Samuel from his thoughts. "We've all been through so much, and we're scared."

"I understand," Samuel said.

The man reached out his hand, "I'm Sherman. Pastor Sherman Hall, and we'd be happy if you'd show us around."

Samuel introduced himself and then slowly ushered the group through camp. He showed them the mess tent, where food was served daily at four. He showed them the pit which was used as a common toilet—the group recoiled at the sight and smell of it. He also showed them the church tent where people worshiped, and the small improvised play area for children.

"What about bathing?" Pastor Hall asked.

Samuel pursed his lips and shook his head. "You have to ration your water and use the little you have to spare to clean yourself up."

"That's barbaric," Hall said. "That's inhumane. It's bound to cause illness of the skin and body."

"Illness is everywhere, I'm afraid," Samuel said as the group responded with muddled gasps. "Measles, dysentery, scurvy—it's unavoidable. But there are a few doctors among us. They can't do much, but they do ease suffering."

The group stood in stunned silence, their faces white with fear and sorrow.

"I'm sorry," Samuel said. "Let me show you to your tents and tepees. We had a few set up knowing you would arrive."

Pastor Hall lowered his eyes and nodded his head. "Very well."

As Samuel led Pastor Hall and the group toward the only available living space in the camp, the Pastor opened up to Samuel. "It's a new world," he said, his voice cracked and shallow. "I came here many years ago with the American Board of Commissioners for Foreign Missions. I thought I could save these people—educate them, give them a future."

"Where did you come from?" Samuel asked.

"Vermont," the Pastor said.

Samuel smiled, naturally, something he hadn't done in months. "I'm from Vermont, too! From Londonderry."

The Pastor smiled in return, but his grin looked out of place on his withered and strained face. "I'm from Weathersfield," he said.

"How strange that we find ourselves here."

There was a brief silence between them before Pastor Hall continued. "I came to this region more than thirty years ago when almost nothing was here. A few trading posts but no civilization whatsoever. I was so excited back then. When I started my mission at La Pointe, I thought I could change the world."

Samuel's ear pricked up at the mention of La Pointe. He knew that was where Waabi had grown up. "La Pointe, you say?"

"Yes. I spent two decades there, giving the best years of my life to the service of God and the Ojibwe people. I loved the people there, but I wasn't making the impact I had sought to make. One day, I decided to move along with my family to Crow Wing in Minnesota Territory. I thought a fresh start might make a difference, but my efforts remained futile."

"I'm sure that's not true," Samuel said.

Pastor Hall remained pessimistic. "No. This war... this war is proof. But I think I understand. I tried so hard to change them when I should have been listening to them. Because I didn't... because we didn't, they've taken it all back. If my message had a chance before, it no longer does now. That much is certain."

Samuel did not try again to uplift the Pastor's spirits. Instead, his mind was fixed on Waabi. He wondered if this Pastor may have been Waabi's teacher. He wondered if he may have been Agnes' father.

They arrived at the group of scattered tents and tepees.

"It isn't much," Samuel said, pointing at the group's new home. "But it is shelter. Try to make yourselves comfortable. I don't know how long we'll be here."

"Thank you," Pastor Hall said, as he and the rest of his group walked past Samuel to settle into their new, undesirable living space.

Samuel found himself unable to leave. He watched as the people claimed their tents and set out their meager belongings. His eyes focused on the young lady who had earlier comforted the panicked woman. He watched as she moved slowly yet gracefully, always keeping an eye on her young child. Samuel looked at her closely and tried to remember how Waabi had described Agnes. Blue eyes, freckled cheeks, and wavy blond hair. But none of those things were apparent now. Her cheeks were sallow and covered with dirt. Her hair was knotted and dirty. Even her eyes looked colorless. But then, as she leaned down and her hair angled away from her forehead, Samuel saw a bean-shaped birthmark on her right temple. *The birthmark*, Samuel thought. *Waabi said that she had a birthmark above her right eye.*

Samuel approached the young woman feeling uneasy, but at the same time filled with a strange excitement.

"Excuse me," he said, reaching out to touch the blanket that was slung around her shoulder.

She turned and looked Samuel directly in the eyes. "Yes,"

she said, her voice soft and youthful.

Samuel paused and swallowed hard. "Is your name Agnes?"

"Yes, it is," she said, raising her eyebrows. "How ever did you know that?"

"That is your father, isn't it?" Samuel said, pointing to Pastor Hall who stood about thirty feet away.

"Oh," she said, cracking a smile that made her look warm and gentle. "Yes, I saw you talking with him."

"He did not tell me your name," Samuel said.

Agnes looked confused. The boy at her side, who must have been two or three years old, clung to her hand silently. She looked down at the boy and then back up at Samuel. Her lips quivered as she tried to form a question.

"You know an Ojibwe named WasabishkiMakwa, from La Pointe?" Samuel said.

The color suddenly returned to her eyes. She reached her hand out, touching Samuel on the arm. "Yes!" she said. "Is he... is he at the fort?"

Samuel's heart sank. He looked away from the hopeful young woman. When he looked back, the hope he'd seen was gone.

"Oh," Agnes said, lowering her chin and dropping her hand from Samuel's arm.

"He didn't fight for the Alliance," Samuel said, as if it somehow made the tragic news easier to bear. "I mean, he could have left and gone home. But he wanted to protect you. He saved me and then tried to help me save my brother."

"I'm not surprised," Agnes said, softly. "He..." Agnes couldn't finish the sentence.

"He died in the battle for the fort. He died saving me." Samuel swallowed hard thinking about how brave and selfless Waabi had been.

A tear fell from Agnes' eye, cutting a path through the dirt on her cheek. She looked down at the boy who looked up at her with big, innocent eyes.

"Is this your son?" Samuel said.

Agnes looked up at Samuel, her eyes pooled with tears. Overcome with emotion and unable to speak, she nodded.

Samuel crouched down, eye to eye with the young boy. "Hello. I'm Samuel. What's your name?"

The boy, hesitant, looked up at his mother who nodded, giving her approval. "Everett," he said.

"I named him after his father," Agnes said, sniffling.

Samuel smiled and the boy smiled back. His freckled cheeks were round and dimpled and he looked happy. "I am Samuel. Would you like to be my friend?"

Again, the boy looked up at his mother. She nodded. Everett looked back at Samuel, squeezing his eyes together and holding back a toothy grin. He nodded enthusiastically. "Yes," he said.

"Great!" Samuel said, feeling almost normal for the first time since he could remember. He felt so much sympathy for this young boy who had lost his father. His sympathy only grew knowing that Waabi wanted so much to protect Agnes and her son. Samuel patted Everett's head and rustled his hair, not unlike his father used to do to Thomas. "We'll play games like hide 'n seek, or tic-tac-toe, or bowl toss. It will be so much fun."

Everett giggled as his cheeks turned red from smiling.

Samuel stood back up regarding Agnes once more. "I'm so sorry," Samuel said.

"I know. I'm sorry, too. No one ever thought it would be like..." Agnes looked around, "like this."

Samuel put his hand on Agnes' shoulder. "I'll be back frequently to check on you and Everett."

"Thank you," Agnes said, then she squeezed Everett's hand a little tighter. "Say goodbye," she said to him.

"Goodbye Mr. Samuel," Everett said, waving his free hand.

"Goodbye," Samuel chuckled, feeling peaceful as he turned to leave.

The days grew shorter as darkness settled in early over the snow covered northern landscape. Cold, icy temperatures became a permanent condition of the camp and the region. Even the midday sunshine, though inviting, was weak and rare. It was winter in Mni Sota Makoce.

Gathered in their small, torn, dilapidated tent, Samuel,

Alexandra, Isabel, Edward, Eva, Agnes, and Everett played a game of charades. Samuel tried imitating a penguin by holding his arms at his sides and placing his feet close together while waddling back and forth.

"Someone who is tied up," Alexandra said, "like a robbery. Is it a robbery?"

Samuel grimaced and shook his head causing everyone to laugh. Then he continued waddling.

"I've got it," Edward said. "It's a mummy! An Egyptian mummy!"

Samuel smiled this time, but shook his head again.

"Oh!" Edward hollered. "I thought I had it."

Samuel waddled again, but this time he added a cooing, whistling sound. Everyone looked at each other with confusion.

"Oh, is it... is it a duck?" Isabel said, quite unsure of herself.

Samuel titled his head and brought his hand up, putting his thumb and pointer finger together to indicate that Isabel was close. He waddled again, this time accentuating the waving of his upper torso.

"Ah!" Agnes gasped. "A penguin! You're a penguin!"

Samuel turned and pointed at Agnes. "You got it!"

Everyone burst out laughing and clapping. Even the young ones, Everett and Eva, threw their hands up and down in joyous celebration of the carefree game.

"Whose turn is next?" Samuel said, as Agnes got up to switch places with him to continue the game.

As Samuel sat down, wrapping himself tight in a wool blanket, he marveled at the pleasantness of it all. There they were, without a home, without a future, without even the certainty of their next meal or their next breath, and yet he felt happier than he could remember feeling in a long time. He missed and he feared for Thomas, but he accepted that it was outside of his control. Instead, looking around the tent, he took stock of those things he did have. Back home, in Vermont, he realized that he had taken the things he had for granted, and he didn't want to make that mistake again, no matter how dire his circumstances.

"A willow tree?" Edward declared as he watched Agnes alternate the swinging of her arms.

"No, she's a windmill," Isabel said.

"Octopus!" Samuel said with confidence.

Agnes stopped and put her hands on her hips. With a face of dissatisfaction she said, "I'm swimming! I'm a swimmer!"

"Oh!" everyone said in unison followed by laughter.

As they settled down, there was a noticeable commotion from somewhere else in the camp. They heard men yelling forceful commands in the Dakota language. Samuel moved as quickly as his leg allowed him to get outside to see what was happening. He was followed by Alexandra and Agnes who trod noisily through the snow.

Under the light of the moon, Samuel could see that a large group of soldiers from the Alliance had entered the camp. The Native soldiers split into smaller groups and began pulling men from their tents and tepees. The men resisted at first, flailing their arms and shouting for their families, but were quickly subdued by the larger armed Native forces.

Alexandra leaned in close to Samuel and put her hands on his shoulders. "What's happening? Where are they taking them?"

Samuel was composed, but his heart beat fast. "They're being arrested, I think," Samuel said. "I'll bet they're being taken to the fort's prison."

Agnes gasped. "Will they come for you?"

"I don't know," Samuel said. Looking on, he could see that they were taking men who had fought in the battle at the fort against the Alliance. "Don't worry. I won't leave my family again."

Alexandra tightened her grip on Samuel's shoulders. "Do you think... Thomas is there—in the prison?"

Samuel knew that Thomas was most likely dead, but he could not say that to his mother. "Yes, he's probably being held in the fort," he answered.

The men who had been targeted had their hands tied and were being led away as their families cried and moaned for their loved ones.

"I can't watch any more of this," Alexandra said. "Let's return to the tent."

Back in the tent the children all sat in stunned silence, the joy they had moments ago suddenly torn away.

"What's wrong?" Isabel asked, almost as mature in demeanor as she was now in age.

"It was just a little disruption," Alexandra said, putting on a reassuring smile. "Everything's going to be all right."

Samuel tried to smile like everything was all right, but he couldn't. Fear and confusion marked the faces of his family. They had been through so much already and still, no one knew what was next. Samuel couldn't fake assurance.

Chapter 32

Samuel
Internment Camp below Fort Snelling
December 1862

The wooden gate made of sheared pine creaked open as Agnes, Samuel, and a small group of camp members waited for their weekly escort to the river. On the other side of the gate stood a dozen Native soldiers armed with rifles and hatchets but who looked almost harmless wrapped in their blankets and standing casually. With the beckoning of his hand, one of the soldiers invited the camp members forward. Carrying their empty pots and baskets of well-worn clothes, the group moved ahead down the familiar path to the river while taking deep, grateful breaths of the air outside of their prison camp.

"You know," Agnes said as she walked alongside Samuel. "It's Christmas next week."

"It is?" Samuel said. "I hadn't thought about it, but I suppose you're right."

"Yes! I wouldn't make it up." She looked at Samuel for his reaction, smiling. "It's hard to celebrate right now, but we should try. I've already made a present for Everett."

"You have? That's wonderful. What is it?"

"It's nothing really," Agnes said, turning her face away. "It's just a little corn husk doll I managed to make from some of the leftover rations."

Samuel forced a smile, trying his best to show some enthusiasm. "That's fantastic, but I haven't gotten anything. Not for mother or Edward or anyone. Christmas just never crossed my mind."

"There's still time," Agnes said, snickering.

"Yes, I suppose there is."

As they reached the river, Samuel collected water in pots as Agnes scrubbed the few extra pairs of socks and shirts they all had—later, she would warm them by the fire. Chunks of ice floated down the wide, slowly flowing river. The air was cold and the water even colder. But, it was a reprieve from the camp—the only reprieve they received each week. Samuel paused to gaze across the river at the grayness of the trees that clashed with the whiteness of the snow. It all looked so barren. A land in slumber just waiting to burst forth with life in the spring and summer. Samuel turned his head upward, looking at the white sky. He breathed in the cold winter air, exhaling slowly while enjoying a moment of peace.

"Let's go," Agnes said, snapping Samuel from his solitude. "They're ordering back to camp."

"Already?"

Agnes widened her eyes and nodded her head assuring Samuel that it wasn't a choice.

The small group of men and women gathered their things and walked quietly back toward their enclosed encampment. They slumped along, some coughing, some limping, like Samuel, because of the aches and pains of daily life in camp. As they walked, Agnes noticed something on the western slope of the island just below the fort. She took a sharp breath, bringing her hand to her mouth. "Samuel," she said. "Is that...?"

Samuel stopped in his tracks causing the rest of the group to stop and look up. Several gasps were followed by distraught calls of, "Oh, my God!"

There, not far from the camp, was a large wooden structure. It was a square platform standing seven or eight feet off the ground and held up by numerous wooden legs. Above the platform, held in place by poles, was a long wooden beam that extended the entire perimeter of the square.

Samuel's mind immediately went to his brother Thomas, whom he promised to protect. But he didn't want Agnes to see his fear and worry. With a steady, emotionless voice Samuel said, "It's a gallows. A mass gallows."

Agnes gasped again. "They're going to execute us?"

"No, no," Samuel said. "They couldn't possibly execute all of us. Don't worry."

The group was nearly frantic now, crying and bellowing over their potential fate.

Their Native guards shouted at them and pointed their

weapons. "Keep walking!" one of them commanded in English. "Continue! Continue!"

The group quieted and then continued walking back to the camp, huddled closer together as if that might somehow protect them.

Entering the camp, Samuel took one last look at the gallows. For a moment he felt grateful—grateful that he had not been taken prisoner in the days before. But then he felt shame and a deep, palpable sense of fear sitting like a rock in his stomach. *Was Thomas meant for those gallows?*

Back in camp, word spread quickly about the gallows though they could not be seen from behind the twelve-foot fence that enclosed them. Some cried out in sorrow and fear, "They'll hang us all! They'll hang us all on Christmas day!" Others were numb to the news. They had already lost their homes. They had already lost their family members. Fear of death had become so common that it had little effect.

When Samuel informed his mother about the gallows, she responded with a blank emotionless stare.

"Do you understand, Mother?" Samuel said, speaking to her outside the tent. A cold wind blew against their legs.

His mother stood there, still blank faced and silent.

Samuel wondered if she was in shock. "I don't think they'll use the gallows on anyone in camp," Samuel assured her. "But I am worried about—" He paused, swallowing his shame. "—about Thomas. He could still be alive, held prisoner in that fort."

"Thomas?" she said.

"Yes," Samuel answered.

His mother looked up at him. "Samuel, it's Isabel that has me worried. She woke up with a fever this morning."

Samuel drew his head back. "Where is she? Is she in the tent?" Samuel stepped to his right to move forward around his mother.

Alexandra put her hand up against her son's chest. "Samuel. You can't go in there. She has a rash, too. Behind her neck. I think... I think it's measles."

Samuel felt a rush of hot, nervous energy. Measles had

already claimed scores of lives in the camp. Without the aid of a good doctor and some proper nutrition, there was almost no hope of survival.

Samuel tried to push past his mother, but she held firm.

"You can't, Samuel!" she pleaded. "If you go in there you'll get sick too and then the rest of the family will get sick. You just can't."

Samuel relented. He closed his eyes, allowing the realization that his sister could very well die wash over him.

"I've sent Edward and Eva to stay with Agnes and Pastor Hall," Samuel's mother said. "I want you to do the same."

"What about you?" Samuel said, his eyes strained with worry.

"I have to stay and care for Isabel."

Samuel tilted his head. "But... You will get sick. You could get the measles and..." He paused. Lowering his voice he said, "and die."

His mother looked down at the snow covered dirt before looking back at her oldest son. "I can't just let her die alone, Samuel. You understand that, don't you?"

Samuel clenched his jaw fighting back his anger and desperation before finally bellowing, "Mother, no!" With broken breaths he added, "I already lost father because I brought us here, I can't lose you too."

"Shh, shh," his mother cooed, putting an arm around Samuel's shoulder and pulling him in tight. "It's not your fault," she said directly into Samuel's ear as he cried on her shoulder. "What happened to your father, what's happening here now, it's not your fault."

"But we've lost everything," Samuel said, quieter now but still sobbing. "We've lost everything."

"You couldn't have known," Samuel's mother assured him. "What happened here was set in motion long ago, and we're just a little piece of it. So small we could never possibly see what was happening—what was meant to happen."

"I'm sorry," Samuel said, pulling away from his mother, face red and wet with tears.

"It's all right, Samuel," she said. "And don't worry about me. I'll take good care of Isabel and she'll be all right, too. Come spring all this madness will be over. Maybe... maybe we'll even go back to Vermont. Or start over somewhere else. We'll be happy yet."

Samuel nodded and wiped the tears from his cheeks. Stepping forward he reached his arms around his mother and pulled her tight against his shaking body. "I love you, Ma," he said. "I'm sorry for this. I'm sorry for all of this. Somehow, I still believe it was my fault."

"No," she said in a soft, nurturing way. "What happened here. This was inevitable. It had nothing to do with you—nothing to do with us. You only wanted what was best for us."

They held their embrace. Samuel finally released and looked with gratitude upon his mother.

"Go on now with Agnes," she said. "Isabel and I will see you soon."

Samuel wiped his eyes and regarded his mother. Streaks of ruffled, gray hair framed her wrinkled face. She looked tired. She looked kind.

"I love you," she said, and turned to enter the tent—an uncertain, though predictable fate ahead.

Isabel passed away Christmas morning. Alexandra, Christmas evening. Their bodies were wrapped tightly in blankets and thrown into a shallow pit just outside of camp. They joined dozens of other bodies who were dying daily. Samuel, Agnes, Edward, Eva, Everett, and Pastor Hall stood outside the pit and managed to say their final goodbyes. Seeing that Samuel was too grief-stricken to pray, Agnes asked everyone to join hands and close their eyes.

"Gizhe-manidoo," she said.

An Ojibwe prayer. Samuel was surprised, but kept his eyes closed, focusing on the words.

"We are blessed by you Lord, you who connect all beings. We are blessed by your Son, you who gives us light and strength. We are blessed by your Moon, you who teach us the importance of reflection. We are blessed by your Land and Water, your circulation supports our living. As we are blessed, we bless others. As we are loved, we love others. As we are healed, we heal others. As we are related to you, we are related to one another. Help us all now. Sing to us all now. Bring peace to all our souls O Lord. Bring peace to the souls of those we've now lost."[2]

"Amen," they said together and opened their eyes. Pastor Hall dropped a small wooden cross into the grave and then threw snow over the bodies. After a few moments of silence, the Indian guards watching over them urged them back to camp. Together, they walked back a changed family—a new family.

Chapter 33

Samuel
Internment Camp below Fort Snelling
December 1862

The morning after Alexandra's and Isabel's deaths was eerily quiet. The frigid air was still, and as the sun rose over the eastern landscape of the river valley, no one stirred or moved about. It was as if life had stopped moving forward. In the tent, Samuel huddled closely to Eva and Edward. He listened intently to the patterned breathing of his still sleeping siblings, and he felt the soft beatings of his own heart against their warm bodies. It was a stark reminder that he was still alive. "What more could we possibly lose?" he whispered to himself. It was the day after Christmas, 1862.

Moments later the grating, abrasive noise of the gate opening broke the silence of the camp. Samuel sat up and with curiosity and drew open the tent flap. Obscured by numerous tents and tepees, he saw only that the gate was open, he could not see who entered.

"Is it morning?" Eva said with innocence.

"Yes," Samuel said, turning back to see the pale, tired face of his young sister.

Samuel then heard the scuffling of feet against the frozen ground and the patter of hooves indicating that a large entourage was entering the camp.

"What's happening?" Edward asked. "What do they want?" He spoke with bitterness in his voice. He was old enough to understand their desperate circumstances.

"I-I don't know," Samuel said, clearing his throat of its early morning raspiness.

A loud voice rose up over the camp. "Get up from your tents and tepees!" the voice declared, speaking English with a clear Native accent. "Take only your coats and blankets, you need none of your belongings!"

"Where are they taking us?" Eva said.

"Just keep quiet," Samuel said, fighting back a sinking feeling of despair. "If we do what they say everything will be all right."

"No it won't!" Edward said immediately.

Samuel whipped his head around giving his brother a heavy glare. "We haven't got a choice Edward. Now grab a blanket and hat. We should get going."

Edward frowned but followed Samuel's command without arguing.

Staying close together, Samuel, Edward, and Eva weaved their way through the camp toward the entrance and the open ground that lay in front of it. As they reached the crowd of assembled captives, they found Agnes, Everett, and Pastor Hall, and joined them. The entire camp, more than two thousand in total, squeezed together awaiting their instructions. At the front of the gate were dozens of mounted and unmounted Native soldiers. They all carried weapons and had their faces painted black.

"What's happening?" Agnes whispered to Samuel.

Samuel looked at Agnes with bleak, empty eyes.

Agnes shook her head as she began to understand what Samuel already knew. "The gallows?" she whispered.

With a drop of his shoulders Samuel said, "I think so."

As the crowd crunched closer together the Indian who had spoken earlier began shouting instructions in broken English. "You follow mounted men outside of camp," he hollered, making his voice carry. "Do not try escape or you killed and scalped."

"Where are you taking us?" a voice from the crowd shouted, but it went unanswered.

Shuffling forward, the captives were led through the gate and made to march in a long column. In front of them, on the corner of the island below the golden-hued bluffs, were the gallows. Ropes tied with empty nooses hung side by side from the top wooden bar. They looked eerie, swaying in the wind. Tension rose from the crowd as they encountered the structure. People cried out in agony realizing what they were about to witness, or take part in: an execution.

"What are those?" Eva said, looking up at Samuel with wide, frightened eyes.

"Don't worry," Samuel assured her. "Just stay close to me."

The front of the crowd of captives were halted about fifty feet from the gallows. After a few minutes, the rest of the captives filled in behind them. They became one enormous group surrounded by their captors and facing a mass gallows.

Up on the bluffs hundreds of Natives from the Alliance gathered on the walls of the fort looking down on the gallows. More crowded the banks of the bluffs and the road leading to the fort. They were a ready audience.

After a few minutes of hushed commotion, a small group of Native leaders were ferried across the still unfrozen river. Once across, three of the men took their places on a platform in front of the crowd. One of the men Samuel knew to be Little Crow. He was wrapped in a red and white blanket which covered his arms and lower body. He also wore a thick buttoned-up wool coat and had a knit scarf around his neck. His posture was subdued and his face was drawn. He did not look happy to be there.

"That's Bagone-giizhig," Pastor Hall said, pointing to the man in the middle. "The Indian leader from Gull Lake. He was always known for being a shrewd leader, but I never imagined he could organize the overthrow of the entire state government."

Samuel remembered him from the day he saw him leading men on the battlefield. Bagone-giizhig was more expressive than Little Crow. He looked down on the crowd like an emperor over his people—chin high, eyes down. A colorful blanket covered his shoulders and was draped over his athletic physique. Around his neck he wore colorful beads and feathers. His long hair was braided and he wore a headdress made of fur and eagle feathers.

"Who is the third man?" Agnes asked.

The man to the right of Bagone-giizhig looked old and wizened, though not feeble. His face was pockmarked from smallpox that he must have endured years earlier. A buffalo robe hung from his shoulders to his feet, and his head was unadorned. Like Little Crow, he bore an expression of dismay.

"I believe that is Inkpaduta," Pastor Hall said, drawing his arms into his chest like he were cold. His voice quivered as he continued to speak. "The renegade Wahpekute leader who instigated the Spirit Lake Massacre and evaded capture. He's been hiding out in the west."

Bagone-giizhig stepped forward to speak.

"Boozhoo," he said and then continued speaking in his Native Ojibwe. He did not speak loud or soft. Through the use of a megaphone his voice carried freely over the crowd and his delivery was calm and confident. After speaking his Native tongue, he translated his own words into English.

"Hello," he said. "I am Bagone-giizhig, known as Hole-in-the-Day to the whites. I have been elected speaker of the Native Dakota-Lakota-Ojibwe Alliance. As you know, we have defeated your people and your government. We now control this region from the St. Croix and Mississippi in the east, to the Pipestone Quarry and the Red River Valley in the west. From Spirit and Okoboji Lakes in the south to the international line with the British in the north."

The crowd gasped, stunned that the Native Alliance had claimed for itself so much territory.

"The whites have fled the region, and your Great Father has sent no one to save you or your settlements. In time, we well set out permanent boundaries where our people will thrive forever, no longer restrained by your laws and treaties, by your greed and avarice, by your death and disease. This is Indian country. Just as it was before, is now, and will forever be Mni Sota Makoce."

The crowd gasped again, shocked by the realization of what had happened to their former homes. Those Natives gathered, thousands upon thousands of them, cheered and whooped. They went on cheering for half a minute before Bagone-giizhig raised a hand to quiet them.

"We have suffered dearly," Bagone-giizhig said, steady and unwavering. "But we will suffer no more. We do not want that you would suffer, only that you would be punished. A wrong for a wrong. You see these gallows before you." Bagone-giizhig turned and waved his hand at the wooden structure. "This instrument of death devised by the white man. Today we use it to end the lives of thirty-eight men guilty of crimes against our people, and we bring you as witnesses."

The crowd of captives moaned and shouted, distraught by truth before them. Samuel looked on grimly—saddened and heart-broken. How had it come to this? How had he been so wrong?

"You should be grateful," Bagone-giizhig said. "We might have hanged hundreds. But we were anxious to not act with so much mercy to inspire your people to fight again, nor with so much severity to be real cruelty."[3]

Commotion rose up among the crowd and a man shouted, "What were their crimes?"

Bagone-giizhig pointed at the man, and he was quickly subdued and taken away by several Native guards.

"We are merciful," Bagone-giizhig said, "unlike your own leaders who stole and cheated and killed, taking away our lives and our culture; forcing us to remove from our homelands; stripping us of our language; crippling us with disease and drink. What does the bear do when you threaten her cubs? What do the wolves do when they are hungry? We are not like the bear or the wolf or the white man. We merely take back what is ours. We merely ask for a place at the council—not a high place, nor a low place. Only equal footing. A puff of the peace pipe, not the whole pipe and all it controls.

"But like the bear or the wolf, we too have fangs and we do not shy away when mistreated. We will not hide when we are hungry. And so you see us today, standing atop the sacred Bdote, a place taken from the Dakota several generations ago. The place where from all living things flow. Now we watch over it in your fort. We protect it with our traditions. We have won back what was lost, and we do not intend to return it.

"You, standing before me—you are captives of this war. Soon enough, we will release you. We will release you back to your own people. But today you are witnesses. Witnesses to our mercy and to our justice. These gallows behind me, they will end the lives of thirty-eight of your countrymen."

Shocked and saddened, the crowd no longer bellowed and moaned. They just looked on in terror and sadness.

Agnes brought a hand to her mouth as her eyes widened with fear. Samuel felt sick.

"Remember what you see," Bagone-giizhig said. "Remember

our mercy that you were not hanged on these gallows. But remember also the swinging, lifeless bodies of the white men, and tell your leaders what happened here. Tell them that we spared you. Tell them that this is Indian country."

The Natives surrounding the fort and gallows raised their fists and voices, celebrating their victory with unabashed joy. The sound of unified, celebratory shouts roared like a wave across the faces of the captive crowd.

Bagone-giizhig stepped back and motioned to his right. Moments later, a string of disheveled, defeated-looking men were led toward the gallows, and up its steps. Their hands were tied in front of them, and their feet were bound, causing them to make small steps. The men ranged in age from young to old and most wore army uniforms that were now torn and hung loosely from their malnourished figures.

"Oh, my God!" Agnes cried, "I can't watch this." She knelt down and wrapped Everett in her arms.

Her father placed his hand on her shoulder trying to comfort her. Samuel was numb, and he thought only of protecting his little brother and sister. "It's all right," Samuel said to them. "Just close your eyes and think of summer."

When Samuel turned his head back toward the gallows, his heart wrenched. Climbing the steps of the gallows was Thomas.

"Thomas!" Samuel cried out, but it went unheard.

Samuel's innocent, rambunctious, often irritating little brother, was not that anymore. The innocence was long gone. Now, he was a political sacrifice. He was a prisoner of war. He looked nothing like the boy who joked and teased and played silly games with his father. His hair was long and his face was sunken and distant. His walk was slow and broken. He was almost unrecognizable.

"Do you see Thomas up there?" Eva asked.

Edward looked at Samuel with narrow, hateful, tear-filled eyes. Samuel shook his head at him. He did not want his young sister to know the truth.

"No, Eva. Thomas is not among them. I was just thinking of him, that's why I called his name."

Thomas took his place on the gallows as did thirty-seven

others. One of the men was older than the rest. He was tall and slender, and wore the fresh, clean, and sparkling attire of a Union Colonel. This was Henry Sibley, Samuel knew, who was governor of Minnesota when Samuel and his family first arrived. The fact that he wore military attire, Samuel reasoned that he must have been tasked with putting down the Native rebellion. He had failed.

As Samuel looked on he fought hard to keep from openly crying, but his heart stung with grief and pain. He was having trouble breathing and he felt dizzy. His mother was gone now. Waabi gave his life for a futile cause. His family was shattered into pieces. There was no one there to console him. And why should there be? He hated himself. He hated himself for bringing his family to this place. He hated himself for allowing his father to die. He hated himself for the words he said to Thomas—for not stopping him from joining the army, for not protecting him like it was his obligation to do.

Samuel looked up to see that the sky was clear and the wind was calm. The men on the gallows stood in their places, hands now free from the ropes. Some, like Thomas, remained silent and kept their heads low. Others wailed like children crying for their mothers. Still others clasped their hands at the belt and prayed for mercy.

From beside the gallows, Native drummers began to strike a repetitive beat. The rhythmic beat echoed loud, its vibration passing through the cold, frozen ground and reaching the feet of every on-looker, making the sound tangible and connecting every captive to the lives of the condemned men. The rhythmic beat was not glori-fying or celebratory. It was strained and painful. It was filled with sorrow and grief. It was an expression of both hope and shame.

Somehow, for a moment, the music helped Samuel calm his breathing and forget his grief and anger. He was no longer there, standing as a captive on the losing side of a war. Instead, he felt as if he were only observing the situation. Suddenly he knew he was taking part in a historic milestone—a precipice where the trag-edies of the past met the conflicts of the future. He didn't know what preceded him when he arrived in Minnesota. He didn't un-derstand what he would come to learn about the real strife and conflict that existed deep within the Natives who were already there and the whites who, in their innocence and their greed, were taking it away. But having lost his father. Having met and befriended WasabishkiMakwa. Having fought and bled, he knew it was more than just a conflict over land. It was a deep-seated and inevitable struggle over the right to be truly human. To have a home and a family. To have a life and choice. To win and to lose based on one's own merit. It was like his mother had told him, this hanging, these events, had to happen one way or another. He was ignorant of it before, but the right to be human had to be fought out. And though the pain and suffering of it belonged to him now, it had to belong to someone.

Under the cold, weak winter sun, the crowd cried in agony while white, muslin sheets were placed over the heads of the soon-to-be executed men. Seconds before Thomas' face was covered, he turned his eyes up toward the crowd and searched. But before he could find Samuel, the cloth made his world dark.

"Don't watch," Samuel said to Eva and Edward. "Just keep your eyes closed."

Edward looked angry and would not close his eyes. But Eva, in her still youthful innocence did as she was told, holding her eyes shut tightly.

"I'm sorry," Agnes said.

Samuel looked at her, then at Everett. "I'm sorry, too," he said.

The drum beat continued. With their heads now covered, several Native men strung nooses around each of their necks. As the nooses were tightened, the men reached for their neighbors, finding each other's hands despite their blindness. They held hands with the man on each side of them, and then several of them began singing *The Battle Hymn of the Republic*. It was almost inaudible at first, but the crowd quieted, and more and more of the condemned men joined in. Even the drum beat stopped and all that could be heard were the stark voices of the men forced to pay the ultimate price.

Glory, glory hallelujah.
Glory, glory hallelujah.
Glory, glory hallelujah.
His truth is marching on.

Whoosh. With the slam of an ax, the rope was cut, the doors in the platform opened, and the men fell quickly and suddenly, their voices silenced and their lives extinguished. Thomas, like his father, his mother, and his sister before him, was dead.

For what was only a second or two, but seemed an eternity, the silence was only broken by the creaking of the swinging ropes. Then, in unison, the Native Alliance of Dakota, Lakota, and Ojibwe men and women hollered joyfully together. They whistled and shouted and beat their breasts in jubilant celebration while the captive men and women stared forward in silent, broken awe. The thirty-eight men were hanged for fighting to protect their homes and families.

Samuel fell to his knees, depleted and heartbroken. "No, no, no," he muttered to himself. As he covered his face with his hands and cried, Edward and Eva stood on each side of Samuel and embraced him. It was a moment of total, unabashed sorrow.

As Samuel, Agnes, and the others were ushered at gunpoint back to their internment, the bodies were cut down from the gallows, each one landing like a sack of potatoes against the icy ground. Samuel learned later that the thirty-eight dead were placed in a shallow, sandy grave because the frozen ground could not be dug up. One day, during a brief and supervised break from the camp, Samuel visited the sandy grave only to find it had been emptied of all the bodies. He hadn't even the energy to weep. But, before leaving, he tossed away his army satchel. Within it, was the copy of *Leaves of Grass* that Thomas had given him.

Chapter 34

The months passed with a dreariness equal to a never-ending downpour. Each week three or four more people died of disease or hopelessness or both. The river iced over, the sun rarely shined through the gray winter clouds, and the temperature regularly dipped below zero. Their world was small. Their captors were indifferent. And there was never once any indication that the government would attempt, nor could attempt, to free them.

"The soup is hot today," Agnes said one evening in April while sitting around the empty fire pit with Samuel, Edward, and Eva. "No meat, but the broth has a bit of flavor."

Samuel was withdrawn and passive, almost inert. He nodded but never moved to get his own bowl.

"He won't answer you," Edward said, using the same bleak tone he had since Thomas' death.

Agnes slurped another spoonful and then frowned. No one spoke for several minutes.

"They made an announcement today," Agnes said, speaking to Samuel because Edward and Eva had already been told. Agnes waited, but Samuel didn't look up. "We're leaving. All of us," she said in an encouraging tone. She leaned in, peering at Samuel, but there was still no response. "They had negotiations with the government. They are going to send steamships next month to take us away from here. We'll be free. Finally."

"Good," Samuel muttered, barely audible.

Agnes sighed. "You can't stay like this forever, Samuel."

Bringing his eyes up, but not his head, Samuel said, "Like what?"

Agnes set her bowl of half-eaten watery soup to the side.

"Like this!" she said, hands held out to the side. "Depressed, morose, defeated."

Samuel snorted, shaking his head.

"I'm serious," Agnes continued. "You've lost a lot—as much as anyone. But we've all lost a lot. Our homes, our futures, our families. Waabi. We both lost Waabi."

Quick and cutting Samuel said, "You didn't lose Waabi, you gave him up."

Agnes drew back. "That's not fair. That's NOT fair, Samuel."

Samuel kept his head low and did not respond.

"I'm going to pretend you didn't say that," Agnes continued, "because I know you're hurt. But whether you choose to participate or not, life will move on. Generation to generation, it will move on."

Still no response.

"It's not your fault, at least know that. There is nothing you could have done to have changed any of this."

A thousand thoughts swirled through Samuel's mind, but he couldn't bring himself to express them. He took a deep breath, letting his mind clear. Without a word, he got up and went into his tent.

"Samuel? Are you coming back?" Agnes said from her seat around the fire pit.

When he came out of the tent Samuel held a worn but beautiful, red, green, and blue beaded, floral bandolier bag. He walked slowly toward Agnes and handed it to her. She looked up at him with amazement and confusion.

"What is this?" Agnes said.

"This belonged to Waabi. And it belonged to Waabi's father before him. I don't think I should have it. I don't know who should, but certainly not me."

Agnes drew her fingers over the smooth, delicate pattern. "It's brilliant. It's the most beautiful thing I've seen since I can remember. But surely it is yours. It is yours to remember him by."

Agnes held the bag out, but Samuel had already turned away from her. Without another word he had retreated to the tent alone.

In early May, when the snow had finally melted, the hard ground had turned to mud, and green leaves were sprouting on the trees, the over two thousand captives that survived the six-month confinement departed their camp never to return again. The world looked different now, Samuel thought, as he, Agnes, Pastor Hall, Everett, Edward, and Eva walked out together, crowded among the others, and carefully watched by their Native guards. The river was lined with canoes that moved slowly and effortlessly with the current. The banks on each side were dotted with tepees and wigwams and Native families dressed not as farmers, but as traditional Dakota and Ojibwe. Even the fort was changed. Thin wisps of white smoke billowed out from somewhere on the parade ground, while deer, elk, and buffalo hides were strung out over the tops of the repaired walls, and where there once waved an American flag, there was a gray cloth inscribed with a crossed circle with four distinct colors—white, yellow, red, and black.

"That is a medicine wheel," Pastor Hall said, noticing what Samuel was looking at. "It's a symbol of unity."

Samuel held his eyes steady on the flag as it whipped and billowed in the wind, standing above the entire territory below it.

While the captives were being loaded on two steamboats, a tall, young, and strikingly handsome Ojibwe walked up to Agnes and Everett.

"Agnes! Boozhoo!" he said, revealing his flawless grin.

Samuel watched and felt a tinge of protective anger. It was the first time he'd felt anything in a long time.

"Chibines?" Agnes answered, her voice soft and uncertain.

"Yes, it's me! It has been many years," he said, now standing alongside Agnes as she held Everett's hand.

"Is this your boy?" Chibines said looking down at Everett and still grinning as if he expected a warm response.

"You know this man?" Samuel said recognizing Agnes' discomfort.

"We were in school together," Agnes said. "He knew Waabi as well."

Chibines' expression changed noticing that perhaps he was not welcome.

"You fought for the Alliance," Agnes said.

Chibines took a step back and nodded. "I never meant any harm. We never meant any harm. You have to understand. We only fought for what is ours."

Chibines searched Agnes' face. Then he looked to Pastor Hall, then to Samuel. Seeing that he could get no sympathy he backed away again. Offering a subtle bow he said, "It's nice to see you Agnes. Pastor Hall. Someday, when the American Government recognizes our right to this land, perhaps you can return to this place."

Seeing that he would get no response, Chibines began walking away.

"Wait!" Agnes said.

Chibines turned and looked back.

Searching through her belongings, Agnes pulled out the bandolier bag. Holding it out she said, "This bandolier bag belonged to Waabi. It was his father's before that."

"His mother made it," Samuel added.

"It's not ours to keep. It belongs here," Agnes said.

Chibines nodded, stepping forward and taking the bag in his hand.

As Chibines took the bag and examined its delicate and colorful pattern Samuel conceded, "Perhaps none of it was ours to keep."

Chibines looked up, his eyes locking onto Samuel's. "Miigwech," he said with a nod. "This is a beautiful and sacred item. It belongs in Mni Sota Makoce." With that he walked away.

After several hours the boats were finally loaded. They were packed so tight with people—with refugees—it was impossible to sit down. But, with the blow of the horn and a puff of smoke, the steamboat began east toward the former capital, St. Paul. The fort faded in the background and the camp disappeared behind the trees. Samuel looked ahead not sure if he was happy to be alive or not. How quickly his life had changed. How briefly he had known this place called Minnesota. How briefly they all had known Minnesota. Some, like Rolf and Karl in New Ulm, came to escape persecution. Some, Samuel was certain, sought wealth. Others, like the Maxfields, were just chasing dreams of happiness. The land was bountiful enough. The people—strong, kind, and well-meaning. There was enough for everyone.

But, standing there on the deck of the ship, being exiled from a place where so much had been promised, Samuel realized that he didn't really want the promises the land had to offer. He wanted his father's acceptance. He wanted was his mother's pride, his brother's friendship, his family's safety. They didn't have to come to Minnesota for that. He considered the Native families who had already lived in Minnesota, whose cranberries they had stolen so long ago. How often he had remembered that day with shame and an impossible wish to go back to before—before the Americans had taken what belonged to families like Waabi's, before they had loaded that wagon. Before his life had been forever changed.

Samuel looked up and saw a hawk floating effortlessly through the air. It reminded him of the day he and his family stood on the bluff overlooking Dubuque. He'd seen the hawk then swoop down and capture a mouse. At the time he didn't know the fate that the hawk foretold. He didn't know how it would end, not only with death and exile, but with a rift so deep it would take a century to understand and a century more to mend. Perhaps, he thought, no matter the reason they came to Minnesota, no matter the righteousness of that thing called Manifest Destiny—perhaps they were just never meant to be there.

Epilogue

Present Day

Aazhooniingwa'on threw open her desk drawer, frantically searching through an array of papers, pencils, wires, sunglasses, batteries, and other loose objects. Unsatisfied, she slammed the drawer shut and turned to her couch and quickly removed the cushions and pillows. Nothing! She felt hot with anger. From outside the car horn blared sounding to her almost like an Indian war-whoop.

"C'mon, Peacekeeper!" her law clerk, Winona, called from the driver's seat. "We're late! We're late!"

Aazhooniigwa'on groaned. Succumbing to frustration, she stood in the middle of her summer tepee, hands on hips, heart racing, and decided she had to leave without finding it. She stepped to her desk, grabbed her briefcase, and walked toward the blue hemp sheet covering the entrance to her lodge.

There it is! Right next to the entrance. She put it there so she couldn't forget it.

Relieved, Aazhooniingwa'on picked up her bandolier bag and slung the old, worn strap over her shoulder.

"C'mon, c'mon!"

Winona waved to her from the driver's side of her brand new cherry red Model S Tesla.

Aazhooniingwa'on walked purposefully but did not run. Looking at the car with the free flowing waters of Owámniyomni behind it, she felt a strange sense of satisfaction.

"What are you so pleased about?" Winona said as Aazhooniingwa'on settled into the passenger seat and buckled her safety belt.

"I'm not sure," she answered, eyes tilted upward searching her mind. "There's just something about stepping out of my tepee and into a Tesla that feels right."

Winona shook her head, put her foot on the clutch, and

298

shifted into first gear. "You sure are weird sometimes," she said as she popped the clutch and accelerated down the winding highway.

After a few moments of silence Winona said, "You don't seem worried about being late."

"I'm not."

"But you're the Peacekeeper and everyone is waiting for you to hear an important case."

"Exactly," Aazhooniigwa'on said as if Winona had just proven her point. "I'm the Peacekeeper and they can wait. No matter when I show up, the council can't go on without me."

"Must be nice," Winona said, cracking a smile. She peered at the bag in Aazhooniingwa'on's lap. "It was that bag, wasn't it?"

"Huh?"

"That bandolier bag," she said, pointing. "That's why you took so long after I pulled up. You couldn't find it, could you?"

Aazhooniingwa'on chuckled. She looked at the bag and then out the window at the mixture of tepees, wigwams, lodges, and modern buildings that marked the rolling landscape. "No, you're right," she said. "I couldn't find the bag, and I had it next to the entrance all along, just so I wouldn't forget it."

Winona exhaled sharply through her nose. "You're unbelievable sometimes—you and that bag you're named after. I can't believe you still use it," she said, raising her voice a pitch. "It's lost all color. It's been ripped, torn, and rethreaded I don't know how many times. You should just put it in a box somewhere. I can get you a new, beautiful bandolier bag before the sun sets tomorrow. I have two aunties who make them."

Aazhooniingwa'on stared out the window, holding her forehead to the glass. "Nah," she said. "This bag's been passed down for generations. It means too much for me to just leave it in some box. What would my ancestors say? What would the peacekeepers before me think if the bandolier bag that has been passed down and protected was just put in a box on a shelf somewhere?"

"I think our ancestors would say 'Get a new bag! That was a long time ago,'" Winona said. "Besides, didn't the bag originally belong to someone who fought for the resistance? Someone who wanted to stop the Alliance from winning?"

Aazhooniingwa'on drew her head quickly from the glass and turned toward Winona. "His name was Waabi, and he fought for everyone. He fought to protect what was right and good for everyone, not just himself."

"Okay, okay," Winona replied, lifting her hand off the steering wheel in concession. "It's just an old, worn out bag is all I'm saying. A new bag with new beads and bright colors would look much better on you."

"I suppose it would," Aazhooniingwa'on said, "but then I might have to change my name."

The wheels of the Tesla hummed over the noiseless engine that powered it across the bridge connecting the bluffs over Bdote. Aazhooniingwa'on looked down at the swirling confluence of the Wakpá Thánka and Mnísota Wakpá, admiring the clarity of the water that reflected the sandy bluffs and lush green trees. Ahead of them, atop the highest bluff where a place called Fort Snelling once stood, was the cultural and government center where Aazhooniingwa'on and Winona worked—the Mni Sota Makoce Multi-Tribal Council Center.

"Almost there," Winona said. "Are you prepared?"

"I read over the case files, if that's what you mean," Aazhooniingwa'on said, casually. "Some dispute over a cranberry patch."

Winona smacked her lips. "It's not just some dispute. Your decision will set an important precedent—public versus private land; American capitalism versus Native communalism."

Aazhooniingwa'on glared at her young law clerk. "Don't worry, I understand the import."

Moments later they pulled up to the front of the council center, a two-story red and black building powered by solar panels and framed with lush colorful gardens. On the roof a large flag marked by the Lakota medicine wheel whipped in the wind. Aazhooniingwa'on and Winona entered the building and walked quickly through the dimly lit hallways until they reached the forum room. As Aazhooniingwa'on opened the door to the large circular room, she was greeted by nearly one hundred turning heads all awaiting her arrival.

She smiled, apologetically, and lowered her head as she walked toward her position at the center of a long pinewood table. The softness of her moccasins against the floor and the subtle clapping of her beaded, frilled vest sounded over the silence of the room. She felt every single eye upon her.

Once she took her seat at the center of the table—elders on each side of her—she looked over the assemblage of Dakota, Ojibwe, and Lakota faces who awaited her judgment as Peacekeeper.

"Pardon my tardiness," Aazhooniingwa'on said. She cleared her throat to fill the awkwardness that followed. "This case has already been through much deliberation," she continued, "and I understand that the council members could not come to an agreement, which is what brings me here today. As the Peacekeeper for our multi-tribal nation, Mni Sota Makoce, I am now prepared to hear your final arguments and reach a just decision."

A handsome man seated at a table opposite Aazhooniingwa'on slid his thumb speedily across the screen of his smart phone. After a few moments he stood, dropped his phone in the breast pocket of his brightly colored suit coat, and spoke.

"I am John Teetonka and I am here to defend my rights," the man said, speaking Dakota which was just one of many languages understood by the people of Mni Sota Makoce. "I came to this country five years ago to reclaim my heritage. Before this, I was living in Montana, in the United States, where my ancestors were forced to flee during the period of treaty making. We made a home there, but were forced to live on a reservation where the land was barren and the game scarce. We have tried many generations to change and live as Americans, but we remained poor. That is why my family and I came here, to Mni Sota Makoce, where we lived before the great war. As it happens, I have recently discovered a cranberry patch near my lodge. The cranberry patch is large, but not so large that it cannot be cultivated by me and my family. Because I discovered this cranberry patch on my own land, where my parents and grandparents are buried, my family and I should be allowed ownership of the cranberry patch and all that it produces. I no longer wish to live in poverty and hunger. I left the reservation and I claim my heritage." Teetonka turned to the audience, his ponytail swinging to keep up with his head. "I did not try to hide this discovery from you. I brought it to the council immediately, knowing them to be wise." He turned back to Aazhooniingwa'on. "But now the council lays the matter at your moccasins. I ask you to be careful in your deliberations and just in your decision. I have done nothing wrong and only ask for what is mine."

Teetonka lowered his head and quietly walked back to his spot at the table. A low murmur could be heard from the crowd of onlookers.

Aazhooniingwa'on looked to her right, nodding at the woman who waited to speak in opposition of Teetonka's argument. Black and red beaded earrings dangled from her ear lobes, and she wore a single eagle feather around her neck. She stood and stepped to the center of the floor.

"I am Agnes Anangokaa," she said.

Aazhooniingwa'on was struck by her name, but she wasn't sure why. She ignored the feeling and listened carefully.

"I am of mixed descent—Ojibwe, Dakota, and American heritage. I value all parts of my background just as I value all parts of my land. There is value in ownership—in boundaries—it is what sets us apart from the United States of America. It keeps us whole. It protects us and our traditions. It is what our ancestors fought for on those fateful summer days in August of 1862. But not all boundaries and ownership have the same meaning and the same value. What springs forth from the earth without any cultivation is meant for all, not just one. Think of the copper that was mined by the Americans on the rocky shores of Gichigami. Think of the timber that was cut across vast regions of our land and taken for the profit of one business owner. We fought and died—fighting each other even—to protect ourselves from becoming the same thing that was destroying us."

Agnes Anangokaa paused, lowering her head. When her head raised back up her eyes were filled with fiery passion. "We live in Mni Sota Makoce, a free and independent nation. The timber of the forests, the fish of the lakes, the sap of the trees, the clouds in the sky, the water of the rivers, the OXYGEN..." she said, slowing her speech and raising her voice, "of our air, the cranberries of our swamps. These things belong to all of us. And all of us should profit from them."

Finishing her speech, Agnes closed her eyes, took a deep breath, and walked back to her seat.

Silence filled the room as Aazhooniingwa'on let the impassioned words of both speakers settle on her heart. "Thank you," she said, standing from her position at the center of the council table. Speaking to the entire audience and all the elders to her right and left she said, "I will deliberate in my chambers and return shortly with my decision."

Aazhooniingwa'on rose to her feet, nodded solemnly at the council members, and went into her chambers. The room was small but vibrant. The walls were decorated with various painted landscapes, flat wood carvings of moose and wolves, and elaborate porcupine quill and birch bark hangings. On her desk were red-stone, long-stemmed pipes, a deer hide painted with a Lakota hunter, and child figurines made of basswood. Aazhooniingwa'on lowered herself into the cushioned seat at her desk, admiring the contemplative space she was provided as the Peacekeeper.

Aazhooniingwa'on read through the statements provided by each side of the argument and then read through the recommendations made by the elders. Then, she thought about the statements made by John Teetonka and Agnes Anangokaa. She felt empathy for both sides of the argument. One must be allowed to make a living upon the land which he or she has settled. But surely the land provides an abundance for all to share equally...

The door swung open and in stepped Winona with a steaming cup of coffee. "I'm sorry," she said, noticing the look on Aazhooniingwa'on's face. "Am I interrupting? I thought you might like some coffee."

"Of course you're interrupting," Aazhooniingwa'on said. "I'm in the middle of an important deliberation."

"I know," Winona answered, biting her lip and placing the coffee on Aazhooniingwa'on's desk. "I was actually a little curious. Have you reached your decision?"

Aazhooniingwa'on smirked. "You are impossible," she said, teasingly. She leaned over and took a sip of coffee. "Your coffee is good though."

Winona stared at her, tilted her head forward and raised her eyebrows. "You didn't answer my question."

Aazhooniingwa'on lowered her cup of coffee back down to the desk.

"I don't mean to rush you," Winona said, a slight sense of urgency in her voice. "Well, maybe I do. I thought we were headed to Mooningwanekaaning-minis to do some ricing. Or, did you forget?"

"No, no, I didn't forget," Aazhooniingwa'on said. "Just let me write my decision and then we'll be on our way."

Winona's face gleamed with positivity. "Good," she said, and turned to leave the room. "I'll let you be."

Aazhooniingwa'on took a deep breath, opened her desk drawer and pulled out a piece of letterhead. On the top it read, *From the Office of the Peacekeeper, Mni Sota Makoce, A Sovereign Independent Nation, Established Time Immemorial, Re-established 1862.* With her pen she began to write:

This case is not about a cranberry patch. It is not about John Teetonka or Agnes Anangokaa. This case represents something far greater. It is about the land the Creator gave us, and our right to live upon and use that land. It extends far beyond just what we see and know today. Rather, this question is rooted in our history and our founding. Did the Ojibwe have the right to force the Dakota south? Did the Americans have the right to force the Natives west? Did the Native Alliance have the right to take it back and force the Americans elsewhere? What appears as a simple dispute over a cranberry patch is an ever-consuming, ever-repeating argument over the right to land and livelihood. I do not condemn John Teetonka for coming here to reclaim his heritage and escape his poverty. Neither do I condemn Agnes Anangokaa for fighting to protect the common good of her people, her land, and all living things on the land. I do not even condemn those white Americans many years ago who came here with a dream to make a better life for themselves. I only condemn those who greedily view their own livelihood as more important than that of their neighbor's. I condemn those who would cheat, steal, and lie to protect their own interests while destroying the interests of others. Unfortunately, around the time this place was labeled as Minnesota, there were plenty of them to find.

There is a time to fight back, and there is a time to relent. There is time to acknowledge and rectify the wrongs of the past and a time for forgiveness. There is a time for grieving and a time for celebration. But above all, in Mni Sota Makoce, let us remember that there is abundance. An abundance of grief and sorrow and wrongfulness, but also an abundance of kindness and joy and forgiveness. An abundance of land. An abundance of beauty. An abundance of wealth.

We were given this land, but we made our history. Now, finally, let us remake it. Or, rather, let us make it in a way that will leave our ancestors proud.

End Notes

1. The smudge or smudging is a common practice among the Ojibwe to cleanse negative energy. It is used to produce vision and healing and to purify the soul.

2. This prayer is called Nana'isanishinaam and is attributed to the website Ojibwe.net. - https://ojibwe.net/projects/prayers-teachings/bring-us-peace-prayer/

3. The sentiment expressed in this statement can be attributed to Abraham Lincoln, who, when explaining his reasoning for reducing the number of Dakota hanged after the U.S. – Dakota War of 1862, stated: "Anxious to not act with so much clemency as to encourage another outbreak on one hand, nor with so much severity as to be real cruelty on the other, I ordered a careful examination of the records of the trials to be made, in view of first ordering the execution of such as had been proved guilty of violating females."

Glossary

Ojibwemowin

Aadizookaan – Sacred Stories
Abitaa-niibino-giizis – July
Baaga'adowewin – LaCrosse
Baawitigong – Sault Ste. Marie
Biboon – Winter
Binaakwe-giizis – October
Boozhoo – Hello
Bwaan – Dakota
Daga – Please
Dagwaagin – Fall
Enya' – Yes
Gaa-mitaawangaagamaag – Sandy Lake
Gaa-zagaskwaajimekaag – Leech Lake
Gaagaagiwigwani-ziibi – Crow Wing River
Gaawiin – No
Gakiiwe'onaning – Keweenaw Bay
Gayaashko-zaaga'igan – Gull Lake
Gegoo – Something, Anything
Gichigami – Lake Superior
Gigawaabamin – I will see you again
Haudenosaunee – Iroquois
Hay' – An expression of dismay
Iskigamizige-giizis – April
Makak – a basket
Manidoo(g) – Spirit(s)
Manoominike-giizis – August
Mashkii-ziibi – Bad River
Mashkiigiminikaaniwi-ziibi – Cranberry River
Mashkimod – Bag
Midewiwin – Traditional way of life, Grand Medicine Society

Mide – Member of the Grand Medicine Society
Miigwech – Thank you
Mino Gigizhebaawagad – It's a good morning everywhere
Mino-bimaadiziwin – The good life
Mishoomis – Grandfather
Misi-zaaga'iganing – Lake Mille Lacs
Misi-ziibi – Mississippi River
Miskwaabikaang – Red Cliff
Mooniingwanekaaning-minis – Madeline Island
Naadowens – Dakota
Nagaajiwanaang – Fond du Lac
Nigozis – My Son
Niibin – Summer
Niimi'idiwin – Pow Wow
Noozhis – Grandchild
Odaawaa-Zaaga'iganiing – La Courte Oreilles
Onnaabaw-giizia – March
Oodenaang – Odanah
Waaswaagan – Lac du Flambeau
Waatebagaa-giizis – September
Zaagawaamikong-wiikwed – Chequamegon Bay
Zaagiwakiing – Bdote or Confluence
Ziigwan – Spring

Dakota

Bdote – Where two waters come together (the sacred creation spot
    for the Dakota)
Inyansa K'api – Pipestone National Monument
Mnísota Wakpá – Minnesota River
Owámniyomni – St. Anthony Falls
Wakpá Tháŋka – Mississippi River

Recommended Reading

Fiction

Cole-Dai, Phyllis. *Beneath the Same Stars: A Novel of the 1862 U.S.-Dakota War*. Bruce, SD: One Sky Press, 2018.

Maltman, Thomas. *The Night Birds*. New York, NY: Soho Press, 2008.

Simar, Candace. *The Abercrombie Trail Series: Abercrombie Trail, Pomme de Terre, Birdie*, and *Blooming Prairie*. St. Cloud, MN: North Star Press of St. Cloud, 2009 – 2012.

Swanson, D. A. *The Thirty-Ninth Man: A Novel of the 1862 Uprising*. Prior Lake, MN: Rainy River Press, 2017.

Urdahl, Dean. *Uprising: A Novel*. St. Cloud, MN: North Star Press of St. Cloud, 2007.

Wilson, Diane. *Spirit Car: Journey to a Dakota Past*. St. Paul, MN: Borealis Books, 2006.

Nonfiction

Anderson, Gary Clayton. *Little Crow: Spokesman for the Sioux*. St. Paul, MN: Minnesota Historical Press, 1986.

———. *Massacre in Minnesota: The Dakota War of 1862, the Most Violent Ethnic Conflict in American History*. Norman: University of Oklahoma Press, 2019.

Anderson, Gary Clayton, and Alan R. Woolworth. *Through Dakota Eyes: Narrative Accounts of the Minnesota Indian War of 1862*. St. Paul, MN: Minnesota Historical Society Press, 2008.

Beck, Paul Norman. *Inkpaduta: Dakota Leader*. Norman: University of Oklahoma Press, 2008.

Case, Martin. *The Relentless Business of Treaties: How Indigenous Land*

Became US Property. St. Paul, MN: Minnesota Historical Society Press, 2018.

Clemmons, Linda M. *Dakota in Exile: The Untold Stories of Captives in the Aftermath of the U.S.-Dakota War.* Iowa City, IA: University of Iowa Press, 2019.

Haymond, John A. *The Infamous Dakota War Trials of 1862: Revenge, Military Law and the Judgment of History.* Jefferson, NC: McFarland et Company, Inc., Publishers, 2016.

Monjeau-Marz, Corinne L. *The Dakota Indian Internment at Fort Snelling, 1862-1864.* St. Paul, MN: Prairie Smoke Press, 2005.

Nichols, David A. *Lincoln and the Indians: Civil War Policy and Politics.* Saint Paul, MN: Minnesota Historical Society Press, 2012.

Oneroad, Amos E., and Alanson B. Skinner. *Being Dakota: Tales and Traditions of the Sisseton and Wahpeton.* Edited by Laura L. Anderson. St. Paul, MN: Minnesota Historical Society Press, 2005.

Paap, Howard D. *Red Cliff, Wisconsin: A History of an Ojibwe Community.* St. Cloud, MN: North Star Press of St. Cloud, 2013.

Schultz, Duane P. *Over the Earth I Come: The Great Sioux Uprising of 1862.* New York, NY: St. Martin's Press, 1993.

Treuer, Anton. *The Assassination of Hole in the Day.* St. Paul, MN: Minnesota Historical Society Press, 2011.

Waziyatawin. *What Does Justice Look like? The Struggle for Liberation in Dakota Homeland.* St. Paul, MN: Living Justice Press, 2008.

Westerman, Gwen, and Bruce M. White. *Mni Sota Makoce: The Land of the Dakota.* St. Paul, MN: Minnesota Historical Society Press, 2012.

Wingerd, Mary Lethert, and Kirsten Delegard. *North Country the Making of Minnesota.* Minneapolis, MN: University of Minnesota Press, 2010.

Acknowledgments

I first learned about *The U.S. – Ojibwe Conflict of 1862* while reading Anton Treuer's *Ojibwe in Minnesota*. At the time I was aware of the rumors that had circulated in 1862 that Taoyateduta, Spokesman for the Dakota, and Bagone-giizhig, controversial leader for the Upper Mississippi bands of Ojibwe, were colluding against the white settler population of Minnesota. But I knew nothing of the tensions at Gull Lake between Bagone-giizhig and white officials in September 1862—tensions that nearly led to an outbreak of war. I only mention this because my first acknowledgment must go to Anton Treuer without whose scholarship I may have never written this novel.

I started writing this novel in June 2018 from my father's guest bedroom at his home in Boy River, Minnesota. It began as a short story—a requirement for my upcoming summer residency with the Augsburg MFA program. I want to thank my father, not just for allowing me to use his space, but for always being supportive of my endeavors. He's been there every step of the way without a single word of criticism or doubt all while pursuing his own artistic dreams and personal enlightenment.

If I continue chronologically, then my next thank you belongs to all of the gracious and wonderful faculty in the Augsburg MFA program. Specifically, I'm speaking of Karen Babine, Cass Dalglish, Jim Cihlar, Stephan Clark, and Lindsay Starck. Also, I should at least acknowledge, if not thank, Andy Raphael Johnson whose criticism in October 2018 catapulted this project forward. Not only that, but he broadened my perspective and opened my eyes to a lot of personal blind spots.

I want to thank my beta readers, whose insight came freely and graciously. They include: Amanda Symes, Mark Mustful, Rachelle Kuehl, Elizabeth Hollenhorst, Teresa Fogle, Carlos Arturro Serrano, Chris Podbielski, Rich Horton, and Sean Beggin.

I owe a huge debt of gratitude to Louise Hare of The History Quill. Louise's structural edit provided the necessary objective criticism to fill plot holes, bolster character development, and push this story into its final stages. I would recommend her to any writer seeking clear and constructive feedback on their manuscript.

I want to thank Robin Henry of Readerly.net. Robin brought me through the query process and helped me distill my story in a way I could never have done on my own. I highly recommend her services to other writers. She also completed a final read-through of the manuscript, checking it for structure, clarity, and overall effectiveness as a narrative. She is very easy to work with and accomplishes tasks ahead of schedule. Thank you, Robin.

I cannot overlook the amazing work of Michael A. (AmikoGaabaw) Loso, an enrolled member of the Mille Lacs band of Ojibwe. As a sensitivity reader, Mike checked my work for cultural and historical accuracy. He has been incredibly gracious in helping correct the cultural and linguistic errors and misinterpretations of my text while always making himself available to counsel and assist me in connecting with Native communities. I sincerely appreciate all his help and guidance.

Thank you to Christine Horner, the Book Cover Whisperer, for her beautiful cover design. Christine is very easy to work with, and I would recommend her to anyone looking for a professional, affordable, and attractive cover design. Thanks for Inanna Arthen for designing the interior of the novel. Inanna is also a great professional that is accommodating, effecient, and a pleasure to work with.

I owe a huge thanks to my sister, Rachelle Kuehl. She has been supportive and helpful for many, many years and has never asked for anything in return.

Finally, I want to thank my readers. If there is one thing I've learned about publishing, it's that there are a lot of books out there for readers to choose from. I am so grateful that you chose to read mine. Whether you enjoyed the story or not, I sincerely appreciate the time and thought you put into reading it. Thank you so much. And I hope, if I gave you anything, I gave you a new perspective.

About the Author

Colin Mustful is an independent author, historian, and publisher. His work helps readers learn and understand the complicated and tragic history of settler-colonialism and Native displacement in the Upper Midwest. He has a Master of Arts degree in history from Minnesota State University, Mankato and a Master of Fine Arts degree in creative writing from Augsburg University. He is the founder and editor of History Through Fiction, an independent press that publishes high-quality fiction that is rooted in historical research. Mustful is an avid runner and soccer player who lives in Minneapolis, Minnesota. He believes that learning history is vital to understanding our world today and finding just, long-lasting solutions for the future.

www.ColinMustful.com

Other Books by History Through Fiction

Resisting Removal: The Sandy Lake Tragedy of 1850
By Colin Mustful

The Education of Delhomme: Chopin, Sand, & La France
By Nancy Burkhalter

The Sky Worshipers: A Novel of Mongol Conquests
By FM Deemyad

The King's Anatomist: The Journey of Andreas Vesalius
By Ron Blumenfeld

My Mother's Secret: A Novel of the Jewish Autonomous Region
By Alina Adams

A Noble Cunning: The Countess and the Tower
By Patricia Bernstein

If you enjoyed this novel, please consider leaving a review. You'll be supporting a small, independent press, and you'll be helping other readers discover this great story.

Thank you!
www.HistoryThroughFiction.com